CLAN NOVEL
VENTRUE

BY MATTHEW McFARLAND

WHITE WOLF

"My lady, have I offended?"

She turned to him. "My lord? What right have I to be offended by the prince's actions?"

Jürgen shook his head. "My lady, I admit to a desire to shield you from the horrors of what we are, and sometimes I forget that you are no less a Cainite than I. But Albin still hangs in his cell, and if it is truly important that you see him—"

"It is not." She stood, but glanced around at the chairs in the room. Jürgen took the hint, and sat. She did as well, but a good distance away. Neither said anything for a long moment.

Jürgen looked away from her face, and said, "Albin claims there is a spy in my court."

"A spy for whom?"

"The Silent Fury. A band of murderous rebels. They sent me a list of their aims some years ago—some nonsense about freedom to do as they would, as Caine said. I should have destroyed Albin before, rather than imprisoning him." He glanced at Rosamund, but she seemed unmoved.

"Is that what you will write in the books? That destroying your enemies is preferable to leaving them intact, since they might one day return?"

"The… book? Oh, Acindynus's letters? Perhaps, why? What would you write?"

Rosamund smiled coldly. "Me? I am no prince, my lord."

Dark ages
VENTRUE

Matthew McFarland

AD 1232
Twelfth of the Dark Ages Clan Novels

What Has Come Before

It is the year 1232, and decades of warfare and intrigue continue among the living and the dead. The Teutonic Knights and Sword-Brothers have embarked on campaigns to conquer and convert pagan Prussia and Livonia, spreading the crusading zeal into new lands. Bloodshed has, as always, followed in its wake.

Away from the eyes of the living, in the shadowy world of the undead, these crusades have dark echoes. The powerful Saxon vampire Jürgen of Magdeburg shares the Teutons' zeal and leads the so-called Brotherhood of the Black Cross, a secret order within both the Teutonic Knights and Livonian Sword-Brothers. He is determined to expand his domain into Livonia, using the banner of Christianity to increase his holdings. Last year he sent his guest-*cum*-rival Alexander to lead the conquest on his behalf, but that mighty vampire fell before the vampiric chieftain Qarakh, who leads a band of pagan blood-drinkers in alliance with Deverra, a blood sorceress and unliving priestess of the pagan god Telyavel. Qarakh's might in battle and Deverra's witchery together brought ancient Alexander low. To eliminate the threat of Deverra, Jürgen turned to Jervais bani Tremere, a blood sorcerer of ill repute.

Now only the Gangrel chieftain, strengthened by Alexander's stolen blood, remains between Jürgen and the conquest of Livonia. But Jürgen's heart weighs heavy at this time of potential victory, for Alexander was more than a political rival, he was betrothed to Rosamund of Islington, an ambassador of the Toreador clan. Rosamund and Jürgen have circled each other for years now, mutual affection, predatory desire, and even courtly love mixing into a heady brew. Can he find victory in Livonia and finally take Rosamund to be his own?

Prologue Magdeburg, AD 988

The young man hadn't been afraid at first when his captors led him into the room, but when he saw the blood on the floor, he blanched. Blood on the battlefield was one thing, and indeed his ears were still ringing, his head still pounding from the chaos. But here, inside, far from where men met with swords and fury, here he wasn't expecting it.

He actually stood there in the doorway until the man behind him shoved him. They chained him to the wall, but didn't bother saying a word. They left, and he stood, shackles around his wrists and ankles, staring at the stain on the floor. It was old, but obviously blood. The stain was nearly two feet long—it looked as though someone had smeared blood across the floor with a cloth, as though trying to daub the stone to a more pleasing hue.

The man started. Footsteps approached the door. Someone paused outside to speak with the guards, but they spoke too low for the young man to understand. He wondered who his captor was, and why he was a prisoner. He was a noble, and should therefore be given courtesy as befit his birth. His father, he knew, wouldn't stand for this. He was certain that the battle was won by now, and that his father would be preparing to find and rescue him, or at least negotiate for his release. He was plucking up his courage to order his captor to move him to better conditions when Lord Jürgen of Swabia stepped into the room.

The man had never seen Jürgen before, but had heard stories. He'd heard that Jürgen was nine feet tall and commanded an army of demons. He'd heard that Jürgen meant to cover the world in blood and the wreckage of anything he came across. He'd heard that Jürgen made sport of anything of woman born, and that looking at Jürgen's eyes meant death for any Christian. The man shrouded in shadows before him looked nothing like a demon, only a man; tall and imposing to be sure, and certainly with bearing enough to be nobility, but only a man for all that. The young man relaxed a little. If Jürgen was truly a noble, he would be reasonable. He would treat his prisoners well.

Jürgen took a step closer, into the light, and the young man gasped. His captor was covered in blood from neck to toes. His hands were stained crimson and his hair, probably fair blond when clean, shone waxy and amber in the torchlight. "Your father is dead," he said flatly. "He fell on the battlefield."

The man stammered. He imagined Jürgen must be lying— his father didn't ride into battle with his men anymore. Jürgen continued. "Yes, he stayed away from the battlefield, like an old man or a coward. Or both. Nonetheless, he is dead. A man who does not intend to fight should not take the field at all, and should certainly watch his flanks if he does." Jürgen craned his neck to the side and the young man winced at the hideous popping sound. "I am tired, boy. You are heir to your father's lands. I am taking those lands from him—from you. Your men will fight me because they assume you are still alive, and I do not know what they will do if I kill you. I have no wish to do so, in any case." He removed his shirt and snapped his fingers. One of the guards handed him a tunic. Before he put it on, the young man could see his body, muscled and smooth, nearly unmarred by scars.

"All I want to know is this: How many men did your father command? And where are they?"

The man stammered again. Jürgen sighed, turned his back, and took a drink from a skin. "It's not difficult, boy. Just tell me, so I can find his men and finish what began on the battlefield."

The man finally found his voice. "Tell you where they are… so you can kill them? Why would I…?"

Jürgen's brow furrowed and he leaned over to look the man in the eyes. "I have men enough to people your father's lands. I have no need of the men who worked them before, and certainly no need of men loyal to the former lord. If you tell me, I shall let you live and even allow you to dwell in your father's lands, though not in his home, of course."

"Let me... live?" The man had not considered this an issue. Jürgen's gaze did not falter.

"All men die, noble born or not." He drew a dagger from his belt and pushed the tip into the man's palm, drawing blood. "All men bleed, all men feel pain. Had the God who granted us the wisdom to rule also granted us immunity from iron and pain, I would have taken it as a divine mandate that I should keep to my own lands. As it is, we are all flesh, and since you are no less flesh than I, and since you cannot stop me, I shall take your lands." The boy's mouth fell open as he tried to decide if his captor was speaking madness, blasphemy, or both.

Jürgen merely sighed. "You truly are a child. Now tell me what I want to know."

"No. I mean, I—" The boy realized his mistake as soon as the first word left his lips. Jürgen beckoned to the servant behind him, and the boy found his right hand jerked forward and held like a pup pulling at a leash. Jürgen brought the blade of his knife down across the back of the boy's hand with a flick of his wrist. Blood welled up around the blade as it chipped the bone. The man screamed in pain; Jürgen covered his mouth with a bloodstained hand and locked eyes with him.

"No?" Jürgen twisted the knife. The boy began to weep, but stopped screaming, and Jürgen uncovered his mouth. "No? I didn't offer you a choice. Tell me what I want to know, and I will let you live. I did not say that I would kill you if you *didn't* tell me, because you *will* tell me. Immediately. If you do not tell me, I will let you live anyway, but I promise you that the condition your body will be in will offer you no kind of life suitable for a man." He pulled the knife out in one quick jerk and wiped the blood and bone from the blade before the man's eyes. He said nothing further.

The young man, however, had much to say.

Later, as one of the guards was walking home, a pair of men approached him. One of the men reminded the guard strangely of Jürgen; perhaps it was his posture or the angle of his features, but something in the man's bearing was similar. The second man never came close enough to the guard's torch to be seen, but the guard could see well enough to know that he had dark hair and wore black. The first man looked at the guard's eyes, and everything in the guard's mind suddenly belonged to the man. The guard stumbled on, confused, violated.

The two Cainites walked on, talking of Jürgen.

"He's perfect, but not for your cause. Surely you must see that, Lasombra."

The dark one gritted his teeth. "I have asked you, repeatedly, not to call me that. My lineage is none of my doing, Hardestadt." Hardestadt offered a curt nod, but both men knew that he would forget. "And as for Jürgen's suitability to my—God's—work, I admit that his zeal is, as of now, unfettered by any kind of morality."

"So you will give up any claim of progeny?"

"Let me finish. Where you see a man unsuited to do God's work, I see an unfinished blade of the finest steel, a man simply waiting for someone to add the Word of the Lord to his already admirable drive." The man smiled, and the starlight itself recoiled. "He is perfect for me. Exactly what I wanted. He could be everything I should have been from the start."

Hardestadt shook his head. "Gotzon, I think I've been remarkably patient with you on this matter. But I mean to have Jürgen as my childe, and since your vow precludes you from—" He had not finished the sentence when Gotzon let out a fierce hiss.

"I have other gifts, Patrician. And for all you know of me, I have seen you. I know you. I have watched from faraway shadows as you committed acts against your road and God, and I know of the parties who would most enjoy burning you slowly for what you have done."

Hardestadt bristled. "No worse, I daresay, than the horrors you have wrought on the world." His hand crept towards his blade.

"Stop," said Gotzon, but he had already half-drawn his own sword. "I've already said I won't fight you over this."

"And if the fight begins, will you flee?" Hardestadt locked eyes with the Lasombra, and the moonlight stopped to watch them. Gotzon opened his eyes a fraction wider, and allowed Hardestadt to see what lay behind them for an instant.

Hardestadt took a step back. He had not backed down from a foe in a century, perhaps more. But then, he had never actually *seen* Hell. "My God," he choked.

"You see, Hardestadt? The horrors that I loosed upon the world never left me. I called them up at the behest of my clan and my mentors. I learned all I could of the Abyss. One word from me could blot out the sun. That is what I carry with me."

Hardestadt struggled for words, but only managed to find the strength to sheathe his sword. "Damn you," he said finally.

Gotzon laughed, and the moon cringed. "I have been damned for many years. But that's not the point. The point is, we can't come to blows over this. Then no one wins." He stopped. "I have a thought. I concede that, even as your childe, Lord Jürgen stands to do God and His Word great service. Do you concede that, even as my childe, he might do much for your... rather worldly causes, even incidentally?"

Hardestadt nodded cautiously. "I also think, though," he ventured, "that he would chafe under your strictures. His time as a conqueror has taught him that, while the meek might someday inherit the Earth, the strong live comfortably in the meantime. I think that he would either wind up an apostate from your Road of Heaven, or a worse tyrant than he would ever become as a Scion of the Road of Kings."

"Well, then, we'll let the man himself decide. We'll offer him the choice—God or glory, the cross or the crown. We'll see what kind of man Lord Jürgen truly is."

Hardestadt smiled. "And you truly think he'll choose your way? The rewards of virtue are largely spiritual. A great number of our kind feel that means that they might as well not exist at all."

Gotzon smiled sadly and held up a palm. His shadow, which stood out despite the low light, did likewise, but with the opposite hand. "The rewards of virtue are spiritual, as are the fruits of sin, Scion. And both are very real."

Chapter One

Parchment, Jürgen mused, was more precious a thing than blood. Rumor had it that the Tzimisce he had fought in Transylvania used the skins of their enemies to that purpose. *Brutal,* he thought, *but assuredly much less expensive.* He sat in his great oak chair, staring at a table nearly covered in parchment, and tried to guess at the value of what lay before him. He couldn't, but then he wasn't a merchant.

Jervais bani Tremere sat on the other side of the table, trying unsuccessfully to fit his huge bulk into the chair beneath him. Jürgen considered sending for a larger one, but decided against it. He was prepared to make adjustments for certain of his servants, but Jervais wasn't one of them. In truth, he had been half hoping that the magician would meet his death in Livonia. But then, if Jervais hadn't returned, he reflected, he would not have nearly the intelligence on the area that he did now.

Jervais finally made himself comfortable enough to begin his report. He unfurled a large map of Livonia, marked in several places with red symbols that Jürgen recognized as crude representations of the crest of Clan Tremere. He clicked his tongue disapprovingly. If those symbols indicated victory for Jervais, they really should have been marked with the Ventrue clan crest, or at least Jürgen's own personal seal, given that Jervais was there under Jürgen's authority. Jervais, for his part, either did not notice or simply did not acknowledge Jürgen's displeasure and began his report.

"The situation in Livonia is still chaotic at best, my lord, and seems unlikely to change." He pointed at one of the symbols. "Here, according to Wigand, is where Alexander fell. You have heard enough stories of that battle, I assume? The bog opening beneath his feet and all?"

Jürgen nodded. "I have. Go on."

"Yes, my lord." The sorcerer ran a finger over the map, attempting to find something in particular. *Hopefully he has some good news for me,* thought Jürgen.

"Here," Jervais said, indicating another of the symbols, "is the village of Auce. Though small, the people there are hale and healthy, and have proven good soldiers against the pagans."

"The Sword-Brothers continue into Livonia, then, just as the Teutonic Knights do God's work in Prussia?"

Jervais smirked a bit; doubtless he thought Jürgen was attempting irony with his last statement. "Just so, my lord."

Jürgen pretended not to notice. "Auce, eh? Very well, go on."

"A bit further south, the river—" Jervais began. Jürgen stopped him.

"This information I could obtain from mortal travelers. What of the Telyavs? Are the pagan sorcerers gone?"

Jervais gave him a smug smirk. "Yes. Their leader is gone, and their peoples are being routed."

"So they are *all* dead?"

Jervais's face fell. "Well, my lord, I can't say with *perfect* certainty—"

Jürgen leaned forward. "Jervais, destroying every last wolf in the forest is not impossible, but knowing that you have destroyed the last one *is* impossible. What I would like to know is if you knowingly left any Telyavs still in existence when you and my knights left Livonia."

Jervais stared back at the Prince of Magdeburg for a long moment. *Trying to decide what I already know,* Jürgen thought. *Tell the truth, Jervais.*

Finally, the Tremere spoke. "Surely, my lord, the knights you entrusted to me have made reports as well."

"They have, but that doesn't answer the question."

A mortal man might have sighed in resignation; Jervais simply slumped his broad shoulders. "As we were returning, and since, I have learned that a few isolated Telyavs may yet remain.

I believe, however," he said, pointing a finger to the map, "that all of their elders—and thus much of their magical knowledge—is gone."

Jürgen nodded. "Fair enough. You destroyed their leader and broke the back of their power. I can't expect a sorcerer to be a warlord." He knew this would chafe the wizard, but he needed to remind Jervais who was the true power here, sorcery or no. "Very well, please continue. Auce, you say, is a potentially beneficial outpost, but I think it is too far north to name as a primary goal. What of this region?" he said, pointing to the Nemen River and its surrounding lands.

Jervais looked over the map. "Livonia, as you well know, boasts no Cainite overlord. Most of the native Cainites are—or were—pagan and feral. As civilization and the Cross come to land, others of our kind come with them, but no one has established power." He peered closely at the Nemen. "If memory serves, this area and much of the south and east of the Baltic owes some loose obeisance to the *Voivodate*, but again, there is no clear ruler."

"The *Voivodate*. Naturally." Jürgen grimaced. In any campaign to the east, he would face Clan Tzimisce. A part of him, the man that understood what the Tzimisce did to their foes, didn't relish the thought of facing them again. But the soldier within him, the soldier he truly was, wanted nothing more. "How secure is their power?"

Jervais thought, choosing his words carefully. His clan despised the Tzimisce as much as Jürgen's. "They claim domain over Livonia and Prussia, but I have seen no concrete evidence that their power is as secure as they claim. Hungary is, of course, largely their domain," he said, "ignoring the lands that your clan has taken."

The Arpad Ventrue ruled the Cainites of several cities farther East, and had alliances even among the Tzimisce, astonishing as Jürgen found that to be. "Yes, but in this area, what elders need I be concerned with?"

"A Tzimisce called Visya once dwelt in, or visited, the area," said Jervais uncertainly, "but has since left for an eastern city. I am not sure which one. And of course the Obertus order—"

Jürgen looked up sharply. "Surely not this far west?" The Obertus's noxious patron, Vykos, had received his lands by brokering a deal between Jürgen and the Tzimisce leader some years ago, but those lands were in Hungary.

Jervais gestured at the map helplessly. "It's possible that the monks were Dominicans, my lord. Besides, no Cainite was ever sighted among the monks." His voice dropped. "If anyone is the true Cainite power in these lands, it is Qarakh."

"The Gangrel warlord," Jürgen muttered. Jervais nodded. Neither vampire said what they were both thinking. Qarakh was more than an animalistic warrior or even a chieftain among his people, though both of those were true. Qarakh had slain Alexander of Paris, the last western Ventrue to march into the Baltic. "He is allied with the Telyavs?"

"He was. I do not know how their leader's destruction has affected any such alliance, and the rules of honor by which the beast is bound are unclear at best."

Jürgen paused and stared past Jervais at the wall. With no other preeminent Cainite powers in the land, claiming Livonia and Prussia as his own would be much more his sort of war—conquest, rather than alliances and courtly tactics. This meant, however, that staying to the west would be advisable, rather than following the Teutonic Knights and their mortal Hochmeister von Salza too closely in Prussia. *I shall have to extend the Black Cross to the Sword-Brothers, then,* he thought, *if I am to have the manpower I'll need.*

"Thank you, Master Tremere," he said. Jervais gathered his belongings and left, probably grateful to be out of the room. Jürgen watched him go, and wondered about sorcerers. Their goals seemed so... strange compared to his. Power could be taken and used by sword and fire. The effort that they went to, the risks their souls must incur—it seemed unnecessary.

Shaking off these thoughts, he turned his attention to the matter at hand. New lands and war beckoned, and he was anxious to leave. His last foray into the east, after all, had hardly been a true victory.

The fact that Alexander had fallen in battle to a Gangrel chieftain of some kind was well and good. *Actually,* he thought,

I couldn't have asked for a better end for him. Jürgen now had to venture east himself if he wanted to take the territory, and that did require him leaving his German fiefs without his direct supervision for some time longer, yes, but if he could succeed where Alexander failed...

What? She will love me all the more?

He ground his teeth and focused on the coming campaign. It required him to put his affairs in the strictest order. *When leaving for battle, assume you will not return,* he reminded himself. He picked up a pen and his few sheets of clean paper.

He first wrote a letter to an agent in the city of Acre—he had not heard from Etienne de Fauberge in many months. The Prince of Acre was nominally his vassal, but Jürgen had heard disturbing rumors that he was casting about for support in Outremer and attempting to sever ties with Europe. Jürgen grimaced and shook his head. Etienne was no Scion—Cainites ruled by their faith could make and break alliances and simply claim God was moving them in one direction or another. Jürgen knew the simple truth—God was one more overlord, and did as was His wont. All on Earth were His vassals and minions, some He favored, some He did not. All done in His name for His glory was good, and all would be measured when the Time of Judgment came. The faithful certainly had respectable Cainites among their ranks, but those cut from Etienne's cloth—those unsure, soft Cainites who harbored notions of damnation or forgiveness—he had no use for them.

But then, it could be worse, he reflected. Some Cainites fancied themselves God's true inheritors, blessed instead of cursed. These Cainite Heretics had never reached Outremer, to his knowledge, and that was well, because his impressionable vassal might well fall in with them. He instructed his agent to investigate Etienne's court and find out where the Ravnos's loyalties lay, and then send word back. Jürgen kept his words in letters simple, true and curt. The written word, so arcane to most of the kine, held power. Jürgen had gleaned that much from the Tremere, and although he did not understand their magics (nor did he care to), he was careful when he wrote letters never to reveal too much of himself. Everything he sent out into the world remained there, and could be discovered by anyone who looked diligently enough. Jürgen of Magdeburg had too many enemies with too many resources—one detail about himself loose in the world was too many.

Which made the question of what to do about Rosamund that much more pressing.

He ignored the matter for the moment. He finished his letter to Acre, and sealed it. As he did so, he whispered, "This is my seal. I lock this seal with my soul and blood, and any who break the seal but the man for whom I wrote this shall be known to me, and he shall face my wrath." He bit his finger and dripped a few drops of his potent blood onto the still-cooling wax, and set the letter aside. It was as secure as he could make it, and there was more business at hand.

He would have to leave Magdeburg in capable hands; he could be gone for years. Many of his vassals were young Cainites, and too many of his enemies would be happy to destroy a fledgling vampire and take the important city from him. His sire could, of course, offer some assistance in guarding the city from rivals, but he was loath to ask Hardestadt for anything of late. Hardestadt was bitter about Alexander's departure and subsequent demise and still looked askance at his childe's failure to acquire new territory east of the Elbe. He had once considered leaving the city under Father Erasmus's guidance, but had since decided he needed to leave Magdeburg in the care of a fellow Scion. He needed a man he could trust, a man sworn to him and who would respect the vows of fealty, but who still had the age and patience of an elder Cainite. Oh, and who could survive having a duplicitous bastard like Jervais in the city, as well.

Ruling as one of the lords of the night, he reflected, was much more difficult than ruling as a mortal. A mortal's reign, no matter how glorious, ended, and so there eventually came a time when a ruler could stop planning new conquests or answering troubles within his realm and instead focus on turning over power to a successor. The transition was rarely easy for the inheritor, but at least for the departed ruler the struggle was over.

And is that what I'm doing now? Preparing to leave on a final journey? Does my time as Prince of Magdeburg end here, no matter whom I put in charge?

It did not, he decided. When he had chosen his road, his ethos to allow him to remain in control of the hunger and fear that was the Beast, he had chosen the only one that made any sense to him. The Road of Kings was a difficult one—it required absolute adherence to sworn oaths and noble behavior at all times—but it was every inch a warrior and conqueror's path.

But not just a warrior's path, he reminded himself, *for Rosamund walks the same road. The Road of Kings holds diplomats and scholars as well as warlord. One doesn't need a sword to be a Scion.*

Jürgen stood and paced his chamber. He would have to feed, he knew, before attending to much more. He idly wondered what sort of fare he might sample; wars in the "Holy Empire," as it was laughably called now, were different from in his day. Prisoners were treated with more respect. Jürgen understood that the kine changed their customs with each setting of the sun, but the practice of ransom did make feeding difficult for him. He opened the door and beckoned for a servant.

The boy was no more than twelve summers and approached Jürgen as though he were approaching a bear tied to a pole with a fraying rope. "Yes?"

Jürgen knew that the boy was afraid, cowed by the aura of kingship that the Sword-Bearer exuded. He also knew that he could do nothing about it, and so did not bother being gentle or understanding. "Tell Christof I would speak to him. Also tell Hans that I shall be visiting him soon, and that I would prefer if he would have a vessel waiting for me." With that, Jürgen turned his back. He had learned not to watch the servants' expressions; many of them felt threatened or even offended when Jürgen referred to prisoners of war as vessels. Jürgen had no time to consider the feelings of his subordinates.

He returned to the matter at hand: What manner of man to leave in his stead? A possibility occurred to him; he could leave Rosamund here as an acting prince. He shook the thought off immediately. Doing that would require him to place a great deal of trust in the young Toreador. She was too recently a Cainite to handle the responsibility, and he feared that her sire in the

Courts of Love might exploit the situation. He certainly would, in Queen Isouda's position.

Besides, the notion of not being able to see her face for months or years...

Is irrelevant, he thought. *Of course the Artisan is lovely. They always are. And besides, it's hardly fitting to take one such as her to war.* He stopped in the middle of the room and closed his eyes as a pang of hunger—or desire?—rose up within him. The Beast stirred, but lazily.

What does the Beast know of love? No more than I do. God is for priests, love is for women, war is for men.

Christof knocked on the door. Jürgen knew the footsteps by their sound, the knock by the tone and force before the knight even entered the room. The prince sat in his chair and smiled. "Christof. I was just thinking of men and women, and here I have both in one body."

Christof shut the door behind her and said nothing at first. The prince knew that discussion of her double unlife—as Sister Lucretia and Brother Christof—made her uncomfortable. She had worked too long and too hard at maintaining both not to feel threatened when the subject was broached. When Jürgen did not continue, she spoke. "There is a messenger here for you, bearing papers and books."

Jürgen frowned. "Where does he come from?"

Christof removed her headgear. Her hair had been cut to just about her ears; Jürgen knew that come the next nightfall it would once again hang past her shoulders. "I don't know, sir. He is a Cainite and his walk and manner suggest he is of noble blood." Jürgen nodded in approval. "But I cannot guess at his clan. One of us, perhaps, but just as easily a Brujah or a Toreador. He is congenial and asks to present himself—and his business—to you at your convenience."

Jürgen nodded slowly. "And what of his thoughts?"

The knight-commander lowered her eyes. "I could not see. I have been practicing, and can read the thoughts of my own ghouls and the other knights. In fact, I discovered that one of them had learned," she gestured down at her body, "the truth about me, and I changed his memories before they had settled."

Jürgen grunted. "Good," he said. She probably deserved more credit than that. Altering memories, even fresh ones, wasn't easy for any Cainite. Jürgen remained silent, however. As capable as his knight-commander was, he had no wish to allow her to grow too proud.

"I could not read this courier's mind. Perhaps he is closer to Caine than I, or—"

"That doesn't matter for reading minds, only for commanding them." Jürgen sat forward and moved some of the papers on his table. Transporting paper on his journey would require more people, and extra care to make sure the papers were not allowed to become wet or damaged. "The Cainite mind is unchanged by age or lineage. Only the blood—which is what powers the command of thoughts and minds—changes in purity when it is diluted by distance from Caine... or mingling with the fallen." He paused, and then smiled. "Which reminds me. I shall be taking Wiftet on my journey."

Christof nodded. Jürgen imagined that she rejoiced, inwardly. "And me, sir? Shall I—"

"You shall remain here." Jürgen stood and crossed the room. He placed a hand on Christof's shoulder and pushed her gently to her knees, and then cut his wrist. "Drink."

Jürgen saw the look of surprise on her face at being made to take blood from him in such a manner. It was degrading to her, both as a woman and as a knight. Normally he would have drained his blood into a cup, asked for a spoken oath along with the strange communion. Why, then, did she not protest? he wondered. Was the scent of blood, her Beast's hunger, enough to make her ignore this indignity?

And more the point, why was Jürgen doing it? His Beast growled loudly enough to drown out the question, and Jürgen brought his hand close to her mouth. Her lips closed around the wound, and Jürgen resisted the temptation to clasp his other hand to her head while she lapped at his blood. He didn't allow her to take much; after only a few seconds, he withdrew his hand. Her lips and then tongue followed the cut, followed the blood, unconsciously. Whatever Christof's feelings for Jürgen as a man or as a companion, her feelings for him as a leader were enforced by the power of the blood and were therefore unbreakable. The wound on his wrist had already closed by the time he reached down to help her stand. "Remain here, my vassal, as acting prince. Remain here and govern as I would over the Cainites of Magdeburg. Use some of the knights as your vanguard and your enforcers should any question your rights to the city. But know that wherever I am, I am still Prince of Magdeburg, and I *shall* take the city's reins again when I return from my journey."

Christof—Lucretia von Harz—nodded, and replaced her headgear. "I understand." She paused, perhaps wishing to leave, but Jürgen fixed his gaze on her. "I swear I shall do as you ask, my liege."

Jürgen nodded. An oath held power for those who walked the Road of Kings. Even hearing her swearing the oath had roused Jürgen's Beast. An oath made was but one word from being broken, and once broken, the Beast edged ever closer to control. Over time, Jürgen had learned to hear the sound of a breaking oath from miles away, listening for the snap of betrayal through the Beast.

The prince licked his lips and again felt the odd pangs of not-quite-hunger. He shook his head and looked at Christof, who was staring at him with a look of fear, or perhaps envy.

"What is it, Christof?" Jürgen walked back to his chair, but realized he would need to feed before receiving the messenger.

"I—forgive me, sir. But while I drank from you I saw your thoughts."

"Did you?" Jürgen kept his words calm, but Christof could surely hear the Beast behind them. Jürgen had agreed to teach her the ways of stealing secrets from others' minds on the condition that she never attempt such a thing on him.

"I did not mean to, but when I tasted your blood, when you touched me—"

"Collect yourself, girl." The voice wasn't harsh, but Jürgen knew the words would sting. "That happens. The blood carries everything, life, mind and soul. It's only natural that you should see something, some random memory of mine, while you drank of my blood."

"Pardon me, but no, sir," she said. "It was something that had never happened, I think."

Jürgen glanced up. "Yes? What did you see?"

Christof cleared her throat. She was stalling, Jürgen knew. The dead had no need for such affectations. "I saw the room as you saw it, while I was drinking."

"Not uncommon, either. What of it?"

"When you looked down…" She stopped, looked up him with eyes so weak they made him wince. "I didn't see myself. I saw *her.*" With that, she turned and left the room.

Her. Jürgen knew who Christof meant, of course.

Rosamund.

Chapter Two

"This is all, then?" Jürgen looked over the prisoners with some distaste. Hans, Jürgen's jailor, nodded. The nod was too familiar, Jürgen thought. Hans was growing too comfortable in his role, taking too many liberties simply because he knew that Jürgen would not drink his blood. Jürgen fed only on prisoners of war. "Those taken in battle, alive or dead, I own, and will claim my tribute," the Sword-Bearer told his troops before any battle. The jailor therefore assumed that, since he was a ghoul in Jürgen's service, he was safe and could behave as though he was the prince's familiar or friend, instead of a lackey.

Jürgen turned towards the jailor, facing the man down. "Answer me, Hans."

"Yes, sir. That is all." Hans looked confused and frightened. He did not realize his crimes; he had meant no offense. Jürgen considered that for a moment, and then let the issue pass. Hans served him well.

"All right, then." Jürgen stepped forward and pinned one of the prisoners against the wall. The man began to protest, but Jürgen didn't even bother trying to place the man's accent. He sank his fangs into the prisoner's wrist. The prisoner—still a soldier, despite his fear, beat at Jürgen's back for a moment before the Kiss took hold, and then slumped against the wall, trying in vain to fight the pleasure that numbed his mind.

Jürgen often wondered about the Kiss. He had only felt it once as a mortal, during his Embrace. He didn't remember the kind of pleasure that most kine seemed to feel, a sensual and carnal euphoria that Cainite poets spoke so blushingly of in their works. He remembered submission, as a vassal submits to a lord or (he imagined) a priest submits to God, but nothing he would describe as particularly pleasurable, ordinarily.

But then there is Rosamund. And that wasn't mere pleasure... that was nothing he could describe.

The man under his fangs shuddered suddenly, and let out a quiet death rattle. Jürgen glanced up, startled, and the wound on the man's wrist released a tiny gout of blood, enough to stain the Sword-Bearer's shirt. He dropped the corpse and looked at the others. They were all pale, but that was to be expected in prisoners. And yet there was something else, something about the way they were sitting, their backs to the walls but hands pressed to the floor as though hiding something....

Jürgen crossed the room and yanked up another prisoner. The man protested, but weakly. Something was wrong with these people. Jürgen never kept vessels long enough for them to become ill—although he knew he had nothing to fear from plague, the illness left a fetid taste on the blood that he found quite unpalatable. These prisoners didn't look sick. They simply looked drained and weak. He turned the man around and examined his back, and then pulled up his arms and looked at the wrists. He found nothing. In frustration, he spun the man around again and peered into his thoughts.

As useful an ability as it was to be able to steal the very memories and thoughts of another, Jürgen detested using it. His line—the Ventrue, the Clan of Kingship—prided itself on ruling because they were meant to rule, not because they could tell people what they wished to hear. And yet, as the most powerful vampires in Europe fought each other, the traditional structures were breaking down, and he was forced to resort to such trickery much more often. Reading the mind of a Cainite, while distasteful, was often fascinating, although Jürgen preferred to avoid it. Using the power on mortals, however, was utterly disgusting.

Jürgen pushed aside the man's will as a woman would clear away cobwebs, but even so, he felt the man's thoughts crowding in him. Fear, loneliness, even lust clung to him like blood and shit from a battlefield. Worse, really—those scents had an earthy purity that Jürgen could appreciate. The stench of a mortal's mind wasn't oppressive or even heady, it was insidious, and his mind would feel it for nights afterwards.

Nonetheless, he continued. He saw the man's capture. He saw the man being led to the room, chained, locked in with his fellows. He saw long nights of prayer and mewling before God, saw their horror when a figure entered the room to drink their blood.

But Jürgen had never visited these people before.

Jürgen withdrew his senses from the man's mind, and the prisoner twitched in his grasp like a peasant woman in the grip of a randy knight. With a scowl, Jürgen dropped him. The Beast hissed for more blood, but Jürgen had quite lost his appetite for these vessels. He turned towards Hans, who was standing in the doorway with eyes with as big as wagon wheels.

"What did you hope to accomplish, Hans?" Jürgen didn't bother subsuming Hans's mind; he knew the jailor would answer a direct question honestly.

"I hoped... to become like *you*, sir."

As infuriating as it was, Jürgen laughed aloud. "Did you think the Gifts of Caine were so easily stolen? That all you had to do was drink the blood of a few captured soldiers and you would walk among them as a god, as a Scion?" He shook his head. "Hans, you amuse me. You disgust me, too, of course, and you have violated my trust and the oaths you swore to me, but you do amuse me. Were it so easy to become what I am, do you not think that others—others more learned or more clever than you—would have found out that secret long ago?" Jürgen walked to the quivering jailor, grabbed him by the shirt and pulled the door key from around his neck. "The Gifts of Caine can only be given, and *my* gifts are given only to those who are worthy. You are simply a jailor who victimizes his prisoners— and that serves no end except for making terrified prisoners. For my purposes, that won't do."

Hans managed to croak out the word "mercy" before the prince threw him against the wall. The jailor fell to the floor, bleeding but alive. Jürgen nodded back to the prisoners. "Take back your blood, if you wish." He shut the door behind him, reminding himself to arrange for the corpse he'd left to be removed within the next few nights. He'd let Christof deal with Hans's punishment, provided the other prisoners didn't kill him first.

The door to the prison led directly out into the night air. While the prison was certainly in better repair than many other such places—after all, to Jürgen it was more like a larder than a jail, and he had no desire to feed in a place that smelled like a privy—the air was stale and smelled of old blood. The night was cool, and Jürgen took a moment to listen to the world around him. Somewhere nearby, two people were sparring with swords—from the sounds of the blows and the timber of their grunts, he guessed it was Václav teaching one of the younger Knights of the Black Cross some of the maneuvers the eastern vampires used. He began to walk towards the sound, but a set of footsteps behind him caught his attention. His seneschal, Heinrich, stopped respectfully behind him and waited to be acknowledged.

"Yes?" Jürgen was aware his tone was harsh, but he wasn't having a pleasant night.

"A messenger, my lord. He wonders if you can see him tonight, or if he should return."

Jürgen glanced off towards the sound of steel on steel, and shook his head. It wasn't battle, but it was as close as he was likely to get for some time. "Tonight, I think. Where is he?"

Heinrich smiled. "Right this way." Jürgen looked down at his steward. Heinrich had a bounce to his step that usually indicated he was moments away from securing a large amount of money or goods. Jürgen didn't ask; he knew Heinrich would tell him within a few seconds. Heinrich was shrewd, but had trouble containing good news. "The messenger is really quite an interesting fellow," he said.

"Do tell," sighed Jürgen.

"He's a zealot, I think. I'm not sure." Jürgen almost groaned. Zealots were annoying—the wrong word could send them into a violent frenzy and he wasn't in the mood to have to write a letter to the messenger's master explaining why sending Brujah on courier missions was risky. He'd already had to do that once, when a Brujah representative from the baronies of Avalon had flown into frenzy after taking a comment about Scotsmen the wrong way. Mithras, fortunately, had been understanding, but the incident was embarrassing. "He's got a book with him—a collection of notes on the *Via Regalis*. It's written by someone called Acindynus."

"Acindynus?" Jürgen stopped short, trying to place the name. "The scholar? What does he want with me?"

Heinrich stopped as well, but fidgeted, obviously wanting to bring Jürgen to the messenger. "I don't know, exactly. He just said he wanted you to read what he brought, as other noble Cainites had done."

Jürgen started walking again. He had heard of this sort of thing. Ashen priests of the Road of Heaven sometime made notes in the margins of their Bibles, notes in languages long dead or in code that only other Cainites would understand. But the enforcers of his own road—the justicars—didn't bother with such obfuscation. And what possible message could Acindynus have for him, secret or otherwise? He was a soldier, not a philosopher. Jürgen was intrigued, but rather feared that it would turn out to be a waste of time. Or, worse yet, that it might be some ephemeral matter of the soul or the mind that he would be happy to hear about but could not, in any way, contribute to.

Possibly Rosamund could, however. Rosamund was much more able to put a poetical spin on matters that Jürgen merely found practical. He knew that many Cainites waxed poetic about the roads they walked, about the moral codes they used to keep their ravening Beasts in check and about the disposition of their souls. Jürgen, of course, knew the disposition of his soul. He had made his own decision in that regard, and had never doubted it.

"You mentioned other Cainites had read this messenger's works, Heinrich. Did he say *who* exactly had done so? And also, what's the messenger's name?"

Heinrich opened a door into the keep for his master, and his eyes rolled heavenward as he thought. "I remember him mentioning Prince Mithras of London, and of course Acindynus. I seemed to recall the name Rodrigo, as well, but I don't know who that is." Jürgen shook his head; "Rodrigo" sounded Italian or Aragonese to him, but he wasn't sure. "The messenger calls himself Rudolphus, but I suspect it to be a name he's using while here in Germany. His accent is strange. It isn't that I can't place it—it actually sounds like he was born and raised in Magdeburg, but since he wasn't—"

"I understand. Pay it no mind. He's a messenger, a professional traveler. Such men are paid to be invisible to all but those meant to see them. Lord knows I hire them occasionally. They are meant be," he paused and grimaced, "ghosts."

Heinrich closed the door behind them. He gave Jürgen a quizzical look, but did not ask. That was just as well. Jürgen had no wish to discuss his own particular "ghost" with Heinrich. A clanless vampire called Albin the Ghost had once served Jürgen, and had subsequently betrayed him. Jürgen had unwisely spared him, but then sent him on a mission Jürgen had assumed was suicide. Albin hadn't returned and now didn't respond to summons. *Just one more thing I should attempt to resolve before leaving,* Jürgen mused, *though I'm sure Christof could handle the wretch should he reappear.*

The two Cainites walked down the hall in silence, and from the hall where Jürgen received new guests, they heard two people, a man and a woman, laughing politely. *It seems,* thought Jürgen, *that my visitor has not been wanting for entertainment.* He entered the room ahead of Heinrich; the seneschal surely noted the breach of protocol, but the breach was Jürgen's to make.

Rosamund stood, and Jürgen stopped. Every fiber in his body willed him to keep walking, to greet—or even look at—his guest, but he could not but stop and look at her. He met her eyes and tried to smile. He dropped his eyes to her red lips and tried to speak.

Rosamund drifted to his side and touched his hand, and for one brief but excruciating second Jürgen saw in his mind's eye what Christof had described earlier—Rosamund kneeling before him to drink of his blood. Jürgen pulled his hand away. Rosamund gave him a strange, slightly hurt look, but Jürgen finally found his manhood and smiled gently at her. Then, at last, he turned his attention to the messenger.

Rudolphus stood patiently, and when the prince finally looked to him, he bowed deeply. He was stained from the road, but only someone with the keen senses of a Cainite would notice. He wore dark robes—a mortal traveling by night might well mistake him for a friar, if the mortal were to see him at all. A short sword lay on a table, well out of arm's reach—he obviously understood the etiquette of court enough to know that a civilized man does not wear arms in the presence of a Cainite prince he does not serve. A leather satchel hung around his neck, and Jürgen could smell ink and wax from inside it.

"My Lord Jürgen, permit me to introduce myself. I am called Rudolphus, and I serve Acindynus, a scholar of the Clan of Kings. I have come to deliver to you a letter and a book from my master." He opened the satchel and pulled forth a folded slip of paper sealed with an imprint Jürgen had never seen and a thick sheaf of bound papers.

Jürgen took the letter and the book, but did not open either. Instead, he looked over his visitor. He looked low-blooded to Jürgen, but that might well have simply been the dust of the road. The man's bearing was impressive enough; he had obviously been trained well, but who knew how many years had passed since that training? The prince glanced at Heinrich, who was still smiling broadly, and then back at Rosamund, who had seated herself and was waiting patiently to be addressed. Jürgen saw no reason to distrust the messenger, other than the fact that he *was* a messenger. "How long do you plan to stay here in Magdeburg, good sir Rudolphus?"

"If I could impose upon you to read the letter tonight and give me the answer to the question it contains, I could leave as early as tomorrow night, my lord."

Jürgen nodded. The letter looked brief enough, and he had no desire to leave Magdeburg with a newly arrived Cainite in the city. "And where will you go from here?"

The messenger looked thoughtful. "Actually, I hadn't made that decision yet. It depends, again, on your answer to the question in the letter."

Rosamund smiled. "Much depends on this letter, it seems. Don't make us wait any longer, my prince."

Jürgen felt his mood lighten when she spoke. He glanced at her face, afraid that she was employing one of the gifts of her clan, but she merely looked beautiful. He took up the letter and broke the seal, and read aloud:

Most honored and revered Prince of Magdeburg,

I am called Acindynus, and am considered something of a scholar among the Nobility of the Night. In an effort to collect thoughts and information regarding the Via Regalis *from those most suited to rule (and therefore to walk our road) I have sent my messenger to you, bearing my written works. You may read them and inscribe whatever comments you feel are appropriate. When you have made a notation, I ask only that you inscribe a symbol or mark that other Cainites will know as yours—this serves to keep the words and thoughts of the great princes separate from the seneschals and keepers who have also committed their thoughts to paper. Of course any Cainite's view may be of interest, but in matters of kings, it is truly the kings who matter.*

While reading the Letters, you may discover notations from allies, vassals, friends and enemies. You may read commentary that is counter to your own philosophies and even offensive. I ask, however, that you not mark out or destroy anything that you read here. "By his fruits shall you know him," after all, and that wisdom extends to foolish or crass words as well as wisdom and insight.

When you have finished, my messenger will take the book and continue on his way. I assume responsibility for any of his actions while he is visiting your city, though he has served me faithfully for many years and has never caused me any embarrassment. If you choose not to lend your wisdom to these pages, I will not fault you for it—there is much to demand your time in the current nights. However, please feel free to keep the book as long as necessary. We have nothing but time, after all.

I thank you for your time and look forward to reading your thoughts on the rights of kings.

Regere Sanguine Regere In Veritaem Est,

Acindynus,

Childe of Phoebe,

Childe of Marcus Verus,

Childe of Mithras,
Childe of Veddartha
Jürgen lingered over the signature and Acindynus's lineage. "Marcus Verus," he murmured, "is one of Mithras's Barons, but I did not know he was a childe of the Prince of London as well." Rudolphus nodded. "Baron Marcus declined to make any comments in this book himself. He said something about it being a waste of time, but I did not spend much time in his fief. The British Isles are strange lands, my lord."

"So I have heard," Jürgen replied, casting a look towards Rosamund. She hailed from England, but had never visited her home as a Cainite. Jürgen had, while still in the direct service of his sire, but it had been years. He remembered the country being prone to rain, and that the wilds were even stranger and more infested with Lupines than the German forests.

The room grew quiet. Rosamund gazed at Jürgen as though expecting him to ask her something. Rudolphus cast a glance back at Heinrich, who smiled cheerfully. Jürgen looked at the book, and then back at the letter. The fire crackled and popped from across the room, far enough away that even the most fearful Cainite wouldn't be unnerved.

After a long moment, Jürgen spoke again to the messenger. "I would very much like to read this book and perhaps to add my own thoughts, though I caution you that I am a soldier, not a philosopher."

Rudolphus smiled. "Other noble Cainites have said as much, and their contributions are much prized. I am sure yours will be invaluable to our road."

"However," Jürgen continued, "I am leaving on a matter of some importance. I cannot give this project the time it deserves before I leave, and I certainly can't ask that you leave the book here or wait while I am gone." The messenger looked disappointed; Jürgen suspected he was as intrigued by this scholarly endeavor as his master. "I have a solution, though, but it requires some trust on your part."

"Yes, my lord?"

"If you will allow me to take the book with me, I shall add my comments to it as a Scion and a soldier, in the field, commanding troops, whenever I have time. I would imagine that such an opportunity has not yet been presented to Acindynus."

Rudolphus smiled and shook his head. "It has not, and I'm sure he would be glad of it. However, you must understand, that book has not been re-copied in several years. Were we to lose it, we would lose the commentaries of many distinguished Cainites, some of whom are difficult to find." He raised his eyebrows thoughtfully. "At least one of which has since fallen to Final Death, actually."

Jürgen nodded. "I understand, Rudolphus. I can only offer to swear to do everything in my power to keep the book safe, and to send a courier immediately west if my own situation becomes untenable. If you are, as you say, a Scion," at this Jürgen cocked an ear to listen for a lie, but heard none, "you know that my word binds me as surely as yours binds you to your master."

The Brujah messenger nodded. "Quite so, sir. I accept your word as binding, though I expect that if the book is lost or damaged, my master might wish some reparation to be made."

"Of course," Jürgen nodded. The paper alone was valuable enough to merit a boon if he lost it.

"I would also ask one other favor. I am not welcome in the lands of the *Voivodate*. I understand that you have had trouble there of late, but if I understand you correctly, you are traveling east, yes?"

"Circumstances may indeed conspire to draw me to Transdanubia, yes."

"Surely some of the Tzimisce walk the *Via Regalis*, but I have never met one, Scion or otherwise. If, perhaps, you chance to come across such a Tzimisce and are on somewhat amicable terms, you might persuade him to write his own thoughts in this book? My master would be overjoyed, I know."

Jürgen laughed out loud, and Heinrich grinned as well. "Yes, of course. And if I chance to meet Our Savior on the road as well, I shall of course obtain his insights."

"My lord, have I offended?" Rudolphus was apparently not as well-informed as he might be, considering the number of Cainites he had undoubtedly spoken with, else he would have known the depth of Jürgen's loathing for the Tzimisce. Jürgen wondered if the courier really understood the value of the book he carried or if he was simply anxious to please his master.

"No, Rudolphus. I apologize for my brusqueness. I do wish you to understand, however, that I am unlikely to speak with a Tzimisce under circumstances that would allow me to make this offer. If, by some miracle, it does happen, I shall of course do as you request."

Rudolphus grinned. "Excellent. In that case, my lord, I will request to stay in Magdeburg only one night, and then I shall be leaving for Hamburg."

"I have heard that Hamburg has a Malkavian prince, is that true?" The voice was Rosamund's, and Jürgen started. She had been quiet since before he'd read the letter, and her voice once again stirred the feeling within that wasn't quite hunger.

Rudolphus turned to face her. "Yes, my lady. Prince Midian is indeed one of the Moon Clan, and I must say that his court is... rather different that my lord Prince Jürgen's."

Jürgen looked down at the book with something like distaste on his face. "Are his notes in this book?"

Rudolphus shifted uncomfortably. "No. I tried to explain my mission, but Prince Midian never quite seemed to understand what I wanted. Actually, he didn't seem to understand that I was there at all, at times. I left the following night, and was halfway here before a messenger from an elder of Hamburg called Lucius Cornelius Scipio, one of my clan."

"I know Scipio, but he's no Scion." Jürgen frowned. Rumors flew about the "true power" in the city of Hamburg, but as the Cainites there were ideologically much closer to Julia Antasia's humanist leanings than he and his sire, he had little verified information. Scipio, from what he'd heard, only held what power he chose, but there were other, more influential, Cainites in the city.

"Indeed, many of those who have made commentary are not. Other viewpoints are useful, to a point, or so says my master. Faithful Cainites may remind us that we answer to God—"

"'Remember, you are mortal.'" Jürgen smirked. "Very well. Godspeed on your journey, Rudolphus. How shall I leave word for you regarding this book?"

"I shall send word to my master that the book, or word of it, will one night await him in Magdeburg. He will advise me from there, though I'm sure he will simply send a minor agent to make inquiries of your seneschal periodically."

"Good." Jürgen nodded at Rudolphus, who correctly surmised that the interview was over and took his leave. Heinrich followed him out. Jürgen sat down and opened the book. The words "Letters from the Lord of the Night" greeted him. He grimaced.

"What is it?" Rosamund could read him. She knew he was annoyed, even if the reason was minor. Could she read his mind as well? *Would* she?

"Nothing. Vanity." He smiled bitterly. "I find it curious that Julia Antasia, who admittedly is much my elder but is *no* Scion, has commented in this book no fewer than three separate times."

"Yet you have never been asked before." She sat down next to him. "It does seem strange. Especially since Rudolphus has been in Magdeburg before."

"What?" Jürgen was fairly sure he had never seen the Brujah before, but then, messengers weren't supposed to be noticeable.

"He was at the tourney. I didn't speak with him, and I don't think he was there the entire time, but I remember him." She sensed his displeasure and spoke before he could. "I didn't say anything before because I wasn't sure. He's a messenger, and he's unremarkable. But before he left, I recognized him."

"How?" Jürgen turned to face her, as difficult as it was to look at her eyes.

"I don't know. His walk, perhaps. The way he smiled at Heinrich. I don't know what he was doing here before, but we could call him back to ask him."

Jürgen considered. "No need. He is, as you say, a messenger, and any business he had at the tourney was concluded then. In any case, we don't need any other distractions. We'll be leaving for Livonia tomorrow night."

"We?" Rosamund was smiling. As beautiful as her speeches could be, one word was enough to render Lord Jürgen mute, and that enraged him.

"Yes." He tried to think of something to say, something that would tell her it wasn't because he distrusted her, it was because she was who she was that he wanted her along. "The thought of not seeing you for months..." he stopped. "Yes. Both of us. And Wiftet, I think."

Rosamund smiled, and glanced down at the book, and then back up at Jürgen. "I look forward to your thoughts on that book."

"Hmm? Oh, yes. I look forward to reading it, although I am a bit confused as to what Acindynus hopes he'll gain by asking the opinions of those who don't walk my—our—road."

"Just what Rudolphus said, I think. You give confession to one of the Faithful."

"Yes. Erasmus." The Toreador priest was out of the city on an errand, and wouldn't be back before they left.

Rosamund lowered her eyes. "That isn't who I meant," she whispered.

Jürgen smiled almost guiltily. "Ah. Gotzon." He shook his head. "I couldn't explain Gotzon if I tried. He's a Lasombra, yes, and yet he is not much like most others of his clan. I trust you know enough of me, my lady, to know my mind on the Clan of Shadows as a whole." She nodded; Jürgen made no secret of his hatred for Lasombra; travelers of the clan in Germany didn't bother stopping in Magdeburg. "He... I have known him since my Embrace. Since that night, in fact." He stopped. He was not prepared to tell the tale of his Embrace—the whole tale, any-way—to anyone, even her. *Especially her*, he thought. Instead, he thought of Gotzon and what he'd done since then. "Gotzon's faith is pure in the way a crusader's should be."

"Is he a crusader, then? What is his crusade?"

"He has many." Jürgen shifted slightly. Talking about Gotzon made him uncomfortable; while he was not bound by oath or propriety from revealing Gotzon's motives, he disliked speaking of his confessor. "If you asked him, he would prob-ably say only that he does the Lord's work, but the manner of work that God demands of him is bloody indeed. Pagans, her-etics, even demons and those who would call them forth—all those have fallen before him."

"I find it strange, then, that more tales don't circulate of his doings. Such a hero should have ballads."

Jürgen smirked. "I don't think that the title 'hero' truly suits him." Jürgen looked upward, trying to think of a way to explain Gotzon to Rosamund. "Consider," he said, "the Brothers of the Black Cross, or even the mortal order to which they are bound. All of those men are clergy, and yet they fight and kill, in God's name."

"I have seen what men do in God's name," said Rosamund coldly.

"Yes, I know." The Church had its own warriors to hunt down vampires, and Rosamund had suffered because of them. "Gotzon is not unlike those inquisitors, I'm afraid. I've often thought that only those who have seen Hell, in some form, are qualified to preach of it."

Rosamund shivered. The gesture was meaningless. The night was cold, but the flesh of Cainites was colder. "I have no doubt that he has seen Hell."

Jürgen took her hand, gently. "Do you fear him?" He winced immediately. That wasn't what he'd wanted to know. Rosamund seemed to understand, however.

"I don't fear him, exactly. Certainly he is frightening, but many elders are." The specter of Alexander seemed to alight on her shoulder for a moment, but then was gone. "I fear… what he has seen. As you say, he has seen Hell. I fear that some part of him might still be there. His eyes—"

"No different than many others of his clan, I assure you," Jürgen muttered. He was thinking of Norbert von Xanten, the Lasombra Prince of Brunswick. Norbert had once harbored desires of taking Magdeburg, having been its archbishop in life. When he had joined the ranks of the undead, the Brujah Cedric had still been Prince of Magdeburg and Jürgen his occasional advisor (though still in service to Hardestadt). After a fire claimed Cedric, Norbert and Jürgen had both been contenders for the city's throne, but with Hardestadt's support, Jürgen had easily emerged victorious. He had often wondered who Norbert's sire was and why he hadn't supported his childe's bid for power—or indeed, why no other prominent Lasombra had stepped forward.

"Yes, but *his* eyes are different." Rosamund was insistent. "His eyes are... so different from yours."

Jürgen blinked. "How so, my lady?"

She smiled again. "Your eyes are strong, my lord. Your eyes are *alive*. I see motion and steel and power in your eyes. Your eyes frighten me at times, too, but not like his. Yours have a vibrancy to them that I've not seen—I've seen such intensity before, but never under such control. You see. You *know*, and it's beautiful to behold." She stopped, and gazed at his eyes. Jürgen knew that she might stay like that for hours if he let her, transfixed by something so simple as his eyes. He reached up and brushed her cheek, and she shook her head and smiled demurely.

"And his eyes... aren't like mine?"

"Gotzon's eyes are lifeless. Not dead or even empty, but lifeless. Like seawater at night. The darkness he's beheld isn't empty, and that's what terrifies me. I think that his faith is so strong because he *knows* what's waiting in the dark."

Jürgen could think of nothing to say, so he reached forward to touch her shoulder. She moved forward to hold him, and he put his arms around her, awkwardly, her small frame pressed close against his chest. *A sword might break against my body*, he thought, *and yet this girl breaks me*. He opened his mouth to say as much to her, and then stopped.

He let her go and turned towards the door with a look of annoyance. Someone was waiting on the other side—Heinrich, by the sound. "Enter."

Heinrich leaned into the room. "Forgive me, my lord. But I knew you would wish to know immediately."

"Yes?"

Heinrich glanced behind him as though afraid of being watched. "Albin the Ghost has been captured...." He glanced nervously at Rosamund. "He was captured in my lady Rosamund's rooms."

Chapter Three

Watching Rosamund of Islington laugh was as close to sunlight as any sane vampire ever dared go. Hearing her sing or recite poetry was to hear a siren. Watching her walk was to see the beauty of God's love in motion.

Watching her weep was unbearable.

Rosamund crouched over the corpse of her maidservant. Jürgen tried to remember her name—Blanche, he believed. She was French, and despite her time here hadn't been able to learn much German. He remembered Rosamund laughing about it.

Rosamund cared for her servants too deeply.

She crouched over the woman's corpse and shut Blanche's eyes, whispering a prayer for her soul. Jürgen had already sent a messenger to fetch Jervais, but it was more to see where the Tremere was than out of any need to have him here. If need be, Jürgen could command the very room to give up its memories, but he didn't think it would be necessary. It was fairly obvious what had happened.

Albin the Ghost, Jürgen's onetime spy, had been charged with spying on a band of rabble calling itself the Silent Fury. Jürgen knew the Silent Fury; he'd discussed them with Hardestadt and with other Cainite nobles. They wished for nothing more than the ashes of the Cainite nobility staining their fingers—what they called "freedom." It wasn't hard to see how Albin, who had always been an imbecile, could have fallen in with them. He had failed to report in for more than a month, and Jürgen had assumed he had either joined them or been destroyed. It seemed that he had returned, although what he hoped to accomplish by this course of action wasn't easily apparent.

He had sneaked into the priory, probably by using the one gift that Caine had seen fit to grant him—stealth. If Jürgen remembered correctly, Albin was among those Cainites who could shroud themselves in another's likeness for a short time. Jürgen personally found the practice crass and cowardly, but it suited Albin well. Jürgen clucked his tongue. Albin was no threat, but a cannier vampire could certainly wreak havoc upon the court using similar abilities. He made a mental note to think of a way to counter such attacks and then went back to surveying the scene.

No one else had been reported missing and no other bodies had been found, so if Albin had had any business other than murdering the unfortunate maid, it remained undiscovered. Jürgen wasn't willing to give Albin much credit for strategy (although he wouldn't have expected *this* much audacity from the clanless wretch), but did dispatch two knights to search the area for anyone lurking in shadows or anything out of place. He admonished them not to separate and not to make eye contact with anyone they didn't know. "You are both good men," he said. "I have no wish to kill you because your minds are poisoned by another Cainite."

Blanche had died to assuage the Ghost's hunger. Her body was chalk-white and two ragged holes trickled blood down her neck. The Caitiff hadn't even bothered to close the wounds.

Rosamund sat weeping, her face stained crimson. Jürgen turned away; he had no desire to see her this way. Vampires could not cry true tears, he knew this, but the sight of Rosamund's perfect face streaked with blood...

He stalked out of her quarters and made for Sir Thomas, her bodyguard. The Englishman saw Jürgen coming and, Jürgen thought, made a mental prayer that his death would be painless. The Sword-Bearer picked the knight up by his throat and pressed him against a wall. "Sir Thomas, is it?"

"Yes," he croaked. "I am sorry, I don't—"

"Silence," hissed Jürgen. He lowered his arm so that he and the knight were face to face. "Where were you?"

"Awaiting my lady outside the priory. She was with you."

Jürgen bared his fangs. "Why were you not here?"

Thomas, his mind caught in Jürgen's grasp as surely as his neck, cried out, "I was waiting on my lady, sir. I was told to wait on her there. She told me. I wait for her every night—I do not guard her quarters."

Jürgen dropped him in disgust. Of course he was right— had *Rosamund* actually been in her quarters, she would have had protectors aplenty. Blanche, a maidservant simply waiting on her lady's return, did not. He turned and walked back to his lady and knelt next to her.

"I am sorry," he said. It was all he could think of.

"Oh, Blanche," Rosamund whispered. Her tears had stopped, but her face was still stained red. Jürgen helped her up and gestured to Sir Thomas and to Rosamund's secretary and assistant, Peter, only now arriving.

"You two, attend your lady. Do not leave her side," he said pointedly at Thomas. The two men led Rosamund off. Christof stepped up beside Jürgen. "This has happened before, Christof. One of her servants dying." Jürgen shook his head. "It's amazing, you know. She knows their names, their minds, their lives."

"Why don't you, my lord?"

Jürgen turned to face his second, but the look on her face was merely curious. She had intended no disrespect.

Jürgen considered the question. "I suppose I could never weep so for anyone."

"No one?" The two Cainites watched Rosamund being led off to the Embassy of the Rose.

"Where is Albin?"

Christof began walking. "This way, my lord. Chained and awaiting you."

Jürgen glanced behind him. "And where is Jervais? More to the point, where was he during all of this?"

"The messenger you sent spoke with Fidus, his apprentice. Jervais has been deep in study all night and left strict instructions not to be disturbed." Christof sniffed. "Deeply involved in blasphemy, no doubt."

"Yes. But if he's casting one of his spells that requires the entire night… Hmm. Either an alibi or a very convenient excuse. He used Albin as a pawn once before, if you recall." Jürgen rolled his eyes. The affair with the Toreador sword had simply been the beginning of a very long debacle. The stars must have been in very strange places that year. "I doubt very much that he is attempting to betray me so soon after establishing his precious chantry, but if he is involved, I'm sure Albin will tell me."

Chapter Four

From the moment Jürgen saw Albin the Ghost, chained to the wall in the priory dungeon, he knew something was wrong. Albin was standing *straight*.

Albin never stood straight. Albin the Ghost was a pathetic fool, a clanless, weak-blooded pizzle. He did have one useful trait—he knew Magdeburg better than any living or unliving soul, Jürgen included. But Jürgen had never allowed him to take pride in even that, instead reminding him at every turn that the Ghost owed his unlife to the Sword-Bearer.

As Jürgen watched, Albin faded from sight. The chains were still there, but they appeared now to be hanging limply from the wall. Jürgen cocked his head and stared piercingly at where he knew his prisoner was still standing. Caine had granted some of his children the gift of vanishing from plain sight, and the implementation of it was unnerving to watch. Indeed, the ghoul who had taken Hans's place gasped as the prisoner disappeared. Jürgen knew that Caine had granted that gift only to vampires who were unworthy of greater power. The deceitful, the mad, the hideous—they could disguise themselves with trickery. Jürgen stared, and the power covering Albin faded away. Albin couldn't command shadows as Jürgen's confessor, Gotzon, could—his power instead caused others to ignore him. *Fitting*, thought Jürgen, *that the Ghost's only notable gift should be the power to become* more *ignominious*. He noted, however, that Albin's control of his power was stronger. Jürgen actually had to concentrate to see him, willing his eyes to acknowledge the fact that Albin was, in fact, standing there. The prince frowned; Albin's power could never surpass Jürgen's ability to find him, but he seemed surer of himself, as though someone had finally treated him like the valuable person he clearly was not.

"Albin, what on Earth are you doing? Even if you could fool me into thinking you had escaped, you're hardly like to do so when I'm standing in front of you."

Albin the Ghost cracked a smile, something else that Jürgen had never seen him do. And then he spit blood in Jürgen's face.

It was by no means the first time Jürgen had suffered such an insult. Men in power, he had come to recognize, suffered all manner of slander and envy from those beneath them. He had long suspected that Albin hated him, but before that hatred had always been submerged beneath a healthy dose of fear and respect. But now the wretch had apparently grown some balls, and thought that this development entitled him to stand up to the Prince of Magdeburg.

And that simply would not do.

The jailor, whose name Jürgen hadn't bothered to ask, was fortunately quick on the uptake. He did not react to Albin's suicidal action, but stepped forward and asked, "What shall I bring you, my lord?"

Jürgen wiped the congealed blood from his face. "Build a small fire outside the room and bring me a sharp knife. And a sharpened stake, please. Nothing else will be required." The jailor left, and Jürgen stepped forward.

"Come closer," hissed Albin. "I would love to bite your lips off."

Jürgen smirked. "You have the look of a man who intends to perish come the dawn, or else be rescued. Neither is likely, Albin." The Ghost's only response was to spit at Jürgen's feet. "Come now. Keep that up and you'll starve yourself into torpor, and then I'll have to sacrifice some perfectly decent rats to bring you around. Isn't that your chosen fare? Rats?"

"I have not supped on rats for some years now, Jürgen." Jürgen refrained from breaking the man's jaw for the slight, but reminded himself to do so later. "And all I mean to do is return to you the blood of yours that you forced me to drink."

Jürgen bristled. "I never forced you into anything, Caitiff. You came to me for protection and I took you as my vassal. You swore an *oath* before me and God—"

"As if I had a choice!" The voice was so bitter that even Jürgen was taken aback. "I came to you to beg for mercy, that much is true, but had I known what you would do to me I would have died in the sun first."

Jürgen shook his head. "Believe me when I tell you that other Cainites have had it much worse than you ever did, Albin. I ask my vassals for very little in comparison to—" he almost said *"Alexander"* but then corrected himself. The Ghost would know little of the former Prince of Paris, and he had no desire to say the man's name again in any case.

"As Hardestadt?"

Jürgen shut his eyes. His Beast politely asked permission to separate Albin's head from his torso. "You would do well to avoid speaking of my sire, wretch. You will wish for the Final Death come the dawn in any event, but whether that wish is granted or not is another matter."

"Really? You love Hardestadt then? You took the oath willingly to him, did you? You find him a kind master? Such things I could tell you of Hardesta—"

Jürgen surged forward and caught the Caitiff under the jaw, slamming his head against the stone wall. He stared into Albin's eyes and commanded him, his words backed by the power and blood of the Third Mortal himself. Jürgen felt Albin's mind like a thin covering of ice on a pond, felt it splinter and then shatter under his power. *"Do not speak of Hardestadt, boy."*

The command filtered through Albin's mind. Jürgen had seen the same look before on many faces, kine and Cainite alike. But the look was different—commanding Albin not to speak of Jürgen's sire shouldn't have any real effect on the Caitiff, emotionally. Yet Albin looked confused, even crushed.

Jürgen did not release Albin from his mental power immediately, but rather searched through his memories, looking for what had happened to the Ghost. He saw his former spy looking in on other Cainites, doubtless members of the Silent Fury. He saw five of them and recognized one, a Brujah called Armin Brenner whom he had imprisoned some eight years before for burning down a warehouse in Magdeburg. The other four, he did not recognize. Two were women, two men. One of the women was wild-looking, surely ruled much of the time by her Beast, but he didn't think her one of the animalistic Gangrel. Such Cainites often sported fur and claws and wolf-like eyes; this woman looked human enough. Her features weren't German, however—possibly Slavic?

One of the men bore the mien of a boy, eighteen summers at the most. If Jürgen didn't know that Brenner was the nominal leader of these fools, he'd have guessed that this one was. He regarded the others with a careful eye, and as the four of them sat crouched around a table in some dingy room, he watched the walls and windows. Jürgen realized that Albin must have been watching invisibly while this meeting took place.

The other two Cainites sat near each other. The man's clothing was French, and Jürgen wondered if Rosamund or someone else in the Courts of Love might know who those vampires were. The woman—a waif not any older (before her Embrace) than Rosamund, clasped the man's hand. Far from looking frightened, though, they both had a lustful look about them. Jürgen stared through Albin's memory at the woman—she looked familiar, but he couldn't quite decide why.

As he watched, the scene began to fade, the colors becoming washed out and muted, the sounds of the memory falling to distant echoes. Jürgen tried to remain rooted in the memory, but minds—even one so weak as Albin's—were fluid things, and holding one was sometimes like holding a handful of water. Albin's eyes cleared. He laughed, and curled his lips back to spit again. Jürgen balled up a fist and broke his jaw before he got the chance, and then stalked out of the room.

Chapter Five

Christof and Heinrich waited outside the prison. Jürgen joined them, wiping blood from his fist. His two vassals looked at him expectantly.

"Well," began Jürgen, "someone of his acquaintance is fairly skilled at manipulating memories. His have been crushed into paste in places."

"Could you decipher them?" Christof had some skill with the minds of others, but not so much as Jürgen.

"Given time, but I don't think it's necessary."

"But there's obviously something they don't wish you to see," offered Heinrich.

Jürgen shook his head. "That isn't the point. It seems fairly clear what the Silent Fury is doing; they've allowed Albin to become captured and made him swear, upon every loyalty he has, not to tell me some inane fact. That I will beat that fact out of him will no doubt come as a great shock to Albin, but not the Silent Fury. When I put that fact, whatever it may be, although I suspect it is the location of a meeting, to use, the Silent Fury intends to kill me, or at least whomever I would send to rout them."

"Could they be so brazen?" asked Heinrich.

"I wouldn't have thought so," said Jürgen, "if they hadn't managed to convince Albin the Ghost to spit in my face." Heinrich gasped. "He's still intact. Mostly." He decided not to tell his vassals about Albin's other insult, speaking familiarly of Hardestadt. It embarrassed him to think of it.

"So what shall we do? Surely you aren't going to play into their hands."

Christof nodded. "Yes, my lord. Leave him chained up here and continue with your journey as planned. If the Silent Fury follows you to Livonia, they are bigger fools than we thought. If they remain here in Germany, my knights will find them surely enough once I piece Albin's memories back together."

Jürgen looked past them, towards the Embassy of the Rose. *Every detail out in the world is another weapon the enemy can use,* he thought. For Albin to steal into the city undetected would be child's play—no one knew the city better. For any other Cainite to infiltrate the priory was almost unthinkable, but Albin the Ghost could accomplish it. Once inside Jürgen's haven, he might remain unseen for nights. Destroying—or even attacking— Jürgen would be difficult if any trace of the blood oath remained, but it didn't seem to. And yet, Albin's role in the "plan" of the Silent Fury seemed clear. He was to be sacrificed to lure Jürgen to wherever they wanted to stage an assault.

"But it doesn't follow," said Jürgen aloud. "The Silent Fury's best hope for harming me would be to send Albin in and have him set a fire, or otherwise cause chaos here. Sending him here to bait me makes too many assumptions—it assumes that I can't repair his memories enough to discover the true plan: I can. It assumes that he'll break under torture. He will, but it's still a gamble, if even a slight one. It assumes that I won't just order him set on fire after killing one of my lady's servants, which I admit is tempting." He shook his head and pointed at the Embassy of the Rose. "Christof, send another two knights to guard Rosamund. Make sure they are sober and alert men, and that they have sworn oaths before the Black Cross." Christof trotted off in the direction of the order's house. Jürgen turned to his seneschal. "Heinrich, bring me Jervais. I don't care if he's communing with Satan Himself. If that sorcerer is going to reside in *my* city I am going to make sure he's useful." Heinrich nodded. As he turned to go, Jürgen stopped him. "Heinrich, one other thing. Have there been any arrivals from Brunswick? Not Cainites, necessarily, but merchants, mendicants, anything?"

Heinrich shook his head. He knew Norbert von Xanten, the Lasombra Prince of Brunswick was a rival of Jürgen's. "No, my lord."

"Good. Do as I ask. Have Jervais meet me at Albin's cell." With that, Jürgen turned and descended the stairs again. The jailor had the fire lit and blazing merrily and handed Jürgen a dagger. Jürgen nodded, and then opened the door to Albin's cell and spoke loudly enough for him to hear. "Now, kindly hold the blade of this dagger in the fire until it glows. When it is ready, knock on the door." The jailor nodded, but Jürgen wasn't looking. He entered the cell and shut the door.

Albin was still working his jaw back into place, which Jürgen imagined was difficult with his hands chained the to wall. He waited patiently for the Caitiff to finish.

"Well, Albin, since you've gone to all the trouble of breaking in here, betraying your master—"

"You are *not* my master any longer," he snarled.

Jürgen ignored him. "—and committing murder in my city, all the while carrying around clumsily concealed memories of the Silent Fury, it's fairly obvious that you want me to find something out."

"I don't know what the Silent Fury is!"

Jürgen shook his head. "If you're going to lie, at least tell a lie that has a *hope* of being believed. I told you to investigate the Silent Fury some time ago. You did. They caught you. You probably begged for your pathetic unlife. I have to admit, I wonder what manner of power they had to infuse you with for you to grow a spine—that unkemptlooking woman in your memories, is she a Tzimisce, by any chance? Did she graft a backbone on you, worm? Perhaps a pair of balls, as well?" He crossed the room towards Albin. The Ghost had apparently given up on spitting and instead kicked his leg out at Jürgen in a futile attempt to strike him. Jürgen batted down Albin's foot. He considered snapping his leg, but decided against it—Albin was stupid enough to waste precious energy on healing himself, and Jürgen didn't want to bother feeding him yet. "Albin, I am a better man than you, and so I shall be honest. You will never leave Magdeburg again. Your ashes *will* float down the Elbe, probably very soon. But you know more about this city than most Cainites, and doubtless you know *me* better than most Cainites. Please consider what I'm capable of doing to you. And don't make me do it."

"Does your pretty Toreador not fulfill you, Lord Jürgen, that you have to torture peasants for your pleasure?"

It was an obvious thing to say, as insults went. Jürgen had endured all manner of slights, both as a mortal warlord and as a Cainite. Part of being a leader was recognizing which slights had to be answered for in blood and which ones were simply born of desperation, a prisoner or foe trying to take whatever he could before the inevitable. This, Albin's petty insult, was very much the latter. The Caitiff knew that he was doomed, and was trying to salvage his own dignity. Jürgen's mind said all of this, but his Beast said something quite different.

Uncharacteristically, Jürgen listened to his Beast.

The look on Albin's face when Jürgen surged forward, teeth bared, eyes fairly glowing with hate, made it quite clear that he hadn't expected such a reaction. Jürgen sank his fangs into the Caitiff's sallow cheek and ripped downwards, tearing away a long flap of skin. The frenzy passed almost immediately, and Jürgen spat Albin's cheek at his feet and wiped the blood from his chin.

Albin was trying to retain his earlier bravado, but it wasn't working. His ruined face was twisted in panic and pain. His own toothless Beast was working its way to the surface. Jürgen decided to leave him alone for a moment. He left the room, and found the jailor busily heating the knife.

"Almost ready, my lord."

"Good," growled the prince. Footsteps echoed down the stairs. Jürgen couldn't clear his mind enough to tell whose they were, but expected them to belong to Jervais. He was very surprised to see Rosamund. "My lady?"

"I wanted to see the prisoner. I wanted to see what kind of creature killed one as innocent as Blanche."

Jürgen shook his head. "Surely you know, my sweet, that to many of our kind innocence is meat and drink. You have met such Cainites."

"I have." Her manner was strange. She seemed cold, numb, but very much in control. "But even so, please let me into his cell."

Jürgen stood in front of her. "Lady, I cannot. I am loath to deny you anything, and I know how you grieve, but you cannot see him, not now."

"Do you think that I will quail at the sight of him? Is he so fearsome?" The words should have been lightly sarcastic, but Rosamund's voice was so bitter that the jailor turned away, tears in his eyes.

Jürgen shook his head. "No. It isn't that I don't wish you to see him." *I do not wish you to see what I did to him, what I can do in your name.* "I cannot allow him to see you, for even the lowliest wretch might find himself uplifted by your beauty."

She didn't believe it, but she acted as though she did, and for that Jürgen silently thanked her. She turned and walked out of the jail, leaving the room colder and emptier in her absence.

"Is the knife ready yet?"

The jailor took a moment to compose himself, and then rasped, "Yes, my lord."

Jürgen took the red-hot blade from the jailor. The blade's handle was hot enough to sear human flesh, but to Jürgen it was merely uncomfortable. "When Jervais arrives, he is to wait here." With that, Jürgen opened the door.

Not more than twenty minutes passed from when Jürgen entered the room to when Jervais descended the stairs, but to the jailor, listening to the screams from inside the room, it certainly felt longer.

Chapter Six

"It is, in fact, Albin," Jervais said flatly, rubbing a drop of blood between his fingers.

"Please tell me something more useful than that, Jervais." Jürgen sat at his table, rubbing his temples. Albin's newfound resolve had lasted less than a minute from when Jürgen reentered the room. It was by no means the fastest he'd ever broken a prisoner, but then he'd never bitten off anyone's face before. Jervais had been tactful enough not to ask about it when he saw Albin.

"You have a much greater gift for rooting out spoken lies than I, my lord." Jervais smiled. "To my infinite regret."

Jürgen smirked mirthlessly. "That's just the problem. All that Albin says, he believes. But some of what he asserts simply isn't possible."

"My lord?"

Jürgen sat forward and glanced over the notes he'd written. He'd scrawled out as much of Albin's "confession" as he could on a wax tablet (and reflected ruefully that Albin was, if nothing else, succeeding in costing him time). "He said that he left my employ because of the way that I treated him. That's not true; I imprisoned him because of *his* betrayal of *me*. He said that he escaped, but then remained by my side for some time. He insists—*insists*—that the Silent Fury has a spy at my court...." Jürgen trailed off and raised his eyes to Jervais.

Jervais's eyes widened. "Surely, my lord, you don't think—"

Jürgen waved his hand at the Tremere. "No, no. I don't flatter myself that you've become entirely loyal to me, Jervais, but you aren't stupid, and you certainly aren't likely to ally with idiots like the Silent Fury." He looked at the tablet again. *Silent Fury has a spy in Magdeburg.* "No one here is, really. Unless a spy snuck in as he did and is simply hiding in the city... but he insisted the spy was part of my court."

"Do you believe that?"

Jürgen brushed aside the notes. "Again, Jervais, it's a strange set of circumstances. What I *know* is that Albin the Ghost has been the subject of a through, if not very precise, reworking of memory. If I, or Christof, or probably even you, had done the job, it would have been nearly undetectable, but as it is, it seems more like someone tried to sculpt new memories for him using a very dull ax. Therefore, while he believes there is a spy here, I'm inclined to think that this was simply something he was made to believe." He paused. "Taking that risk, however, is problematic, especially as I am about to leave the city."

"Christof is competent. I'm sure he would find the spy, if such existed."

Jürgen looked sharply at the warlock. "At present, Jervais, you and I know about this alleged spy, and no further does the story need to travel. Understood?"

"Yes, my lord."

"I have no need of panic in my courts." Jürgen looked at the rest of his notes from Albin's ramblings. "He described the other members of the Silent Fury, although he didn't know—or was not allowed to recall—most of their names. Apparently the coterie consists of only six, including him."

Jervais laughed. "Albin the Ghost, a slayer of kings?"

Jürgen, in spite of himself, chuckled. "I wouldn't have believed it, either. I still think it's mostly to do with their reworking of his mind. In fact, perhaps the clumsiness of the job is because he didn't submit to it willingly. At any rate, the other members are mostly high-blooded, if that's to be believed."

"Oh, yes?" Jervais spoke pleasantly enough, but Jürgen could still hear the bitterness. The Tremere courted the favor of the High Clans, but were never considered such.

"Yes. Two Toreador, sire and childe, one Brujah, and a Tzimisce." Jürgen was pleased that he had guessed the wild woman's clan correctly.

"And the last?"

"Clanless, like Albin. German, though. That's something."
He looked over the names; the German Caitiff was called
Christoffel Weiss. He didn't recognize the name, but then, why
should he?

"What else did he confess to?"

"Well, naturally the Silent Fury gave him information on
where they might be found during the day. A little makeshift
hovel on the road to Frankfurt. I imagine that if I were to send
knights there to kill them while they sleep, I'd find that they've
set up some sort of trap. If I send anyone during the night, the
trap still applies, and they'll be awake and waiting. I have no
intention on marching straight into their hands." He regarded
Jervais thoughtfully. "Perhaps you could summon some kind of
storm over the area?"

Jervais shook his head. "Not really my area of expertise, I'm
afraid."

"Ah, well."

"Perhaps you or Christof could summon them here? Is that
not one of the powers of the Ventrue?"

Jürgen shook his head. "I thought of that, but summoning
someone requires having met the person, as I understand it.
With only a name, it's possible we might call some poor man
from his bed."

"What of their leader? You said you've met him."

"Yes, but if I summon him, no doubt his compatriots will
restrain him. And the compulsion only lasts until dawn. The
sun breaks the summons as it breaks many of our powers. God
takes His due, like any lord." Jürgen stood. Dawn was approaching. He had hoped to resolve this issue and put Albin out for
the sun, but it seemed the matter would require more attention.
"Towards the end, his will broke entirely. He just kept singing
a song about a pig."

Jervais chuckled. "That wouldn't be a 'pig in a shining
crown' by any chance?"

Jürgen stared at him. "Yes, actually. How did you know
that?"

The Tremere looked up, startled and perhaps a bit frightened.

"It was a song—something the peasants used to sing in Paris sometimes. A ballad about the king."

"A ballad about the king featuring a pig in a crown?"

"Well, perhaps 'ballad' is the wrong term. It was an insult, frankly, but skillfully written. Actually, once you've heard the tune it's very difficult to lose it."

Jürgen nodded; he had, in fact, been unable to get the melody out of his head since Albin had started singing it. "But who wrote it?"

"Some dog called Pierre Cardinal. He was somewhat famous for a brief time; I'd always assumed the king's men had caught and hanged him."

Jürgen smiled. "Maybe not." He nodded towards the door. "Thank you, Jervais. We shall speak more tomorrow night." Jervais bowed slightly, and took his leave.

Jürgen sat alone for a moment, and then addressed the empty room. "Well? Have you any thoughts on this?"

A figure stepped forward from the shadows, slowly taking form, until a woman stood before Jürgen's table. Boils and pustules covered her gray-green skin. Her hair was only present in patches, most of them not on her head. She covered herself in thick robes, and looked on Jürgen with love and devotion. Her voice was soft and beautiful, and wrenching to hear from such a hideous frame. "My lord, I have heard that tune as well. I made it my business to learn the entire song, in fact."

Jürgen smiled. Akuji, his master of spies, collected stories and songs of all types. Her near-perfect memory was only one of the reasons she excelled at her post. "And can it help us in locating these Furores without them seeing us coming?"

"I think so. From what the Caitiff said in his confession, I think that they destroyed most of his memories of the Silent Fury, except what you were meant to see. Obviously, the German Caitiff—"

"Christoffel Weiss," murmured Jürgen.

"Yes. He was allowed to remain in Albin's memory for a reason, though I'm not sure why."

"It may have been a mistake on their parts, of course."

Akuji shook her head. "Perhaps, but I'd be more inclined

to think that it was a mistake if they *had* been more careful in changing his memories. As it is, that name was the one that they left—if the manipulation was as clumsy as you say—"

"Then it took more effort to leave the name than it would have taken to erase it. I see your point. But the song?"

The Nosferatu shrugged, the boils on her arms cracking and leaking slightly. "As you say, once you've heard the song, it stays. I think they just didn't notice."

"But that still leaves the question of how to find them on our terms."

"True. Perhaps I might be allowed to think on it and speak with you tomorrow night?"

Jürgen smiled. It was a pity Akuji was so hideous; he had known her for more than a century and she was one of the few Cainites he could bring himself to trust. *And yet the beautiful one, who so obviously wants my trust...* he didn't finish the thought. Instead, he nodded to his spymaster. "I shall be here tomorrow after sunset, awaiting your wise council." Akuji opened the door and faded from view. Some Nosferatu adopted masks, changing their appearance to something more palatable. Akuji preferred not to be seen.

Jürgen left his chamber and walked towards the Embassy of the Rose. It was late, he knew—Rosamund was probably preparing to sleep—but he felt restless. As he approached, he saw Sir Thomas step out of the shadows, sword half-drawn, and then step back just as quickly. "Your vigilance does you credit, Thomas," Jürgen said in his direction. He knocked on the embassy door; Peter, Rosamund's steward, opened it.

"My lord?"

"I would speak with Lady Rosamund." He watched Peter's face change, but subtly. These mortals had spent time with Alexander, where one false twitch of an eye could spell death. Peter seemed to disapprove of Jürgen's visit, but of course said nothing. The seneschal led Jürgen to Rosamund's chamber and knocked.

"My lady? Lord Jürgen is—"

"I know," came her voice. She opened the door and dismissed Peter, but did not welcome Jürgen into the room. Jürgen was shocked; any breach of etiquette was unheard of for her.

"My lady, have I offended?"

She turned to him. "My lord? What right have I to be offended by the prince's actions?"

Jürgen shook his head. "My lady, I admit to a desire to shield you from the horrors of what we are, and sometimes I forget that you are no less a Cainite than I. But Albin still hangs in his cell, and if it is truly important that you see him—"

"It is not." She stood, but glanced around at the chairs in the room. Jürgen took the hint, and sat. She did as well, but a good distance away. Neither said anything for a long moment.

Jürgen looked away from her face, and said, "Albin claims there is a spy in my court."

"A spy for whom?"

"The Silent Fury. A band of murderous rebels. They sent me a list of their aims some years ago—some nonsense about freedom to do as they would, as Caine said. I should have destroyed Albin before, rather than imprisoning him." He glanced at Rosamund, but she seemed unmoved.

"Is that what you will write in the books? That destroying your enemies is preferable to leaving them intact, since they might one day return?"

"The... book? Oh, Acindynus's letters? Perhaps, why? What would you write?"

Rosamund smiled coldly. "Me? I am no prince, my lord."

Jürgen's brow furrowed, and then relaxed. Obviously, Rosamund was upset that he had not invited her to make her own notes in the letters. He reproached himself; she was an Ambassador of the Rose and a diplomat and courtier of considerable standing, and no doubt her insights would be at least as interesting as his. Probably more so, he admitted—hers would be far better written. He opened his mouth to apologize, and then stopped. He wasn't sure how to make the offer to her without it sounding as though he was simply doing so to placate her. A woman like Rosamund did not deserve placation.

Jürgen's Beast stirred, drinking in his frustration and pain. It asked permission to look at Rosamund, to show Jürgen what it saw when it beheld the English rose. Jürgen denied it, and then slowly spoke. "My lady, I am sorry."

"For what?" Her tone was still cold, but softening. She had the same senses that he did, and could hear his sincerity.

"Chiefly that I did not say earlier, when Rudolphus was here, that I would make sure that your insights were added to Acindynus's letters along with mine. But also..." he faltered. "I do not know. I have no poetry, no verse from scripture or proverb of the ages that conveys what you are to me. I have no way to explain myself, for matters of the heart are not matters of the battlefield. I can construct no plan for breaching your heart the way you have breached mine."

Rosamund stood and took a seat closer to Jürgen. She took his hand and they sat there, her looking at him, him looking at the floor, for a long moment. Jürgen reflected that their hands did not warm to each other—mortals took much for granted. Even two hands warming each other by touch was a deliberate thing for vampires.

Jürgen's Beast exercised a rare moment of strength and asked Jürgen a question. *Does she make you miss your mortal life?* Jürgen declined to answer, but removed his hand and looked at his lady.

"Rosamund, a question." He hummed a snatch of the cardinal's infectious tune. "Do you know that song?"

She nodded. "Yes. I'd heard it in France, but I don't know where it comes from." She paused. "Why, my lord?"

The Sword-Bearer looked up at the door. He needed to leave; he could feel the dawn tugging at his soul. It wouldn't be proper for him to spend the day here, as much as waking up next to her the following evening might appeal. "Because of your time in France, I thought you might have heard the song and perhaps tales of its author." He frowned and shook his head. "And because—" he turned to face her—"I hold you in esteem, my lady, and recognize that you have the right to know the goings-on of this city. Your advice and knowledge are assets I have placed too little value on before this." His Beast snarled in frustration, and the soldier in him demanded that Rosamund be made to drink from him after this admission.

Rosamund said nothing. She had no need. Jürgen could see

her pride and jubilance, and that was enough to quiet both of those urges. He stood and took her hands, kissing them both, and then turned towards the door. He stopped before opening it. "I expect our journey might be slightly delayed as I deal with this 'Silent Fury'."

"Can I be of assistance?"

Jürgen opened the door, and heard the guards outside snap to attention. A thought struck him, and he smiled. "Perhaps, my lady. Tomorrow night, I may have need of your help."

"I am only too happy to be of service, my lord." He turned to look at her once more before leaving for his own haven. "And I am glad I will be allowed to help to avenge poor Blanche."

Jürgen nodded, and began the walk to his bedchamber. *Of course she is a true Scion,* he reflected, *and I should have recognized that earlier. A true Scion answers all debts and slights, and of course the murder of her servant must be paid for in blood.*

Chapter Seven

Albin the Ghost wept bitterly in his cell. According to the jailor, he had cried and gibbered all throughout the day in a kind of hysterical half-sleep. As soon as the sun had set, he had attempted to pull himself free of his bonds, but when that had failed, he could only stand and bawl.

Jürgen was about to ease his pain considerably.

He'd warned Rosamund that the creature in the cell was not so much a Cainite as the remains of one. He'd warned her that he might boast to her about killing her servant, about any number of foul deeds. Rosamund had taken these warnings to heart, of course, but Jürgen wasn't worried. Cainites of skill and age could reduce even other vampires to tears with a glance and a few well-chosen words, taking knowledge from their opponents' minds and backing that knowledge with the force of Caine's curse. Rosamund had experienced the worst of such manipulators; Albin the Ghost was hardly a threat.

Jürgen waited outside the jail for only an hour. Other Cainites and their servants, and even unknowing mortals wandered by, and he resisted the temptation to seize each of them and wrest whatever they knew from their minds. *Everyone knows something,* he thought, *but they don't usually understand the significance of what they know.*

The Beast asserted its boredom and reminded Jürgen of what he had done the night before. Jürgen slapped the voice down and buried it under thoughts of his erstwhile servant.

Albin the Ghost hadn't known his sire or his clan. Such Cainites were called "Caitiff" and were the lowest of the low, more debased and despised even than the cursed Malkavians or the deformed Nosferatu. But Jürgen had found uses for Albin, and set him to work in Magdeburg as a spy. When Albin had betrayed him, Jürgen had first imprisoned him, and then released him to find and report on the Silent Fury.

But apparently, there was some lost time here, somewhere. Not much—a year or two—but even so, Jürgen had let his attention to Albin slip. It was easy to do; the wretch was easy to ignore. Somewhere in the course of his travels, Albin had fallen in with the Silent Fury. *But the time still doesn't work,* thought Jürgen. *I imprisoned him... perhaps seventeen years ago. I released him shortly thereafter to trail these rebel bastards.*

Jürgen's Beast snarled a reminder. Albin hadn't been released, he'd escaped. Jürgen had simply caught him skulking around the city thereafter and erased the escape from his mind. In the years since, Jürgen had quite forgotten, just as Albin had. *But that still doesn't answer where the Ghost was between his escape and his recapture. It couldn't have been more than a few months, but much can happen in that time.*

"My lord?" Rosamund walked up to him from the jail. She wasn't disheveled in the slightest, at least not physically, but her expression told Jürgen that something else was very wrong. "We must speak alone."

Moments later they sat in Jürgen's chambers, the door guarded by ghoul knights and a fire blazing away. Jürgen hoped the noise from the fire would mask their conversation from any Cainites in the area. "My lady, what did he tell you?"

She looked at his chest as if afraid. "Did you... command him last night? To refrain from speaking of your sire?"

Jürgen shifted uncomfortably. "Yes, but what of it?"

Rosamund nodded. "That is why he was so muddled, and that is why his mind was unclear, I think. But as I am unable to command minds or reorder memories—"

"What have you found, my lady?" Jürgen was growing nervous. He was beginning to suspect what had happened.

"He was commanded by the woman—the Tzimisce in the Silent Fury—to reveal to you his true allegiance. He has been in the employ of your sire since his release from imprisonment." Rosamund's eyes didn't move.

Jürgen shut his eyes. "And in what capacity?"

Rosamund's words were a whisper, but Jürgen heard them well enough. "He was spying on you on Hardestadt's behalf."

Jürgen felt his fangs elongating, and his eyes snapped open. He made the mistake of catching his lady's gaze for a second, and saw her own eyes widen in fear. *Have my eyes that vibrancy you so cherish now?* he thought. "He told you this, even with the command I gave him?"

Rosamund shook his head. "He never said so much, not directly. But I saw it. I saw the way his colors and mind changed when I spoke of you and of Hardestadt. I think he has taken blood from your sire."

Jürgen ground his teeth. "Yes, I suppose his blood might well wash away the oath Albin had with me, especially since he has not received my own blood in so long." Jürgen took a moment to put the pieces together. The Silent Fury never went too far from Magdeburg, which meant that Albin could spy on both them and Jürgen without too much difficulty, especially if he and the rebels were allied. But Hardestadt... what did the lord of the Fiefs of the Black Cross think to gain here?

He stood. "Very well. I understand their plan, and I know what must be done. I ride tonight, alone." His Beast leapt up and howled in delight, but Jürgen shushed it. He walked to the door, and then turned. "My lady..." He moved back to her and took her hands. "I do not know how to thank you for this. I can only say that I knew that there was more to learn from Albin, but that finding it myself would take time, as he would resist me." He stepped closer. "But no one resists you."

He leaned in and kissed her. His fangs were still extended and they brushed gently against her lips, but drew no blood.

They kissed, and he lost time. He lost rage and blood and honor. He lost everything but the kiss, but her, but what she had done for him without thought of boon or advantage.

Love?

The soldier refused to allow it. He stopped and pulled back. She looked surprised and perhaps a bit frightened—this was unlike Jürgen. He turned and left the room, instructing the guards to make sure that Rosamund was kept safe.

Heinrich joined him immediately. "My lord, what is happening?"

Jürgen grimaced. "I am leaving, Heinrich. I have important business." He nodded towards the stables. "Go and make sure my horse is saddled, and tell Christof that he is to act as prince until I return. I doubt it will be more than a few nights."

"Alone, my lord?"

"Yes." He stopped at the prison door. "I am only staying to feed and get my sword, and then I ride." He started to descend the stairs, and then turned back to his seneschal. "Heinrich, Albin must not know that I have left, under any circumstances." Heinrich nodded and darted off to the stable. Jürgen continued down towards the prisoners. He would need his strength.

He knew where to find the Silent Fury.

Chapter Eight

Jürgen rode south, his horse's hooves deafening in the still night. He dearly wished he could dull his senses and hear as a mortal, but he could not—when riding at night, he needed to be able to see the road by the dim moonlight. While that was all very well, his hearing was similarly sharp, and the pounding hooves drowned out any other sound.

Trabitz. He had never been there. It wasn't a large town. It was significant only insofar as Hardestadt's court stopped nearby. Hardestadt never held court in the same place for too long. Every few years, he would send word to Jürgen as to his traveling schedule for when and where he expected to see his childe. Hardestadt paid very little attention to what happened behind him, as ever more concerned with what was before him. Jürgen couldn't find too much fault with his sire's practices—his sire was unquestionably one of the most powerful Cainites in the world. But he hadn't noticed the Silent Fury following him, dwelling ever in his shadow, probably only a week behind him. Feeding on his scraps like the dogs they were. Small wonder, then, that Albin had found them so easily.

Small wonder that Albin had such incomplete information on Jürgen—he had traveled with the Silent Fury instead of gathering information for Hardestadt.

Still, Jürgen could not help but pity the Ghost of Magdeburg. The Caitiff had no idea that he was meant to be a sacrificial lamb, simple bait to lead Jürgen into conflict with his sire. Jürgen rode on; he reasoned that he could reach Trabitz before daybreak. Once in the vicinity, he should have little trouble finding the Silent Fury—Cainites left evidence of their passing if they were not careful, and these Furores had most assuredly proven careless.

His horse's hooves flew over the uneven ground, but the steed—strengthened on Jürgen's blood and trained with Akuji's skill with animals—didn't slow. Jürgen's thoughts drifted to Rosamund. *Would she have come on this mission, had I asked? How have I any right to ask such a thing? This mission is nothing more or less than war, and Rosamund is no warrior.* That thought troubled Jürgen. All Cainites, no matter clan or road, possessed the capability for battle. The Rose Clan, known commonly as the Toreador, possessed skills of perception and speed that made them fearsome combatants. Some of them, like Rosamund's brother-in-Blood, Josselin, did choose that path; others chose more artistic pursuits. Jürgen wondered if Rosamund's sex held her back; he knew that sheer age and necessity made warriors out of many female Cainites.

He heard the river to the east and urged his horse closer to it. Hardestadt's court had followed the river for a time, and so the Sword-Bearer assumed that the Silent Fury had as well. He ducked under a branch and slowed slightly. He'd been riding for hours; his quarry should be somewhat nearby. Their leader had been a merchant in life, and if he was correct in his assumption that Pierre Cardinal was now a Cainite, spreading his tunes as he had in life, the pack of them wouldn't be too far from Trabitz. They must sleep outdoors or in a wagon, perhaps with a ghoul guard, and enter the city to feed at night. Now Jürgen only had to track them.

Trabitz wasn't a large settlement—the population wouldn't support five Cainites easily. As he rode, he smelled tilled earth. People, farmers perhaps, were nearby. He dismounted and walked his horse, having no desire to tire the stallion out too much. He would need to ride back as quickly as he'd come, after all.

From the distance he heard someone singing. The words were German, but the tune was familiar.

Sits in his castle on the Elbe,
Happy in his sty, happy in his swill.

Jürgen noted with some distaste that the lyrics had been

reworked to fit him. He drew his sword.

Spends nights at the teat of his fair French whore,

The pig, the pig with the shining sword.

Jürgen crept closer. He had no gift for stealth, but the Cainites of the Silent Fury seemed not to notice. He peered out at them—the moonlight was enough for him to see by, and of course they had no fire lit. Fire only served to frighten Cainites, for it could not warm them and many of them had no need of the light.

He only saw four. One sat near a small wagon and played on a lute. His clothes and accent marked him as Pierre Cardinal, the Toreador. His childe was nowhere to be seen, but she wasn't the one Jürgen was most concerned about. Christoffel Weiss, the Caitiff, stood near the Toreador and sang along. Armin Brenner stood off, peering towards the river.

Where is the Tzimisce?

Members of this clan, often called the Clan of Dragons, were dangerous in ways that no other Cainites could be. The merest touch of a Tzimisce could reshape flesh, splinter bone and even—if legends were to be believed—draw the blood from an unliving body. Jürgen wished to kill the wild-looking woman first, but could not see her.

And then Jürgen's horse shrieked, and he knew that she was near after all.

He heard the music stop and a warning called out in a language Jürgen had heard before, but did not understand—some bastard Slavic tongue.

The Sword-Bearer leapt to his feet and strode towards the Cainites. He had no need to hide, or to sneak, or to cower. He was the Prince of Magdeburg, and he had no fear of the peasants before him.

They attacked as a group—they had clearly been training for the night when they might face Jürgen in battle. Pierre darted in more quickly than a human eye would have been able to follow, stabbing at Jürgen's face with a short blade. Jürgen deflected it easily, and lashed out at the Toreador. The blow caught him by surprise and Pierre stumbled backwards, out of Jürgen's reach. Jürgen raised his sword and advanced, just as Christoffel leapt on him from behind.

The Caitiff's fangs pierced the back of Jürgen's neck, and Jürgen realized with a trickle of cold fear that they intended to take his blood and soul as well as his unlife. He wasn't surprised, of course—while performing the Amaranth on another Cainite, especially a prince, was tantamount to blasphemy, surely nothing was beneath these wretches.

Jürgen's Beast roared in frustration, but Jürgen quieted it. He stabbed his sword into the ground, reached behind him and seized Weiss with both hands, and flung him against a tree. He heard bones crack in the impact, and more break as the Caitiff tried to regain his footing, but ignored them. Weiss would have to waste precious blood and time healing himself, and Jürgen did not intend to give him the chance. He snatched his sword from the ground and rushed at the Caitiff still struggling to his feet. Christoffel's eyes grew wide as Jürgen drew back his sword to decapitate him—but the blow didn't land.

Armin Brenner tackled the prince, and Jürgen mentally chastised himself for not keeping his attention to the side. Brenner, as was typical of his clan, was much stronger than his small frame would indicate. Also characteristically, he was on the verge of frenzy.

Jürgen dropped his sword again. He grabbed the Brujah by the throat and groin, raised him above his head, and brought Brenner's back down on his knee. Brenner's spine shattered with a sickening crunch, and he screamed in pain. Jürgen threw him to the side—repairing a wound of that magnitude would take only minutes, but minutes would be enough. He picked up his sword and saw that Weiss was retreating towards the wagon, obviously as the precursor to an attack by the others.

Jürgen had no intention of playing into their hands. He sprinted towards the wagon and jumped on top of it. Looking down, he saw Weiss, Cardinal, and Cardinal's childe waiting for him. The girl was terrified—almost in Rötschreck, Jürgen guessed. He glared down at her and bared his fangs, his gaze cutting through her mind as surely as his blade would her head. She shrieked and ran. Cardinal looked after her and shouted, "Mathilde!"

Weiss kept his eyes on Jürgen, but he was still trying to set the bones in his legs. The Sword-Bearer leapt nimbly down from the wagon and landed behind the Toreador, grabbed a handful of hair, and drove his blade through the small of Cardinal's back. He fell to his knees as Jürgen's sword severed his spine, and, shoving the musician to the ground, Jürgen turned his attention to Weiss.

"Christoffel Weiss, isn't it?"

The Caitiff said nothing, but held his ground. *Stupid*, thought Jürgen. *In a Ventrue, someone who has a hope of dying honorably, it might be brave, but from this rabble?*

"Your minstrel here gave you away." Jürgen ground his booted heel into Cardinal's back with enough force to shove his broken spine out through the stomach wall. "He apparently is very fond of that pig song, as he has managed to leave it in villages all over the Empire. Those villages match my sire's route, as it happens." Jürgen heard someone rushing towards him from behind; he could tell by the force of the steps and their speed that it must be Brenner.

Jürgen spun, but kept his foot planted on Cardinal's back and his sword pointed at Weiss's head. Brenner, as he expected, was charging him, but his angle of attacking was wrong. *A feint*, Jürgen realized. He jumped forward to meet the Brujah, whipping his sword around in front of him. Brenner might have had enough time to dodge if Jürgen had stayed in place and attacked, but the sudden jump towards him surprised him. Jürgen's sword pierced Brenner's stomach and exited from his back. The Sword-Bearer looked down into the Brujah's eyes and saw humanity and reason melt away—Armin Brenner had given way to his Beast, and was now much more dangerous. Jürgen spun and threw him off his sword towards Cardinal's prone body. Then he turned to meet the fiend.

Mathilde—Cardinal's cowardly childe—was a weakling, but the Silent Fury's other female member was obviously anything but. She carried no weapons, but the bones of her fingers extended past the flesh and came to wicked-looking points. Her hair was gone—the top of her head boasted only a thick layer of skin and Jürgen realized that she must have removed her own hair to prevent him from using it to his advantage in battle. He opened his mouth to comment, but then stopped. She would not be able to hear him. Her own Beast guided her, but she stalked Jürgen with the single-minded ferocity of a trained hunting dog preparing to bring down a hart.

How does her Beast know me? Does she command it?

Jürgen's own Beast cackled and demanded leave to fight this battle. Jürgen refused and shouted a challenge. The Tzimisce crouched and pounced like a cat.

Jürgen braced himself and then swung his sword at the tips of her outstretched fingers. He knocked her hands aside, splintering the bone claws she had fashioned for herself and, more importantly, knocking her hands away from his face. He had no idea if the fiend could use her foul flesh-crafting powers while the Beast rode her, but he had no wish to take a chance on having his skin reduced to jelly. She landed from her pounce awkwardly, her hands bloodied, and crouched again.

Jürgen drew back his sword. If she leapt at him again, he could probably take her head off and end this battle before the others could regroup. Already he heard splintering wood from the wagon and a yelp of pain, but dared not turn his head to see what had happened.

The Tzimisce leapt, and Jürgen stepped forward to meet her. Too late, he realized that she had twisted in midair and landed beyond the reach of his sword. She reached out, grabbed the weapon by the blade and locked her fingers around it. Jürgen pulled and saw the blade part her flesh, but she was much stronger than he would have thought possible. However, both of her hands were now engaged.

He released the blade and grabbed her by the throat. Immediately, she dropped the sword and drove her fingers— had the bones regrown already?—into his wrists. The pain was bearable, but Jürgen knew that if she were to use her powers of flesh-crafting now she might sever his hands, and he had no idea if he could repair the damage. A tiny sliver of fear entered his mind—what was a warrior without hands? In that sliver, his Beast slipped its leash.

Jürgen pulled the woman close as though to embrace her, and then sank his fangs into her throat. She howled in rage and dug her claws deeper into his wrists, but Jürgen's pain was lost in the throes of the Beast's hunger. His mouth filled with her blood, he drank in great, hurried gulps. The taste was strange— he had fed from other vampires before, of course, even in battle, but never from a Tzimisce. The blood burned his tongue as heavily spiced food might burn that of a mortal, and his Beast faltered.

Jürgen seized control of his Beast and forced it to the back of his mind. He pushed the woman back, knocked her prone and looked down. For a moment she looked pitiable, and Jürgen felt that he should spare her—she could fight, after all, and so perhaps he had a place for her?

He shook the thought off and retrieved his sword. The Tzimisce struggled to her feet, but by that time Jürgen was already swinging the blade. The sword's edge met her throat at the same point his teeth had, and cleaved her flesh just as readily. Her head fell to the ground, her body already decaying. The pity and respect Jürgen felt faded just as quickly. All Cainites could enslave others merely with a drop of their blood, and Jürgen knew well the power of the blood oath.

He turned towards the wagon and saw Cardinal and Weiss wrestling with Brenner. Weiss raised a jagged chunk of wood—probably torn from the wagon—and stabbed it into the Brujah's heart. Jürgen smiled. If they had been better tacticians, one of them would have led Brenner back towards Jürgen and the Tzimisce and then let the three of them destroy each other. Jürgen wasn't sure, in fact, that he would have been able to defeat them both so easily. Now, battened on the blood of the wild woman, he strode towards the two Cainites.

Cardinal saw him coming and jumped to his feet, but Jürgen willed himself to become faster. He sprang forward and sliced at the Toreador's face with his sword, cleaving a section of bone away and putting out both of Cardinal's eyes. He dropped to his knees, screaming, and Jürgen's sword flashed downwards to separate his head from his body.

Weiss backed off in horror. Jürgen advanced, stepping over the torpid body of Armin Brenner. He would remain insensate until the stake was removed, and Jürgen didn't see the need to let him watch the demise of the Silent Fury.

From the nearby brush came a scream and Mathilde came charging towards the wagon, fangs bared, blind with rage over her sire's death. Weiss turned to face her for an instant, and Jürgen took his chance. The sword stopped at his spine, and Weiss collapsed forward, trying to speak around the steel cleaving his throat. Jürgen pinned him to the ground and worked the sword through his neck until his head fell away. For a mortal man, this would have taken minutes; for Jürgen, it took only the time for Weiss to gasp the words *"Pater noster—"*

Mathilde flung herself onto Jürgen's back. The Sword-Bearer reached behind him with his left hand and snapped her neck, and then flung her to the ground. She was obviously weakened from fear and hunger—rather than heal herself, she simply lay there and twitched. Jürgen took the moment to heal the remaining wounds on his wrists and study her more closely.

She had once been his prisoner, he realized. Some three years before she had been caught skulking around one of the outlying towns of Magdeburg, but Jürgen had been busy with matters involving the Church's inquisitors and hadn't bothered to interrogate her. She had either escaped or been freed; at the time, Jürgen had berated the agent that had found her, but was just as annoyed at himself for not immediately transferring her to his own prisons. Now he had even more cause to regret the mistake—she was a member of the Silent Fury. Had he questioned her then, he could have learned enough about the Furores to avoid this waste of time.

Jürgen smacked his lips. The Tzimisce blood dried against his lips like rancid milk. He would need to wash his mouth before leaving. He wondered if he could reach Magdeburg before dawn. Even if he couldn't, he could probably reach some sort of haven closer to his city. He briefly considered taking Mathilde back with him for questioning, but decided against it. Best not to let anyone survive who had escaped his grasp. He growled as he thought of Albin—he should never have let the Ghost back into his service.

He did Mathilde the service of cleaning the blade of his sword before decapitating her: Weiss's death had no doubt been painful and he had no desire to inflict that on the woman. He crouched down next to Brenner.

"Armin, I know you can hear me," Jürgen whispered. "I haven't decided what to do with you yet. My thoughts so far include setting you on fire, leaving you here for the sun, taking your head as I did with your filthy band of traitors and peasants, or simply carrying you with me to Magdeburg so that you may enlighten me as to the desires and practices of other such coteries."

Brenner did not answer, of course. He couldn't even blink.

"My personal preference is for taking your head. That's a fairly clean and quick way to die..." he glanced at Weiss's corpse, the neck ragged and the bones splintered... "normally. Any thoughts?"

Again, Brenner could say nothing, but Jürgen could feel the hate and rage emanating from him.

"Have you nothing to say? No last cry for freedom? No wish for final combat or poetics on the rights of Caine?" Jürgen smiled, and then stood over the Brujah. "Take this thought with you to Hell—you did not lose this battle because I am your master or rightful ruler, although I am. You did not lose because you planned poorly, because your scheme, although clumsy, was actually somewhat inspired. You lost—you *died*—tonight because *you failed to control your subordinates.* I found you because of Cardinal and Albin. Had you acted like a leader, like a Scion, you might have bested me in time."

Jürgen raised the sword over his head, and then stopped. Something in Brenner's eyes, or perhaps the colors surrounding him, intrigued him. Jürgen sighed and peered into the Brujah's mind. As always, it disgusted him, but he was looking for a very specific piece of knowledge. When he found it, his eyes grew wide. He carried Brenner on the back of his horse all the way to Magdeburg, and arrived at the priory just before dawn.

"Take this one to the dungeon, but do not remove the stake," he said to the knights who met him, and wandered off towards his bedchambers. Christof found him before he reached his door.

"My lord?"

"The Silent Fury has fallen," said Jürgen quietly. "All but Albin and Brenner, and Albin shall be ash on the wind before I leave for Livonia."

"And what of Brenner? Why is he here? Does he have information we need?"

Jürgen nodded. "In a sense, Christof."

She frowned. "My lord? In what sense?"

Jürgen looked back towards the jail and furrowed his brow. "I had to know, Christof. I took him because I want to discover what brings a man like him to this state."

"What kind of man?"

Jürgen opened his door. The approaching dawn tugged at his undead body, but his mind still grappled with the question. "He's a Scion, Christof. He walks the *Via Regalis* as we do." Jürgen rubbed his wrists; they would not scar or ache in the morning, but they had a strange tingle now. "And I would like to know what *happened* to him."

Chapter Nine

The next night, as Jürgen left his bedchamber, Heinrich approached him. Right away Jürgen could see that Heinrich was uncomfortable: The usually cheery gait was gone, replaced by a wary sidle. Heinrich was on an errand for someone else; Jürgen could already guess who.

"My lord, regarding what happened last night—"

"Christof disapproves?"

Heinrich smiled slightly. "In a word, strongly. He feels that you put yourself in grave danger—"

"Christof, of course, is not the prince here."

"I feel the same, my lord." Heinrich looked about as though hoping the walls would tell him what to say. "You are the prince, and I am to serve you. Consider, though, that I am your seneschal and it is my duty to make sure that this domain is run smoothly even in your absence."

"You knew that I was leaving and when I would return, and unless you have grown considerably stupider over the past few nights, I'll guess that you knew I was going to battle." Jürgen began walking; Heinrich kept pace.

"That isn't the point, my lord."

"No?" Jürgen smiled. Heinrich was taking this rather seriously. "What, then, is the point, dear seneschal?"

Heinrich took a breath. "The point, my lord, is that you swore an oath to us." Jürgen stopped. "To all of us. Myself, Christof... all of your vassals have your word. Part of the oath that you swore is that you would not bring us harm so long as we were faithful in our own oaths."

Jürgen turned to face his servant. "Bring harm upon you? By slaying rabble?"

Heinrich cocked an eyebrow. "My lord, please be reasonable. How many things could have gone wrong? How many different chances did you have to meet Final Death last night? More than one, I'd guess. And if you fall to enemies, it endangers us, and therefore your oath to us. Not to mention your oath to—"

Jürgen's head snapped up. He locked eyes with Heinrich and glared, ready to command him never to speak of Hardestadt, as he had with Albin. He stopped, and released the seneschal from his gaze. "I am sorry, Heinrich."

"My lord?" Heinrich was unaware that anything had happened.

"I am sorry for my behavior last night." The Beast screamed that he retract that apology, and then remove Heinrich's arms for his temerity. Jürgen ignored it. "You are right—Christof is right—had anything gone wrong, the city and indeed the Fiefs of the Black Cross might have been endangered. You do well to bring such things to my attention."

Heinrich smiled. "Well, my lord, I flatter myself that is why you keep me." The two Cainites began walking again.

"Please tell Christof what I said, Heinrich," Jürgen said as they reached the door to his room.

"I shall, my lord." Heinrich walked off into the night, and Jürgen sat down at his table. He had much to do—planning his route, first and foremost, but he had awakened with the strange feeling that he would receive a visit tonight.

His visitor was not long in arriving.

"Doing the Lord's work?"

Jürgen raised his eyes from the map on his table. The door was opened, but he hadn't heard it. The man standing before him, however, wasn't a threat.

"Gotzon."

The Lasombra didn't smile. Jürgen, in fact, had never seen him do so. The shadows he cast in the light from the fireplace recoiled as though being attached to the magister was painful to them. Gotzon lowered his hood and stared at Jürgen, and Jürgen could see what Rosamund had meant. Those eyes were devoid of life, but not of intelligence. Gotzon, despite anything else that might be said about him, was brave and pious in a way only someone who had seen Hell could be.

"What brings you here?"

Gotzon closed the door and sat down. "You're leaving soon." He nodded towards the maps. "Setting affairs in order?"

"You know me, Gotzon."

Gotzon nodded, and peered at the map. "Following von Salza?"

Jürgen grimaced. "Up to a point. Von Salza is in Prussia; my target lies somewhat farther west. The Sword-Brothers, though not of my order, do much the same work. I am stuck in the unfortunate position of having either to follow these knights to defend them from a horror that killed Alexander of Paris, or leave them to their own devices and let Alexander's death go unanswered. The former is unpalatable, the latter impossible. So onward we march." He smirked, but stopped when he met Gotzon's gaze.

"God cries out for justice and for His Light to grace the pagans of the land. Despite your feelings of how 'unpalatable' this situation is, Lord Jürgen, this *is* what God intends."

"Amen," murmured Jürgen. "But what brings you? Do you intend to follow?"

Gotzon narrowed his ebon eyes and Jürgen looked away. He should have known better; Gotzon never answered direct questions about his plans. He trusted in God to direct him in all things.

Jürgen stood. "Surely you have heard of the happenings with the Silent Fury." Gotzon nodded. "I intend to leave their leader with a splinter of wood in his heart until I return."

Gotzon didn't respond. He knew something of secret societies. His clan had taught him in the blackest arts possible, the mastery of the shadows of the Abyss. A paltry bunch of rebels were probably beneath his notice even as a crusader. Jürgen felt the need to justify his decision.

"He is a Scion. That's why I want him kept alive."

"We are none of us alive."

Jürgen checked himself. Of course Gotzon was right; some Cainites were more particular than others in their terminology. "Kept intact, then. I want to know how a Scion came to this."

"And you'll wait until you return for this?"

Jürgen shrugged slightly. "You disagree?"

"Your reasons for not destroying him are your own, Jürgen. I think, however, that if you are following your usual protocol of assuming you will not return—"

"Yes, you're right." Jürgen glanced outside; he guessed he had enough time before daybreak to speak with Brenner. "I'll visit him tonight."

Gotzon nodded and picked up a map showing Jürgen's route. He traced the line with his finger, stopping at a domain circled in red. Jürgen didn't bother to wait for the question.

"The prince of that domain is a Tzimisce. My spies inform me that he is outcast from Rustovitch's *Voivodate* and has been casting about for allies." Gotzon turned to glare at Jürgen. Jürgen sighed in exasperation. "I know what you think, Gotzon. But for all I know, this fiend might be Christian." Gotzon coughed quietly. "Unlikely, I know. But I can't simply kill other Cainites in power wantonly, no matter how wicked they might be. If for no other reason than that to do so is a breach of the order that Caine and God handed us."

Gotzon set the map down. "We have differing notions of God's order, Jürgen, and always have."

"And yet you never doubt my piety or my ability to do His work."

"I never doubt that you do God's work, that is true. Whether you do it deliberately or not is sometimes more of a mystery." Gotzon stood, and the shadows which had been creeping up around him fled.

Chapter Ten

Brenner's mouth shut with a snap when Jürgen removed the stake. The Brujah pulled against his chains, on the verge of frenzy. Jürgen decided to wait and see if Brenner could control himself. After a moment's thrashing, he calmed enough to speak.

"Why am I not ash on the Elbe, Jürgen?"

"Why do you not address me properly, Armin?"

Armin spat on the floor and Jürgen almost groaned. *God, not another Ghost.* "Properly?" Armin said. "That I address you by your name at all is only in acknowledgment of what you said last night."

"Go on," said Jürgen. A wax tablet sat behind him; he intended to copy any notes he took into the Letters of Acindynus later.

"You were right. Had I controlled the others better, I might have beaten you. We might have found freedom." Jürgen shook his head. "Were you mentored, Armin? Taught on the Road of Kings? You must have been."

"I was, yes. My sire instructed me, but neglected to point out that childer could be violated and used at whim."

Jürgen reached for the tablet. "I beg your pardon?"

Armin gave Jürgen a withering glare. "Surely you remember, Jürgen. I burned a house here in Magdeburg, perhaps ten years ago. The others freed me while I awaited justice."

Jürgen nodded. "I remember. I don't think I was actually in the city when it happened. I rather doubt they would have attempted it with me here."

"Don't flatter yourself, Jürgen." Brenner shifted his arms a bit, but the chains held him tight. "They would have done. They might not have succeeded, of course." He leaned his head back against the wall and looked up. "They wanted for a leader."

Jürgen rolled his eyes. "They might have come to me. I don't turn away capable Cainites."

"No, but you do ask them to drink of your blood, Jürgen. And they didn't understand oaths—all of the Cainites in the Silent Fury had seen only broken promises from their sires and leaders, lies from powerful elders meant to lull their childer into doing their dangerous work. And before you open your mouth to deny you do any such thing, Lord Jürgen, please remember that one of *your* servants wound up serving under *me* because you mistreated him, threw him down a well and forced his mouth to your wrist." Brenner had started to pull against the chains again; his Brujah blood was evidently working him towards frenzy. Jürgen noted what he'd said and allowed him to calm down before speaking.

"Surely you know that no true Scion makes a one-sided oath. The lord must swear to the vassal; that is how the world stays on course." This was the most basic tenet of the Road of Kings. *If Brenner doesn't know this,* Jürgen thought, *then he is truly of no use to me.*

Brenner laughed out loud. "Then there are a great many false Scions in the world tonight, Lord Jürgen. A *great* many." He looked at Jürgen's eyes, unflinching and defiant. "I was Embraced one year before Constantinople fell, and so I was very much a neonate when my sire instructed me to burn that house. He taught me that oaths are always two-sided, that both parties must swear. What he did not tell me was that God does not strike down oathbreakers with a thunderbolt, nor does the Beast immediately and permanently claim the soul and mind of any Scion who dares renege on a promise."

Jürgen set his tablet down, nodding. "Go on."

"All that a broken oath truly represents is a *risk*, Jürgen. My sire lied to me. He knew that the man who lived in that house was under your protection, but he sent me on the errand anyway. He thus broke an oath to you *and* to me, but when that man was dead, he had accomplished whatever his goal was and so fled Magdeburg. He accomplished his goal by breaking an oath—does that make him a better Scion for the task?" Brenner shook his head. "Had the Silent Fury not 'saved' me, I might have sworn fealty to you, Jürgen. As it happened, they did, and

I saw in them my own followers. I vowed I wouldn't abandon them or use them, and now they are gone and I am awaiting the sun."

Jürgen stared at him for a moment, and then wrote his words on the tablet. He then stood. "I cannot spare you," he said quietly. "You have engineered murder in my domains, and I am vowed to avenge it. I cannot break my vows as easily as your sire, even when I am tempted otherwise."

Brenner nodded, but Jürgen could see his fear. The Beast was what drove all Cainites from fire and sun, and moved them to murder their own childer to save themselves. Brenner's was probably howling loudly enough to wake the dead at present.

"I can offer you confession and a swift end. That is all."

The last of the Silent Fury looked up and met Jürgen's gaze. "Then I accept that offer, Lord Jürgen."

Jürgen left the room, and saw Gotzon waiting outside. "How do you do that?"

"What?" Gotzon stared past Jürgen into the cell.

"Appear when needed."

"Am I needed? I only came to find you. You'll give confession before you leave?"

Jürgen nodded. "Yes. I shall meet you in the chapel. Speaking of confession, the Cainite in the next room faces the sun tomorrow, and would unburden himself before he does." Gotzon nodded and began to walk into the cell. "Gotzon?" He stopped, but did not answer and did not turn to face the prince. No other Cainite in Europe, save perhaps Hardestadt, would have dared that. "Can Cainites love?"

"Love God, Jürgen." The dark figure did not turn.

"But another of our kind—"

"Love God, and that is all. That way lies salvation. All else is darkness, pain, and eventually the fires of Hell." He turned, and Jürgen rather wished he hadn't. His eyes were still lifeless, but the intelligence behind them had begun to move. The blackness, as Rosamund had pointed out, wasn't empty, and Jürgen reassured himself that Gotzon had taken a vow never to use his power over shadows and living darkness.

"I would ask something of you, Gotzon. Will you hear Lady Rosamund's confession before we leave?"

Gotzon's expression told Jürgen everything. Gotzon was disappointed and perhaps even offended that Rosamund was accompanying Jürgen on the journey at all, but he was bound by his vows as an ashen priest to hear confession from any Cainite who asked. The Lasombra nodded, and walked into the cell to hear Brenner's last words. The light changed as the shadows and the flames assumed their usual relationship.

Lady Rosamund would be terrified, Jürgen knew. But he had his reasons. If Rosamund had something to confess involving Jürgen, he didn't want anyone except Gotzon to know it. Gotzon, despite everything else, was a devout priest and warrior of God, and took his vows as seriously as Jürgen took his own.

And besides, thought Jürgen, *if anyone can make him see that Cainites can love, it's her.*

Chapter Eleven

"Those with no domains to call their own are like beggars in the streets, or thieves in the night, taking what does not rightly belong to them. It is just for the lord of a domain to seek and punish them for any crimes against him and his own." Jürgen was reading aloud from Acindynus's letters to Rosamund. From outside the wagon, they heard the knights trying to move a fallen tree from the path. They could see the fort of Kybartai ahead, and Jürgen had sent a runner to ask for help from the prince, but nearly three hours had gone by and no one had returned.

"Your thoughts, my lord?" Rosamund was wrapped in furs, and even remembered to shiver occasionally. Jürgen didn't usually bother—undead flesh did not suffer from chills. As much as he enjoyed winter, as the long nights made possible extended campaigns and battles for him, remembering to exhale and react to the temperature was a bother. He preferred simply to avoid contact with mortals.

"I think that this sort of comment, taken on its own, is fodder for idiots like Brenner." Jürgen shifted carefully; the wagon wasn't very spacious, and he had no wish to scatter his maps. "Some Cainites aren't meant to hold domains. Look at Wiftet. He's most certainly a Cainite, but can you imagine him as a prince?"

Rosamund giggled quietly. "I admit, the nights in his city would be amusing."

Jürgen nodded seriously. "Yes, amusing until some band of rebels swept through and took his blood. Or until someone like Rustovitch—or, to be fair, myself—took his territories. Or until the humans found the Devil in their midst and sent out their own—" Rosamund looked away, and Jürgen fell silent. He returned his attention to the book and read quietly to himself, but could not focus on the words. "I am sorry," he whispered.

Rosamund shook her head. "You have no reason to be, my lord." She moved closer to him. "Read further, please."

Jürgen read more of the page, silently, making sure he could correctly read all of it aloud. The hand was of an author he hadn't seen yet. He turned to the first page, where all of the commentators had made their mark, and saw none he could match to the handwriting. "Curious."

"What?"

"An anonymous author." Jürgen read a bit further, and then nodded slowly. "And I see why. This commentator is no Scion, but a member of the Heresy."

Rosamund didn't react visibly. The Cainite Heresy had caused her less grief than the Church from which it sprang, after all.

"He writes, too, on the nature of domain. Listen: 'All domain is not physical, and in fact, all that is physical is base and impure. Therefore a Cainite who concerns himself solely with the capture of land only damns himself, whereas he should be claiming domain in spirit.'" He paused and looked up at Rosamund. "What on Earth do you suppose he means by that?"

"Followers, perhaps? Power over souls instead of land?"

Jürgen shook his head, and might have crossed himself had both hands not been on the book. "God save us. He continues. 'No Scion has ever been a true leader in this regard, commanding power over the spiritual. Instead, you followers of the Road of Kings simply are content to fight your wars and dwell in castles, never realizing what lies beyond your reach. True power rests in the hands of the likes of our archbishop, Nikita of Sredetz—'" Jürgen broke off suddenly. "He's even drawn us a picture, my lady." He turned the book to show Rosamund the drawing. The anonymous author had indeed drawn a sketch of, Jürgen imagined, Nikita of Sredetz, the so-called Archbishop of Nod.

"What does the author hope to achieve by drawing Nikita's

picture here?" Jürgen wondered aloud.

"Perhaps he is mad or obsessed," offered Rosamund. "And besides, is not the Archbishop of Nod a Tzimisce?"

Jürgen nodded. "Yes, and that means he could reshape his face, anyway."

"What of his claims to spiritual dominion?"

"I think that being the leader of the Heresy offers Nikita power, though I'd hesitate to call it a domain. A domain represents more than just power. It is a symbol to one's foes, and thus it is quite important that it be visible." Jürgen set down the book. "I'm interested to know your thoughts on domains, my lady. What would you do with your own territories? How would you govern the Cainites therein?"

Rosamund glanced down at the page. "You know, my lord, that I was educated under the Queens of Love. I think that their style of governance suits me best—patronage of the arts, adherence to the courtly ideals."

Jürgen raised his eyebrows. "Such ideals make claiming new territory difficult, of course. And even proper defense of one's own city is often compromised by having to adhere to someone else's laws."

"Fortunate that Hardestadt was a Scion, then, my lord. I fear you would be terribly confused following another path."

He scoffed. "I have seen what the other roads offer their followers. Lies, tempting promises and a slow stroll towards destruction." A great yawning crack from outside and some muffled cheers indicated that the tree was finally beginning to shift. Jürgen turned a few pages back. "Here, Acindynus refutes the notion that kings are granted the right of rule by God Himself."

Rosamund nodded. "And Antasia supports that view." Jürgen rolled his eyes.

"Yes, which isn't so surprising. What I think is that the *Via Regalis*, like the very act of ruling, is not one, decisive action but a continual struggle. Some Cainites simply give themselves to God, and others let their Beasts hold sway. But we," he took her hands, "we must fight nightly to remain what we are. Perhaps your ideals are somewhat more," he paused, trying not to offend her, "*pleasing* than mine, but we do walk the same road. We struggle in the same way, but while yours is a struggle of words and glances, mine is blood and steel."

"My struggle is not free from blood," she whispered.

"Of course not." Jürgen's mind flashed back to a night in Magdeburg, when he had heard her seducing a young knight to take his blood. "Forgive the insinuation, my lady."

She shook her head, eyes cast downwards. "Do you forget that I am the same as you, my lord? The same curses, the same gifts, separated in clan only by a whim of fate?" She raised her head and Jürgen saw that she had allowed her fangs to extend. "I feel what you do when I bestow the Kiss, I'm sure."

Jürgen moved forward, running his tongue briefly over his own fangs. "Do you, Rosamund? I believe we have never discussed it." He kissed her hand, lingering for just moment, his senses sharpening to pick up her perfumes, the rustling of her garments, even the change in her hair as she lowered her gaze to watch him. "What do you feel when you give the Kiss?"

"Surely, my lord, you could read my thoughts at such a moment." She was teasing; he had already told her how much he despised peering into others' minds.

"I could, my lady, but I was taught it was uncouth to spy upon a lady in such an intimate act."

"And yet you wish me to spill my secrets to you." She reached up and ran a hand down his face. "And if I wished to hear yours, Prince Jürgen? What do you feel when you feed?"

Jürgen paused. He had no wish to ruin the mood—Rosamund was beautiful, and the conversation changed her. The colors surrounding her grew slightly brighter. Vampires gave off pale haloes; the spark of life, which many pious Cainites believed to be the soul, vacated at the moment of death. That Rosamund's halo shimmered so meant that she was enjoying this discussion, much as two mortals might enjoy reciting poetry or kissing and touching before a tryst. But to tell her of his Kiss? The mortals upon whom Jürgen preyed were not lovestruck waifs or anyone so romantic.

And yet, I do derive pleasure from them.

"If you wish to hear, I will tell you, my sweet," he said.

Rosamund moved closer still. Their legs touched, and Jürgen ran his hand down the back of her head, savoring the softness of her hair, the cold flesh of her neck. His gaze stopped at her throat, and he thought back to a different night in Magdeburg, when they had shared more than words and secrets.

A Cainite could labor under only one blood oath, but even the slightest drop of blood engendered feelings of respect or love. Jürgen and Rosamund had already drunk once from each other. *But I felt for her, and her for me, before that night.*

The Beast snapped its jaws, and Jürgen looked away. The Beast pressed, reminding Jürgen of the last time he had fed from a female Cainite—just before severing her head. The strange, burning sensation from the Tzimisce's blood returned to his mouth, and his wrists began to itch....

"My lord?"

Jürgen fought the sensations away, and turned back to her. "I am sorry," he said. "Now, please, favor me. Your Kiss—what do you feel?"

Rosamund met his gaze, and then lowered her eyes; Jürgen felt them linger on his lips and neck. "Had I the power, I would blush to say." She shifted her dresses. "The feeling is... impious."

Jürgen smiled. "Really, lady Rosamund?"

"I cannot say for certain, my lord Jürgen, as I was but a maid when I received the Embrace. But I imagined—" She stopped. Jürgen reflected that notions of the act of love were very different now than when he had last drawn breath, and probably very different in France than in his native lands. He took her hands to reassure her. "I imagine that the Kiss might be like that union." She shook her head, and Jürgen sensed her frustration. She was trying to describe something so basic, so natural to Cainites that even her talent for words failed. Jürgen waited patiently—Rosamund would find the words. "I feel my teeth pierce his skin," she said, "and I blush. Perhaps my face does not warm or grow red, but I remember the sensation from my mortal days. I remember the heat, how it blooms on the cheeks and spreads to the neck."

Jürgen kissed her cheek gently. "Go on."

"My lips find the wound, and it always surprises me, the

outpouring of blood. The first time I fed, it filled my mouth. I wasn't ready." She shut her eyes, lost in the memory. "But the taste—the feeling of life. I have learned to savor it, to keep the wound closed with my tongue and then reopen it with another bite. And all the while I can hear his breath, growing shallower, but whispering to me not to stop." Jürgen leaned in and kissed her neck. She did not draw in a breath the way a living woman would have, but turned her head slightly to give him better access. "And his voice is not the only one—the Beast rises up like a serpent in my ear, tempting me, telling me to kill."

"How do you fight it off, my lady?" To Jürgen's knowledge, Rosamund had never killed while feeding.

Rosamund smiled and bit her lower lip. "I know the Beast has no power to make me break my vows of courtesy. I view it as spice to the meal, a hint of danger, that knowledge that I could simply bite harder, take one more swallow, and his life would wink out." She reached behind him and trailed her fingers through his hair. "But thinking and doing aren't the same thing, though the Beast can be tricked with such thoughts." She kissed his throat, just below his jaw. Jürgen cast his mind back and tried to remember if a woman had ever done that during his mortal life, when he had had a pulse for her lips to find. He couldn't recall. Jürgen had never married, but as a soldier had known women—it was traditional for warriors to take women as spoils.

He wondered if Rosamund, as a Scion, would understand that. He decided not to ask. Her voice drove the thought away.

"Now, my lord, what of your Kiss?"

Jürgen leaned down and ran his tongue from the base of her jaw to her earlobe, and brushed her ear with his fangs. "What, indeed, my sweet? I think perhaps I should have spoken first, for after hearing your descriptions my thoughts lose their meaning."

She smiled. "Poetry is honesty, my lord. Great poetry is simply the most honest rendering of feeling and beauty into words." She kissed his neck again. "Tell me something true."

He nodded gently, and pulled back enough to see her face. "My Kiss..." he stopped. True? Was this a test, and if so, who was being tested? "My Kiss is barely a Kiss. It is not a gift to be bestowed or a favor to my servants, for I grant it—inflict it—only to those I have bested. Those captured in battle. I suppose," he met Rosamund's eyes to see if she was frightened or disgusted, but she looked intrigued, "I suppose I consider it a more fair way to feed. A warrior killed in battle, who dies with honor, has nothing to fear. A warrior who escapes the battlefield has nothing to fear, but those who become prisoners—"

"Should fear? Do your prisoners gain no pleasure from the act, then? I find that difficult to believe. I took great pleasure when you favored me with your Kiss."

Jürgen smiled. "You accepted my Kiss freely, beauty. The men whom I visit in the prisons do not."

"Tell me more."

He shut his eyes and pictured the cells. "I can hear their fear before I set foot in the prison. Sometimes they pray, other times they are indignant at first. They think that I should ransom them or allow them more comfortable rooms." He chuckled. "I've actually met blood-servants who believe themselves to be a kind of nobility simply because of the masters they serve."

"Can not the master elevate the servant?"

"Yes, but there is as great a gap between ghoul and Cainite as between hunting dog and master. The master relies upon the dog, perhaps even feels some affection for it, but come what may, it is still a dog." Rosamund did not respond, and Jürgen mentally reproached himself. She cared too much about her servants to hear such things. "I approach the cells and choose one."

"How do you choose?"

Jürgen stroked her hair casually. The intimacy had changed, grown dull, since he had begun speaking. He suppressed the urge to grow angry that his words did not carry that sort of passion. "It varies, I think. Some nights the options aren't very wide. Some nights I choose someone weak, that he might not suffer, and others I choose a strong man in recognition of his strength." He smiled, perhaps a bit maliciously. "Sometimes the Beast chooses for me." Rosamund glanced upwards, surprised. "My Beast does rattle its chains off the battlefield, my fair Rosamund. It whispers to me as yours does to you, and sometimes it chooses a vessel to assuage its hunger along with mine."

"And you let it make that choice?"

"Occasionally. Throwing a scrap to a dog does not mean that the dog has trained the master, after all." Rosamund nodded. "The prisoners aren't kept chained, and it's happened occasionally that they harbor thoughts of attacking me when I enter the room. Only once has anyone actually done so—a ghoul whom I later discovered had lived well beyond the years God would have otherwise granted him through the blood his mistress had granted him."

"What happened to him?"

Jürgen kissed her ear and lingered, feeling her skin against his lips. He kissed her again and noted that neither his mouth nor her ear grew warm; the winter chill would not leave their bodies unless they sat near a fire or willed the stolen blood within them to well up and warm them. "I fed well that night," he whispered. "In fact, I can think of only one other night when I have fed better."

She craned her neck, rubbing her cheek against his. The passion was returning, and Jürgen felt something stir within him, that feeling of hunger and desire he'd come to associate with Rosamund. "What about the woman? The Tzimisce? Surely she fed you well."

Jürgen's Beast leapt on the question, and the strange sensations returned. They were muted, but more pervasive—the strange tingle started at his wrists and then spread. Jürgen pressed his fingertips to the back of Rosamund's neck, gently, and felt her flesh yield slightly. She gasped slightly, and pulled away. Jürgen pulled his hands from her skin and stared at his fingers. There was no change, even to his heightened perceptions. He reached for her, slowly, and stroked the back of her neck. The skin was smooth and even—nothing had changed.

My Beast, then, he thought. *A simple taste of Tzimisce blood cannot impart their blasphemous gifts.*

Rosamund stared at him. "Have I offended?"

Jürgen shook his head, "No, my lady, no. I was—"

"Someone's coming," she said. A second later there was a

knock at the door. Jürgen wondered briefly why he hadn't heard the visitor approaching.

Opening the door, he found Sir Thomas standing there, clothing disheveled, smelling of sweat and wood. A wooden cross, which Jürgen guessed he had made as a boy, judging from the craftsmanship, hung around his neck. It was far too large to be comfortable under a mail shirt, but Jürgen presumed the knight thought it a protection from enemies. "We have finally cleared the road," his German still tainted with his strange English accent, "but the runner has not yet returned." He stared past Jürgen at Rosamund, who demurely nodded to him.

Jürgen glowered at the knight. "Sir Thomas," he said, "kindly escort Václav to the fort and find out what has happened to my runner, and if we may enter freely or not. If we may enter freely, tell Václav to return bearing his standard visibly. If we are refused, tell him he is to cover it with a cloth."

"Yes, my lord." The knight didn't know why Jürgen was annoyed, but like most of the prince's subordinates, didn't wish to remain in the area when he was. He jogged off towards the head of the caravan, calling to Václav.

"Will they be all right, my lord?" Jürgen knew what Rosamund was really asking: *Did you just send one of my servants to die?*

"Thomas will be fine. Tzimisce have rules of hospitality strict enough to make the Courts of Love look like anarchy by comparison. Václav, of course, is my childe, but he understands those laws better than any of the rest of us. It may be that since the runner I sent was mortal, the fiend in charge of this domain simply slaughtered him rather than listening." Jürgen ground his teeth and shot the bolt on the wagon. "In which case, I shall have words with this prince. But in any event, Václav is not only a Cainite but one of my own blood, and the Tzimisce would not dare harm him *or* anyone accompanying him."

Rosamund nodded, relieved. "What about the covering of his standard, then?"

Jürgen took Acindynus's book and wrapped it tightly in cloth, replacing it in its locked chest. He then pulled his mail shirt from another chest and pulled it over his head. "If Václav returns with his standard covered, then we have been refused entry. That will also mean that the mortals who live in the fort will refuse entry to the mortals among my knights." He pulled the white mantle with the black cross on the chest from his belongings. "And that simply won't do. We have need of supplies and information, and if they refuse to honor their own traditions, we shall simply have to take what we need."

Rosamund stood. "My lord, may I accompany Václav and Thomas? They can't have reached the fort yet, and I can catch up with them easily enough."

Jürgen stopped in his dressing and turned to face her. He already knew what she was about to suggest.

"I am a stranger to these lands, and to yours, in many ways. My home is France and my sire is many miles away. If Václav and Thomas are accompanying me, then neither of them will be hurt, but I can ask for hospitality in ways that won't seem threatening to this fiend."

Jürgen nodded. "Go, then. Tell Václav that you are to speak for me and he is to offer only his name and his lineage, and only if asked." He hardly needed to mention that Thomas, as a ghoul, shouldn't speak at all if he valued his life. Rosamund stepped forward and Jürgen kissed her cheek. She turned and opened the door of the wagon. Outside, moonlight turned the snow a strange blue-white color.

Rosamund stepped down from the wagon. "My lady!" Jürgen called after her. She turned. "Do not let the prince touch you."

She nodded, and ran off into the snow.

Chapter Twelve

Long hours had passed since Jürgen had watched Rosamund run across the frozen ground towards Václav and Thomas. The sun would rise soon; two hours at most, Jürgen guessed. No word from the runner, from his childe or from his lady.

Jürgen was angry enough that his Beast wasn't even bothering to exacerbate the situation. He paced outside of his wagon, sword in hand, face set in a vicious snarl. "How strong could this prince possibly be? On the very edge of Tzimisce territory? I'll take his fief, his head and his blood!" The other knights and servants stood well away from Jürgen, even the other Cainites. Any vampire was capable of losing himself to the Beast if his anger built too far, and despite his usually iron-clad control, Jürgen was no exception.

Only Wiftet the Simple stood by his lord, cradling his shivering dog in his arms. The Malkavian fool's usually colorful garb was obscured almost completely by his winter clothing, and he seemed decidedly out of his element, so far from the stone walls of Magdeburg. "My lord?"

"What?" snarled Jürgen. The dog cringed and whined.

"Oh, oh, ssh. There, there, Albion. The lord didn't mean it, he's only upset because he's not the lord of *this domain*."

Jürgen turned to face his fool, and decided that the little man had until the next gust of wind to say something amusing.

"After all," Wiftet continued to his dog, "the lord kept a man waiting for nearly this long just before we left. And then there was the time that the emissary from Mithras's court fell into the jaws of his own Beast at the merest mention that the people of his homeland were wild-haired men who copulate with sheep, and did Jürgen respond with any behavior inappropriate to the lord of the domain?" Wiftet held the dog up for it to lick his face. "No, he didn't! He broke all four of the messenger's limbs and imprisoned him for a fortnight. For just a fortnight!" Wiftet placed the dog under his shirts and regarded Jürgen again. "I'm sorry, my lord? What were we saying?"

Jürgen chuckled just as a gust of frigid air swirled the snow around his fool's feet. "Wiftet, you are truly an inspiration to all those who survive solely on God's sufferance."

"An inspiration to all the world? Oh, you are too kind, my lord."

Jürgen turned his gaze towards the fort. Not only was this delay intolerable, it was dangerous on a number of levels. If the sun rose and he had no word from Rosamund, he would have to ask his men to bring the wagons into the fort and then perhaps sprint—in daylight!—to wherever they might find her. As unpalatable as that thought was, the option was to wait for nightfall in his wagon as he had during many a long day on the Nemen river, and he was far too close to hostile forces for that. If Rosamund had already come to some harm (which would mean that her knight and Václav were already dead), he would have to exact revenge on the entire place, which would cost him time and probably mean that the *Voivodate* would send troops and monsters after him. He wasn't here for them this time, (although conflict with the Tzimisce was, of course, inevitable), and had no desire to fight them before discovering what kind of opposition he might still face from the Livonian Gangrel. Alexander had died fighting one of them, after all, and although Jürgen had sent scouts into the forests, no incident had yet occurred. His knights had accompanied Jervais on the Tremere's quest to destroy the Telyavs, of course, but at present the pagan inhabitants of the Baltic seemed reticent. Surely Jürgen wasn't so fearsome to them?

But beyond any consideration of tactics, beyond any concern he might feel for Rosamund's safety, every minute he allowed this princeling to leave him, Prince Jürgen of Magdeburg, out in the snow was one more rung that his Beast could climb to taking control. Hand-in-hand with control over his Beast was control over his surroundings, which meant that to submit to this treatment risked his soul as well as his unlife. Wiftet's point that sometimes the duties of a prince did not allow entirely gracious treatment of visitors helped somewhat, but time was getting short. Jürgen called his lieutenants together and nodded towards the fort. "It was originally my intention that we storm the fort if we were refused entry." One of the knights—a Cainite called Klaus, whom Jürgen recognized as subscribing to the same ethics as Rosamund—winced at this. Jürgen continued. "I understand that this sort of attack might be unpalatable to some of you, but I'll ask you to remember two things. First, Lady Rosamund awaits us in that den of fiends, and if this prince is as vicious as some of his clanmates, we would not recognize her lovely face when he had done with her." This had the desired effect; the knights reached for their swords, and the one who had reacted before bared his fangs in anger. "And second, the Fiefs of the Black Cross will *not* be treated this way, not even by a prince, not even by a Tzimisce."

A shrill whistle from one of the scouts caught Jürgen's attention. He bid the knights remain where they were and jogged up to the front of the caravan. The scout, a sharp-eyed lad of perhaps fourteen years, stood shivering under a fur cloak. "There," he stammered. "Something's coming. Maybe a horse."

Jürgen peered into the distance. There was indeed something very large plodding towards them, and someone rode on its back. The gait was wrong, though—it walked like a dog, not a horse, and it stood too high. Jürgen had seen its ilk before, though he'd never seen one meant for riding.

He clasped the boy on the shoulder. "Round up the other scouts and go to your wagon. Lock the bolt and do not come out until after sunrise." The boy scampered off to find his fellows, and Jürgen drew his sword and waited for the *vozhd* to reach him.

The creature was moving slowly, but Jürgen knew that the massive war-ghouls that the Tzimisce fashioned from the still-living bodies of their victims were only sluggish when they didn't have to be otherwise. He had seen them in his last campaign into fiend territories, but had never personally fought one. He turned and gave a brief shout for the knights—three of them ran to attend him but the rest scattered around the caravan. Jürgen suspected that the *vozhd* might be a distraction. It was a superb means of getting attention, after all. He turned his unearthly senses to the woods around the wagons, but heard nothing except his own people taking their positions. *Perhaps this is simply a message,* he thought. *But why in God's name send a messenger on a* vozhd?

The creature moved as though stuck in a bog, and it took nearly half an hour to walk the remaining distance to Jürgen and his knights. This had the effect of allowing even the mortals, who possessed no way to see except for moonlight, to behold the monster. It stood nearly twelve feet tall at the shoulder and was easily as long as one of the wagons. While Jürgen knew that all such creatures were fashioned from human bodies, piecing together which parts had once been legs and which had once been spines was a challenge—until the creature opened its mouth. At least six human spines had been used to fashion each jaw, and the ribs left intact and sharpened. Jürgen guessed this creature could easily bite a man in two.

The beast was seamless—the *vozhd* Jürgen had seen before, he realized, must have been constructed hastily for combat. Those creatures were thrown together and only barely attached with a flap of skin or a length of bone at strategic points, but this monster must have been the product of a master flesh-crafter. The notion of flesh-sculpting as art sickened Jürgen, although he imagined the noxious magic probably replaced poetry among the Tzimisce.

Jürgen stood firm as the *vozhd* halted several yards in front of the knights; from behind him he heard one of them begin praying quietly. He took a step forward and the creature bared its teeth. From above, Jürgen heard the rider cluck something in an unfamiliar tongue and the *vozhd* lowered its head slightly. It sniffed loudly at Jürgen, its nostrils opening with wet cracking sounds, and in a sickening moment of realization, Jürgen saw where the jaws of the human contributors had gone.

"Lord Jürgen of Magdeburg," said the rider. Jürgen peered

up and saw a middle-aged man in armor, black hair woven into a tight braid. "I am Jovirdas, *tysiatskii* of this domain and childe of Geidas, the *kunigaikstis*."

Jürgen had never heard the terms before, but based on the tone of the man's voice as he said them, he assumed that "*tysiatskii*" was roughly analogous to a lieutenant or sheriff. The second term obviously meant "prince." Jürgen waited for the *tysiatskii* to finish.

"You are welcome to enter our domain, but your people must sleep in their wagons. Our men will ensure that the mortals of this place do not disturb you. You need not fear; all are loyal to us."

"Of that, I have no doubt," answered Jürgen. Many Tzimisce, especially in smaller settlements, ruled their mortal herds openly rather than skulking in the shadows. While pulling strings from behind the scenes and working through puppets was an interesting challenge, Jürgen still envied the fiends their freedom. Of course, they were also much more visible in times of turmoil.

The *tysiatskii* continued. "You will be given quarters along with your childe and your consort." Jürgen wondered what Rosamund had told them; it certainly wasn't in her character to lie, so the prince must have assumed her to be a consort. Or perhaps this *tysiatskii* was simply trying to anger him by insinuating that the Cainite acting as a diplomat was nothing but a bedmate to the Sword-Bearer. He decided not to waste anger on this minion.

"Very well, *tysiatskii* Jovirdas. Lead on." The beast turned, and led the wagons into the fort.

Chapter Thirteen

Jürgen slept fitfully that day. He had not believed, when he was shown to a rather dank bedchamber, that he was in any real danger, but that was because he assumed his host to be a Scion. *But what if the* kunigaikstis *follows one of the lesser roads, or is ruled completely by his Beast? Such a Cainite would have no qualms about slaughtering us in our beds.* He awoke at sunset none the worse for the day, however, and found a servant waiting outside his door when he'd dressed.

"Is the prince ready to attend us?" Jürgen didn't bother looking at the servant, merely followed him out of the room into the cold. The servant didn't answer, but gave Jürgen a look that indicated he did not understand. Jürgen shook his head in disgust. His treatment the night before had been shameful enough, but sending a guide who didn't understand a visitor's language was inexcusable.

Jürgen saw Rosamund and Václav nearby, being led by another slack-faced peasant. He imagined that Geidas was in the habit of dominating his subjects' minds so thoroughly that little remained of their own personalities. He began to walk towards his childe, but his guide stepped in front of him as if to block his way. He batted the man aside with his left fist and kept walking—he could not brook such insolence from a page, not if he ever wished to face himself again. Václav began to take a step towards his sire, and was similarly blocked. He refrained from knocking the man aside, probably for Rosamund's sake.

"Good evening, sire," said Václav.

"Is it? Not as far as I've seen," muttered Jürgen. "Have you seen anyone else?"

Václav nodded. "Everyone else is still in the wagons. The same guards that were posted when I was shown to a room were still there in the morning. I don't think that they'd moved."

"Prince Geidas certainly commands his subjects' loyalty," Rosamund remarked. Jürgen's guide joined them, blood dripping down his face from where Jürgen's mailed fist had cut him, and the three Cainites followed their guides towards a malformed stone structure.

"This is slavery, not loyalty," said Václav. While of the same line as Jürgen, he had mastered only the most rudimentary gifts of mind control.

"I suppose a Cainite who can reshape a servant's flesh at whim might be less inclined to appreciate the usefulness of an unsullied mortal servant," whispered Rosamund. "But it's eerie, nonetheless."

Jürgen guessed that she hadn't seen the *vozhd.*

The servants led them to the door of the structure. From inside, Jürgen could hear a fire crackling and movement that indicated at least seven people. One of the servants knocked at the door and then opened it, but did not enter. He stood at the threshold and spoke in the same strange tongue that Jovirdas had used the night before. His voice was flat and gray—had Jürgen not been listening, the voice would have faded into the noise of the fire and voices from elsewhere in the fort.

The voice that answered it, however, was quite the opposite. "Enter, Prince Jürgen of Magdeburg. Enter, Václav, childe of Jürgen. Enter, fair Rosamund of Islington." Geidas's German was accented so thickly that Jürgen barely recognized the name of his own city, let alone Rosamund's. The *kunigaikstis's* voice was nasal and biting. It reminded Jürgen of creaking floorboards. As he and his companions entered, the room, he was reminded of the night in Magdeburg that he'd met Rosamund for the first time. There, in his own court, surrounded by visitors and making ready to announce his campaign to extend his lands east of the Elbe, he'd felt completely in control, the epitome of the Scion and warrior he'd wanted to be. It hadn't lasted the night.

Jürgen wondered if Geidas felt a similar sensation of power when the Prince of Magdeburg entered his court.

Geidas sat on a chair fashioned of wood and what resembled bone. The bone, however, looked as though it had been added to the frame of the chair rather than actually used as a building material; embellishments of white caught the firelight and made the chair seem to glow slightly. Jürgen knew that only very old bone caught light that way, and wondered if he'd been misinformed as to Geidas's age. His sources had indicated that this Tzimisce was barely a century from his breathing days, but the *vozhd* and his décor (not to mention his disregard for the rules of hospitality, which indicated that he was powerful enough to ignore them) seemed to belie those claims. The *kunigaikstis* appeared to be a boy of only twelve years, possibly less, but then Tzimisce could shape their flesh the way a sculptor did clay. His clothes were simple and, Jürgen noted, a bit ragged. *Perhaps they have a dearth of tailors here,* he mused.

Jovirdas stood next to his sire, and had Jürgen not met the man the night before, he would have assumed the *tysiatskii* to be the prince. He stood tall and straight, and wore his armor and sword as though ready to take to battle at any moment. Jürgen peered at the two Cainites—there was a strange feel in the air between them, as though they had a different connection than childe and sire.

Jürgen had guessed correctly at the door—besides the prince and his sheriff, five other people shared the room. Two were servants, shuffling around the room with the same deadened eyes and demeanor as the ones that had guided Jürgen. The other three were peasants, tied at the hands and feet and laid out on tables like roasted pigs. They moved occasionally, and as Jürgen watched one of them began to mouth the Lord's Prayer, but no sound escaped his lips.

"Welcome, Lord Jürgen." The floorboards had again begun to creak. "This is truly an unexpected delight." Jürgen frowned. The prince was either mocking him or was having difficulty speaking German. He decided to assume the worst.

"*Kunigaikstis,* I cannot imagine that my arrival comes as any surprise, considering that we waited half the night at your gates." Jovirdas glanced sharply at Jürgen, as though giving him a warning.

"I attend visitors at my own sufferance," the boy-prince said peevishly. "You would have waited the winter had I known you would be so impertinent."

"Well, I *am* here," said Jürgen, not wishing to trade insults any longer. "I do not intend to stay long, however. Your domain cannot support the Cainites I bring with me, and we have urgent business east of here."

The prince muttered something to Jovirdas, who stepped forward. "The *kunigaikstis* has heard stories of your brazenness, Lord Jürgen," he said, "but he is surprised to find that the truth is even worse. You would impose upon our hospitality on your way through our peoples' lands in order to make war upon them?"

Jürgen creased his brow. "I did not declare an intention to war."

Geidas leaned forward sharply. "No, but von Salza and his knights have certainly made no secret of their intentions. And it is well known that where the Order of the Sword goes, the Sword-Bearer follows." He smiled, and Jürgen noted that each of his teeth had been sharpened to a fine point. "Apropos, actually."

"Then what would you have of me, *kunigaikstis*? Tribute? Sacrifice?" Jürgen intended to give him no such thing. He reasoned that between himself and Václav they could kill the prince and his childe while Rosamund rallied the other knights, if necessary. "The Teutonic Knights do God's work in this land, and, yes, I follow. My reasons for doing so are far simpler than you might think."

"Enlighten me." The fiend's tone was slightly less peevish now.

"I intend to claim territory in these lands, yes. I have servants among the Knights; when von Salza brings the Savior to the pagans, he must also impose the rule that God intended upon them. The same should be true for these lands at night, when God-fearing men are safely in their homes and those such as we awaken."

"These lands are already well-governed, Sword-Bearer, especially at night," said Jovirdas. Jürgen glanced at him; it was rude for a servant to interrupt when his betters were speaking. Jürgen decided not to answer him.

"The Ventrue have already taken land and domain east of the Danube, Geidas. There is no stopping the inevitable, but I have no quarrel with you personally. You are wise enough to rule, so surely you are wise enough to—"

"Bow down before you? Swear fealty?" Geidas laughed bitterly, and Jovirdas clenched a hand on the hilt of his sword. "I think, Lord Jürgen, that before I become a vassal to the Ventrue," his tone made it quite clear to Jürgen in what regard the prince held his clan, "I shall wait and see how you fare against the Cainites of this land." He smiled. "Your predecessor did not fare so well."

Jürgen smiled back. "Which predecessor? Jervais returned with some very encouraging reports."

The change on Geidas's face was immediate and, even to Jürgen, frightening. The prince's fangs extended and twisted until they resembled hideous blackened barbs jutting from his lip. His nose wrinkled and his eyes narrowed until he looked more like a demon than an adolescent boy. Jovirdas took a step back, and Jürgen tensed himself—if the prince attacked him, he would arguably be within his rights to destroy the fiend.

The attack never came, however, for just then the door flew open and two of Geidas's guards rushed in. They babbled for a moment in their native tongue, and Geidas listened, his face returning to normal. He stepped down from his throne and approached Jürgen; Jovirdas followed close behind him.

"How many Cainites did you bring with you, Jürgen? Of what clans?"

Jürgen had no intention of enumerating his forces to the enemy, but saw no harm in the second question. "Most are of my line or my lady Rosamund's. My fool is a lunatic, but he's quite harmless."

Geidas nodded. "No others?"

Jürgen glanced at Jovirdas, and then sideways at Václav. "No, Prince Geidas. Why?"

The prince whispered something to his sheriff in their language, and then motioned for Jürgen and the others to follow him. "A Cainite was captured on my lands. He killed my *vozhd*. I just wanted to make sure he wasn't one of your company before I have him put to the torch." Jovirdas opened the door, and the Cainites filed outside. Rosamund caught Jürgen's sleeve and started to whisper something, but Jürgen shushed her. The fiends could probably hear them, and besides, he knew what she was going to say.

Gotzon was here, and the Tzimisce had captured him.

Chapter Fourteen

Gotzon stood in chains, surrounded by guards. He had healed himself from the wounds the Tzimisce guards and the *vozhd* had inflicted, but his clothes were in shreds and soaked in blood. His eyes were closed, and his lips moved silently as he recited the Lord's Prayer.

Jürgen's Beast howled in pain. He fought it down. He could not help his confessor by flying into a frenzy; the guards would simply incapacitate him and then he would have to make restitution for the loss of control.

"So this man did not come to Kybartai in your company, Lord Jürgen?"

"No, Geidas, he did not." That much was true.

"Very well, then." Geidas nodded, and Jovirdas plunged a sharpened stake into Gotzon's heart. Jürgen winced. Gotzon could, of course, have freed himself at any time before that, but his vow prevented him from calling upon the shadows to aid him. With the stake in his heart, however, he was immobilized just as any Cainite would be. "We shall leave him for the sun tomorrow morning." Geidas smiled viciously. "I understand that Lasombra burn especially slowly in the sun. I shall endeavor to remain awake to see it." He turned back towards Jürgen. "Where were we?"

Jürgen stared at him numbly for a moment. "We were discussing—"

"Your predecessor, I remember. I was referring, of course, to the other one. The Ventrue elder."

"Alexander." Behind him, Jürgen felt Rosamund shudder. It took some control for him not to do so as well.

"Yes, Alexander. He fell in battle to... well, it's not so important. Suffice it to say that you would have far greater threats than me to face, Lord Jürgen, if you wished to claim domain in these lands."

"To be sure." Jürgen nodded, and looked to Gotzon's torpid body. *My confessor, what would God have me do? Save you? Carry on your work and slay these pagans?* The fact that Gotzon was here at all was strange; possibly he had followed Jürgen, but just as likely his own crusades against heathen religion had simply crossed his path with the Sword-Bearer's. The fight against the *vozhd* had clearly weakened him; since he eschewed his command over shadows, he had only his strength and skill to aid him in battle. These were, of course, considerable, but costly, especially for a Cainite who fed sparingly. Jürgen wondered if Gotzon had chosen to stay his hand against the mortal guards or if they had merely worn him down. The condition of his clothing suggested the latter.

He turned slightly and looked helplessly at Rosamund. He was at a loss; he did not have enough information to make threats or entreaties, as he wasn't sure which was more appropriate.

Rosamund responded, her thoughts filtering through his like the scent of burning sweet grass across a battlefield—*Test. Find his weakness. Show him why you are so feared.*

He smiled his thanks to her, and then faced the Tzimisce ruler. "Consider this, Prince Geidas. Suppose I leave your domain and face whatever manner of creature felled Alexander, or members of your clan farther east, and fall. You can be sure that I will take many of them with me, and you can be sure that if I fall, others of my line will attempt to exact revenge. You will then not only be in the way of Ventrue coming from my homelands, but I am sure that the sires and overlords of the Tzimisce I destroy before dying—for rest assured, Lord Jürgen Sword-Bearer will not fall easily—will wonder why you did nothing to warn them or prevent me from intruding."

"You assume I will not." Geidas was faltering a bit; Jürgen realized that Gotzon's attack had shaken him quite a bit more than he was letting on. *So Geidas did not create that beast,* Jürgen realized, *else he would be bemoaning the loss of his own handiwork. Instead, he acts like a young lord who loses a favorite horse—he laments the thing itself, not the time it took to rear and train it.*

"I think, Geidas, that I could prevent you." The Tzimisce began to speak again, but Jürgen raised his hand. "Let me finish. Now, consider what happens if I leave here and go on to face whatever killed Alexander… and win." A look of fear crossed Geidas's eyes, for only a second, but both Jürgen and Jovirdas saw it. "You are then stuck between my forces to the west and my new-claimed territories. Von Salza's knights would find this fort before too long. And then…" Jürgen didn't bother finishing the thought. He simply waited for Geidas to realize the truth of it all.

"Of course," the prince said slowly, "I could simply destroy you all before you leave here."

Jürgen smiled. "Possibly. But you are now missing your warbeast and several of your guards. Most of your servants are near-mindless, so without you to lead them, I seriously doubt they would pose much threat to my knights. And at the moment, you and your sheriff are outnumbered." Rosamund was no combatant, of course, but Jürgen reasoned that neither the prince nor the *tysiatskii* would risk that. "You have until sunset to decide on a course of action, Geidas."

"And then?" Geidas had a sickened, gray look upon his face. Jovirdas shifted uncomfortably; Jürgen looked over the sheriff and decided that if it came to combat, the *tysiatskii* would have to be the first to fall.

"We shall leave." With that, Jürgen turned and walked towards his wagons. Václav and Rosamund followed.

"What stops them from attacking us by day?" hissed Václav.

"Nothing," answered Jürgen, "save that they are subject to the same restrictions we are. I expect they know how many of our knights are Cainites and how many are ghouls—if they have spies worth the title, they'll have noted which of our company visit the privies and which do not. I am hoping that the prince realizes that my knights and his guards are not equals by any means—he'd have a better hope defeating us if he attacked now."

"Why doesn't he?"

"I believe I have turned the tables, thanks in large part to good counsel." Rosamund said nothing, but her eyes told Jürgen the compliment did not go unnoticed. "Where before I was concerned about Geidas's true strength, I believe that he is now equally worried about mine." Jürgen turned to stare back towards the building where Gotzon was being held. "That does not entirely quell my concerns, however. I have merely made him uncertain; it could well be that Geidas is older and more power-ful than any of us. But in any case, I have given him a choice—we must come to accord or to blows." They reached Jürgen's wagon, and he nodded to Václav. "Post extra guards here. There's no point in trying to conceal where we sleep, so we'll just move the wagon there," he nodded towards an immense, snow-covered tree, "and make it clear that we expect treachery." Václav ran off towards the waiting knights. "As for you my lady, I recommend that you stay here with me today." Rosamund nodded. The sug-gestion wouldn't be proper in Magdeburg, but out here in the wilderness, the rules of court changed.

Jürgen's men began moving the wagon towards the tree. Geidas's numb-minded servants occasionally blocked their way, but the knights brushed them aside like flies. "Rosamund, you spoke with Geidas?"

"Yes, briefly."

"What… *happened* here? Who is Jovirdas, do you think? Certainly not Geidas's childe."

"I don't think so either. I think that Jovirdas is the elder of the two, but not by too many years." She paused, and took Jürgen's hand. Something else was troubling her, he could see, but she didn't put voice to it. "Geidas reminds me of István, somewhat."

Jürgen tried to place the name. "The emissary from the Arpads, yes? The one who pledged himself to Alexander?"

Rosamund nodded. "He always seemed… trapped. So many of us are, I suppose."

"Cainites?"

"Scions. We're trapped by orders and oaths just as a fish is trapped by the mud of the pond. Make too few oaths, and you are seen as untrustworthy and having something to hide. Too many, and your own words bind you tight and cut you to the bone." A light snow began to fall, and Jürgen cursed under his breath; another delay. Rosamund pretended not to notice. "Oaths are blades, my lord. They are of benefit only when you wield them deliberately, and they care not whom they cut."

Jürgen squeezed her hand gently. "We have hours before sunrise, my lady. Perhaps we could read from Acindynus's letters?" Rosamund turned to look at him, and then spoke so quietly that even Jürgen's heightened senses could barely hear.

"Let me go and speak with Jovirdas." Jürgen glanced up and saw that the *tysiatskii* had left the prince's side and was giving orders to some of the more competent servants. "Let me determine what is truly happening here. At the least it would give us more information."

"It is a risk, my lady. I have already made my move to Geidas; sending you to speak with Jovirdas might only worsen matters."

"Then do not send me. I shall go on my own, should anyone ask."

Jürgen glanced at her. The suggestion was a departure from courtly practice in many ways, but then, they were hardly in court. "My lady—"

"Maybe we can free Gotzon," she said. Jürgen paused, unsure of what to say.

"Such a risk for a man you so feared, Rosamund?"

Rosamund smiled. "He heard my confession, as you asked, Lord Jürgen. What he thinks of me, I do not know, but I saw more of him than I wished. Whatever else he may be, Gotzon is a godly man, and I think it would be a sin to let him perish here."

"Possibly so," he said. "But I still think it too much a risk. I cannot give my consent." He looked at Rosamund's eyes, and saw the realization she knew he'd make—she had not asked for consent. She had informed him of her course of action, not asked for permission to take it.

Rosamund walked off into the falling snow, and Jürgen stood there, wondering what had passed between her and Gotzon in Magdeburg. *What had she to confess?*, he wondered. *And did Gotzon follow us here? Too many questions*, he thought, *and only one way I know to answer them.*

Chapter Fifteen

Jürgen stood before his confessor. Three guards stood between them, swords drawn, all looking nervous. At least three more men were hiding nearby. Jürgen imagined they had orders to summoned Geidas and Jovirdas and probably set Gotzon on fire—one of them held a torch a little too close to the paralyzed Lasombra for comfort—if Jürgen tried to free him.

Jürgen had considered it, of course. But snatching the stake from Gotzon's heart wouldn't be the end of it—he'd have to open the chains, too. Despite his clan's reputation for fearsome strength and powers of the mind, it was the unholy command of shadows that Gotzon had chosen to master...

The same mastery that he had forsaken in a vow to God. Jürgen didn't feel that he could successfully free his confessor without causing the entire fort to erupt in chaos and burn any chances he had at leaving behind an ally rather than a troublesome enemy, and that gnawed at Jürgen's heart like a jackal.

But perhaps, he had thought while waiting for Rosamund, *Gotzon can help me to help him.*

Jürgen had never attempted to read his confessor's mind. His usual distaste for the process aside, the prospect terrified him beyond words. Gotzon was something more than a Cainite; the shadows that he had dedicated untold centuries to commanding had made a hornet's nest of his undead body. The man actually *bled* blackness, as Jürgen had once been unfortunate enough to see. Gotzon was always reticent, saying only what he needed to say, and to Jürgen it had always seemed that Gotzon was careful because the blackness inside him was merely waiting for the right word, the right gesture, to facilitate its escape.

Indeed, Jürgen had strong suspicions about the eclipse some two years past, but had never asked Gotzon about it.

Jürgen hadn't bothered to ask Geidas's permission to approach the prisoner. He didn't expect that anyone here could recognize Gotzon or make any connection between him and Jürgen (the enmity between Ventrue and Lasombra was famous, in any case, and it would be a surprise to most Cainites to learn of Jürgen's relationship with Gotzon) but he didn't wish to bring suspicion upon himself, either. He stared past the guards at Gotzon, trying to look past the shadows on his face, past his paralyzed flesh, past the frost growing over his eyes.

Blackness. Staring into the night sky wasn't truly black—there was always light from somewhere. Being underground, in dungeons or caves was closer to this, but...

Jürgen pulled back. He couldn't face it. He was afraid.

Jürgen's Beast laughed and demanded that he scream in terror. Jürgen refused, and forced his consciousness into the murk once more.

Gotzon's body was immobile, but his mind still functioned. Jürgen wanted to know why his confessor was here.

Jürgen saw the blackness once more, and mentally cast about in the dark as a drowning man might hope desperately to find something to cling to. The blackness chilled him, infested him, clawed at his mind. His Beast shrank back in fear, and Jürgen mentally grinned—the Lasombra's reputations for ironclad control made perfect sense, if the blackness within so cowed their Beasts.

Of course, the blackness had its own plans for their souls, or so Jürgen surmised.

Gotzon? Most Cainites were easy enough to communicate with this way, even while paralyzed so. Gotzon's mind was apparently spacious enough to become lost in.

—Jürgen? What in Heaven's name do you want?

Gotzon, I...

The blackness roiled, and Jürgen felt Gotzon next to him.

—Jürgen, are you going to try to save me? Consider, my son, I am already saved.

To be sure, but Rosamund insists upon trying.

The blackness changed. Jürgen was still lost at sea, still foundering in pure nothingness, but now that nothingness grew colder.

—*Rosamund? Why? What does she care of me?*

I was hoping you could answer that. She gave you confession—

—*You know I can't speak of confession to any except God, Jürgen.*

Of course not. Jürgen had expected this response. *Can you tell me why you followed me?*

—*No. Perhaps later.*

You do realize you will be burnt in the sun come the dawn?

The darkness began to recede, and Jürgen realized with sick fascination that he was drifting away into the depths, away from Gotzon's mind. The last thing he heard—felt—from Gotzon's mind was...

—*No, I won't.*

The voice echoed, but Jürgen was stuck, trapped floundering in the black mire of Gotzon's memory. He heard chanting in a language he did not understand, and moved towards the sound. He saw something—not light, just a place in the murk where the darkness was simply less complete, and saw Gotzon.

Cainites did not age physically, and so Jürgen had no idea how long ago the scene he beheld had taken place. Gotzon's eyes still had the same intensity, his form the same control, but it was different here. He was somewhat, just somewhat, less sure of himself, a tiny fraction less rigid than when Jürgen had met him.

He wore black robes, and was surrounded by Cainites—all Lasombra, Jürgen guessed—dressed just the same. The shadows in the room pooled about their feet like stagnant water, and periodically a tendril would reach up to caress one of them. One of the vampires spoke, and although Jürgen did not understand his words, in Gotzon's memory he saw their meaning.

"We will learn the word. With one word, we can bring darkness to the world and walk during the day."

As Jürgen watched, Gotzon's face grew hungry. "The cry that slays the light? But who among us—"

"Need you even ask?" The man ended the sentence with a

name, and Jürgen understood it to be Gotzon's true name, the one he had been born with. But he could not repeat it, not even mentally. Gotzon had worked very hard to obliterate that memory. "Of course it shall be you. None of us is so favored by the Shadowed One and by the Abyss that we are worthy to learn the word."

One of the vampires turned and stared at Jürgen. Jürgen started, and pushed himself backward as though trying to swim through the blackness to safety. As he left the memory, he heard a voice remark, "Shadows ripple through time as well as space. Pay it no heed."

Jürgen cast about, first for Gotzon, then wildly for Rosamund, and then finally began to recite the Lord's Prayer. And as he did so, he saw light—true light, not just a wrinkle in impenetrable blackness. He pushed towards it, and found himself in another memory.

This one had to be more recent than the last. Jürgen recognized the surroundings—they were in Swabia, his homeland, but probably centuries before his birth. Gotzon lay on the ground, his undead body torn and savaged. His assailants were nowhere to be seen, but he held a broken sword in one hand.

"Good Lord," whispered Gotzon, "what is it you would have me do?"

Jürgen reached to his confessor, but of course he could not touch a memory.

"Shall I wait here for the sun?"

Jürgen looked up and saw that the clouds covered the moon. The night was almost completely dark, and Gotzon carried no light.

"Or shall I wait for the shadows to consume me?"

Jürgen looked around, and saw the shadows gathering, growing stronger. He debated pushing away again; he knew that Gotzon must escape this event, as it *was* only a memory, and he was therefore in no danger.

And then, a miracle occurred.

The clouds parted and the full moonlight streamed down on Gotzon. The shadows around him wailed in pain and backed away, and Gotzon pulled himself to his feet, glaring at the creatures in the darkness. Finally, after the last of the shadows had retreated behind trees and stones, Gotzon knelt.

"Then I shall not wait," he said. "I shall spread Your Word and I shall hunt those like myself."

Jürgen pushed away. This moment was between Gotzon and God, and he had no right to it.

"And I shall not use the tools of Satan to do Your Work, my Lord," was the last thing he heard Gotzon say. He flew upwards towards the moonlight, and found himself standing there in front of Gotzon's chained body. The guards standing in between them looked nervously at the Sword-Bearer, then back to their captive. One of them stepped forward protectively, as if Jürgen might lurch forward to grab at the stake in Gotzon's heart. Another waved the torch closer to Gotzon.

Jürgen glared at him. "If that man so desired," he said, "everyone here would already be dead." He shook his head in annoyance. "But he keeps his word, and trusts God for the rest." With that, Jürgen turned and stormed back towards his wagon to wait for Rosamund and the coming dawn.

Václav intercepted him before he reached it. "Your wagon is beneath the tree, but by morning it will be buried in snow, if this continues." The snow had been lightly falling for hours now, and the fort was slowly becoming amorphous and white.

Jürgen shrugged. "No matter. We'll dig it out if necessary. Thanks be to God that it *is* winter; if the days were longer I think Geidas might be more tempted to have his men take advantage."

Václav leaned in closer to his sire. "Did you speak with him?"

"In a sense," murmured Jürgen.

"What is he doing here?"

"He wouldn't say, but I imagine he was pursuing demons. Exacting God's justice, as usual."

Václav looked back towards the main structure. "Do you think we can save him?"

Jürgen did not answer his childe, but clasped him on the shoulder and nodded towards the wagons. Then he continued on his way towards his own makeshift haven, safe beneath the massive tree. If he had to wake up during the day, Jürgen reasoned, the shade might provide enough cover to fight, and the snow would keep the wagon from burning easily.

He glanced back over his shoulder again, and then walked on through the snow. Nothing to do now but wait. His Beast spoke up petulantly, asking for blood, but Jürgen had no answer. He agreed with his Beast, however—this was not the kind of warfare he desired, either.

Chapter Sixteen

He reached the wagon and climbed inside. Lighting a candle, he pulled the letters of Acindynus from the box and began to page through them. He came across a passage that caught his eye:

"Cainites do not change; the Creator freezes us in time when our mortal lives end. Our sires, of course, make the initial choice as to when exactly this occurs, but I believe that the fact that we do not change is indicative of the role that God wills us to play. Our unchanging nature enables us to be forces of stability, for even as men reshape the world, we remember it as it was, and can guide the mortals towards the best of their past."

Jürgen scoffed. He shook a bottle of ink and dipped his quill into it, then added his own notation:

"Cainites do not change in the way that mortals change; we do not age, mature or die. We cannot bear or sire children, nor can we alter such superficial things as our hair or skin (barring, of course, the hellish arts of the Tzimisce). But we can change; surely you have met or heard of Cainites who stepped off their former roads and adopted others? We must fight to change, this is true—our natural inclination is towards stability, and that is why Cainites such as myself, who strive to gain as much domain as God will allow—are rare creatures indeed. But of more significance than a Cainite who wills himself to chance is an event that, in and of itself, becomes the impetus of change in a Cainite. A mortal who witnesses a possible miracle can more easily rededicate his brief life to God's service, but a Cainite with only eternity ahead of him? That Cainite must be very moved indeed to make such a change in his unlife.

"Respect, then, the Cainite who can change, for he has retained one of the best gifts of humanity—the best of the past, as Acindynus says. And also respect the force that can change him, for that is true power."

Jürgen signed the notation with a quick sketch of his arms, and scattered sand across the page to dry the ink. He sat back to consider his own words.

Wasn't that why he had asked Rosamund to give confession to Gotzon? To change him? Gotzon had already changed. All Cainites followed codes of ethics, but honest and pragmatic vampires admitted that these roads existed more to hold the Beast in check, to avoid the decline into madness and bloodlust, than any true feeling of moral obligation. And yet, the feeling of obligation had to remain, else the Beast would see through the sham and seize control. Thus Jürgen walked the *Via Regalis*, the Road of Kings, and spent every night of his unlife, every moment he was awake, being the leader and warrior he was born to be. He had never seen any other option.

But Gotzon obviously had. Gotzon had told him cryptic stories, but now Jürgen had seen more in the darkness of his confessor's mind. He had hoped that Rosamund would do as Acindynus suggested and help Gotzon to remember humanity, to help Gotzon understand that passion for forces other than God was still possible. But it was Rosamund who had changed— now, instead of feeling terror at the Lasombra, she was working to free him.

Had she found *beauty* in those shadows? Was she trying to indebt Gotzon to her? Jürgen winced at the thought—Gotzon would not feel the slightest bit indebted to anyone who risked himself to save him. He considered his soul resigned to God and his unlife ever a second away from being forfeit. Jürgen wondered if she would merely consider it a breach of some ethic not to save Gotzon, but he felt that was unlikely. After all, Jürgen followed the same rules of decorum as she, or nearly so; why did he not feel the same compulsion? True, he would save Gotzon if given the chance, but he didn't feel he was violating any trust by letting him die in retribution for invading another Cainite's domain. Jürgen himself knew full well that he could expect a similar fate if he was ever captured by an enemy—he often hoped that, if his time on Earth should ever end, it would end either on the battlefield or at the hands of a stronger Cainite.

A sound of footsteps outside snapped Jürgen to attention, but the light rap at the door told him it was Rosamund. He opened the wagon's door and helped her in, shutting the door against the snow. He then took a moment to look her over, to make sure that she was intact.

Her skin seemed to shimmer softly in the candlelight, and both her eyes and her halo told Jürgen that she had something to report, something that she considered good news. She leaned forward and embraced him, and then pulled back and whispered in French.

"We can save him. He's to be taken out of his chains and imprisoned until sunset, and then you can, if you so choose, challenge Geidas for his unlife."

"Challenge him?"

"Yes. To a duel of minds."

Jürgen's eyes widened. "A duel of minds?"

Rosamund nodded enthusiastically. "It's his greatest source of pride, his control over minds. He doesn't have the command of flesh that most of his clan does; that's why he's out here. He was Embraced only—"

"His greatest source of pride, Rosamund?" Jürgen was fuming. "If it's his greatest source of pride, there's a *reason* for that. Do you know what is involved in such duels?"

Rosamund's smile faded. "I have seen similar duels, my lord, and—"

"At court, yes? In France?"

"Yes, I—"

"This is rather different, my lady. This is war." Jürgen ground his teeth. "Most such duels are fought within the mind of a mortal, one unconditioned by either party and unbiased by inclinations. We are in a very small settlement; every mortal here has probably been bent to his whim to some degree. But that is not even the worst of it. I have no idea how close to Caine Geidas is. If, by some strange quirk of God's will, he is closer to his clan's accursed founder than I am to Veddartha, I stand to lose much more than Gotzon in this duel."

"But I have seen Cainites of differing lineage duel before."
Rosamund looked crushed. Jürgen tried to calm down.

"Plucking at heartstrings is one thing, Rosamund. Caine
decreed that the minds of his children are sacrosanct, at least
from those further removed from his blood. While your powers
over the heart function well on mortal and Cainite," he stopped
and took her hand, "mine are not so... versatile."

"My lord, I am sorry." She pulled her hand away and cast
her eyes downwards. Jürgen smiled.

"Don't be. The plan is sound, and provided that Geidas's
blood isn't any thicker than mine, he doesn't stand a chance of
harming me."

"If the duel is fought with a mortal, how could he?"

Jürgen sat and drummed his fingers on his knee. "Mortals'
minds are like unformed clay. They can be shaped into a number of different forms, even a funnel to allow his mind into
mine. This is a risk to both of us; while it's impossible for him
take command of my mind while filtered through that of a mortal, he might learn much. Again, the closer to Caine, the more
danger I am in." He paused, trying to remember what he had
learned of Tzimisce lineages, but the languages were unfamiliar, the names long and arcane. "I think it's unlikely, frankly,"
he said finally. "You said something about his Embrace—perhaps you heard his sire's name?"

She shook her head. "No, I'm afraid not. I learned that he
was Embraced recently, not even a century before I was."

"Meaning he isn't even two hundred years from his breathing days," Jürgen mused. "Still, age is no indicator of lineage.
Pity we don't have Jervais with us; perhaps his sorcery could
help."

"How are such duels won, my lord? What is the object?"

"It varies." Jürgen stretched out his legs. "Sometimes it's
something as simple as picking up a cup—if the mortal picks up
a cup marked with a contestant's blazon, that contestant wins.
And remember that these duels are not always fought with
mortal go-betweens. Once I saw a duel where the loser had to
plunge his hand into a fire. That duel lasted almost until sunrise." He chuckled at the memory. "A Lasombra lost that duel,

and he very nearly lost his hand as well." He looked over at Rosamund, and debated telling her the unpleasant truth, but decided it was better that she hear it now. "The problem is, if I issue the challenge—and I must, since this is Geidas's domain— he decides the terms."

"What is the worst he could ask?"

Jürgen considered. "Not the fire, of course—that I could withstand, probably better than he could."

"Could he stipulate that you will engage each other's mind directly?"

"If he does, the risk is as great to him as to me. Probably the worst he could do is stipulate that the loser must drink of the winner."

Rosamund gasped. "Oh, my lord, what have I done?"

Jürgen grinned. "Do you think I shall lose? Moreover, even with one drink, do you think I would be bound to him more strongly than to my sire?" Rosamund calmed, and smiled slightly. "Or more strongly than to you, my lady?" He sat up and took her hands. "I shall win this challenge, and I shall do so in your name, if you will let me. When he sees into my mind, he'll see you, and a creature of such a hideous nature must fall before your beauty."

A strange look crossed Rosamund's face. "He'll see your thoughts?"

"Part of the duel, I'm afraid." Jürgen shrugged. "When two Cainites attempt to command one another, one usually yields right away, or averts his gaze, thus breaking the contact. But in such duels, both must search for any handhold in the other's mind that they can find, especially if we must duel in the unfamiliar territory of a mortal's mind. No matter who wins the duel, we'll come away knowing a great deal more about each other than we do now. In fact, I've heard of very cocksure Cainites engaging in such duels with the express purpose of gaining information rather than actually winning."

"That seems a dangerous game," Rosamund whispered. She seemed distracted now.

"To be sure." He lifted her chin up. "What is it, my lady?"

She said nothing, but kissed him. Jürgen, surprised,

remained still for a second, and allowed his own lips to soften and accept the kiss. He felt her tongue probing at his fangs, and wondered if she intended him to drink from her again. They had tasted of each other's blood once before, but it had been an act of passion, of mourning, possibly—he had dared to think at the time—of love.

But then there was the matter of Alexander and the sorcerers she had neglected to mention to him. Rosamund could use love, when she needed to.

Jürgen kissed her back, and ran his hands through her hair. Eyes closed, he reached over and snuffed the candle, and pushed Rosamund to the makeshift bed on his floor. Outside, the wind howled and pushed snow against the wagon—mortal lovers would have found the wagon intolerably chilly. Jürgen barely noticed, except to note how cold his lady's mouth felt.

He kissed her neck, and she stretched her head back as thought inviting him to bite. He felt his fangs extending and his Beast silently urging him to drink, to keep drinking until she rotted in his grasp. He quieted the voice, but refrained from biting her—was she inviting him to bind him closer? Absurd; if he drank, then so would she. Was she trying to distract him from something, from some vital part of the duel with Geidas?

Rosamund can use love. She has before.

Love God, and that is all, came Gotzon's voice in Jürgen's memory.

Rosamund reached up and ran her tongue along his throat, and then closed her mouth against it. He knew she wouldn't bite without his permission, but the feel of her fangs against his throat scattered his thoughts. He pressed his hand against the back of her head, and whispered, "Yes."

Her fangs worked to pierce his skin, tearing jagged holes in his throat. A mortal would have died in seconds from the outpouring of blood; from Jürgen's dead throat, the vitae oozed almost sluggishly, and Rosamund sucked it from the wound, daintily at first, and then with growing urgency. Jürgen felt the pleasure of the Kiss wash over him, and shut his eyes. He didn't want to look at his lady again until after he had drunk of her also; he knew that the next time she looked at him the full force of the second drink would hit her.

If she is not already under oath to another.

Jürgen felt her lick the wound, and the itching pain on his neck abated. She stretched our her neck before him, and he heard the rustling of garments in the dark. If she is under oath to another, he thought, drinking from her again will almost enslave me. Am I willing to risk that?

He lunged forward so quickly that Rosamund gasped, but Jürgen had no thought of violence. He was merely moving quickly to escape the argument in his head, his own voice clashing with his Beast's, Gotzon's, Christof's....

His fangs met her throat, and he was lost. Her body, soft and cold under his hands, seemed to yield like water as he drank. He knew that the next time he saw her, he would love her.

If he drank of her blood again, he would love her without question, without thought, and without hope of recourse.

He drank deeper, and blood washed these thoughts away.

Chapter Seventeen

Jürgen woke the following night expecting to hear servants at his wagon door, or perhaps his childer rousing him. He heard nothing. He raised his head and listened, sharpening his senses in hopes of catching some hint of events outside his wagon. He heard movement, but muffled, and Jürgen guessed it to be men and horses at the far side of the camp. *Von Salza? Impossible. We're well to the northwest of his route.* Even with the influence Jürgen and Christof wielded in the Sword-Brothers, he had no desire to see them here.

Why so quiet, then? Rosamund, not sleeping (as no vampire slept past sundown) but not stirring, either, lay next to him, pale, cold, a sculpture of flesh and time. He couldn't see her; the wagon was, of course, designed to admit no light from outside, and he didn't bother lighting a candle just yet. He stood and donned his shirt and his mail, and then pulled his sword from the wall. Silence could mean an ambush, but if that were so, why not just burn the wagon?

He pushed against the door, and found it blocked. His Beast leapt in fear and Jürgen drew back a fist to break the door, but stopped himself.

"My lord?" At her voice, he felt the urge to kneel. He heard her reaching for the candle, and realized that to *see* her would be...

"Stop, my lady." He wondered if his voice, so coarse and boorish next to the music of hers, engendered any of the same feelings. "Please. The door is stuck, and I hear nothing from outside."

He heard her stand and approach him. She touched his

chest, and even through the steel of his mail, at her touch he felt the urge to weep. He stepped forward to embrace her, and felt something shift on top of the wagon.

"Moving snow," suggested Rosamund. Jürgen smiled; that was most likely the case. A snowfall during the day, or wind strong enough to cause drifts, might easily have sealed him in the wagon. He could have escaped through a panel in the wagon's floor, if necessary, but now there was no need. He listened again, and heard the scraping sounds of spades on snow above him and outside the door.

"I have been too long at war," he said, but both Cainites knew he didn't mean it. "I have no place of respite, no place that isn't a battle."

"No place, my lord?" The voice in the dark was a siren's, the touch on his chest was God's own succor.

"Perhaps..." he frowned. He knew that last night he had been leery of Rosamund for some reason, something about using love for her own benefit. Surely, now that she had drunk from him a second time, surely she wouldn't deceive him. "Perhaps there is a place for me, my love, where I can rest, and leave my sword far from my reach without fear."

His Beast reminded him that he was not in that place, in any event. Jürgen agreed, but did not release her from his arms. "We must be ready; they'll dig us out soon." He kissed her, and found her lips to be somehow warmer, somehow fuller, than the night before. He lit a candle, but kept his eyes shut until the light filled the small room. Then, and only then, did he turn his gaze on her.

She wasn't watching him, concentrating on dressing herself. The statue was moving now, but still so lovely, so perfect that no living woman could ever dream of what she embodied. She *was* woman, all of woman-kind, and Jürgen stared at her and knew again what a young man feels. His Beast hated the sensation, and let him know by screaming every foul epithet it could at Rosamund, but Jürgen batted it down with no effort at all.

Love God, and that is all, Gotzon? Impossible, he thought. How could anyone look upon her and not love her? A streak of jealousy shot through him and he opened his mouth to say that she must never give confession to Gotzon again, but then stopped. That was the madness that had doomed Alexander, the desire to own everything that he loved. Jürgen of Magdeburg decided he would not make that error—he would love her as she deserved to be loved, as a Scion and a lady.

She finished dressing, and turned to him. Her eyes met his, and he realized dimly that she was seeing him for the first time since they had shared blood the night before. The look in her eyes told him everything, and yet there were no words he could think to say, no move he could think to make, that would prove him worthy of the love in her eyes. And yet the look wasn't the slavish adoration of a ghoul knight; Jürgen had, in his time, put many such mortals under the blood and never seen emotion such as this behind their eyes. They had all been men, of course, but even so, in Rosamund's eyes he saw trust that he did not even have in himself.

The spades' scraping grew louder, and Jürgen heard Václav's voice calling to him, but did not respond. He took a step forward, his eyes locked on hers, and knelt. He caressed her hand, kissed her palm, and brushed his fangs over her wrist. He savored the scent of vitae through her skin, prolonging the moment when he would drink of her again, and know salvation.

She pulled her hand away, and Jürgen's Beast howled in triumph.

He stood, his eyes burning into hers, intending to seize her mind and command her to drink. She spoke one word: "Wait."

Possibly it was the fact that her eyes hadn't changed; instead of showing fear when he'd surged towards her, they had remained loving, trusting and genuine. Perhaps it was simply her voice that the Beast feared. In any case, Jürgen stopped, and angrily sent the Beast back into the recesses of his mind. "My lady—" he began.

"No need," she said, and kissed him lightly. "I know. I understand." The spades stopped, and both Cainites glanced up as Václav stepped up to the door of the wagon and knocked. Jürgen slid past Rosamund to open it. Václav stood at the threshold glancing nervously about, and Jürgen noted that the people digging out the wagon were all knights, and all armed. Wiftet stood a small distance off, his dog clutched to his chest, staring at the fort.

"My lord, we must hurry," said the knight. "We have only a few hours now."

"What's happened, Václav?"

"Geidas sent a messenger during the day. He eluded our spies and escaped into the forests, and the watchman was afraid to send knights after him for fear of an ambush."

Jürgen nodded. "Wise."

"But we don't know what message he carried, only that he traveled east. Our scouts found evidence, though, that some regular travel occurs between this fort and some destination east of here, but not by mortals."

"This trail wasn't erased by the snowfall?"

Václav leaned in to his sire and whispered. "It didn't snow today, my lord, except *on this fort.* One of the knights walked outside of it, and said that he was staring at a wall of snowflakes, but not a one touched him."

"I see," said Jürgen. Could the Tzimisce control the very weather? He'd heard that some of Jervais's compatriots could do so, but had never heard any such ability ascribed to the Clan of Dragons. But there were Tremere here, Jürgen knew, so perhaps they had...? *That is ridiculous,* he thought. *Tremere allying with the Tzimisce? That's as preposterous as...*

...as a Ventrue prince giving confession to a Lasombra priest, he realized.

"My lord? What shall we do?"

Jürgen surveyed the camp. A fresh layer of snow covered everything, but if the snow indeed had only fallen on the camp, and Tzimisce reinforcements were on the way, they would be trapped. "Did anyone else leave the fort, or anyone arrive from outside?"

"No, my lord."

"Good. Then we'll proceed as if nothing has changed. I shall issue my challenge to Geidas, and attempt to free Gotzon. In the meantime, keep your men alert and note any movement beyond the fort." He looked to the other side of the wagon, where Peter, Thomas and Raoul were leaning on their spades, red-faced from exertion. "And make sure they guard their lady well, Václav."

Chapter Eighteen

Geidas and Jovirdas stood behind a small wooden table. The only objects it held were two iron cups. Jürgen grimaced as he walked into the room—as he'd feared, the loser of the duel would become partially bound to the winner. While one drink wasn't enough to stop one Cainite from murdering another, it could provide critical lapses in judgment and timing. He could ill afford such mistakes.

Jürgen's gaze left the table and the cups and circled the room. It was a different place from the one he'd been in the night before—obviously Geidas wanted Jürgen to be in as unfamiliar a situation as possible. He had not even been present when Jürgen had issued the challenge; Jovirdas had heard it and issued the terms. "A duel of minds, to be lost by the first Cainite to drink from an iron goblet containing the other's blood." But Jürgen had not heard any talk of a second, so why was the *tysiatskii* in the room at all?

And worse, why was no mortal present?

"Am I dueling you both, Geidas?" he asked.

Geidas sneered at him, his reedy voice especially grating tonight. "You are unfamiliar with our ways, of course. You may have an observer present, Lord Jürgen. Under no circumstances may the observer speak or interfere with the duel in any way."

Jürgen nodded, thinking. If they intended to attack him, Václav would be the best choice. Wiftet, although nearly useless in a fight, would not be missed outside, and he might well be able to help keep Jürgen's mind away from secret topics. But as Jürgen walked to the door and called out for a servant, he already knew whose presence he'd request.

"She's quite a diplomat, Sword-Bearer," remarked Geidas as they waited for Rosamund. "She obviously has great faith in your abilities, as well. Suggesting a duel of minds with me... When I've beaten you in this duel, would you like some time to discipline your servants?"

Jürgen glanced upwards at the prince. "So sure you'll beat me? Have you so much control over every mortal you see?"

Geidas looked honestly surprised. "What have mortals to do with it?" Jovirdas said something in their native tongue, and Geidas nodded expansively. Jürgen had the distinct feeling that this exchange had been well rehearsed. "My *tysiatskii* informs me that among your people, duels of the mind are often fought with mortals as the battlefield. We find that unnecessary here."

"Would you enter a sword-duel without knowing until the last moment if your sword was made of clay or iron?" Jürgen glanced about the room, sizing up possible escape routes or weapons. Jovirdas's hand crept towards his sword. Jürgen decided to stall. "You can't possibly be less than nine times removed from Caine. I expect this duel to be over in seconds."

Geidas smirked like a child about to tattle on his brother. "Nine times? I assure you, Lord Jürgen, that the blood of the Eldest runs more thickly in my veins than that." He glanced to Jovirdas, who nodded grimly. "Much more thickly."

Perfect, though Jürgen. He cocked and ear and listened carefully to the specter of Geidas's words, still hanging in the air. The lingering memory of the sound held still the truth of what he had said—or the lack thereof, to a Cainite skilled enough to hear lies.

Jürgen of Magdeburg was indeed skilled enough to do so. He listened, and heard the words again, but in a tinny, echoing timbre. Geidas, however close to Caine he might actually be, did not fully believe what he had just said.

It was still a gamble to duel directly. But if Jürgen wished to avoid it, he would have to renegotiate the terms of the duel or back down. Neither was acceptable. Trying to decide on a course of action, he turned his attention to the sounds outside the room. A moment later, footsteps in the snow announced her retinue's approach, and she knocked lightly on the door.

When she entered, hope entered with her. Doubt and fear slunk quietly away into the snow. Jürgen turned to Geidas and looked at him carefully, studying his bearing, his manner, his clothes and his face, and found nothing but a child-prince, a boy pretending to greater power than he could understand.

A true duel of minds, then, he thought. Jürgen admitted Rosamund into the room and quietly explained the rules. He looked into her eyes and saw confusion there—she wondered why she had been chosen to accompany him. *I shall explain later, my love,* he thought, and turned to face Geidas.

Geidas stood across the table from him and cut his wrist with a dagger from his belt. Jürgen did the same, and both Cainites dripped a small amount of their blood into the iron cups. Jürgen glanced down at the cup before the first drop of Geidas's blood reached it; it was clean and smelled of nothing but iron. Geidas apparently intended to win this duel on skill alone, and that worried Jürgen more than any possible treachery. He glanced behind the prince at the *tysiatskii*. Jovirdas stood impassive, staring at Jürgen as though he expected the Sword-Bearer to speak to him. Jürgen heard Rosamund shift her weight behind him, and behind that, heard her guardians waiting in the snow. If there was to be treachery, Jürgen was not without protection.

But the snowfall during the day nettled him. Either Geidas had allies among Jervais's so-called "Telyavs" or the Tzimisce held much deeper secrets than Jürgen had suspected. Or, he considered, it was possible that the knight had exaggerated and that the snowfall had fallen on a larger area, perhaps simply more heavily upon the fort.

Jürgen lowered his hand, the wound already sealing. He drummed his fingers against his side, letting his thoughts clear. He glanced about the room, and realized that if violence broke out, he would be limited to the tiny knife in his belt or break-ing a leg from the table. Geidas wasn't obviously armed, but Jovirdas's hand rested casually on the hilt of his sword. Jürgen's Beast suggested, insistently, that he simply attack the two fiends, now, before this absurd duel began, before Geidas had the chance to invade his mind, to see what he felt for Rosamund, before he saw…

Jürgen silenced the voice, but knew that he could not allow Geidas to see Rosamund in his mind. Geidas seemed to have changed his opinion of Rosamund; where once he had assumed her to be Jürgen's consort, he now regarded her as a servant, perhaps a specialized mediator. For Geidas to learn what Rosamund truly was to Jürgen would give him an advantage Jürgen could not allow.

Jürgen's Beast snickered, and slunk off into the dark of his mind. Jürgen knew that his Beast would become inaccessible during the duel, as focusing on controlling it would provide his mind the distraction it needed to avoid giving information to Geidas. But he couldn't focus on anything trivial; if Geidas felt so confident in his powers as to allow this challenge, especially with no mortal go-between, he would sweep aside any flimsy memory that Jürgen could call up.

Jürgen's hand stole to the cross around his neck. There was a memory, he knew, that he could call up if necessary.

"Ready, then?" Geidas's voice was even, but his eyes were unsteady. Jürgen simply nodded, and the two Cainite princes locked eyes. Geidas's were the color of dead leaves, and he locked his hands behind his back. Jürgen didn't bother; if he allowed Geidas enough control to force him to move his hands, it wouldn't matter where they were.

"Drink," they chorused, and their minds went to war.

Chapter Nineteen

Jürgen had never participated in such a duel before. He had been both the victim and (more often) the user of this form of mental control, but never both at once. He felt Geidas's power like a leaden weight upon his eyes, working its way back into his skull at the same time that his own gaze forced its way past the Tzimisce's eyes. His eyes seemed to offer no resistance to Jürgen's mind, but then he found his will caught in a net, trapped in many layers of commands and counter-commands. And Jürgen understood why Geidas had been both confident and unsteady about this duel.

Geidas was a pawn. Another Tzimisce, an elder whose name Jürgen could not find amidst the morass, had sired this boy and installed him as the *kunigaikstis* of this tiny domain, and then lent him the *vozhd* as both protection and a way to make him seem more powerful than he was.

But who is your sire, Geidas? No sooner had Jürgen mentally asked the question than Geidas's assault on his mind tripled in strength. Jürgen withdrew his own will, nearly shutting his eyes, to stop himself from succumbing. Obviously that particular line of memories was too well protected to plunder, at least for now. Jürgen had no such protection for his own memories. He would have to rely on misdirection.

Geidas's fierce barrage had abated in force, but not in intensity. He was trying to wear Jürgen's resistance down. Jürgen allowed him deep enough into his mind to see the destruction of the Silent Fury, and suddenly he was there, listening to Brenner thrashing against his fellows in frenzy and battling the Tzimisce woman. He drank her blood and threw her down, as he had before, and knew that next he would destroy her....

But this time something changed. The sensation he felt when he saw her on the ground wasn't the slight, easily ignored respect of the first drink, but the all-encompassing adoration of the *third*. He knelt down beside the Tzimisce woman, and suddenly knew her name—Masha—and she tilted her head back, black curls falling lightly over her neck, and beckoned him to drink.

Jürgen glanced down in the memory and saw his hand reaching forward. He stopped the motion and locked eyes with the woman, his gaze bearing down upon her like a hawk to a mouse. He drew back a mailed fist and smashed it into her face, fighting through the false blood oath. He heard bones crack, but underneath he felt something else give, something more ephemeral than bone or flesh, and the scene faded. He was standing in the snow, now, looking out into a storm, and cold, angry....

This wasn't his memory, he realized. He foundered for control, but was stuck in the vision. The snow covered him; he could find no handhold, no way to regain himself.

He was Geidas, the man, the youngest son of a mortal *kunigaikstis*, a boy who lived in fear of the night-monsters his mother told him about. He had seen his older brother carried off into the night by a man on a horse, and now he waited in the snow, waited for the man to return his brother to him, waiting for sunrise, waiting to find his way home.

The man on the horse returned. Jürgen peered up in hopes of seeing and perhaps recognizing this man, but the snow and wind obscured his face.

Geidas. The man's voice barely carried over the wind, and yet Jürgen shivered anyway. *Your brother is dead. He chose to fight me, and the Beast claimed him.*

Jürgen's eyes burned with tears. He still could find no way to fight this; he *was* Geidas, and Geidas was inside his mind.

Geidas, the man continued, *you are young and weak, and so I despise that I must take you into the night. But I have need of one such as you.*

"Such as me?" Jürgen found his mouth forming the words.

The man didn't answer, but spurred his horse on and grabbed Jürgen by the scruff of his neck. He hoisted Jürgen up to his horse and closed his fangs around the boy's neck.

Jürgen grabbed for the knife in his belt and found it was missing.

The Kiss began to overwhelm him. It began with searing pain and then became a smooth coolness that covered his entire body, numbing him to the stinging wind, the ache of the saddle beneath him, the pain of the fangs in his neck.

He felt himself dying. He tried to raise his arm and found he could not.

The man bit open his own wrist and lowered it to Jürgen's mouth. *Drink*, he said.

Jürgen's lips opened. The blood would save him. The blood would save him from the cold, from the pain, the blood would bring back his brother.

Jürgen's eyes met the man's. The man's eyes were blue.

The man was a fiend. His eyes were blue, like Jürgen's. Jürgen was staring into his own eyes. Whose eyes was he using?

Jürgen screamed in rage and leapt for the man's throat. No longer was he wearing Geidas's frail, mortal body but his own, fully armored form. He knocked the horseman to the ground, then lashed out in rage. His fist connected with the horse's neck and the animal fell dead.

"What kind of coward sires a helpless boy?" Jürgen stared down at the man, whose form seemed to be shrinking. "What kind of Cainite places such a weakling in charge of any domain?" The man's armor disappeared, and Geidas's robes faded into view. The man's eyes changed from blue ice to dead leaves. Jürgen bit his wrist and grabbed Geidas by the back of the neck. "Drink."

The snow vanished, and brown leaves began to swirl around them. A savage howl echoed from the woods, and Jürgen glanced upwards. Geidas vanished from under him.

Jürgen looked around carefully. He was still himself; he had evidently not fallen into another of Geidas's memories. The forest around him was familiar; the trees were not the same blackened, foreboding things of the eastern forests, but the majestic spires of his homeland. Indeed, in the distance he could see the city of Magdeburg. He began to walk towards it, looking forward to Akuji's stories and Wiftet's jests, not to mention—

A scent of roses came up around him, and he stopped. Without thinking, he grabbed for the cross around his neck and the moon was covered in shadow. The night became black as pitch and the howl he had heard before sounded again, this time joined by several others. *Lupines*, thought Jürgen, and his Beast spoke up in fear, telling him to run for the city, run until his knights could hear him, he was no match for the wolf-men.

Jürgen took two steps, and then stopped. He heard panting in the brush, and the trees rustled as though something very large walked between them. He fought the urge to run, for he knew that wolves would chase anyone that fled from them. Instead, he approached.

Jürgen had never seen a Lupine before, only heard tales of their ferocity. And yet, he *knew* that the creature he saw as he stepped from the path into the forest was a werewolf. It was an immense, black-furred thing, standing on two legs and towering over Jürgen. It had hands like a man's but they ended in dagger-like claws, so unlike a wolf's that any doubt about these creatures' demonic origins faded from his mind.

And yet... Jürgen saw a nobility in the beast. It was obviously powerful, and its eyes showed intelligence; this creature had once been a man. It had brown, thoughtful eyes.

Eyes the color of dead leaves.

Jürgen took a step back. The werewolf followed him. Jürgen desperately looked to the trees, and found they had turned from the German forests to the cursed place that he had come to conquer. The werewolf raised a claw and snarled; Jürgen stood fast. The creature's vicious paw flashed downwards with a speed that any Cainite would envy. Jürgen tried to dodge, but the claw caught him across the midsection and sent him sprawling. He crashed against a tree and saw more wolves emerging from the woods, all with the same eyes, all bearing down on him.

The lead wolf, now less like a man and more like a beast, raced at him on all fours and sprang, and Jürgen reached up and caught it by the throat. He slammed it into the ground, tearing off a strip of its flesh, and was rewarded by a jet of blood against his chest. *Such strength in that blood,* he thought. *If I am to best them all, I'll need to drink.*

His hand found the cross again, and he forced his gaze up into the wolf's eyes. "Coward," he said. "The beasts of the forests are for the low-blooded to control, and yet you attack me in their form like a base Gangrel. Very well." If this was Geidas's memory, Jürgen reasoned, it must be a frightening one. Jürgen stood, and the other wolves circled him, snarling. "If they are wolves and men both, then let their man-halves serve me as their wolf-halves serve you. Which do you think is stronger?" With that, Jürgen became the leader, the warlord, the Sword-Bearer, and called out to his new followers.

And the wolves answered.

They leapt upon the Geidas-wolf, tearing at him, pulling the fur from his body and then the flesh. Jürgen stood above him and cut his wrist, and shouted to the hapless abomination beneath him. "Submit, and I shall call them off. Drink."

The Geidas-wolf fought its way to its feet and reached for Jürgen's wrist, desperately, as the wolves worried at his legs and ribs. His face ran like water and became Geidas's. His lips trembled as he reached for the drops of blood on Jürgen's hand....

And then the forest erupted in fire.

Chapter Twenty

Geidas's body burned away in seconds, but Jürgen found himself standing on a island in the midst of a sea of red fire. The ground cracked and shook, and geysers of hot magma erupted from below. *Is this a memory?* Jürgen thought in horror. *It can't possibly be. When would any Cainite have seen this and not gone mad or been destroyed?*

Jürgen's armor began to melt. He fell to his knees in pain, and saw the rider coming towards him again, the same figure, the same eyes, riding to him across the lake of fire. *He's coming to make me drink, and how shall I resist this time?* Jürgen's Beast concurred, begging him to drink, to submit, anything was preferable to death in the fires, Gotzon would understand, anything was better than this Hell....

Gotzon has seen Hell, thought Jürgen. He snapped his head up and saw the man before him, slitting his wrist, ready to offer it to Jürgen and demand that he drink. Jürgen grabbed his cross and remembered.

The scene faded. The heat dissipated, replace by the cool of Jürgen's mortal home in spring. Two men sat before him. Gotzon, a quiet figure in black, his eyes black as the Elbe at night, regarded him with a look that bordered on hopeful. Hardestadt, dressed in finery as befit a warrior-prince, stared at him with eyes that...

Those were not Hardestadt's eyes. His sire had blue eyes. This man's eyes were dead leaves.

Jürgen sat before the men, unsuspecting, a warrior and soldier entertaining distinguished guests.

"We have not told you our true names or purposes, Lord Jürgen," said Gotzon. "We are here for your life." He said it so casually that Jürgen thought he was joking, and chuckled.

Hardestadt spoke, and his tone made it quite clear that this was a serious discussion. "Lord Jürgen, we are offering you a choice." He bared his fangs, and Jürgen gasped. "We are not living men, and have not been such in many centuries. At times, beings like ourselves—"

"The damned," murmured Gotzon.

"—wish for childer, and seek out those worthy."

Jürgen knew that he should feel afraid. Instead, he puffed up with pride.

"We are here to offer you eternity to do with as you wish, within certain restrictions. But your choice is this: the cross or the crown?"

With that, the two Cainites fell silent, and Jürgen stared at them. He remembered that there was once more to this conversation, but it was buried so deeply in his mind that not even Geidas's probing could recall it.

Jürgen remembered his words well enough, though.

"God knows and directs all things, or so I am told. If it is God's will that I become what you are, then I shall. If God is offering me this choice through you, then I shall make it, and do God's bidding."

Gotzon smiled, just as Jürgen remembered.

"But I choose the crown. I choose to do God's work as a soldier, a leader and a king, not as a priest. I cannot convey God's word, I can only enforce it, and I cannot labor under the strictures that God has seen fit to set for His Church."

Hardestadt stood, just as Jürgen remembered, and shot his companion a glance. The shadows in the room fled as Gotzon stood, and Jürgen saw the Lasombra's fist clench. The shadows gathered around his feet, fawning like whipped dogs, and Gotzon turned away from his would-be childe.

Hardestadt's fangs met Jürgen's neck. Jürgen died, his body cold, and Hardestadt pressed his bleeding wrist to Jürgen's mouth. His eyes—still dead leaves—looked down on Lord Jürgen as he drank.

Gotzon grabbed Hardestadt and threw him through the wall. Jürgen smiled, and stood.

Gotzon's eyes changed from deep black to dead leaves. The shadows fell away and the Lasombra howled in rage.

"You are an idiot, Geidas," asserted Jürgen. "You are transparent. You are a child. Now drink." Jürgen reached to cut his own wrist, but Geidas fled through the ruined wall.

Jürgen followed. He knew where Gotzon had gone that night, and the scene hadn't faded. He followed Gotzon's fleeing form into darkness, followed it to the tiny shrine on the hill. He found Geidas-Gotzon kneeling before it, still lost in Jürgen's memories.

He knelt beside Gotzon. The Lasombra's impassive face was taking on more of Geidas's young features every second. The black clothing was fading away to Geidas's robes, and yet the Tzimisce could only kneel and recite the Lord's Prayer. "Think of it as a first communion, Geidas," said Jürgen. He cut his wrist and lifted it to Geidas's lips.

This time, it was the sky that answered.

A lightning bolt lanced down and shattered the cross that they knelt before. The rain began a split second later, so hard that it completely obscured Jürgen's view of Geidas. Jürgen looked down and found himself on a riverbank. Before him, the dark rider, Geidas's sire, stood on top of the water. The waves rose up around him, but parted before touching him. Jürgen noted with fascination that even the raindrops moved to avoid him.

"You cannot win this fight, Jürgen."

"No?"

"I will not let you."

"Then you have broken the rules of the duel." Jürgen took a step towards him, but the rain only drove harder.

The man nodded. "I have, but my childe has not. He loses no honor. And besides, you won't remember this after you drink of his blood."

"I have no intention of losing," said Jürgen. "You might act through your childe, but even you cannot break me. I did not come here to return a flesh-crafter's lapdog."

"You came here to steal, Sword-Bearer. You came to here to behold the dust of Alexander of Paris on the forest leaves, to sigh in relief that he won't be returning. Why didn't you kill him yourself? Why did you send him to his death? Surely your Tremere lickspittles knew about their stupid Telyav cousins."

Jürgen smiled. "But it wasn't the Telyavs that killed Alexander. I learned as much from Jervais. So what did kill him? I don't trust you to tell me; you have no respect for honor."

The man nodded. "You can't shame me that way, Sword-Bearer. My ethics lie elsewhere than shame."

Jürgen smiled, and shifted his eyes for a split second.

He saw the room, saw the cups, saw Jovirdas, saw that Geidas's hands were now at his sides. He saw that the cup of his blood was perhaps a half-inch closer to Geidas. He saw Geidas's eyes, and bore down again. "Drink," he said, and he was once again in his opponent's mind.

But now, Geidas's eyes were not his own. Whoever his sire was, the fiend was taking greater control of the childe. If Jürgen was to win the duel, he would have to best them both—and although Geidas might actually be further from Caine than Jürgen, his sire's assistance more than made up the difference. His Beast, roused into wakefulness by this violation of honor, cried out for blood and domination. Jürgen inwardly promised that it would have its chance.

Chapter Twenty-One

Jürgen kept his mind moving from one topic to the next, and the scene around him flowed like quicksilver, sluicing across his field of vision and reforming every few seconds. While the effort was exhausting, it was the only way to keep his opponent—opponents, actually—off balance long enough to strike. The cascade of images flowed and ebbed before him, showing him fragments of whatever memories came to mind...

...learning that Norbert von Xanten, the former Archbishop of Magdeburg, had joined the ranks of the undead under Clan Lasombra and wished to take the city from Jürgen...

...seeing Rosamund for the first time, presiding over his court at Magdeburg, the beautiful woman bearing a gift for him, how could he have stupid enough to think that the gift was a forgery, to buy into Tremere trickery?...

...the day so many decades ago when he won his first battle, took his first woman, killed his first man, the scent of blood on his fists and his blade, the screams of the dying, the grim faces of those who walked the battlefield to administer last rites and mercy killings...

...the night that he killed his first undead opponent, not in battle but in self-defense, the Cainite's rage loosed on Jürgen for some reason he did not know, nor would ever know, now that the vampire was long dust...

...the hatred he bore for Vladimir Rustovitch, the sight of the *voivode* of *voivode*'s forces emerging from the trees, his reliance on sorcery instead of tactics, and the compromise with Vykos that had...

...stop.

Something had changed; the memories he saw had changed perspective somewhat. He had not been happy with the compromise of seventeen years ago, which had left him back in Magdeburg with no new territory and Vykos in his "Obertus State" between the Fiefs of the Black Cross and the *Voivodate*. The memories that he had seen, however, were beyond displeasure. They were fury, they were death and fire.

He recalled that meeting again, where the terms of the compromise had been sealed. This time he allowed the memory to form, bracing himself for the inevitable mental onslaught as Geidas and his sire tried to force him to drink. He saw the tent again, saw the maps on the table and the dim candlelight, saw the assembled Cainites, Vykos included.

Somewhere, outside the tent, he felt the rage of the forests. It certainly wasn't Geidas; the rage was older and far too powerful for that. Jürgen considered for a moment that it might be Rustovitch, that this might be his childe ruling over a petty domain, but the rage didn't feel like that of his old enemy. Rustovitch, while he probably had no love for Vykos, hated Jürgen even more. The fury that Jürgen felt was directed almost entirely at the Byzantine Tzimisce.

Jürgen stood in the tent, immersed in memory once again, but this time more aware of his true position. He left the assembled vampires huddled around the map, and walked out into the campground.

The forests and the camp were as he'd remembered, but there was something different, a tension in the air that he hadn't felt. Had this Tzimisce been here even then, watching? But if he had, why hadn't he joined the battle on Rustovitch's side?

The answer presented itself as soon as the thought was complete—he was Rustovitch's enemy as well, or perhaps his rival, just as Julia Antasia was to Hardestadt. No sooner had this realization hit him than the scene faded and Jürgen was left in nothingness.

In other circumstances, Jürgen might have been worried, even frightened. Now he smiled. "No more secrets left, then?" he said to the darkness. "No more memories to show me? No matter." Jürgen summoned up his strength, and dove downwards into the murk of the Tzimisce's mind. He passed by memories that he knew belonged to Geidas, memories of the *vozhd*, memories of Jovirdas coming to watch over him, visions of scouts telling Geidas that Jürgen was approaching. He ignored them. He dove deeper, past Geidas's pathetic mortal life, past his Embrace again, past the moment where his sire had first revealed his name….

…Visya.

Jürgen had heard the name before, but wasn't sure exactly why. He continued his dive, focusing his will on Visya, ignoring Geidas. He came to a barrier, a web woven of memories and pure willpower, and tore through it. All traces of Geidas vanished. He was inside Visya's head, now.

All Hell loosed its fury against him.

The driving rain, the earthquake, the winds and the lake of fire from before were nothing compared to the rage of the Earth that now bombarded Jürgen. He felt his armor, then the skin flayed away by the driving rain, and his exposed sinew seared by white-hot sand. His bones snapped like twigs under a horse's foot as the mountains came down to meet him. And yet he pressed onward, through the pain, through the winds, looking for the source of this power, the first moment that Visya had beheld it.

The ground rose and coalesced into a horde of riders, wearing styles of weapons and clothing that Jürgen had never seen. He knew, however, the look in their eyes—the alien, naked hunger of underfed ghouls. This, then, was the land of the Tzimisce before the Ventrue had arrived to civilize it. How ancient, then, was this Visya? Jürgen faltered as the riders bore down on him, and then leapt, seizing two by the throats but dropping them just as quickly. These phantom memories meant nothing. He would know Visya or die trying; there was no other acceptable conclusion.

None, Lord Jürgen?

The fury of the storm, the hoof beats of the riders' steeds, all sound died away. Jürgen was once again floating in nameless darkness.

"Too afraid to show me even a middling memory, Visya? Who are you?"

You are in my domain now, warlord. Beware. The darkness stabbed Jürgen like a heated knife. Jürgen fought off the pain; it was merely a memory.

"I will know you, Visya. I know enough already, but I will know you for what you are before this ends."

And if sunrise comes first and the duel remains unresolved?

Jürgen dove again, forcing his will towards the voice, fighting through a torrent of power. He knew that if the sun rose, the contact between himself and Geidas would break and he would be forced back into his own body and mind... or would he be trapped here, imprisoned in the mind of a fiend for all eternity? The thought was almost enough to make him retreat, to return to Geidas's mind and finish the duel, but he had come too far already. He would know this Cainite's identity.

"You're no Scion, Visya. Did any sort of true ethics even reach these forsaken lands? I know that Rustovitch at least pretends to the mantle of a king."

He felt no answer, but the darkness thickened. Jürgen extended his mind like a dagger, probing, stabbing, digging into the Tzimisce's will.

"Certainly not a godly man, either. You've not time for shame, you say? Are you some slavering beast who makes a show of being a man, but then ruts with the animals at night?"

No response. Jürgen stabbed deeper.

"What will you say when I am lord of these lands, Visya? Will you rail against me, shaking your fist at my keep? Will you command the flies to sting my horses or the dogs to nip at my heels? You fight like one of the low-bloods, Visya. You fight like a skulking leper."

This garnered a response, but not the one Jürgen expected. Instead of fury or offense, Jürgen felt a glimmer of satisfaction. He pressed on.

"And what when Rustovitch's skull is crumbling in my hands, Visya? Will you have lost a favored ally? Will you long for his attentions?"

Your attempts to bait me are pathetic, Sword-Bearer. You already know my feelings towards Rustovitch.

"So why fight me, then? You obviously don't reserve the

same hate for me that Rustovitch does. What do you gain from this? Whom do you serve?"

I serve no one. A slight rise in aggravation. Jürgen had apparently found the right nerve to touch.

"Rustovitch? Are you even now fighting against an oath to him?"

Oaths mean nothing to me. I serve no one.

"Why all this effort, then? Why the elaborate ruse to make your childe seem so much more powerful than he is? Whom do you serve?"

You know nothing of my childe. The voice shook Jürgen with fury, and Jürgen had to steady himself against it. *I serve no one!*

"Some ancient fiend, lurking on a mountaintop, too afraid of Lupines and Tremere to descend? Who is your master, Visya?"

I serve... no one. The voice was weakening. Jürgen could see shapes in the darkness, beginning to form. A Cainite, not Visya, but a vampire of some power. A Scion, the prince of a city... but which one?

"Your childer do tend to claim domain, don't they, Visya? Do you place them there? Arrange for them to be tutored on ways of kings? I can see why; it wouldn't do for Cainites like yourself, feral bastards with no sense of how civil folk interact, to rule cities."

I serve no one! Not another Cainite and not the Beast! The explosion of fury knocked Jürgen back and nearly dissipated the shapes. He surged forward again and tried to recognize the man and his surroundings, but could not.

"No?" Jürgen smiled in realization. "To what purpose your actions, then? Placing Scion children in outposts, to act as honey-traps for travelers, for diplomats, for Westerners."

A whirlwind of rage and humiliation swept Jürgen back. He fought against it, but Visya was obviously trying to shut his connection with Geidas, forcing Jürgen back into the younger Tzimisce's mind. Jürgen pressed his advantage.

"You tolerate Westerners, don't you? That's why Rustovitch hates you so. That's why you don't have any place to go, because you can't claim domain of your own. You hide behind your childer. Is Geidas the weakest, I wonder, or the strongest? Do

your childer betray you to the *Voivodate*?" Jürgen grasped at
any insult he could, any accusation that would drive Visya
into revealing something. "What about Vykos? Was he one of
yours?"

For a moment, the rage died down, and Jürgen found himself floating, the darkness around him eerily calm and empty.
Then he felt a rumble, much like the thrum of the ground when
men on horseback were riding to battle. The rumble built, and
Jürgen waited with sick fascination as the darkness around him
exploded into memory, color and pain. He saw the man again,
and knew now that the Tzimisce Scion he'd seen *was* Visya's
childe, Radu, the Prince of Bistritz. But there was another
Tzimisce standing with him, lording over him, an invader, an
interloper…

Rustovitch.

The rage overwhelmed him, shoved him back. He tried to
cry out, to coax more information out of the deluge, but all he
received in return was hunger, pain and fear. His own Beast
woke, and howled in unison with the winds and screams
around him, and Jürgen realized with a mixture of fear and
pride that he must have driven Visya to frenzy. Rather than
struggling against it, he submitted, letting Visya's Beast sweep
him out of the Tzimisce's mind. He came to rest slumped in a
chair, a table before him, one cup on the table and the other in
his hand.

Geidas was smiling triumphantly at him.

Chapter Twenty-Two

Jürgen slowly stood and looked around. Geidas, Jovirdas, and Rosamund were all present. Jürgen held the cup in his hand and tasted blood in his mouth; it had the same burning sensation as the blood of the Tzimisce woman he had killed. He looked at Rosamund's eyes; they were the same lovely hazel-green as he remembered. He turned to Jovirdas, but the *tysiatskii* stood impassive, blue eyes steady. Geidas's eyes were the same: dead leaves.

Have I lost, then? Jürgen looked down at the cup. It still contained some lingering vitae. He looked up at Geidas and felt the urge to drink the rest, to raise the cup and complete Geidas's victory.

He heard nothing from outside. The entire world stood still. He searched with his senses, desperate for any sign that this was a trick, a constructed memory, another ploy. He found nothing.

He raised the cup, and then locked eyes with Geidas again and reached out, trying to read his thoughts, see his halo. He expected to feel the usual sickening sensation of violating another Cainite's mind. He expected to see colors of victory, triumph in his halo. He expected to see plans for Gotzon's death.

Instead, he saw only one word: "Drink."

Jürgen dropped the cup and smiled. He walked towards Geidas, grabbed the cup of his own blood from the table, and seized Geidas by the jaw. "Drink," he growled, forcing the Tzimisce's mouth open. Geidas struggled, but had lost the support of his sire. Jovirdas, Rosamund, and the room faded away. Other scenes played themselves out around the two Cainites, much as they had in Visya's mind, but Jürgen squeezed down on Geidas's face, snapping his teeth and piercing his cheeks. "Drink, now."

He tipped the cup, and poured his vitae towards Geidas's mouth. The *kunigaikstis* strained his lips, trying to force them shut, and then closed his eyes, trying to focus his way out of the memory. The colors around them began to solidify, changing into a clear night on a mountainside, Geidas together with…

"Enough," said Jürgen calmly. He released both the cup and the prince, but neither moved. Geidas stood, locked in the same position Jürgen had held him in, and the cup stayed in midair, a drop of blood suspended on its lip.

Jürgen was numb. He no longer felt the constant intrusion in his own mind, the emotions of the scene around him, the burning sensation on his tongue from Geidas's trick—nothing. He felt cold, his mind slipping through this dream-world like an icicle through a child's fist. He waved a hand, and the scene vanished. Geidas stood before him, naked and alone, hair hanging limply at his shoulders, hands covering his manhood like a boy caught pleasuring himself.

Jürgen raised his hand, and Geidas fell to his knees. The Tzimisce tried to resist, but Jürgen didn't feel it. The prince had no strength, and could only watch as Jürgen cut open his wrist, and beckoned. Geidas surged forward, and his lips clamped down on the wound.

The scene before him grew patchy and indistinct, and then his vision cleared. He smelled the ashes in the fireplace, the horses from outside, the oil on Jovirdas's leather, and his own blood on Geidas's lips.

Geidas set the cup down, and looked up at Jürgen with the resentful respect a boy gives his father. He nodded, and made a gesture of acquiescence.

Jürgen didn't bother to acknowledge it. He merely glanced to Jovirdas. "Kindly go and release Gotzon immediately."

Chapter Twenty-Three

Jürgen sat in his wagon with Gotzon. Gotzon looked disheveled—his shirt still bore a large hole from the stake, and the pale white flesh showed through like a moon in a starless sky. His sword hadn't been returned yet; one of Geidas's servants had been dispatched to retrieve it. He stared at Jürgen, impassive as always, but Jürgen saw displeasure in his face.

"You would rather have burned in the sun, then?" Jürgen was still recovering from his victory, still shaken from what he had learned. "You would have burned, and I would still be ignorant of Geidas's sire and his rather strange position."

Gotzon shook his head slowly. "The risk was too great, especially on my account. You have other methods of extracting information from such heathens."

"In another Cainite's domain, I cannot take such liberties without risk to my soul, as you well know."

"That is your choice."

"I do not regret it, Gotzon." Jürgen stared his confessor in the eye, but the Lasombra's eyes did not change. "I made my decisions for reasons you well know, and I cannot afford, as a leader and a soldier, to second-guess every decision I make based on whether God would approve. I can only take my chances, act in good faith and with clear purpose, and confess my sins."

Gotzon did not smile, but his face relented somewhat. "Amen." He relaxed somewhat. "And now?"

"And now," said Jürgen, "I must prepare to move. The prince is a weakling, but has now taken blood from me. I might be able to exact an oath from him to leave us in peace while we are in his lands, but even under a more complete blood oath, I can't imagine a Tzimisce agreeing to such a thing. Besides, I'm sure Visya has Geidas under a blood oath."

Gotzon nodded slowly. Jürgen continued.

"What I think is most significant is that Visya is an enemy of Rustovitch, and a sometime ally of the Arpad Ventrue. I think that he wouldn't be particularly interested in an alliance with me personally, but he might be inclined to non-aggression, were there something I could offer him."

Gotzon leaned forward and beckoned to Jürgen. "Who killed Alexander?"

Jürgen frowned. "An animal called Qarakh. Why?"

"Animals can be trained."

Jürgen's eyes widened slightly. "Surely you aren't suggesting I try to *use* the being that consumed the soul of Alexander of Paris?"

Gotzon's black eyes shimmered like puddles in the rain. "I am suggesting nothing, Jürgen. You long ago proved that neither I nor your sire have any need to give you advice." Jürgen gave him a sidelong glance, but Gotzon gave no indication of sarcasm. "I am merely saying that for all their posturing, those who obey their Beasts are not truly animals. God gave higher reason to men and therefore Cainites, and so while a beast cannot parley, a Cainite can, no matter what road he walks."

Jürgen considered this. "According to Jervais, this 'Qarakh' has followers, evidently other Gangrel of these forests. He has no love for the Teutonic Knights or anyone else who marches in under the cross." He pursed his lips. "He reminds me, actually, of a Gangrel woman that burst in on my court some years ago. Morrow, I believe she called herself." He stood, remembered the wagon was too small to pace in, and sat down again. "Those animals might have joined with the Tzimisce out of spite, but I don't think that they would have delivered messages and intelligence about our approach to Geidas. I think it more likely that they'd simply have attacked us. So some other faction was carrying information to Geidas, someone who knows the area and can either avoid von Salza's men or not trouble them."

"What sort of people wouldn't trouble them?"

"Von Salza's men are here to convert the pagan inhabitants

of the forests." Gotzon didn't respond to this, but

Jürgen knew his mind on the subject; von Salza's methods of conversion suited the Lasombra well. "Someone already Christian, then, monks..." he trailed off. "Of course."

He opened a chest and dragged out a map he hadn't looked at in nearly a decade. It was the map that had been on his table when he, Vykos and Rustovitch had drawn out the Obertus State. The Obertus had monasteries in this area, and the inhabitants could easily meet von Salza's men and even give them shelter, advice, or friendly words. He then found the map that Jervais had shown him in Magdeburg before he'd left. The Obertus held monasteries near towns that Jervais had mentioned—Auce, far to the north; Taurag, perhaps twenty-five miles northwest... and one not more than twenty miles away, on a western off-shoot of the Nemen, not far from a village called Ezerelis.

Jürgen sat down to think. "Vykos and his Obertus are vassals of Rustovitch, meaning any information that those monks acquire is probably known to Rustovitch as well."

Gotzon shook his head. "Vykos is a base and vile sinner. Whether he swore an oath or not—"

"Means nothing to him, true. So he might well be hoarding information for himself. I'm not even certain he is in this region anymore, actually. Meaning, if the monks are collecting information on anyone's behalf, it might well be Rustovitch's."

"Or someone close to him, issuing orders in his name."

Jürgen smiled. "Brazen, that. I'd deal none too kindly with any vassal who treated me that way; I can only imagine what Rustovitch would do. But if you're right, and if what I saw in Visya's mind is accurate, Rustovitch is in Bistritz." He absently wished that he had taken Akuji along with him; given a few nights, she could probably determine the truth of the matter. "In that case, the Cainite closest to him of any real power is Radu, Visya's other childe. If Radu is using even a few of the monks on behalf of his sire..." Jürgen stopped and rubbed his temples. "And that doesn't address the possibility that Visya might be acting under orders. He probably is, as vehemently as he denied it."

"So what will you do?"

Jürgen studied the map again, and then nodded. "The Tzimisce obviously have capabilities that I was not aware of, both in terms of sorcery and in terms of manpower. I shall need to understand both further before I can make any real progress here."

"Both are connected, in this case." Gotzon's voice was more hushed even than usual. Jürgen turned to face him.

"I'm sorry?"

"The Obertus are intimately connected with the Tzimisce, Jürgen. Vykos is younger under the Blood than you, or so you have said. But the Obertus predate him by many years, and have had ample time to spread west and north from the forests of their Tzimisce masters."

"How do you know this?" To Jürgen's knowledge, Gotzon had never been here, but after what he had seen in his confessor's mind, he was prepared to admit that he knew far less about the Lasombra than he had previously believed.

"I have been doing the Lord's work for quite some time." Gotzon shut his eyes, something that Jürgen had never seen him do. The shadows in the room crowded close to see. "Before that, however, I was involved in blasphemies of which I dare not speak."

"You have said as much before."

"Yes, but I have seen blasphemies here, in these lands, that rival even the perversities that I wrought. I have seen them, though I never set foot in these lands until recently."

Jürgen sat down and brushed the maps aside. "Gotzon, tell me what you have seen."

Gotzon's eyes snapped open and the shadows recoiled like cats from a cracking fire. "Do you wish to hear? Having gazed at the darkness, do you wish to return?"

Jürgen's brow furrowed in confusion. "No, Gotzon. I only wish to know the nature of the foes I face."

Gotzon sat forward and stared directly into Jürgen's eyes. Jürgen looked back, and within seconds was lost in the same sea of blackness he had faced before, when he'd read his confessor's mind. Those eyes contained the ocean, and as Jürgen gazed, he remembered what Rosamund had said—*the darkness isn't empty.*

"Jürgen," Gotzon said. "To show you what I have seen, I would have to break my vow. At my command, the shadows would open to show you any place or person I have ever met, and allow you to step through those shadows to face them. All of this and much more I could command of the Abyss."

Jürgen shook his head before Gotzon finished speaking. "Not only, my friend, could I never request such an act of you, I have no desire to win my battles based on a broken oath."

The Lasombra's face softened. "Very well, then."

"God created the Heavens and the Earth," Gotzon said, staring past Jürgen into nothing, "but more, He created the order that governs both. Sun rises, sun sets, living things grow and die. Mortals don't understand it until they are no longer mortal, and even we, separated from life and death, can grasp little of it." He turned his eyes on Jürgen, and Jürgen saw the rigid control in his face slip a bit.

The papers on the floor rustled, but there was no breeze to rustle them. Only the shadows had moved.

Gotzon steeled himself and continued. "We among the undead, outside of God's grace but not his plan, we experiment with things best left undisturbed. I do not know how the first of my clan learned to command the darkness, though I imagine Satan offered him the power and he accepted. Possibly the same is true for the Tzimisce and their control over flesh. Your clan, Jürgen, has remained perhaps the most noble of all of the high-blooded, and that is one reason I respected your decision to choose Hardestadt over me." Gotzon cast his gaze downwards and the candlelight on the table brightened a bit. "You recognized Hell when you saw it."

Jürgen drummed his fingers on the table. "I chose my fate for the reasons I gave then, Gotzon," he said carefully, "but not for those reasons alone. I saw your eyes and what your presence did to the light. I admit it frightened me." Jürgen's Beast laughed, and Jürgen let it, in shame.

Gotzon seemed to see his thought. "Jürgen, there is no honor lost in fear. God gave man fear for good reasons—we are to fear God as a boy fears his father, fear Satan for the monster he is, fear the beasts of the forest for their claws and fangs, and so on.

Your feeling fear when looking upon me reflects your wisdom, and, perhaps, your piety."

Jürgen smiled. "Perhaps so," he said. "You were saying?"

"The flesh-shaping powers that Satan offered the Tzimisce were not the greatest of his blasphemies. He gave them power over the land and the elements, as well."

Jürgen thought back to the explosions of fury he'd faced in the duel. "But why have I never heard of this?"

"For the same reason that many Cainites know that the Lasombra command shadows, but do not know the power taught to the true masters of the arts." Gotzon was again looking down, and again his face had softened. The shadows in the room were creeping closer. "There are few of them, as there are few of the Tzimisce sorcerers. When I was one of those masters, hundreds of years before your birth, let alone your Embrace, I saw the Tzimisce *koldun* and what they wrought upon the land." The shadows widened. The candle flame guttered, but Gotzon seemed not to notice. "I watched through shadows from hundreds of miles away as the Tzimisce called up the blood of the earth, parted the waves, and called down storms." His voice dropped to a whisper, and Jürgen heard it echo in the chasm that the small room had become. "I envied them. I coveted their power."

"Gotzon?" Jürgen glanced around and saw that the shadows had begun to take shape. Some of them looked human; most had too many legs. "What is happening?"

Gotzon looked up. "You wanted to know. I cannot use my hell-born knowledge without violating an oath before God, but I can show you by inaction. This is what I must repel, every moment of every night." The shadows moved forward, lock-step, and Jürgen felt ice growing around his feet. "You talk of the Beast, Jürgen? Of losing control? Of fear? These creatures use my mind as their conduit to God's Earth."

Jürgen stood, but a pair of hands pushed him back into his chair. "Gotzon, please." His voice did not quake, but he knew Gotzon could sense the fear.

Gotzon raised a hand, and the creatures vanished. The room brightened again. Jürgen stood and paced, trying fervently to lose the chill on his neck and feet where the creatures had touched him.

"So, you see, Jürgen, what Hell can grant?"

"I saw it before, in Visya's mind," he said quietly. The room was cold, and he considered calling forth the blood to make his skin warm, just to drive away the unclean feeling. "I saw what these *koldun* can do."

Gotzon nodded. "When I saw it first, I envied it. After God saved me, after I forsook the shadows and took up the sword of the Lord, I knew one night I would have to venture to these lands in person to face these *koldun*, these blasphemers who seek to warp God's order. When I saw you were traveling here, I knew it to be a sign."

"But what of the Obertus?"

"The Tzimisce Embrace from certain families, including what became the Obertus order. The Obertus are lore-keepers. If their order dies, much of the history of the clan dies with them." Gotzon stooped and picked up the maps from the floor. "Your theory of the order doing Rustovitch's work is sound, but the order must not be allowed to infest von Salza's men. Their 'scholarship,' coupled with his numbers…"

"Yes, I see." Jürgen studied the map again. "I shall need to send scouts, I think. Knight and Cainite both. Some can travel ahead to Taurag, but I won't send anyone as far as Auce; it might be as much as a hundred miles. But Taurag and Ezerelis both contain Obertus monasteries, and I need to know what kind of resistance we face. I shall discover what the monks there are doing and under whose direction, and I shall use them to lure Qarakh out of hiding." He folded the map again and tucked it away. "But I do not intend to go forward without securing what is behind me. Which leaves the somewhat thorny problem of what to do about Geidas."

Gotzon stood. "Geidas is wretch and a sinner."

Jürgen looked sharply at his confessor. "Did you come here to kill him, Gotzon? Is he one of the *koldun*?"

Gotzon simply shook his head.

Jürgen reflected that Gotzon had said more this evening than he had heard the Lasombra say in their entire acquaintance.

"I've never heard you call someone a sinner that you didn't want dead."

The Lasombra didn't reply, but turned for the door.

"What are your intentions?"

Gotzon stopped. "I don't intend to sleep here, Jürgen. I intend to find an alternate shelter for the day. We can talk again tomorrow night, if I decide to stay here any longer." He opened the door.

"Do you intend to—"

"No," said Gotzon flatly. "His unlife won't end for at least one more day." With that, he shut the door and walked away. Jürgen heard his footsteps stop, and then continue, and he guessed that the servant had returned Gotzon's sword.

If Gotzon kills Geidas, thought Jürgen, *how would Jovirdas respond?* The *tysiatskii* seemed competent and even honest, but Jürgen hadn't been able to guess at his ethos yet. If he followed the same codes as Jürgen, he might be able to secure an oath. But where did his loyalties lie? Jürgen didn't for one moment believe that he was actually Geidas's childe, but the duel hadn't told him that Jovirdas was in league with Visya, either. Perhaps Jovirdas was of a different line altogether, maybe a vassal of Rustovitch or some other Tzimisce monarch, sent to watch over Geidas in the name of the *Voivodate*. Or perhaps Jürgen was wrong; perhaps Jovirdas really *was* Geidas's childe and had simply been Embraced recently, too recently for Visya to have had anything to do with it. The fact that Jürgen hadn't seen Jovirdas at all in Geidas's memories was strange, but then, he hadn't called up any memories of his own childer, either.

There were too many possibilities, too many permutations, to make any informed decision. Sending scouts to the monasteries was Jürgen's only firm plan at the moment, so he concentrated on that. Wishing he had Christof and Heinrich with him, he pulled the map once again from the chest and began to pore over it. He knew he had little time before sunrise, and knew also that Rosamund might well visit him before sunrise, but he wanted to have some preliminary plan before sleeping.

Chapter Twenty-Four

Plans did not come, and Jürgen was forced to wait for nearly three weeks before taking more action. He watched Geidas carefully for signs of treachery or action, but the boy-prince seemed to slip into a kind of depression. Gone was the bravado he had first shown Jürgen and the assurance of his own position.

On the night that a young knight, a ghoul named Dieter, came running into Kybartai shouting for Jürgen, the Sword-Bearer was in fact planning to give Geidas another drink of his blood, just to see if it would make him slightly more useful.

Jürgen heard Dieter's shouts and left the stone room where he had dueled Geidas, now serving as his planning chamber, to find him. The young knight was flushed, sweating, and on the verge of collapse.

From the look in his eyes, he was also nearly dead from fright alone.

"My lord... oh, God. Help me. I saw him. I saw..." Dieter fell into the snow, writhing as though trying to put out a fire.

Jürgen picked him up and carried him into his chambers, dispatching a servant to bring Václav and Rosamund at once. He set Dieter down on the floor and stood up, unsure of what to do. The boy wasn't injured, at least not visibly, but the madness in his eyes made Jürgen afraid to read his mind. He always felt dirty after looking into a mortal's thoughts; God alone knew what filth this mind was carrying.

Václav and Rosamund arrived together, and both looked down at the knight in shock. Rosamund knelt down next to him and took his hand, trying to soothe him. Václav stood close to Jürgen. "Where did you send this knight?" he asked.

"Northeast of here," answered Jürgen. "To a town called Ezerelis to look into a monastery there."

"Alone?"

Jürgen's eyes widened. "No," he said. "Klaus was with him."

Rosamund looked up. "Klaus? But he is—"

"Yes, I know. One of us." Jürgen crouched down beside Dieter, who was beginning to sob quietly. "Dieter, please, tell us what happened."

"I saw him," whispered Dieter. "A man in robes of blood."

Rosamund looked up at Jürgen, but Jürgen only shrugged. "Go on."

"He called to Klaus, and Klaus went to him… like a man to his lover. I tried to stop him, but he pushed me away." Dieter began to shake again. Rosamund touched his face, and Dieter's eyes flickered over her for an instant. He calmed somewhat, and then began to breathe quickly and shallowly. "Klaus went to him, and he took Klaus's head in his hands… and turned it to blood."

"My lord, what can—" Václav began. Jürgen shushed him.

"And then what? Dieter, then *what*?"

Dieter did not answer at first, but only breathed harder. After a moment of this, he began whispering a phrase, over and over, so quietly that even Jürgen had to listen carefully to hear it.

"Not a drop spilled, not a drop spilled, not a drop spilled—"

Jürgen caught the boy's eyes and commanded him to sleep. He looked confused for a moment, and then his eyes shut and his breathing slowed. Jürgen motioned out the door for one of Geidas's servants to take Dieter off to a comfortable place to sleep.

"What will you do, my lord?" Václav had posed the question, but Jürgen had already decided.

"We will visit this monastery in Ezerelis. If the being there can so easily destroy a Cainite, even a neonate like Klaus, I do not wish to leave it behind me, undefeated."

"So we attack?"

Jürgen nodded. "I have to answer for Klaus's death. Go, and begin preparation with the other knights." His childe left, and

Jürgen turned to Rosamund. "My lady, would you give me a few moments? I have things to prepare, but—"

"But you won't leave without telling me first," she said. Her voice told him not that she was afraid or angry, but that she understood. She gathered her garments around her and left the room, leaving Jürgen alone with her scent and her memory.

Rosamund. How can I bring her with me? The attack on the monastery would involve slaughtering many of those present. While they might be monks, the Obertus order was largely composed of ghouls, and he had no idea what the capabilities of Tzimisce blood-slaves were, to say nothing of the being that Dieter had seen. The attack would be dangerous, but moreover, he had no desire to show her what he could do in battle. *My father told me that battle was his mistress,* he thought. *Was this what he meant? Can I not share conquest, the first part of my joy, with the one who so inspires my soul?*

Jürgen shook off the thought and considered the monastery. He would be best served by attacking near dawn, with only an hour or so to spare. Certainly some of the monks would be accustomed to functioning at night—there might even be a Cainite overseer present—but close enough to dawn would find those who moved by night bedding down and those who moved by day still abed. It would leave him precious little time to escape if something went wrong; that simply meant that he would have to make sure nothing did.

Taking too large a force with him would be a mistake. He needed to cross the ground quickly, preferably in one night. That meant moving on horseback and not dragging wagons. So he would have to leave Rosamund, Wiftet, and anyone else not able to fight. It also meant that he would have to find some way of ensuring her safety. He couldn't leave behind any Cainite knights; he would need them for the attack. He couldn't send his knights on without him—if Christof had been with him, he would have let her take command of the assault and remained to supervise Geidas and Jovirdas.

His Beast suggested an obvious solution—kill the two Tzimisce. He considered this for a long moment, and could find nothing wrong with the idea. He had been loath to attack before because he was unsure of Geidas's relationship with the *Voivodate* and of his personal power, but now that he knew that Geidas was a weakling and Rustovitch wasn't exactly his staunch ally, he reasoned he could burn both Cainites to ash without repercussions.

But then, what of Rosamund? The thought stopped Jürgen in his tracks, and he listened almost guiltily for the sound of her footsteps. Could he truly leave Rosamund behind after murdering two Cainites? Would she approve? Did it truly matter? *Of course it matters*, he reproached himself. Displeasing her would sour his victory, and how could he concentrate on the next phase in his campaign if she were here, surrounded by the ghosts he'd created?

But what if Gotzon were to kill them both? No, he might kill Geidas, but Jovirdas (who might very well be the more dangerous one, anyway) hadn't earned the Lasombra's ire as of yet. Killing them both would be a breach of courtesy of the worst sort, and while that wouldn't have mattered to Jürgen even a week ago, tonight it was important to him... because it was important to her.

Chapter Twenty-Five

Jürgen wasn't the least bit upset when he woke the next morning and found the *kunigaikstis* dead. He was, however, rather surprised to find Jovirdas holding the sword.

The Sword-Bearer had risen immediately upon waking at sunset, donned his armor, and summoned up his knights to bring Geidas out and burn him. When he entered Geidas's "throne room," he'd found the *tysiatskii* standing over his sire's decomposing body. Jürgen noted with some satisfaction that he'd been correct in assuming that Geidas was a young Cainite— the body decayed slowly enough to give off a noticeable stench.

Jovirdas turned and faced Jürgen and his knights. "He was a weakling."

Jürgen nodded. "I know."

"I am not."

"So I see."

Jovirdas took a torch from the wall, with some effort. "I do not intend to die easily, Lord Jürgen. I also do not intend to drink of your blood."

Jürgen took a step into the room, but waved to his knights to stay close. "I hope you don't flatter yourself to think, Jovirdas, that—"

"That I could best you? I don't. But I hope you don't think that I am the only Cainite remaining in this forest not marching under your banner. What one starts, another can finish." He set his sword on a table, still in easy reach, and shifted the torch to his right hand. "I do not wish to burn tonight, but I'll sooner taste cinders than your boot."

"Admirable." Jürgen began to peer into the man's mind,

but Jovirdas leapt forward and shoved the torch at the Sword-Bearer's face. Jürgen's Beast cried out in alarm and screamed at Jürgen to run; Jürgen slapped it down, but did jump backward. Jovirdas took a step back, right hand extending the torch, left hand hovering near his sword.

"Stay out of my mind, Teuton."

The insult at being so addressed paled next to the bitterness in Jovirdas's voice. "Geidas was in the habit of—?"

"Yes!" Jovirdas's voice twisted into a snarl, the fangs extended, his grip on the torch tightening to the point that Jürgen could see the wood fracturing. "I never drank of him, for he had no need of the oath. He saw all he needed to know."

Jürgen sheathed his sword. "Go on."

Jovirdas shook his head as though trying to clear it. "He claimed me as his childe, but that was a lie."

"I guessed as much."

"He made me take this post as his *tysiatskii*, but he never made me drink of his blood. He looked into my mind and took what he needed to know, and forced me to serve him."

Jürgen nodded. Jovirdas was evidently unaware that the ability to read minds was not the same as the ability to command them. "So how, then, did you manage to summon the strength to destroy him?"

"I..." He stopped, his voice catching in his throat with a strange hiccuping sound. "I felt... everything... grow cold."

Jürgen's eyes widened, and his hand slipped to the hilt of his sword. "Go on."

"I don't know." His voice seemed to return to normal, and the *tysiatskii* lowered the sword. "I approached him with no ill intention, but then the hatred I felt for him came up around me, as though I were dropped into the river in winter." Jürgen nodded. "And I felt nothing. No pain, no hate, nothing but the need to kill him."

Jürgen dropped his eyes momentarily. "And the Beast? Did it guide you in this?"

Jovirdas looked shocked. "My Beast does *not* guide me, Jürgen. Ever."

"Never?"

Jovirdas lowered the torch, but eyed it uncomfortably. "Geidas would indulge in play with his meals. He would break his oaths and treat those beneath him like shit on his boot. I cannot do this. It sickened me to watch, and yet I could do nothing."

Jürgen smiled. "I understand how you feel."

Jovirdas's eyes narrowed. "That does not mean, Sword-Bearer, that I have any intention of bending knee before you or anyone, ever again."

Jürgen cocked an eyebrow at the Tzimisce. From his talk of oaths and treatment of lesser, Jovirdas followed Jürgen's ethos, but this was strange behavior from a Scion. Most of them were willing to swear oaths when necessary, especially if the result were advantageous. But Jovirdas seemed positively repulsed by the idea—why? It couldn't be because he fancied himself a tyrant and ruler absolute; Jürgen guessed he had never ruled his own fief. More likely, then, he equated being a vassal with being a slave, as he had been to Geidas.

Jürgen, of course, treated his vassals much better than Geidas, and Jovirdas's less-than-perfect knowledge of Cainite politics would make him an acceptable, if not ideal, minion. This fief wasn't important enough to leave one of Jürgen's knights to rule, but for an experiment, a placeholder like Jovirdas...

Of course, the problem remained: How to convince the Tzimisce that he would do well to accept?

"Jovirdas," said Jürgen carefully, "who mentored you on your road?"

Jovirdas replied only with a blank stare.

"What I mean is, after your Embrace, you must have been taught the methods of keeping the Beast under control, especially to excel at it as you apparently do. So who taught you? Obviously Geidas walked a different path, possibly taught to him by his sire, but you've never met Visya, have you?"

"No," Jovirdas shook his head slowly. "No, and I never mean to."

"Yes, I understand. So who was it that fostered you and taught you? For that matter, Jovirdas, who is your sire?"

The *tysiatskii* turned and replaced the torch on the wall, and gave the only response that could have truly shocked Jürgen. "I do not know." Seeing the Sword-Bearer's expression, he continued. "I came across this fort shortly after Geidas had taken over. I don't believe Visya ever knew of me."

Jürgen shook his head. "He must have. If he kept such loose control over Geidas—"

"And yet, I don't think he does. The communications between them were brief; I always assumed that Visya was busy and perhaps in danger."

"Possibly so. You were saying—your sire?"

"I was a guard, once. Under the command of a true *tysiatskii*, serving a true *kunigaikstis*, not these unliving mockeries." He sat in Geidas throne, trailing a foot through the dust that had once been his master. "One night my company was attacked. I know now it was by a Cainite, probably my sire. But I have no idea why he left me alive."

"He did not," Jürgen muttered. Jovirdas nodded wearily.

"I left and made my own way. When the Beast raged, I remembered my training and the discipline that my commanders had taught. I arrived here and... you know the rest."

"Amazing," said Jürgen softly. "The letters mentioned Cainites such as you, but I never believed it."

"What letters?"

Jürgen smiled. "I carry with me the Letters of Acindynus. Have you heard of him?" Jovirdas shook his head. "He is a Ventrue scholar of the *Via Regalis*. His letters are a collection of his thoughts on my road—*our* road—with annotations from other Cainites." Jürgen paused to gauge Jovirdas's interest; he looked rapt. "Some mention is made of Cainites who have found the Road of Kings—or something much like it—independent of any mentor, but I confess I always thought the road too complex, the teachings too difficult, to be mastered without a guide." A tiny worm of jealousy crept into Jürgen's heart; he crushed it with the thought that Jovirdas's precociousness could well be the means to elicit an oath from him.

Jovirdas shifted uncomfortably. Jürgen decided to spare him the embarrassment of asking to see the letters. "I'd be happy to share these documents with you, but I must, of course, ask for something in return."

The Tzimisce's face fell. "I will not submit to you—"

"You have much to learn, Jovirdas, about the difference between vassalage and submission. Becoming a vassal to a noble Cainite, a true Scion, does not involve losing yourself or submitting your free will because the oath of vassalage *must* be undertaken freely. Likewise, I must swear an oath to you as well, and both oaths are binding."

"Why?"

"Did you swear to serve Geidas?"

Jovirdas looked at the floor, fingers clenching into fists. "I promised him I would aid him in exchange for the right to feed here. He violated that agreement."

Jürgen shook his head. "Not if all he promised was that you could feed, though I must admit that subjugating the will of a vassal is disgraceful behavior for a Cainite."

Jovirdas looked at Jürgen with a sardonic smile. "You have never dominated the mind of an underling, then? Your vassals do as they please?"

"I do not take steps that are unnecessary, Jovirdas. I do not destroy the wills and souls of even my lowliest servants, because I value the ability in those servants to choose to serve. The choice to eat from the Tree of Knowledge was a bad one, yet God let Eve do it, because she so chose." Jovirdas nodded hesitantly; theology was apparently not his strong suit. "My vassals may do as they please so long as what they please does not violate what they have sworn, or their station. This restricts some of them more than others, but I have found that binding Cainites too tightly in service simply spells," he gestured to the dust on the floor, "disaster."

Jovirdas stood and spat in the dust. "You mentioned a price for reading those letters."

Jürgen nodded. "Several, really, and all in the form of oaths." Jovirdas glowered, but not with nearly the same intensity as before. "First, I would ask that you swear that no harm will befall the letters themselves—they do not belong to me and I am honor-bound to return them in the same condition they were given to me."

"Done," said Jovirdas.

"Second, I would ask for your word that some of my retinue, including Lady Rosamund, may remain here for the time being. I have urgent business farther north, and I can take only my knights with me. You must swear to me that no harm shall befall her or any of my other companions while in your care."

"Done, but I should like to know where you are going."

"Of course. That actually ties into the third oath somewhat." Jürgen drew himself up to his full height and stepped over Geidas's remains to stand in front of Jovirdas. The two men were nearly the same height and Jovirdas showed no sign of backing down. Jürgen did not look him in the eye, not yet— Jovirdas would still equate that with mental domination, and Jürgen did not wish to frighten him. Instead, Jürgen focused on himself, willing himself to become regal, inspiring, the very picture of the warlord and noble leader. Jovirdas did not meet his gaze, but stared at his face. The Tzimisce's stony countenance softened somewhat; Jürgen laid a hand on his shoulder and spoke quietly, as though to a trusted lieutenant, or even a friend. "I would like you to swear fealty to me, and I in turn would take you as my vassal."

"Which, of course, requires tasting of your blood."

"It does."

Jovirdas did not respond, and Jürgen did not press the issue for the moment. "If you swear this oath, you are therefore under my protection, ruling this domain in my name. When I take Livonia for my own, the rewards will be great." Jovirdas met Jürgen's eyes for an instant, but then looked down at his chin. "And what of the *Voivodate*? Rustovitch and his ilk? Geidas feared them; I think even Visya did."

Jürgen smiled. "I fought Rustovitch once before, and I failed. I have no intention of failing this time. I do not ask you to come into battle beside me—I'm best served by you remaining here so that I have a base to return to."

"What makes you think I will not swear an oath and then break it when you leave, slaying your lady and her guards and calling for help from the *Voivodate*?"

Jürgen recognized the true purpose behind the question. "Because, Jovirdas, while I may not trust you any more than I trust any Cainite, I do trust that your adherence to loyalty has served you well. You are in no hurry to begin fouling the well that has sustained you on the nights—and I know you have had them—when the Beast threatens to make a true monster of you." Jovirdas nodded. "And in any case, should you break the oath, I shall know. Just as your former master could see into minds, I can hear a breaking oath from miles off." Jovirdas looked skeptical. "How else am I able to hold territory in Acre, in Magdeburg, and elsewhere?" Jovirdas nodded. Jürgen still wasn't sure the other believed his boast, but he also didn't believe Jovirdas would test his luck in any case. "If I should fall in battle," Jürgen continued, "Rustovitch won't know your loyalties and you may do as you please without dishonor."

"But you don't intend to fall."

"Of course not." Jürgen smiled, but did not relinquish his grip on Jovirdas's shoulder and did not allow his bearing to fade. "I intend to win, and become lord of this land as I am Prince of Magdeburg. It is no less than God intends, as both you and Rustovitch will see." He leaned in closer, and spoke directly into Jovirdas's ear. Jovirdas's hand reached up, unconsciously, as if to clutch at Jürgen's side, and then fell. "Will you swear fealty to me, Jovirdas of Kybartai? Will you taste of my blood, and bend knee to a leader who sees your worth, who prizes your strength, as a warrior and a true Scion?"

Jovirdas took a step back, nearly tripping over the throne. He regained his footing—and his dignity—and looked Jürgen squarely in the eye.

"I will, Jürgen of Magdeburg, but I have one other requirement."

Chapter Twenty-Six

"I am unsurprised."

Gotzon stood outside Jürgen's wagon, staring out at the snow with his ebony eyes. The moonlight cast a long shadow from Jürgen, from the tree sheltering the wagon and from the wagon itself, but Gotzon's shadow remained pooled at his feet as though the light were directly above his head. Every so often, the shadow would begin to creep away, but Gotzon tapped his foot and it returned to its place like a whipped dog.

"I *was* surprised. If Geidas were still in power, banishing you would make some sense, but why Jovirdas chose to ask for such a boon is beyond me." Jürgen looked around, wondering where Rosamund was. In the distance, he saw Wiftet sitting on a drift, gathering snow around his body until only his head remained visible. His dog sat patiently at the bottom of the drift, waiting for its master.

"Like you did when we first met, he recognizes Hell."

"Has he seen your eyes so clearly?"

Jürgen glanced back at his confessor, but Gotzon made no move to reply. Jürgen continued. "I should like to leave by tomorrow night." Still no response. Gotzon's shadow reached out towards Jürgen's hungrily; Gotzon glanced downward and it receded. Jürgen cast about for something to say. "I should also like to have your blessing on this battle." He looked off into the distance. "Given the targets."

"I have told you before that I have no special regard for monks, Jürgen. Especially not those fouled by Cainite blood. And after what I told you before Geidas fell, you should have no doubt that I have no love for the Obertus." Gotzon did not turn to face the Sword-Bearer, but continued staring down at his shadow, as though trying to make up his mind about whether to sever it entirely. Jürgen didn't doubt that this was possible for the Lasombra.

Jürgen walked around Gotzon to the door of the wagon. "I also have a favor to ask you, Gotzon." He reached inside and pulled out a folded piece of paper, sealed with his signet and his blood. "I would like you to give this to Rosamund if I should fall."

Gotzon glanced upwards sharply; his shadow took its chance and sprang from his feet, slithering across the snow like a gigantic black eel, making a beeline for Wiftet. Gotzon raised a hand and it stopped, but did not recede. It simply thrashed like a dog on a leash. If this caused Gotzon any strain, his face did not show it. "I do not deliver love letters, Jürgen."

"You assume you know the contents of the letter?"

"I know *you*, Jürgen." He clenched his fist and the shadow pulled back somewhat. "I know you, and I know her. You asked me if Cainites could love, and I answered. And yet you ask me to deliver this letter—"

"If I should perish, yes. I have no intention of doing so, therefore this letter never need be delivered. If you cannot or will not undertake this for me, I shall find someone else, Gotzon. But if the letter is with you, the chances of someone else breaking the seal are much reduced." Jürgen hadn't expected this kind of answer to his request. Gotzon was by no means a servant, of course, but even so, he had always been willing to shoulder such burdens for Jürgen before.

"In the event of your death—your final death?" Gotzon considered. "Very well." He reached forward and took the letter, slipping it into his shirt. "And since I am banished from this domain, I had best be on my way."

Jürgen didn't bother to ask where he would go. He knew that he wouldn't receive an answer. He simply watched Gotzon walk off into the trees, his shadow now giving up on escaping and huddled around his feet as if trying to escape the cold. Jürgen turned, and went to find Rosamund.

Wiftet, now only a head on top of a huge snow drift, called

out to him. "My lord! Look! I am interred, frozen for the winter! In spring, I shall blossom, I shall burst forth in glory!" Albion let out a yip as Jürgen approached; he ignored the dog. Wiftet continued. "I am planted for the winter, my lord. Such bliss!"

Jürgen nodded. "Indeed. Where is Lady Rosamund, Wiftet?"

Wiftet's face became dour and pinched, and he dropped his voice to a mocking tone of Jürgen's. "Why, I don't know. When last I saw her, she was with her man Peter."

"Thank you." Jürgen continued on. He was in no mood for Wiftet tonight, but the lunatic called after him.

"My lord! Shall I remain here, planted, until the snow thaws?"

Jürgen turned. "You shall remain here, Wiftet, and keep my lady and the new lord of this place entertained." He walked on, mentally reminding himself to instruct Jovirdas to simply tell Wiftet to shush if he became too annoying.

He heard Peter's voice from around a corner, but almost immediately heard Rosamund shush him. He found them waiting for him, obviously nervous, their conversation cut short. Jürgen resisted the temptation to pry what he needed to know from Peter's mind, and dismissed the ghoul with a glance. Peter bowed and retreated, but Jürgen saw the look he gave Rosamund.

"My lady, what troubles you?" he asked when Peter had gone.

To her credit, Rosamund didn't bother trying to skirt the issue. "I am concerned, my lord. Can Jovirdas be trusted?"

Jürgen nodded slowly. "I think so. He realizes that he has a much better liege in me than in Geidas, and that he isn't safe in these lands without allies. Plus, I think that he is genuinely interested in learning more of our road." Jürgen smiled. "I have told him that the Letters of Acindynus shall be left in your keeping when he is not reading them. You, of course, are welcome to continue where we left off; I shall regret missing the opportunity to read them with you but I have no idea how long I shall be gone."

"My lord," Rosamund's voice dropped slightly, "what about the duel? You won, clearly, but... I felt something."

Jürgen's brow furrowed. "What, my lady?"

She shook her head. "I don't know. A chill in the room. A sudden weakening—as though the heat left the fire and every bit of life and warmth suddenly vanished. The room didn't change, not visibly, but I swear that it grew larger, as though we were all miles away from each other. And then, an instant later, he reached forward and drank of your cup."

Jürgen stared at her warily. Was she telling the truth? The chill that he had felt before he'd won, the detached feeling of power and inevitability—how could she have known about it? Had she read his mind? He doubted it; that would be a breach of etiquette for her. Her own powerful senses might have detected something that he, while engaged in the duel, could not, and therefore she might be able to shed some light on what had happened.

But the sensation she'd described—it was so similar to what Jovirdas had mentioned when he had killed Geidas. Something, then, was aiding them, helping Jürgen to establish his power.

With inaction, thought Jürgen, *Gotzon does not violate his vows.* Could his confessor have aided him during the duel? But how, while in torpor with a stake in his heart?

While in torpor, did his soul—or his shadow—roam free?

Jürgen shuddered, thinking of the creatures that had emerged from the blackness after only a few moments' lapse in Gotzon's concentration. He considered running after the Lasombra, asking him more, asking him if and how he had managed both to aid Jürgen in the duel and aid Jovirdas in slaying his master.

But he was about to leave, to go into battle, and Rosamund stood before him, confused. He considered telling her his suspicions, but he had no desire to leave her behind with that knowledge.

Jürgen only took her in his arms. "Strange, my lady, very strange." He held her close, feeling her forehead against his chin, cold, smooth, perfect. "I must go. I have preparations to make and very little time." She did not release him, but merely tightened her grip, and Jürgen did not discourage her. "I will send for you as soon as I may, and if anything should happen—"

He meant to tell her about the letter, but she kissed him instead. When the kiss was over, she walked off towards her own wagon, leaving Jürgen in the snow. In other circumstances, he might have felt hurt or slighted that she hadn't bid him farewell, but he merely stood there, the kiss lingering on his lips, watching her disappear into the distance.

Chapter Twenty-Seven

Jürgen stood in the snow, staring at the monastery. He had come to Ezerelis with the intention of laying siege to the place, but had the strange suspicion someone had beat him to it.

The place was silent as a grave. Jürgen guessed the time at two hours to daybreak; the monks should be up and moving, even if there weren't any active Cainites in the monastery (which Jürgen rather doubted, given Dieter's testimony). They should be saying their Nocturns, preparing for the day, singing hymns. Of course, it was possible that these monks did not observe the same practices as those of Jürgen's homeland, but even so, he should be able to hear *something*.

Jürgen stood completely still. His hair began to crystallize on the back of his neck. He blinked once and discovered that his eyes had begun to freeze. He could hear nothing from the monastery, feel no warmth, see no light.

And yet, he did not think this place was empty, or even bereft of life, only that "life" was a relative term.

With a series of muted cracking sounds as the ice on his armor broke, Jürgen turned and walked back to the horses and his knights. He spoke in a whisper to Václav. "Something is wrong. The place looks dead—empty. I saw no lights."

Václav shook his head. "Impossible." He nodded back to the ghoul knights, who were huddled together around the small fire Jürgen had allowed them to build. "Our men are nearly frozen. The building would provide some respite from the wind, but without heat—"

"Yes." Jürgen glanced back. "I saw no tracks. Perhaps the place is abandoned."

"In that case, we should use it. We'll need shelter for the day and the men need rest. Even if the hearths are cold now, we could warm them."

Jürgen tapped his fingers against his side thoughtfully. "If this place is abandoned, what killed Klaus? And why would it be abandoned, anyway? There's no evidence of a fire or some other catastrophe."

"Attack? Lupines, perhaps? Or maybe the thing that killed Klaus also killed the monks?"

Jürgen nodded. "Where are the bodies, then? Why is the structure undamaged?"

"Plague?"

"Maybe, but why didn't we hear of it sooner? The snow hasn't been harsh enough to preclude all travel; surely one of the brothers would have made it to Ezerelis. It isn't that far away."

"Then what?"

Jürgen shook his head, and drew his sword. The sound was unnoticeable, ordinarily. This night, when a breath seemed to carry for miles, it was loud enough to gain the knights' attention. Even the fire seemed to die down as Jürgen approached.

"Ready yourselves. We attack immediately." The knights looked at one another; perhaps they still had misgivings about attacking a monastery, or maybe their nerves were simply wilted by the cold and the quiet. Jürgen frowned; that wouldn't do. He took a step towards the fire. The Beast whined loudly. "You have all seen the Black Cross, brothers. You know what lurks behind shadows, away from daylight. Surely you don't think that all Cainites are as benevolent as I?"

The knights murmured to themselves—they knew very well that most Cainites were true monsters, and demons besides.

"Yes, the place seems empty, but I believe that something else is afoot. Perhaps those monks are dead and the monastery deserted; if so, then so be it. But if they are dead and whatever killed them, and perhaps your brother, too, waits for us there—or if they are dead and they still walk," his men shuddered a bit more visibly, and one crossed himself, "then we have a duty to cleanse the place." He bade them stand, and pointed towards the monastery. "We shall enter through the front. The place looks deserted, so we shall proceed as if it is. If we are attacked, then we shall respond in kind. If any living thing does inhabit that monastery, we shall meet it like men and soldiers of God."

"What of the horses, my lord?" one of the knights asked.

"Bring them a bit closer to the monastery and then tie them. We can see what shelter the place might give them once we determine if it is safe." He pointed at two of the knights. "You carry torches. We'll need light, and we'll need to be able to light the hearths if it's safe."

He left the men to their preparation and walked back towards the monastery. Václav was already standing in almost exactly the same spot that Jürgen had been only a few moments before. "Anything?"

Václav did not turn. "My lord, look at the ground."

Jürgen looked. Even his acute vision took a moment to register what his knight meant, but once he saw it, his eyes widened. There were no tracks in the snow, and none behind him. "My God."

"There's something else. Listen." Václav reached up and grasped a small branch on the tree above him. He broke it—but the branch made no sound at all. "This is sorcery like nothing I've ever seen."

Not for the first time, Jürgen wished he had asked Jervais to accompany him on this trip. He thought back to the conversations he'd had with the Tremere about his talents and those of the Telyavs he'd encountered, but Jervais was often maddeningly vague when speaking of magic. He did recall, however, the Jervais's skills didn't include controlling the weather. But Gotzon had spoken of this sort of blasphemy.

"*Koldun.*"

Václav turned to look at Jürgen. "Who?"

Jürgen shook his head, trying to remember what he'd seen while inside Geidas's memories. The skies, the earth, the water— all had risen up to defend the Tzimisce. Were Gotzon's fears justified? Could the fiends reshape the world along with the flesh? Jürgen's Beast cried out that they should run, flee into the night and leave the knights to their fate, for surely whatever was blanketing this place in secrecy was powerful enough to kill them all.

"Should we change plans?"

"No," said Jürgen, more to his Beast than to Václav. He raised his head and peered at the monastery. Not one stone had changed. "Consider, Václav, that secrecy and illusion are the tools of the base and low-blooded, those who have to hide rather than stand proudly against their foes. We attack. I think that this is a bluff, meant to ward off the cowardly."

The two vampires walked towards the monastery, the rest of the knights not far behind. Jürgen noticed that he could hear the torches crackling until the two knights carrying them reached the spot where he and Václav had been standing, and then the noise ended. The horses, likewise, made no sound as the knights tied them.

Cowardice, thought Jürgen, *or a trap?* A Cainite old enough to produce such terrifying effects might use such an area as a battleground, or a place to capture prey. After all, a scout or traveler could scream all they liked, but never be heard outside the silent zone.

And yet, Klaus had apparently died in a place where sound carried, because Dieter had seen and heard it happen. He wished he had been able to save his ghoul's mind and life; a guide would have been quite useful here. But Dieter had died of a fever days after his return to Kybartai, ranting all the while about the man with robes of blood.

Why did the man not kill Dieter, then?

They left the trees and entered a large clearing before the monastery's door. Halfway across the clearing, Jürgen stopped. Václav held up a hand to halt the knights, and then looked to his sire. "What is it?"

Jürgen didn't answer, but held up a finger to shush Václav. He was hearing chants.

The monastery *was* still inhabited. As he concentrated, Jürgen saw lights in the monastery, faint, but certainly present. The feeling of unnatural stillness faded away, and Jürgen could hear incidental noises in addition to the chants—footsteps, whispers, rustling, noises of life. He started walking again, this time more briskly.

When they reached the door, Jürgen whispered to Václav to

prepare the men for battle, and then touched the door and commanded it to give up its secrets.

While it wasn't as uncomfortable as peering into a living or unliving mind, Jürgen didn't enjoy looking at the memories of objects, either. He feared that the same memories might betray him some night, and hoped that by avoiding the use of this particular gift, it would not be used against him. Tonight, however, he wanted to know who else had entered this place. He looked into the past and saw shadows, saw men opening and closing the door by daylight and by night, but saw only gray reflections of those men. The more passionate the man who touched the door, the more colorful his wraith became, but Jürgen could see little passion in these monks.

Where is their passion for God? he thought. He felt his heart lift. While he would have taken the monastery in any case, he would not have wished to slaughter monks who were truly doing the Lord's work. Gotzon, apparently, had been right—the Obertus were servants of the Clan of Dragons, not the Lord Almighty. Now he could continue without guilt.

The memory of a man opened the door, and Jürgen noted that his colors were vibrant and full, but much subtler than a living man's would have been. A Cainite, then. Jürgen peered at him, but looking through the shadows of memory attached to this paltry piece of wood was like trying to find his reflection in seawater. The Cainite walked outside and left the door open, and looked around the clearing at the trees. He raised a hand, and an owl fluttered down to him.

The Cainite whispered to the owl, but Jürgen could not understand his words. The owl took flight, and the Cainite watched it go without expression.

The murk cleared somewhat, and Jürgen looked carefully at the Cainite's face. He was clean, tall and slender. Dark hair fell to his shoulders, and his face was almost angelically beautiful. The man's hand was still extended, as though feeling the air the way a chef might test the temperature of soup. A small gold ring glistened on that finger.

Jürgen looked as closely as his limited perspective would allow. Something was familiar about the man's face, and yet he didn't think he'd actually seen it before. He concentrated hard, coaxing the wood of the door and the very ground to paint him a clearer picture.

When they did, Jürgen saw the man's face, and then suddenly realized where he'd seen it before. He had never seen it in person, but had seen a drawing—a very good one, too. What he didn't understand was how that man could be *here*, among Obertus monks.

The man was Nikita of Sredetz, the Archbishop of Nod, leader of the Cainite Heresy.

Jürgen released his grip on the door and allowed the scene to fade. He almost staggered, but managed to retain his footing. His mind reeled, and he tried to remember what he knew of the Heresy and of its leader. He knew that Narses, the Lasombra who had preceded Nikita as archbishop, had been slain and his soul and blood consumed by his own childe, Guilelmo Aliprando, now Prince of Venice. He had heard that Nikita had traveled recently to Paris. But as far as Jürgen knew, the Obertus order and its annoying patron Vykos had no love for the Heresy—he expected they might even be at odds enough to consider each other blasphemers.

So what in God's name was Nikita doing here, the obvious master of an Obertus monastery?

Václav noted his expression and whispered, "My lord?"

Jürgen raised a hand and signaled the men to be ready. He stood back and looked at the door—it was solid and well maintained. The Sword-Bearer looked at his childe and shook his head. "We must attack, now. The lord of this domain already knows we are here, and I seriously doubt he would accept any attempt to parley."

"Why, my lord? Did you recognize him?"

Jürgen shook his head. "Explanations later, Václav. We must take this place before daybreak."

Václav's expression was still confused, but he obeyed. Jürgen stood back and waited as the knights moved into position.

From inside, he heard movement stop, and then the sounds of running feet.

Jürgen raised his sword and shouted a battle cry. As the

knights surged forward to smash in the door, the Sword-Bearer dearly wished that Rosamund could see him now, in battle and glory, and feel what he felt.

Chapter Twenty-Eight

The door withstood the knights' onslaught for several minutes, and Jürgen fought with all his will not to look to the eastern sky. If the sun rose while he, Václav and the knights were still exposed, he would have nowhere to run.

In the end, though, the door splintered inwards. Jürgen's wolf-sharp ears caught the sounds of metal and gasps of fear—the monks were arming themselves. He told his knights this, and saw their expressions grow confused. Members of clerical orders were forbidden to spill blood.

But these are not the Dominicans and Franciscans of your homelands, brothers, thought Jürgen. *These are monks tainted by Tzimisce blood and Eastern heresy.*

Jürgen stepped through the ruined door into the monastery. As he did so, the remaining jagged chunks of the door fell from the frame. He leapt forward, out of the way, and nearly impaled himself on a sword.

The monk holding the sword was clearly a ghoul—his face was flushed, the vein in his neck throbbing. He had appeared as if from nowhere, the shadows hiding him in the same way that they hid rabble Cainites like Albin. Jürgen deflected his sword, snatched it from his hand, and tossed it casually behind him. The monk turned and tried to run; Jürgen caught the back of his robe, jerked him backwards, and sank his fangs into the back of the man's skull.

The blood was tepid, thick, as though this man was already half dead. Jürgen had never tasted such blood before—midway between that of a Cainite and that of a mortal. Even ghoul's blood wasn't normally this rich.

The blood had some of the tang that the Tzimisce woman—Masha's—did, but it didn't burn his mouth. Instead it filled him, woke him to the dwindling night. Time stopped, the knights behind him moved as though through mud, the sounds of the monastery slowed and deepened until he could hear nothing but a series of smooth, bass notes.

He released the now-dead ghoul, and time reasserted itself. Jürgen peered into the dark of the monastery and licked his lips. His Beast growled, and Jürgen allowed it—there would be blood enough to sate the Beast here.

"Beware, my brothers," Jürgen said in German. "These monks are dangerous. Watch the shadows and watch each other." He hazarded a glance back at them, and when they saw his face, lips stained with blood and eyes blazing with the fervor of conquest, they shared in that glory. They straightened themselves, shook fear from their hearts, and stepped into the hall ready for battle. *This is why I chose Hardestadt over Gotzon,* thought Jürgen. *Battle for God's sake is noble, but battle for battle's sake is pure.* "Those taken in battle, alive or dead, I own, and will claim my tribute," he said, and the knights let out a cheer at hearing his familiar mantra. Jürgen charged forward, the knights behind, Václav only a few steps to his right.

Jürgen scanned the halls of the monastery carefully. All ghouls boasted enhanced strength, but he had never seen one appear from nowhere before. He knew that certain Cainites—Albin the Ghost, for one—could do such a thing, but he had always reckoned this power beyond the scope of a ghoul. He saw three monks together in a corner, waiting to ambush. Václav saw them as well, and leapt at them. One of the monks was dead before he realized he was being attacked. The other two stepped from the shadows and raised their swords, eliciting gasps from the mortal Knights of the Black Cross, who hadn't seen them hiding. One of the knights moved forward; Jürgen stopped him. Václav could handle himself. *And if he can't,* Jürgen thought ruefully, *it only shows I wasted the gift of the Embrace.*

Václav parried a strike from one of the monks and drove his sword through the Obertus's chest, then turned and shoved the

last monk towards Jürgen. The Sword-Bearer caught the hapless brother by the arm and twisted, wrenching the shoulder
and sending him to his knees in pain. "Bind him," said Jürgen
over his shoulder. He had many questions, but they could wait.

The knights began to spread through the monastery, and
Jürgen could hear the sounds of steel on steel, the cries of
the wounded, the splatter of blood on stone. He heard a few
shrieks in German, and lamented—with his senses, he knew
even from the tone of a cry of pain who had been wounded,
and how badly. He shook off the thoughts and charged ahead—
he needed to know this monastery before daybreak, to know
where its Cainite patron was. He was quite sure that he could
slay Nikita in battle, but he was not quite as confident about his
knights' chances against the Archbishop of Nod.

He and Václav pushed on, deeper into the stone halls,
looking for stairways down. They entered a large room with
a dozen writing desks, but no paper or ink in evidence. "They
must keep their books locked away," muttered Václav. Jürgen
nodded. He didn't smell ink in the air, and the room had no lit
torches or fire. He motioned to Václav to fetch light and waited
just inside the door—he had no intention of being trapped in a
pitch-dark room fighting an unknown opponent.

Václav snatched a torch from the wall outside the room and
handed it gingerly to Jürgen. Jürgen walked carefully into the
room and looked to the corners, but didn't see anyone lurking.
He crossed to the fireplace and quickly built a fire; it was a skill
that many Cainites allowed themselves to forget. He hung the
torch above the hearth and looked back at Václav. His childe
shrugged. "Empty, then," said Jürgen. "Very well." This room
would serve nicely—it had only one door and was deep enough
in the monastery to be a superb barracks.

A scuffle of movement to Jürgen's left caught his attention. A
monk stepped from the shadows, but was not carrying a sword.
He was murmuring something, perhaps a prayer, although the
language wasn't Latin. Jürgen looked back to Václav. "Do you
understand him?" Václav wasn't Livonian, Jürgen knew, but it
was worth asking.

Václav cocked his head to listen to the monk. "No." Jürgen

drew his sword and stepped forward, but Václav stopped him. "Wait! It's changed."

Jürgen listened, and nodded. The monk was still muttering, but had changed from the local tongue to one that both Cainites understood—Greek.

"He has touched me, and thus I change," stammered the Obertus. Jürgen took a step back and glanced at Václav.

"I don't understand this, either," he said.

"He has touched me, and given unto me the means to—" the monk stopped in mid-sentence with a choked gasp, and fell forward. Jürgen smelled blood and bile coming from the man's clothes, and raised his sword, but then stopped. The man lay on the ground shuddering, blood seeping from his ears. He looked as though he was already dying.

A thick gurgling sound caught Jürgen's attention. He looked past the man at the wall. A puddle of red-brown liquid sat at the base of the wall, but was receding into a crack in the stone. Jürgen watched, fascinated, as it disappeared, leaving not even a stain behind it.

"Václav, did you see—"

"My lord, look out!"

Chapter Twenty-Nine

The monk sprang from the ground, his robes tearing themselves free of his body. He had swollen to over seven feet in height, but remained hunched over. His arms had elongated until they nearly touched the floor, and his mouth was distended enough to bite off a man's head.

"Changed!" the beast roared, and lunged at Jürgen. It swung its hand—now ending in claws the size of spearheads—at him. Jürgen managed to raise his sword in time to parry the blow, but the creature struck with enough force to knock him off his feet. It stepped forward and drew back its claws, and then screamed in pain as Václav stabbed it from behind. Jürgen lashed out with his own blade, expecting to disembowel the creature, but only left an angry red streak across its stomach.

The creature swung its arm backwards and Jürgen noticed that its arc of motion didn't stop—its shoulder joint simply popped and allowed its arm to fold fully behind its massive back. Václav, who had been standing safely out of reach, or so he had thought, grunted as the beast's immense fist slammed into him, sending him flying against the wall above the fireplace. He fell to the ground, and Jürgen shouted a warning—the torch he had placed there was about to fall.

The beast took advantage of Jürgen's distraction. It drove its claws into the Sword-Bearer's left leg, picking him up and lunging at him with its fangs. Jürgen drew back and punched it in the face; bones snapped under the blow and blood gushed from the creature's nose. It dropped Jürgen and staggered backwards. Jürgen landed in a heap and rolled to his feet, taking time only to grab his sword.

He glanced over at Václav. His childe was clambering to his feet, healing himself slowly. Jürgen took a step and winced; the claws had pierced him straight to the bone. The monster pawed at the ground like a bull about to charge. Jürgen tried to lock eyes with it, thinking that perhaps he could command it or at least slow it down, but the creature was all rage and blood. *Changed*, thought Jürgen. *It said that someone touched it and now it could change.*

The monster sprang forward. Jürgen had healed his leg enough to move, and dove out of the way, but couldn't quite clear the monster's reach. It caught him by his shirt and tore his mantle away, leaving Jürgen flat on his back. The beast balled both fists above its head and brought them down on Jürgen's chest like a blacksmith's hammer. Jürgen felt pain as his ribcage gave, and then sharp, tearing agony as his skin split and his shattered ribs tried to poke their way through his mail shirt. His undead flesh began mending immediately, but he couldn't muster the strength to roll out of the way.

Something grabbed his feet and pulled just as the creature's fists struck again. The stone floor cracked under the assault. Jürgen looked up and saw Václav, looking pale and wild-eyed from hunger. Healing the wound the creature had dealt him had cost him dearly. "Václav, go and find the knights. Feed, and bring me a prisoner."

The creature had backed up into the corner and was preparing to charge again. Václav never took his eyes off it. "My lord, are you certain—"

"Go, childe!" Jürgen pulled himself fully to his feet and shoved Václav, wincing at the pain it brought his chest. Václav ran from the room; the beast charged at him like a hunting dog. Jürgen hit it from the side, stabbing where a man's kidneys would have been and sending it sprawling into the corner.

The creature stood almost immediately and lashed out with both hands, trying to knock Jürgen off balance again. Jürgen's sword flashed upwards and severed one of the creature's fingers, deflecting the blow, but its other hand caught him amidships, hurling him through the desks and against the far wall. *Better*, he thought wearily, *than being stabbed by those claws again.*

The wound in his leg hadn't fully healed yet, and he suspected that the creature could probably tear his heart from his chest with its talons.

The beast charged again, smashing desks out of the way and howling the word "changed" again. Jürgen grabbed one of the desks near him and smashed it to pieces against the floor, then threw one of the shards at the creature's face. It lodged in the beast's right eye and the monster veered off and ran into the wall, its howls winding up in pitch to crow-like shrieks.

Jürgen flanked the beast and kicked one of the desks towards its feet. The monster responded more quickly than Jürgen would have guessed, smashing the desk to kindling and flailing blindly with its other hand. The Sword-Bearer darted under its swing and plunged his sword into its back. He worked the blade back and forth, trying to sever the creature's back-bone, but it was like working the blade through a wooden post. The creature tried to round on Jürgen, but he had no intention of taking another blow from it. He left his sword embedded in its back and backpedaled out of reach of its arms.

While it was certainly still capable of fighting, the creature was slowing. The blade in its back limited its movement—when it tried to extend its arms to their full length, its hands began to spasm. Jürgen circled the creature; he didn't want to get backed into a corner, and certainly not the corner where he'd seen the moving blood.

He could hear footsteps approaching. They were loud, the footsteps of warriors, not monks, although he didn't think the creature could differentiate between friend or foe anyway.

"Stay away from the door!" he shouted. The creature was blocking the entrance to the room; anyone who entered would walk straight into its arms. Jürgen looked about for a weapon and seized a loose flagstone from the fireplace. He ran for the creature, stopping just as it leapt forward to grab at him, and threw the stone.

The stone hit the monster in the mouth, shattering most of its teeth. It spat blood, stone and bone on the floor and roared with hate, but Jürgen had already moved behind it to retrieve his sword. He stepped back out of the room to see Václav and two knights running towards him. Václav had a monk over his shoulder, whom he dropped at Jürgen's feet.

Jürgen knelt and grabbed the monk's wrist, then impatiently exposed the throat and bit. This monk wasn't as filling as the last—he didn't have the same odd richness to his blood. Jürgen ignored this, gulping down great mouthfuls of the blood, feeling it leak from his mouth to stain his face, and cast the now-desiccated Obertus aside. Picking up his sword again, he braced. The monster was charging at them.

The two knights stepped forward to engage it, but Jürgen waved them back. He had no desire to bury any more knights than necessary and, even wounded, this creature was beyond the skill of any save the Sword-Bearer himself. He would lead the attack; he, after all, could heal any wounds it dealt him. He lunged forward with the strength of the monk suffusing his limbs, and thrust his sword forward and up.

The blade entered the creature's chest just below his rib cage, and its bellow changed to a wet gurgle as blood filled its lungs. Jürgen pushed on the blade, shoving it up, into the monster's throat. The creature lashed out with its arms, but only managed to strike the doorway. "Now!" cried Jürgen.

Václav and the other knights leapt forward and began hacking at the creature with their own blades. It tried to stand, but Jürgen pushed it down with his boot. Finally it slumped over, bleeding from uncountable wounds, and heaved a dying breath.

"It was alive?" Sir Thomas wiped the creature's blood from his blade. He looked green. Doubtless he wished he could have stayed behind with Rosamund, but his compatriot Raoul had apparently won that right somehow.

"It was a ghoul," muttered Jürgen. He was staring at the creature. It was dying—he could hear its heartbeat slowing—but there was still *activity* on some level. He could see whirling, maddened colors around the thing.

"Like us. Mother of God." Thomas crossed himself and staggered against the wall.

Jürgen looked up at him sharply. "No, Thomas. Nothing like you. If you wish to be defined by blood, be defined by the English blood in your veins, or by the blood of Lady Rosamund, or by the blood of Our Savior and your vows before Him. This *thing* was defined by Tzimisce blood." Jürgen glanced back at it. The colors were muting somewhat. "It was human, until he touched it."

Václav stood close to Jürgen and spoke under his breath. "Can a Cainite *do* such a thing to a man? What if it touches one of our knights?"

Jürgen whispered back, "I am rather hoping that Nikita can only do this to someone who already carries his blood, but let us pray the theory is not tested." He thought again to Gotzon's envy and fear of Tzimisce power, and felt somewhat sickened.

From behind them, Sir Thomas cried, "My lords, look!" Václav and Jürgen raised their blades and stepped back from the creature, but the body wasn't moving. The other knights looked with confusion at Thomas and then the creature. Jürgen, however, saw what he meant.

Something was rising up from the creature's corpse. It looked like a black mist, but seemed to be shot through with streaks of red. The mist swirled into a vortex around the body, emitting an angry hissing sound. The knights recoiled from it, and one of them clapped his hands to his ears. Jürgen and Václav, however, simply stared.

Jürgen's Beast growled, and then purred. It ordered Jürgen to touch the mist; Jürgen refused. Václav reached out for it and his sire caught his wrist just in time. The mist rose and oozed along the ceiling, slipping into the same crack in the wall that the blood had.

"What in God's name..." Thomas's question went unanswered. For a long moment, not one of them moved or spoke. Jürgen could still hear sounds of battle from elsewhere in the monastery, but they were growing faint. His knights were winning.

"Václav," he said quietly. "Please find out a way into the room behind that wall." Václav took a step, but stumbled. Jürgen didn't bother to ask his childe what was wrong; he knew. Dawn was coming.

Chapter Thirty

Jürgen sat at one of the few undamaged writing desks, carving a crude sketch of the monastery into the wood with a knife. His knights stood around him, some watching the cracks in the walls, others watching the door. Václav and Thomas were out searching the monastery—since only the two of them and Jürgen had seen the foul mist rise up from the monster's corpse, Jürgen guessed that Thomas had learned the gifts of perception from his mistress and could therefore ferret out any remaining monks hiding in the corners.

Jürgen doubted that the place would have held any more, though. Many had died in the fighting, but despite the fact that these Obertus seemed quite willing to pick up swords, they were poor warriors. Most of them lay about the room, bound and gagged, eyes bulging with fear. Jürgen had ordered his knights to drag the corpses outside—three brothers who had sloughed off some of their flesh to escape their bonds joined the monks who died in battle, the two he had fed upon and the once-human monstrosity. One of those monks had actually fled as far as the doorway before a knight tackled him. Jürgen simply drained those monks white; he would need every drop of blood his body would hold.

The monastery was large, but not vast, and he didn't think that it housed catacombs. That meant that there had to be an entrance to the room on the other side of that wall. In that room waited Nikita of Sredetz, and Jürgen intended to take his head.

The trouble was, he didn't have enough time. Daybreak was coming. He could sleep here for the day, guarded by his knights, and attack come the following sunset, but he wanted to be sure of where his foe slept, first. Now, he could only wait for news, and plan.

He stood and paced the room, looking over his men. Some of them were wounded; two had died in battle. He turned to a young knight named Friederich. "Do you have the chalice?"

Every knight in the room glanced up. Friederich nodded, and took a silver cup from a pouch at his side. Jürgen took the chalice in his right hand and bit open his left wrist, and then bled into the cup until it was almost full. He looked around the room again; he would have to refill the cup at least twice before all of the knights could drink, but it would be well worth it to have strong, loyal, alert troops at his command. He raised the chalice and looked around the room, meeting each knight's eyes in turn.

"You have each sworn to stand under the Black Cross, to fight against the enemies of God, to bring His Holy Word to those who have not heard it. You have seen what lies beyond the light, what your fellows in the Order of the Teutons are not prepared to behold. You have taken your drink from me and you have been judged worthy to fight this crusade, for as long as the night lasts.

"I have sworn to give you strength and guidance, and so I have. I have sworn to lead you to glory, and so I shall. Marvel not at the horrors you have seen here tonight or will before another sunset, for you have the strength you need to defeat them. Your souls are made pure by God." He handed the chalice to Friederich. "And I, Jürgen the Sword-Bearer, I make your hearts strong by my blood."

The knights passed the chalice, and the wounded among them drank deeply. By time it was over, four more monks lay dead and drained at the door, but all of the knights could stand and walk, Jürgen's blood knitting flesh and resetting bones in moments. All of the knights looked upon Jürgen with devotion, and although the dawn was upon him, Jürgen was not tired.

"Blasphemy," came a hoarse whisper. One of the monks had worked his gag loose. Jürgen rounded on him and picked him up by the throat.

"You, heretic, dare to accuse me of blasphemy?"

"I know no heresy," the monk hissed. He was speaking Latin, but his accent wasn't local. It was Greek. Jürgen realized that many of these monks must have traveled here after the fall of Byzantium. "I follow the rule—"

Jürgen's grip on his throat tightened. "Where is your master?"

"I do not know." Jürgen wasn't surprised; most Cainites kept their havens secret from even their most trusted servants. The man's face began to turn purple from the pressure, and Jürgen dropped him. The monk lay there on the floor gasping like a fish, his reddened face changing to a more healthy hue.

Healthy?

Jürgen looked around to the other prisoners. All of them were healthy-looking. None of them had the haggard, sallow look of mortals in habit of giving up their blood for Cainites.

And yet, he had seen no evidence of travelers, nor had any of his knights reported it. So upon whom was Nikita feeding?

Jürgen snatched the monk off the floor again. "Does he feed on you?"

The monk looked confused, and then frightened. He started babbling in a language Jürgen did not understand. Jürgen locked eyes with the man and bared his fangs. "Talk, worm. Does he feed on you or your brothers?"

"No," whispered the monk. The knights looked on with interest.

"Who, then? Travelers? Hunters?"

"No," he stammered. "Cainites."

Although he had been expecting this answer, the horror of an elder who fed only on the blood of vampires stunned Jürgen. "Where do these Cainites come from?"

"He... calls them here. They all arrive wearing the robes of the Church, but they do not leave. He does not tell us who they are. He simply lets us go on about our business. He does not even see us, except for when we pray. He is beyond us, exalted, he does not—"

Jürgen dropped him and nodded to one of the knights. "Gag him. Tightly, this time." He sat back down at the desk. Suddenly the impending dawn seemed only moments away, and sleep tugged at Jürgen's heart. He felt the fire in the room grow warmer, and the heat felt uncomfortable; he longed for the chill of death that the day-sleep granted. His Beast yawned loudly, demanding that he sleep, trying to force his mind to shut down, to die for a few short hours.

Jürgen could not allow it.

He stood and strode towards the door. One of the knights called after him; he ignored the voice. He listened in the hall, heard footsteps, and walked towards them, carefully stepping around the beam of sunlight now coming in the main door.

He heard a sound like a peddler's sack being dropped from a wagon. Sleep had apparently claimed his childe for the day.

Jürgen rounded a corner and saw Thomas standing over Václav's inert body. The knight looked helplessly at Jürgen. He brushed Thomas aside and raised Václav's head, slapping his face lightly. He received no response.

Grunting in frustration, Jürgen bit into his finger and smeared the blood across his childe's lips. Václav's eyes flew open and then fluttered. "Stay awake," Jürgen growled.

"My... lord," said Václav slowly. "We have found the entrance, I think." Jürgen looked behind him and saw that they had smudged a section of the wall with ash. The entrance was there, blocked so that only a Cainite of superlative strength could open it.

"We must attack. Now. We cannot allow Nikita to survive until sunset." He waved at Thomas. "Fetch the others. Bring them all here; leave Friederich behind to guard the monks. Go!"

Thomas fled down the hallway. Jürgen helped Václav to his feet. "But, my lord, how can we fight during the day?"

Jürgen glanced at the wall, listened, and heard nothing. "I think that Nikita will have a much more difficult time functioning while the sun is high than I will, or even you. And that is why we must face him now."

Václav only looked confused.

"He feeds only on Cainites, Václav. The Thirst of Caine has taken him." Václav's eyes grew wide. "Yes," said Jürgen, shaking his head. "That is why Dieter escaped. He has grown so old, so far from the world of man, that he doesn't even see mortals anymore, except those who know how to attract his attention. Had I known, I would have brought not only Jervais on this trip but Christof as well. But there's nothing for it now. We must fight by day."

"But my lord, if we fight by day, when we are so weak—"

"Then how much weaker must an ancient be, one who commits the sin of diablerie on his own kind, one who manipulates God's Church, a traitor? During the day, the Beast holds sway over him completely, and during the day, the Beast wants nothing but slumber." Jürgen heard footsteps approaching and stared at the door. "We will take his head while he fumbles with consciousness."

Jürgen's Beast began to speak, but then shied away. Jürgen stood and pulled Václav to his feet. He stared at the door, still tired, but unflinching. The knights came down the hallway towards them, and Jürgen set them to the task of moving the stone. He watched as the wall began to give, then crack, and finally fell inward in a heap of rubble.

Jürgen threw a torch into the room, but could see nothing but stone and dust.

"Here, then, is the lion who called the animals to him to pay him respect," murmured Jürgen. "But you will not add my dust to your parlor, nor my soul to your memories." He drew his sword and stood straight, the distant sun irrelevant, a minor nuisance. He stepped through the fissure in the wall to meet the Archbishop of Nod.

Chapter Thirty-One

The room couldn't have been large, but it seemed to swallow sound and the firelight both. Václav and Jürgen stood just inside the hole the knights had made, waiting for some indication that their quarry was present. They heard nothing.

The room was filled with dust; it sat several inches thick on the floor. This dust wasn't simply from time, Jürgen knew. As he walked, his feet caught on the remains of clothes that had once belonged to dignitaries of the Cainite Heresy. He felt a snarl catch in his throat as he glanced down and saw Klaus's shirt amidst the dust.

The torch he had thrown into the room before had ignited some of the clothes. Jürgen strode forward and cleared a furrow in the dust so as not to burn the entire room.

"My lord?" Václav's whisper was enough to bring the point home—why *not* burn the room? Jürgen did not have a chance to answer his childe, however, before another voice filled the chamber.

"My lord, the wall—" Sir Thomas's voice echoed against the stone walls, and Jürgen turned to see that the wall to his left was covered in blood. A long tentacle lashed out from this obscene tapestry and splashed against Thomas's face.

Thomas didn't even have time to scream. His entire head liquefied. His mantle turned a deep crimson, and his body collapsed to the ground, twitching. The blood-tentacle receded into the wall, and the sheet of blood did not move.

Václav gaped. Jürgen ground his teeth and glanced towards the aperture in the wall. "No mortal steps through that opening!" he shouted, and stepped towards the pile of burning rags.

Václav looked at Jürgen. "My lord, what now?"

Jürgen picked up a burning length of cloth, possibly a stole or sash of some kind. He flung it at the wall. The cloth hit the blood-sheet and sizzled a bit, but the blood pulled away from the fire, leaving a section of clean stone behind.

Jürgen smiled. "If you won't fight, Nikita, then burn." He nodded to Václav, who gingerly picked up a burning rag with his sword and flung it at the wall. Again, the blood receded, but no other reaction was evident.

Jürgen and his childe continued their assault, but the Sword-Bearer was growing concerned. They didn't seem to be doing any real damage to the blood. While Jürgen assumed this unsightly mass to be Nikita, he had never heard of any first-cursed vampire being able to transform himself so. The low-blooded were typically more apt towards this kind of metamorphosis, but then, the Tzimisce's horrid power seemed unbound by such limitations.

Jürgen stopped and stared at the blood, trying to find a mind within it. He had never tried to read the mind of a Cainite he couldn't see, but since he could read the memories of base objects and the Earth itself, he did not think it would be difficult, provided there was anything at all to be found. He stared at the blood, gazing at the way it flowed away from fire, from pain, at the way it roiled when it moved….

He saw into it, saw nothing but red. He saw fire and soot… a city burning? He saw time.

Time. Endless, black nothing, followed by fire, water, pain, mud, trees, metal, men, beasts… blood. Then nothing again, for a thousand ebon eternities. And on the heels of that pain came something else, but not from Nikita's—the blood's—mind.

Jürgen heard a sound, a crisp, dry crack, as though something had broken—a bone, a branch… or an oath. Somewhere, someone who had sworn an oath to Jürgen had violated that oath.

Jürgen felt a surge of anger, and that anger met with the grief and hate he saw in Nikita's mind and plunged him into fire and blood again.

Jürgen backed away, shaking his head and grunting in pain.

Václav turned his attention from the wall to aid his sire. Jürgen tried to cry out, but couldn't find his voice.

The blood on the wall gushed outward like a geyser, but stopped in the middle of the room and coalesced into a man. The firelight dimmed, and Jürgen felt the heat from the flames die down. Even with his acute senses, he couldn't see the man well. He had seen this sort of thing before around Gotzon; lights seemed to dim and shadows darken to keep his confessor hidden. This seemed different, somehow. The shadows didn't lengthen, rather, the light seemed to die. The man stepped forward, and Jürgen noticed that the ring he had seen earlier was gone, and he was dressed in dark, almost blood-colored robes.

"Surrender," said Jürgen. He expected a laugh or a flippant remark, a challenge, something. He did not expect the response Nikita gave. The archbishop's face grew sad, as if in mourning. Jürgen took a step towards him, brandishing his sword. Václav wavered a bit, sleep eating at his mind, and then followed.

Nikita's eyes were half-shut. Jürgen could sense the power coming from this Cainite, but could also sense that he was weak, the Beast pulling his heart to the temporary death of the day. He lashed out in a feint, testing his opponent's reactions.

Nikita did not move. The sword slashed at his robe, but it mended itself immediately. Jürgen stared at the cut, and realized that the archbishop's "robes" were actually folds of skin.

In disgust, Jürgen thrust his sword forward, intending to impale the Tzimisce. This time Nikita did react. He grabbed the sword from Jürgen's hand and flung it out of the room. A cry of pain told Jürgen that it had not landed harmlessly. Jürgen tensed himself to tackle the archbishop, but stopped and circled. The Tzimisce had wrenched the sword out of his hand with more strength than Jürgen could ever muster. He couldn't grapple with this foe; doing so with Masha had been dangerous enough. He would have to outlast him. Jürgen smirked; he had no fear that he would fall asleep before Nikita would. Jürgen stood firmly on his feet, while Nikita swayed uneasily. The room brightened every time Nikita leaned too precariously to one side.

The archbishop seemed to realize his predicament, and

launched himself at Jürgen. His speed, however, did not match his strength, and Jürgen leaped to one side and grabbed a double handful of the skin-folds on the Tzimisce's back. He tore upwards, showering himself in blood and flesh, and realized that the skin that Nikita wore was still alive somehow. He was wiping the blood from his eyes when the fiend wrapped his hands around Jürgen's throat and began to squeeze.

A mortal would have been dead instantly. Jürgen felt his windpipe collapse, his skin split and his neck begin to crack. He willed the wounds to heal, but the archbishop only pressed harder. Jürgen grabbed the Tzimisce's wrists and tried to pull them free, but they felt like two iron bars in his grip. *How many years my senior can this Cainite possibly be?* Jürgen thought desperately. *I never heard of Nikita of Sredetz being so powerful....* His hands released Nikita's wrists; he was losing feeling in his limbs.

Jürgen heard what sounded like a sword hitting a tree trunk. He cast his eyes up—for he could no longer move anything below his jaw—and saw Václav standing behind Nikita. His childe drew back his sword for another strike, but this time stabbed rather than slashing. Jürgen saw Václav's arms and the hilt of his sword, and then the look of rage on his face as he thrust it forward. Václav, while not nearly so old and powerful as his sire, was a warrior and a Cainite trained and Embraced for the purposes of fighting. Jürgen had seen him swing his sword through men wearing the finest armor, behead horses to bring their riders down, and crush men's skulls with his fists. A strike with all of his strength behind it should have driven the sword through its target and very likely into Jürgen's gut as well.

Nikita, however, barely budged. He did not remove his hands from Jürgen or even acknowledge that he was being attacked. He simply squeezed harder.

Jürgen's Beast rose up, the red fear blotting out the pain and the rage of the assault. Honor and courage, the nobility of the battle and the cunning of attacking by day... what were these if all that was left of them at the next sunset was dust and memories? What was the noblest of plans if it *didn't work*? Jürgen began to thrash, kicking his legs out at his assailant, but couldn't tell if he was connecting or not. Somewhere, the still lucid part of his mind realized that he was being held off the ground.

He thought back to the monk he had questioned, and how easily he had broken that man. He thought back to Albin the Ghost, and how quick he had been to dominate the Caitiff's mind. He knew that Nikita must have those same gifts of command, and was surely close enough to Caine that he could break Jürgen just as easily.

Jürgen's Beast howled in rage and frustration, screaming that it would not be caged, would not be held down, would not be commanded. It demanded release, demanded that Jürgen allow it out to fight, demanded to tear Nikita limb from limb before he tore Jürgen's head cleanly from his body.

Jürgen refused.

A sickening cracking sound issued forth from Jürgen's breast. From outside, he heard the knights gasp, and heard a scuffle as one of them tried to rush in and was held back by the others. Jürgen's Beast whimpered petulantly to Jürgen that frenzy was the only chance for survival.

Jürgen disagreed. He forced every drop of blood possible to his neck and chest, strengthening them, forcing the bones to knit and the flesh to mend. Feeling began to return to his arms. The Beast howled for more blood; Jürgen felt himself growing hungry, and yet he pressed on.

Nikita squeezed harder. Václav struck again, this time stabbing the archbishop in the back of the neck. Nikita's head bobbed forward a bit, but he still didn't turn.

Jürgen grew stronger still, the blood of the Obertus monks infusing his arms until he could lift them again. He grabbed Nikita's wrists and pulled, and felt the fingers budge a little. Concentrating every bit of will that he had, he stared past Nikita and looked into Václav's mind, sending him one very specific thought.

Václav blinked, as his half-unconscious mind tried to comprehend what Jürgen was telling him. Then he moved to Nikita's side, raised his sword, and brought it down squarely on the archbishop's outstretched arms at the elbows. At that precise moment, Jürgen pulled against the Tzimisce's wrists and kicked him in the chest. The two Cainites broke apart, Jürgen landing on his back near the entrance to the room and Nikita staggering backwards towards the fire.

Jürgen picked himself up and stretched his neck. Most of the flesh there was mended, but he could still feel prickles of pain where his collarbones were broken. More importantly, though, the blood in his limbs hadn't abated—and he was still as strong as the archbishop. He glanced down and saw Sir Thomas's headless body, blood seeping from his neck. He imagined Rosamund's face when she heard the news—she had lost another servant to an enemy she had no claim to.

Jürgen reached down and picked up Thomas's sword. It was nothing near the quality of his own, but it would do. He stepped forward to Václav's side. Nikita had recoiled from the fire and was now staring at the two Ventrue dully, as though trying to remember where he was.

"Hungry, Nikita?" Jürgen asked, smiling. "The blood of mortals no longer sustains you? Why is that? Too many years supping on your own deformed childer?"

The archbishop, if he understood, did not respond. Jürgen advanced, circling around to Nikita's right, while Václav moved to his left.

"A vow, perhaps? I understand your clan harbors notions of honor."

Still, Nikita did not answer, but he turned his back on Václav to watch Jürgen. The Sword-Bearer thought he saw something like anger in the archbishop's eyes.

"A curse, then? A further curse from the Almighty for your further perversion of His—"

Jürgen broke off his taunt as Nikita lunged forward, fangs bared, the flesh on his fingers peeling back to reveal sharp bone. Jürgen's eyes glinted—he had seen this tactic before. He swung his sword downward, aiming not for Nikita's steely arms but his fingertips. He knocked the Tzimisce's hands aside, spun the sword, and stabbed it into Nikita's back. He intended to sever the spine, and indeed managed to penetrate his foe's disgusting clothing and the flesh on his back. The force the blow knocked

Nikita forward onto his face, but he lashed out with a foot and knocked Jürgen towards the fire.

Jürgen wrenched his sword from the Tzimisce's back and planted it in the burning clothing to steady himself. The point of the blade slid against the stone floor. Out of the corner of his eye, Jürgen saw Nikita standing. If Nikita pushed him now, while he was off balance, he would fly into the flame. Jürgen's Beast hissed in fear, but Jürgen could do little to right himself.

Václav grabbed Jürgen by the back of his shirt and pulled him up, the knight swinging his sword wildly at the archbishop. Nikita didn't acknowledge Jürgen's childe, but leapt at Jürgen himself. Jürgen raised his sword; Nikita caught Jürgen by the wrists but did not push. He merely held Jürgen's arms in place. Jürgen felt the Tzimisce's finger move, caressing his skin....

Jürgen's Beast screamed in panic as the flesh peeled away from his wrists. The bones beneath began to weaken, and Jürgen realized with horror that Nikita, while no longer strong enough simply to tear Jürgen to pieces by brute force, could certainly sever his hands this way. Jürgen glanced at Václav. His childe chopped at the Tzimisce's wrists with the sword, but couldn't gain a strong enough arc to do any real damage without hitting his sire. Jürgen felt his hands begin to weaken as the bone rotted. He kicked at Nikita's knees, trying to knock him down, but he might as well have been trying to kick down a castle wall.

Václav dropped his sword, grabbed Nikita by the hair and bit him in the shoulder, tearing off a hunk of his fleshy clothing and exposing the skin beneath. Nikita dropped Jürgen's wrists and staggered backwards. Jürgen looked down at his hands— they were intact but for the skin; he could see the bones and sinew clearly. He willed himself to heal and saw the blood welling up at the edge of the wound. The skin and muscle should have replaced itself in seconds, but the flaps of skin hanging on his arms moved at a snail's crawl. Jürgen glanced up at his foe and saw him standing calmly as Václav, on the verge of frenzy, sank his fangs into Nikita's shoulder again.

Suddenly Jürgen smelled sulfur and burning blood. Smoke rose up from his childe's mouth. Václav staggered backwards and doubled over as if to retch.

Nikita stepped towards Václav, now with a ravenous scowl on his face. Václav stood up and Jürgen watched in horror as his childe's jaw melted. Blood cascaded down his chest, smoldering, and caught fire as it reached his shirt. Václav fell to his knees, burning.

Nikita grabbed him by the hair and opened his mouth, revealing three rows of wicked fangs. A six-inch black tongue lolled about the maw for a moment, and then he lunged downward towards Václav's exposed neck.

Jürgen charged forward, drew back his sword, and swung. The blade sliced cleanly through his childe's neck and came to rest in the fleshy folds of Nikita's robes. Jürgen dropped the sword and shoved the archbishop back against the wall, and then hazarded a glance down.

Václav's body was already decaying. The fire consumed him all the more quickly now. His head rolled off towards the burning clothing, crumbling to ash. Jürgen's Beast howled for retribution. Jürgen promised that it would have it.

Nikita stood and stepped towards Jürgen. The ravenous look on his face had intensified, and Jürgen realized that destroying his childe had probably cost Nikita the vitae in Václav's veins. Jürgen shifted the sword in his hands and braced himself. A Cainite in the throes of a hunger-born frenzy could not plan or fight with intelligence, but was in some ways more dangerous for it. He had no intention of giving up his blood to this monster.

Nikita sprang at him. Jürgen struck with his sword, but failed even to break the archbishop's skin. Nikita swung a fist downwards and knocked the sword from his hand, then lashed out with his other hand and sent Jürgen sprawling.

From outside the room, Jürgen heard a commotion. His knights were, perhaps, making ready to rush in. *If they all give their lives to help me defeat this fiend,* he thought, *how will I take and hold the territory? But it won't matter if I don't win here.* His Beast seized the opportunity and forced him to his feet just as Nikita landed on him. The Tzimisce opened his maw and lunged downward; Jürgen's fist shot upward and into his mouth. Nikita's jaws closed... but on the bone that he had exposed earlier. No blood flowed there without Jürgen's will, and so Nikita

could take no sustenance from this attack. Jürgen grabbed the
knife from his belt and stabbed it under Nikita's chin, pushing into his flesh until he felt its point tickling his palm. Nikita
grabbed at Jürgen's arm, but Jürgen pushed harder, trying to
force the whole of the knife into Nikita's mouth.

The Tzimisce let go and backed off, pain apparently over-
riding hunger. He spit out the knife and crouched like a spider.
Jürgen stood and glanced about the room for a weapon. His
sword was somewhere outside the room, Václav's was near his
body, Thomas's was in a corner. All were out of reach.

A pair of footsteps echoed, and the back of room darkened,
as though the shadows were fleeing from something. Nikita's
head snapped around to face this new threat, but Jürgen didn't
bother.

"Gotzon."

The Lasombra did not respond, merely tossed Jürgen his
sword. The blade still glistened with blood from whatever
unfortunate knight it had struck when Nikita threw it from the
room. Jürgen's Beast smelled the blood and demanded that he
lick it from the blade. He refused, instead lowering the blade
and staring at Nikita.

Nikita leapt towards Gotzon, but the ashen priest simply
sidestepped and brought his sword down on Nikita's back.
Jürgen didn't waste the opportunity, he cleaved away a large
hunk of the Tzimisce's flesh-robes, exposing skin that was as
smooth and white as a child's. Nikita reared up and lashed
out at both foes. Gotzon parried the fist with his blade; Jürgen
allowed Nikita to hit his shoulder and sliced a red furrow down
his foe's back as he fell to the ground.

Gotzon slashed at Nikita's stomach, trying to keep clear of
the archbishop's talons. Jürgen stood. "He's weakening." Gotzon
didn't respond, but nodded towards the fire. Jürgen saw that his
confessor meant to force Nikita back to the dying flame, to burn
him to ash as Nikita had Václav.

No, thought Jürgen. *I cannot allow that. He does not deserve so
quick a fate.* He moved behind Nikita and slashed at the back
of his knees, trying to knock him forward. Gotzon, confused,
stepped back and Nikita followed the obvious foe, lurching out

at the Lasombra's throat. Jürgen raised his sword again, and brought the hilt down on Nikita's back, splintering several ribs.

The archbishop stumbled, and then straightened. *He is forcing his Beast down,* though Jürgen. *I cannot allow that, either. If he can think, who knows what unholy sorcery he might produce?* He plunged his sword into Nikita's shoulder and spun the Tzimisce around to face him. He locked eyes with his foe and bared his bloodied fangs, at the same time willing his arm to bleed, to heal.

This had the desired effect. Nikita howled in hunger and lunged at the Sword-Bearer. Jürgen barely managed to raise his sword in enough time to deflect Nikita's attack. Gotzon, fortunately, did not falter, but drove his sword into the Tzimisce's back and pulled downward. Jürgen knew that no Cainite could feel pain while under the Beast's sway, but he was certain that Nikita felt that wound. He saw a chunk of the archbishop's rib fly free and land on Sir Thomas's body.

Nikita rounded on Gotzon and wrenched the sword from his hands, bending the blade double in the process. Jürgen had never seen his confessor look shocked before, but the Lasombra's brows furrowed—he, like Jürgen, hadn't expected such power from Nikita of Sredetz. Nikita didn't slow in his assault, but lunged like a serpent, seizing Gotzon's hand and pulling it towards his mouth. His wounds were not healing—Jürgen could see a fist-sized hole on the left side of Nikita's back where Gotzon had carved away on his ribs.

Just above his heart.

Gotzon winced as Nikita clamped down on his hand. He looked to Jürgen for help, but Jürgen was scanning the room again, looking for a torch, a broom—anything made from wood.

The long furrow on Nikita's back began to close. Gotzon reached back and punched Nikita in the forehead, but only succeeded in knocking them both back a few feet.

Jürgen dove across the room to the entrance, meaning to ask his knights to fetch something made of wood, but he stopped. His Beast growled encouragement, but he couldn't leave this fight, this room, until his foe was vanquished. He looked outside the room and saw the glow of the sun from around the corner, and remembered how insignificant it had seemed before.

He had made an oath to himself, he realized. If he left the room now, his Beast would leap on that broken oath like a wolf on a spring lamb, and he might well collapse into sleep.

"Jürgen." Gotzon's voice, but it had a waver to it that Jürgen had never heard. His confessor was losing vitae, and could not free his hand from the savage grip. Jürgen turned and prepared to launch himself at Nikita, cursing his luck at having to give up the advantage.

His foot struck Thomas's body. He could smell sweat and offal from the poor knight's corpse, and it reminded him of when Thomas had interrupted him and Rosamund outside Geidas's domain....

Jürgen lunged downward and tore open Thomas's mantle. There, around his neck, was the wooden cross he had seen that night. "Thank you, Thomas," he whispered, and pulled the cross from its leather string.

Gotzon had fallen to his knees. Jürgen didn't know when his confessor had last fed, but did know that he fed only rarely. He wouldn't have much blood to give to Nikita, but he also wouldn't survive long under such an assault.

Jürgen snapped the cross into two jagged pieces and moved behind the archbishop. The wound Gotzon had made was closing rapidly; in another few seconds, it would be gone, and Jürgen would never be able to pierce Nikita's skin with this tiny chunk of wood. He raised it above his head with both hands and shoved downward, aiming for Nikita's foul heart.

Nikita arched his back as Jürgen's attack landed. Jürgen felt bones give under his fists, but still the archbishop moved. Gotzon, now free, rolled away and staggered to his feet. Nikita tried to round on Jürgen, but stumbled. Jürgen stayed behind him. He could still feel the wooden shard in his hands, but was afraid to withdraw it.

Nikita started to straighten again. The frenzy was ending.

Jürgen raised the shard again and brought it down lightning quick. This time, he felt it strike flesh, thick, sinewy flesh.

The wall of Nikita's unbeating heart.

Nikita collapsed forward, the tiny shard of wood already

paralyzing him. Jürgen grabbed his shoulders and pulled, dropping him onto his back. Jürgen noticed with fascination that Nikita's lips were still moving.

"The Dream is dying," he said in Greek, and then lay still.

Chapter Thirty-Two

"Doing the Lord's work, Jürgen?"

Gotzon had refused to feed on the monks at first, but blood had won over asceticism. He had taken his fill from one of the brothers and now stood in front of the Sword-Bearer, his face as stoic as ever.

"I should hope so, Gotzon."

"Then why have you not put him to the torch, or taken his head?"

Jürgen had ordered that Nikita of Sredetz be kept immobile. He had ordered his knights to pound a much larger stake through the archbishop's heart, and had then collapsed into sleep. Gotzon must have as well, otherwise he probably would have dispatched Nikita himself.

The Sword-Bearer glanced at his confessor with irritation. "While I don't wish to seem ungrateful, Gotzon, my decisions in war are my own. When I am certain that this fiend holds no use for me undead, I will kill him, but not before."

Gotzon's expression didn't change. "You lost a favored knight and a childe in battle with this foe." He didn't say *and very nearly your confessor as well*, but he didn't need to. "It's dangerous to leave him like this."

Jürgen stood up from the abbot's desk. "Is there something about Nikita you wish to tell me, Gotzon, or have you said your piece?"

Gotzon narrowed his eyes at Jürgen, but did not respond for a long moment. Finally, he shook his head. "No, Jürgen. I have nothing to tell you of him."

Jürgen sat again. "Very well, then. I'll hear no more of it."

Even Jürgen couldn't really explain why Nikita was still extant in any form other than ash and war poetry, but he was quite certain that he didn't want the Archbishop of Nod dead quite yet. Nikita could potentially tell him much of the Cainite Heresy (which should have interested Gotzon as well), to say nothing of the *Voivodate* and the fiends in general. Really, though, Jürgen felt that not killing him allowed him to savor the hard-won victory even more.

Or is it, Jürgen thought, *that I know I would have lost without Gotzon's help? That leaving Nikita intact means my victory is incomplete—but I therefore do not owe anything to my confessor for his help?* He shook off the thought. Honor was honor, and no true Scion left a debt unpaid. He had thanked Gotzon as much as Gotzon would expect to be thanked, but had no intention of brooking any liberties from the Lasombra.

The two of them stood there outside the shattered door of the monastery, staring out into the forest. They had heard wolves earlier, and Jürgen wondered inwardly if the howls were born of natural animals.

"What will you do now, Gotzon?" He didn't expect his confessor to tell him any of his plans, but he always asked.

"The Lord's work, Jürgen." Gotzon did not move, merely stared out into the snowy woods. "There are still demons here. Witches, and those ignorant pagans who labor under them."

Jürgen glanced over at the Lasombra, but Gotzon didn't budge. "Witches?" He received no response. "Would these be the 'Telyavs' that Jervais spoke of? I understood he destroyed them all."

Gotzon's head moved side to side so slightly that it might have been a trick of the light. "You believe a Tremere?"

"I—"

"You sin, Jürgen, by keeping him as close as you do."

Jürgen ground his teeth. "Should I behead Jervais, then, because he violates God's law?"

"Should I follow man's law rather than God's, because it is convenient?" Gotzon's eyes still had not left the trees. "Should I claim domain over a city, plunge it into darkness, and command the kine therein to follow my whims? Should I send out my shadow to collect tribute in souls and libations of sweet blood?"

Jürgen turned his body to face Gotzon, curiosity vying with rage in his heart. This was perhaps the most he had ever heard his confessor say at once. "Kindly remember, Gotzon, that you gave me the choice. The Cross or the Crown, yes? I have never regretted my choice."

"Even in the face of losing a childe and a loyal knight?"

Jürgen glanced past Gotzon. He could see several Knights of the Black Cross still attempting to dig graves for those who had fallen in the siege. They had managed to dig one grave—for Thomas—but the hard, frozen earth held its virtue jealously. "I have lost more than—"

Gotzon turned to face him. "The choice we gave you was a travesty. I know that now, but back then I was as a child pretending to his father's wisdom. There *is* no choice—you do God's work or you burn." The Lasombra's eyes deepened, and the murk therein began to move. The lifeless energy of the void began to seep from his eyes like hideous, inky tears, and the moonlight and shadows both fled the area, leaving a nimbus of color and perception that could scarcely be called "light."

Jürgen took a step back. If Gotzon were to attack him, he was unsure how effectively he could defend himself. "Am I to burn, then, Gotzon? Or will you summon up shadows to take me?"

Gotzon stopped and shut his eyes, and light and shadow made peace and returned. "After all I have told you, you know nothing," he said quietly.

Jürgen's lips curled into a sneer before he could stop them.

Ordinarily, Gotzon wouldn't have bother responding to this, but something was different tonight. "You know nothing," he repeated. "You know nothing of shadows and fear."

Jürgen's eyes narrowed. "Don't insult me, Gotzon, and don't belittle me. The Beast howls within me as it must within you."

Gotzon's eyes glimmered like onyx under candlelight, and the corners of his mouth twitched. It was closer than Jürgen had ever seen him come to smiling. "The Beast, Jürgen? My Beast fled in fear before what I have seen, centuries ago." He turned back to the forest. "The Beast, that howling *thing* that drives you on the battlefield to take the blood from every throat, the life from every heart? My Beast is afraid to speak for fear of awakening what dwells beside it within me."

Jürgen was silent. He wanted with all his heart to contradict his confessor, to belittle his words with stories of his own terrors and battles with the Beast, but he knew that nothing he had seen could compare.

"Did you have nightmares as a mortal man, Jürgen? Did you ever awaken from one and fear to move from your bed, because although you knew you were safe, you also knew that the things from your nightmares still waited?"

Jürgen shifted a bit. "Yes, I suppose so."

"I brought my nightmares to life, Jürgen. They wait behind every shadow, in every glass, in every pool, and my reflection no longer blocks my view. You remember the sensation, Jürgen, of dreading to open a door in a nightmare because of what you might find? I *know* what waits, and the nightmare doesn't end.

"*You* know nothing," he said, and walked off into the snow.

Jürgen watched as his confessor vanished into the trees. He heard the howls again and feared for Gotzon's safety, but he knew better than to act on those fears. Gotzon did as he would, and had been doing so for longer than Jürgen could imagine. If the wolves were to find him tonight, Jürgen could only hope that Gotzon gave them the mercy of a quick death.

Jürgen turned and walked back into the monastery, mentally cursing himself for his rudeness. He knew now what Gotzon had seen in those shadows centuries ago, what the *koldun* were capable of doing. Nikita should be Gotzon's kill, not Jürgen's. He had ordered Nikita's body moved to the abbot's office and stashed under a windowsill. The light never touched the body during the day, but it came within a few short inches; Jürgen hoped that the proximity to the light would keep the archbishop safely in slumber. He knew that, with a stake in his heart, Nikita was paralyzed—but Nikita had surprised him once too often already.

Two knights guarded the door. Jürgen dismissed them. He entered the room and shut the door behind him. A tiny sliver of moonlight from the window revealed only an oddly shaped lump on the floor; it could have been clothing but for the huge chunk of wood sticking up out of it.

Jürgen stepped up to it and drew his sword. "I swore I would take your head, Nikita," he whispered. He brought the sword down on the archbishop's neck...

...and stopped a bare inch above it.

Gotzon had spoken, if indirectly, of following the proper laws regardless of expectations. But what, indeed, was proper here?

Nikita of Sredetz had many enemies, to be sure. Dispatching him would mean that those enemies would be well-disposed towards Jürgen and the Fiefs of the Black Cross. Or, perhaps those enemies would loathe Jürgen for robbing them of their chances to kill the archbishop? Would destroying Nikita bring retribution down upon Hardestadt in Germany? Upon Rosamund, so close to Jürgen, yet far enough away that he could not protect her? Perhaps even upon her own sire and clan in France... Jürgen sheathed his sword and sat at the abbot's desk.

The Tzimisce were not normally supporters of the Cainite Heresy, but they did tend to look after those of their own blood. Destroying Nikita would inflame the blood-war between Ventrue and Tzimisce. It might also cement relations between Tremere and Ventrue....

Jürgen shook his head in disgust. *Relationships between my clan and the sorcerers?* He had suffered Jervais in Magdeburg badly; one of the few things he agreed with the Tzimisce in general upon was that the Tremere were untrustworthy and should never be allowed any measure of true authority. Killing Nikita would drive a wedge between the Black Cross and any Cainite power who had ever allied with the Tzimisce, and that list was longer than Jürgen cared to consider.

Another blood-war, he thought. Such an undertaking, if his power here were certain, would be much to his liking. But it wasn't—establishing himself as Cainite lord of these lands would require months, if not years, of study, effort and war against any native forces in the savage forests. Killing Nikita would simply draw too many enemies. But then, what to do with him? Allowing Gotzon to destroy him was another possibility, but one that he would rather consider in a larger city. In Magdeburg, word would spread quickly that someone had killed a prisoner without Jürgen's consent, but here in God's nowhere, that distinction wouldn't be made.

Jürgen stared down at his captive. Nikita's face was set in the same pained scowl it had taken on when Jürgen had driven the shard of wood into his heart. And yet, the face looked somehow different, as thought the lips had curled upwards an infinitesimal fraction of an inch....

Jürgen looked away. *I cannot kill him, and I cannot keep him here.* His Beast whimpered in fear and reminded Jürgen what Nikita had done to his wrists. The Beast urged him to kill the Tzimisce, burn him, set him out for the sun, take his blood, something, anything, just make sure that the nightmare that was Nikita never troubled them again. Jürgen refused, and buried the fear.

I can use him. I can send him as a message to an enemy, someone who would fear to awaken him but know what it means that I delivered him. Jürgen smiled. The recipient would have to be a Tzimisce; another of Nikita's clan might well understand what Jürgen had gone through to best the archbishop. But who? It certainly couldn't be Rustovitch; the so-called *voivode* of *voivodes* would take it as a challenge and begin the blood-war that Jürgen wanted to avoid. Visya, through his childe in Bistritz? No, Radu was too obscure a figure, and besides, he wanted that particular branch of the Tzimisce clan to continue its dealings with the Arpad Ventrue. He needed someone intelligent but careful, powerful but not a true power in the War of Princes. He looked down again, but this time his eyes came to rest on the archbishop's hand. The palm was smooth, flawless, like a child's, so different from Jürgen's callused paw. The Tzimisce could make themselves beautiful in moments; other clans were stuck with their mortal shells. He wondered how many Tzimisce he had seen disguised behind veils of flesh.

He wondered how many Tzimisce diplomats stole their visages from beautiful village boys, pretty Eastern lasses, nobility long since dead, their features preserved by undead ingenuity.

He wondered about this, and then the answer hit him. He knew of the perfect fiend to receive his gift.

Vykos.

Chapter Thirty-Three

Jürgen, despite his misgivings—or, honestly, fears—about Nikita remaining in the monastery, allowed his knights to finish burial of their brothers before setting them to building a casket for the archbishop. It took a full week for the burials to be complete (owing more to the hard, frozen ground than the number of casualties) and even then they wouldn't be truly done until a priest could say Mass for the dead.

Jürgen imagined that one of the monks had been ordained, but rather doubted that he could persuade a prisoner to say a Mass for the knights. They wouldn't have accepted it, anyway.

The casket for Nikita took another two weeks to build. The wood of this land was no more yielding than the frozen earth, and the knights refused to leave the monastery after dark without direct orders. Jürgen didn't blame them. One of the knights—a careful, constant man named Bertolt—was a superb hunter and tracker. He told Jürgen that wolf tracks surrounded the monastery and grew more numerous with each passing dawn.

Jürgen took this at least partially as good news. At least the wolves were *leaving* tracks. He couldn't fool himself, however, into ignoring the probable significance of this development. It was possible that these wolves were natural animals, attracted by the smell of flesh from the corpses interred in the earth around the monastery. Perhaps the scent of burning flesh (for Jürgen had ordered the slain monks burnt, rather than waste the knights' valuable time and energy burying them) had even attracted them from greater distances. But he had heard tales of the pagan tribes and their Gangrel patrons, of the feral Cainites who stalked these forests, and he knew they could walk as wolves. He also knew that they could enslave normal wolves, and had heard tell that they made pacts with the cursed Lupines, the men who took the skins of wolves and made vows to Satan in exchange for shape-changing power.

His knights did well to fear the howls at night, Jürgen knew. But he feared Nikita more, and with every passing night, he dreaded walking down the long hallway to the abbot's rooms. He dreamed daily that he would find that room awash in gore, that the archbishop would take the blood of the two ghouls assigned to guard him and then leap on Jürgen as a wave of vitae, dissolving him, consuming him, becoming him.

Tonight, Jürgen sat in the former scriptorium watching the knights sleep. The casket, currently housed in the dining hall, was nearly finished. The trick now was keeping Nikita's body secure en route to Vykos. While he couldn't know for certain, he imagined that Vykos was probably lurking in Brasov, but even knowing where Vykos was he still faced the thorny problem of not having enough knights to send on such a potentially dangerous mission.

Shaking off that problem for a moment, Jürgen pored over the latest message he'd received from Jovirdas. The Tzimisce seemed to be holding his end of the bargain quite well; he had been sending supplies and men along as promised, allowing Jürgen to send some of his troops back to Kybartai occasionally. He always rewarded men who traveled to the monastery with a healthy drink of his blood from the chalice, both to strengthen them for the trying nights ahead and to reinforce the blood oath to him, for although Jovirdas *seemed* to be upholding his end of their agreement, Jürgen could not forget that, on the night he had bested Nikita, someone had broken a promise to him.

He read Jovirdas's letter again, looking for any signs of betrayal. The letter was brief and to the point; the only informal matter it discussed was the Letters of Acindynus, and Jovirdas only mentioned the topic to inform Jürgen that he would be sending the letters with the next knights to venture to the monastery. The Tzimisce had found them fascinating, and had in fact asked permission to make a copy when and if time allowed.

Along with Jovirdas's letter was one from Rosamund. Jürgen had not read it yet, for it was the first one he'd seen since he'd left her behind at the fort. He was surprised that she had taken so long to write; she was normally verbose and the fact that he had sent a sincere (if admittedly somewhat brief) note for her back with the first knight he'd sent to Jovirdas should have driven her to write immediately. But she had not, and that only made him worry more. Had she betrayed him? Was the broken oath he had heard hers?

He could peer into her mind even now, even at this distance, and yet he dared not. He dared it not for the same reason that he feared to look in on Nikita's torpid body. He feared to open the door, lest he find himself in a nightmare, just as his confessor had said. His Beast laughed at that fear, and with a snarl he grabbed Rosamund's letter and broke the seal.

Jürgen read the letter at first with anxiety, then with sorrow. She was not angry with him for his brief letter, but had been in mourning for Thomas and had not been able to summon the words. Plus, she had been helping Jovirdas read the Letters—apparently, his literacy had improved dramatically in the last month. She did not ask about the siege of the monastery nor about Nikita, though since Raoul had undoubtedly heard details from his fellow knights by now, Rosamund surely wasn't wanting for information on the subject.

Her final paragraphs read:

I know that you are a soldier, and knew when you left that you would be away some time. But has it only been six weeks? Not even two turnings of the moon, not so long to mortal time and an eyeblink to us? Shall we be apart for years or decades, watching the mortals around us grow old? Shall we meet again as young and strong as we were when we parted?

Will you remember me, and what we shared before you left? Do you remember now? I assure you that I do, and I think of it nightly, as the eastern side of my room grows warmer and I hear the mortals stir before blackness and silence claim me.

My lord, when can I join you? I can do much here, and I know that, but I could do much by your side as well. Though I am no warrior, I am a Scion, and I am of your kind if not of your blood. If it please you, write quickly and allow me to join you at the monastery. Jovirdas tells me he is finished with the Letters; perhaps we can read them together again. Perhaps I can simply be of company, but I am certain that you have other needs than company that I can meet.

I await your response. Though the days grow longer and the season changes around me, the only change in the world that matters is seeing you again."

Yours,
Rosamund

Jürgen read the letter again several more times, finally simply running his hand down the parchment and feeling the texture of the ink beneath his fingers. *The only change in the world that matters is seeing you again.* Jürgen reflected again that a force that could change a Cainite was mighty indeed, and longed to feel that force again.

He placed the letter carefully aside and began to study the maps of the area. He needed a way to find Vykos; again, while he could simply find his mind with a moment's concentration, he did not wish to give anything away by such tactics. He relished the image of Vykos's shock when he opened the casket and saw Nikita before him. He smiled at the thought, absently, staring at the wall of the scriptorium.

"Something amuses my lord?"

Wolfgang stood at the door, about to wake the next knight for the watch. "Nothing I think you'd understand, Wolfgang," murmured Jürgen.

Perhaps I can simply be of company, the letter had said. Jürgen had not spoken to another Cainite since Gotzon had left. Václav had been the only one he had taken with him from Kybartai. Jürgen hadn't needed much incentive to invite her here, and this realization—the knowledge that no other thinking being in his immediate area could truly understand him—was enough to set his hand to writing. Jürgen picked up a fresh piece of parchment and sharpened his quill.

My dear Rosamund...

Chapter Thirty-Four

"Dawn is coming, my lord."

Jürgen glanced up from his maps to see Friederich standing in the doorway. Jürgen had taken over the abbot's rooms as his own, after making certain the window was securely blocked. Nikita rested in his casket outside of the monastery, between the burial ground and the pile of bone and ash that constituted the remains of the monks.

"I suppose winter couldn't last forever." Jürgen frowned. The days were growing longer, meaning his ghoul knights would become even more important. He had considered granting the Embrace to one of them—Bertolt, perhaps, or even Friederich himself—but at present he needed his forces to be strongest by day. "Inform the men that tomorrow they shall drink from the chalice."

"Yes, my lord." He turned to go.

"Has an envoy from Kybartai been sighted?"

Friederich shook his head. "No, my lord. I could send a scout farther from the monastery to see if…"

"No need. They probably won't arrive by night, anyway." He nodded at the knight to dismiss him and went back to his own thoughts.

Having the men drink from the chalice was risky. It required Jürgen to feed heavily, and while enough of the monks survived for the ritual to take place, it would probably kill the last of them. And yet, if he did not give the gift of his own vitae to his knights, they would lose their strength and their devotion in short order.

A hunter must leave his home in the harshest winter if he is to eat, thought Jürgen. *If I am to survive here, I must find prey as well.* He had spent too long worrying about his "message" to Vykos, combing through maps and sending out scouts to other settlements to find the best routes. Jürgen considered simply sending the archbishop to a closer monastery, but if the brothers there inadvertently exposed him to the sun or (worse) removed the stake from his heart, the effect would be lost.

Nikita could wait, Jürgen decided. It was time to make war once again, before the days grew so long that he would be incapable of going to battle. But upon whom?

He had assumed that the Obertus order had been a pillar of support for Rustovitch, since Vykos was technically his subordinate. If Jürgen was to claim territory here, he would need to knock out any of the other supports that Rustovitch was using. He suspected that sending Nikita to Vykos would send a clear enough message. Vykos probably wouldn't risk freeing the archbishop, for fear of his unlife, and if he did, Jürgen would be more prepared for Nikita next time.

The Obertus order had other monasteries in the area, of course, but Jürgen was unsure of the necessity of attacking them *and* sending the archbishop to Vykos. It might be seen as overkill, as zealotry that Jürgen did not wish to exhibit. *But who, then, is left?*

He knew from Jervais that the beast that had slain Alexander had allies here, allies that performed arcane rituals in sacred groves, but according to the Tremere, their leader had been destroyed. Going after them would be pointless, simply a waste of resources. *Let those Telyavs die out along with their pagan peoples,* Jürgen thought dismissively.

His Beast snarled in disagreement. It demanded that he hunt those beings down and take the blood of their human followers, burn their blasphemous groves and reduce them to dust.

Jürgen paused, and for once decided he'd listen to his Beast, after a fashion.

Rustovitch was a Scion—perhaps not a proper one, perhaps following some debased version of the *Via Regalis,* but a Scion nonetheless. He would take whatever advantage he could, using the Obertus monks one night and the Telyavs the next. The

Gangrel of the forest, one of whom had slain Alexander, might patronize the Telyavs and their people, but Jürgen very much doubted that Rustovitch received no tribute or boon from them. *It makes sense for the pagans, anyway,* thought Jürgen, *to choose the devil they know over "invaders" like Alexander... and myself.*

Jürgen wrote a letter to a knight of the Teutonic Order. If von Salza had stuck to his original travel plans, they shouldn't be too far away from the monastery at present. Jürgen didn't have the manpower to send Nikita's casket to Vykos *and* launch any kind of assault, but he knew that at least seven members of the Order of the Black Cross were traveling with von Salza. That should be enough to destroy the fragmented Telyavs... if he could find them.

Jürgen stood and left the offices. He heard the knights saying their prayers, some rising to greet the day, others bedding down after a night watch. Jürgen insisted that the monastery be guarded as if it could be attacked at any moment.

He left the monastery and walked out onto the grounds. The snow was melting and the earth was growing softer beneath his feet. He walked to the edge of the trees and looked down at the ground; he could see tracks from various animals. Wolves, deer, rodents. He wasn't the tracker that Bertolt was, but he could see this forest teemed with life.

And all of it useless to me, he thought. *Except perhaps the wolves.*

He walked back towards the monastery, wishing that he could sleep somewhere else today. He felt sleep tug at his senses, and for a moment, just a moment, he wondered about the sleep of ages, wondered whether he should simply fall into torpor and awaken in some new era, with new enemies to fight, new blood to spill.

Ridiculous, of course, he realized. Such thoughts were for old Cainites, those so out of touch with the world and the mortals that they fed on that they could not relate to anyone but others of their age... but others of their age were more often plotting against them than exchanging reminisces. Jürgen wasn't so old as that, even as many wars and years as he'd seen.

But slaughtering monks? Even given the horrific battle with Nikita's creature and then the archbishop himself, the battle hadn't been what he'd wanted. He would rather have fought in the outdoors, in the open, where he could truly revel in the glory of battle. It seemed a sin to do it indoors, monastery or not.

He heard something in the forest and immediately gave a shrill whistle. Four knights rushed to his side. Jürgen listened, sharpening his hearing to what was coming.

Whatever it was, it was wounded. It stumbled and walked irregularly, bumping into trees, falling, but continuing on its way as though being chased.

Chased?

Jürgen listened more closely and heard the pursuers as well. But they weren't men. "Wolves," he whispered. "Wolves are chasing something towards us."

"A hart?" The knight who asked sounded fearful, and Jürgen didn't blame him.

"I don't think so. Wolves wouldn't chase a hart towards the smell of fire." He cocked his head again. "Besides, their prey is running on two legs." One of the knights stepped forward as though to enter the woods. Jürgen stopped him. "No. It could be a decoy, and in any case, if we intercept the wolves' prey we join it. We will wait—the victim is heading straight for us."

The knights spread out, drawing weapons. Others came to join them. Jürgen stood still, sword still sheathed, listening to the man running in the woods. He was close enough that Jürgen could hear his breath coming in ragged gasps, and could hear something splattering to the ground around the man. Sweat? Blood, more likely. Jürgen's Beast stirred, but he only shook his head helplessly. The man was no enemy of Jürgen, no prisoner of war, and so that blood would go to waste.

The man broke into a run. The wolves did likewise. Some of the knights gasped; they could see flashes of movement in the trees.

The man burst through the trees into the clearing. Jürgen had enough time to register that he was wearing the mantle of a Sword-Brother before the wolves broke the clearing.

Jürgen gave a quick rallying cry and his soldiers fell back, making a defensive circle around the man. The wolves closed in on them, and Jürgen peered at the animals, searching for a human mind within them. To his relief, he found only one—a huge, gray wolf with red, gleaming eyes and a bloodied snout. While the other wolves sported the dull, featureless haloes of true animals, this one crackled with violets and reds... but pale, bloodless.

Jürgen stepped out of the cluster of men towards the Gangrel. The wolves, sensing the power of the Sword-Bearer, flanked their leader. Jürgen glared down at the undead wolf and bared his fangs in challenge.

The natural wolves—probably battened on the Gangrel's blood—snarled and snapped at Jürgen, but their vampiric alpha didn't move. Jürgen locked eyes with him and hissed, "Become a man."

The wolf took a step back, but did not change. He looked over the monastery grounds and past Jürgen at the wooden casket, and then back at Jürgen.

Jürgen heard sound from the road, off to his left. The envoy from Kybartai had arrived... and that meant Rosamund.

He leaped forward and kicked one of the wolves hard enough to splinter its skull. Another bit his leg, but Jürgen grabbed it by the scruff of the neck and threw it against a tree. The other wolves backed off, snarling. The Gangrel glanced at them, probably trying to retain control, but as Jürgen advanced, they retreated into the trees.

The envoy was now in view. The Gangrel glanced over Jürgen's shoulder; Jürgen had no need to do so. He could hear her footsteps on the muddied ground, smell her hair, feel the bond between them.

He drew his sword and struck at the wolf. It dodged to one side easily, but did not attack.

From behind him, Jürgen heard one of the knights say, "He's dying. He's been bitten."

"Good God, will he change?" another asked.

If he dies, thought Jürgen, *I shall have to rely on reading the memories of his clothing to see what happened to him.* Grimacing, Jürgen slashed at the wolf again. He fought the urge to look back at Rosamund, to see her running towards him.

The wolf tensed, as if to spring, and then backed away. It

bared its teeth to Jürgen, and then turned and ran off into the forest. Jürgen listened for a few seconds to make sure it wasn't doubling back, and then turned to see her.

She stood near the casket, mud from the ground staining her dress. He sheathed his sword and opened his arms, wanting nothing more than to hold her. *That is what I wanted*, he thought. *Those arms could hold me against torpor and time, could—*

"My lord?" Friederich looked up at him. Jürgen's head snapped downwards, away from his lady. "This man is dying."

Jürgen crouched next to the injured knight. His left arm had been savaged and he was soaked in blood. He would surely die within a moment. He began to whisper in a language Jürgen did not understand, and then his eyes focused and he saw the knights' mantles. "Save me," he whispered in Latin.

Jürgen closed his eyes. "The chalice, Friederich."

"Sir?"

"Chalice, boy! The rest of you leave. Take Lady Rosamund and the others from the envoy inside."

Friederich pulled the chalice from the pouch at his side and handed it to Jürgen. "Lift his head up," he instructed. Friederich did so. Jürgen leaned down to whisper to the man. "You were brought low by demons, my friend." The knight's eyes widened. "But you have another chance, if you devote yourself to fighting against those demons. If you swear loyalty to the Black Cross and to me."

Friederich's eyes grew wide. He had never seen anyone come fully under the Black Cross before, of course. Jürgen wondered if the chalice-bearer harbored desires to do so himself. "I don't understand," whispered the dying knight.

"I have no time to explain. You must choose. You may die and be taken into Heaven... but understand, no priest is here to hear your sins or to say your Mass." The man looked about to cry. "Or, you may come unto the Black Cross and do the Lord's work on Earth, forever, as a soldier to God and to me."

The Cross or the Crown, thought Jürgen. *Am I giving him the same choice, in a way? Go to Heaven or stay here with me? But would he go to Heaven? Has he sins on his head?*

The man's lips moved, but no sound came forth. Finally, he choked, "You."

Friederich's face was a combination of terror and fascination. Jürgen leaned down and bit into the man's throat, taking the rest of his blood. The taste was foul, unclean—Jürgen could take no sustenance from a man who was not his enemy, but if the knight had blood remaining in his body, the Embrace might not work. Jürgen bit his wrist and filled the chalice with his blood, and then lifted the cup to the knight's lips. The knight drank, swallowed, and then was still.

Friederich's brow furrowed in confusion. "But I thought—"

"Wait," said Jürgen.

The knight's eyes fluttered open. His back arched and his arm, still mangled and useless, began to flex. His eyes deepened in color from the light brown they had been to a rich, dark mahogany and dilated as if in response to a blinding light. He began to thrash in pain, and Jürgen pulled Friederich up to standing to avoid him being injured.

"What's happening, my lord?" whispered the chalice-bearer.

Jürgen shook his head. "The Becoming, Friederich. This knight made his choice, and now has seen the Black Cross." The knight tried to stand, but failed. His mouth opened in a silent wail of pain, and Jürgen saw the fangs extending past his lip. "The revelation is never easy."

Chapter Thirty-Five

Rosamund and Jürgen sat together in the monastery, in one of the cells, so as to afford them some privacy. Jürgen had already ordered his men to make it as comfortable as possible; he intended to let her sleep here while he continued his practice of sleeping with the men in the scriptorium.

They sat there as dawn stalked nearer the monastery. Several times, Jürgen had thought that he should leave—he should tend to his new childe, currently in prayer with the other knights. He should return to the scriptorium before sleep overcame him and he would have to stumble in like a drunkard, rather than striding in confidently.

But staring at her, he found he could not. He found he felt like a man reunited with his lover, not like a soldier on the front lines of a war.

"My lord, your thoughts?"

Jürgen smiled. "Do you know, my lady, that I cannot recall the last time I heard you say my name?"

Rosamund lowered her eyes. "Would it be proper for me to use it?"

"I promise, if it is indeed an impropriety, I shall not think less of you, nor shall I tell anyone of it." Jürgen watched her carefully, but she showed no signs of discomfort. Instead, she leaned over to him and whispered gently into his ear.

"I missed you, Jürgen."

Jürgen shut his eyes, and he felt the soldier slip a little further away from the man. His mouth opened, and then shut—he wasn't sure what to say. He could tell her of wars he was planning, but that seemed distant and frankly offensive to him now.

He could tell her of his battlefield Embrace earlier, for although wolves and not soldiers had killed the young man, those wolves had acted under direct orders.

Instead, he told her a truth. "And I you, Rosamund."

He kissed her, and the soldier departed entirely. His Beast yowled in protest, reminding him of blood, war and metal, but the soldier was gone, and the man who remained didn't care about such things. He kissed her deeply, and felt the hunger-that-was-not-hunger rise up again. *Love,* he thought. *We can love, we can love each other, even if no Cainite can ever love a living human, we can—*

But someone had betrayed him, and he did not know whom.

Jürgen broke the kiss, a little more abruptly than he'd meant to. Rosamund's face was hurt, soft and lovely in the candlelight, but Jürgen's was hard and critical again. He saw recognition in her eyes, and he studied that expression, trying to decide if it was simply her noticing his change of heart or if something lurked deeper. The soldier returned, quietly, without spite or malice, and Jürgen let it happen. There was still a war to win.

"My lord?" she said, and Jürgen looked away.

"Rosamund," he said, "I wish to ask something of you."

"Yes?" Jürgen heard hope in her voice.

"I wish to look into your thoughts. You know I am loath to do this to any Cainite, most of all you, but I have my reasons. May I do so?"

Jürgen did not look at her. He did not wish to see her face as she thought it over, but he could imagine the pain in her eyes. He knew her thoughts already—she wondered if the second drink had meant nothing, wondered if their time apart had changed him.

It has, my love.

Finally, she said, "You may."

Jürgen stood, unsteadily—dawn was breaking. He took her hands and kissed them both. "I have no need to look, then," he said.

"But you felt the need to ask?"

He nodded, unsure of how to broach the topic. "I have an errand for you, my lady," he said. "A dangerous one, and one

that I wish with all my heart I could entrust to someone else."
He thought of Brenner, hanging in his cell talking of sires and
elders and how they sent vassals to destruction. *But she is not
my vassal, she is...* He didn't finish the thought. "I wish you to
deliver the casket outside."

Rosamund nodded slowly. "To whom?"

Jürgen met her gaze. "To Vykos," he said evenly. "In Brasov."

Rosamund didn't respond, and Jürgen could see she was
trying to decide his reasons for this request. She would realize,
he knew, that he was not simply trying to protect her from the
battles to come—the mission he had asked of her was just as
dangerous, and required leaving the area for a long period of
time as well. Would she assume it was a test of trust, then? A
way to get her out of the way?

Those assumptions wouldn't do. Jürgen needed her to know
why he was sending her.

"My lady, you are the best suited for this task. No matter
what Vykos truly is, no matter how much a monster, you can
make him see the power that the Black Cross wields. You can
convince him not to revive the archbishop, and you can escape
unharmed." He took her hand, and she smiled gently. "I know
you can. I have seen what your words can do."

"But then how long will I be gone? How long until—"

"Months. Maybe more." He nodded sadly. "I know. But
when you see me again, I promise I will not be old and gray."
She laughed quietly, he smiled. "And moreover, I promise I will
hold greater lands—" he stopped. It sounded like a boast, like a
braggart's wooing. "I promise I will still..." He searched for the
words. "Still be yours," he said, wishing he was the poet that
Rosamund deserved.

Chapter Thirty-Six

Jürgen walked to the scriptorium, and found Friederich outside the door. He felt for the note he had written earlier, meaning to find a courier to take it to von Salza's camp, but stopped. His new childe sat inside the scriptorium, staring at the floor, lips moving. Jürgen heard no sound, not even a whisper of breath. He looked towards the chalice bearer quizzically.

"He came in from praying a short while ago, my lord," said Friederich. "He's been there ever since." Jürgen nodded. "You said the revelation was not easy, but—"

"It isn't, Friederich. And once you have seen the Black Cross, there is no way back." Friederich swallowed hard and Jürgen walked past him into the room. He pulled a chair next to the knight and sat down. "What is your name, my childe?"

The man looked up sharply. *Good*, thought Jürgen. *At least he hasn't completely lost his senses.* "How am I your child, sir?"

Jürgen nodded. "A fair question, but one I do not have sufficient time to answer tonight. We must sleep soon."

The knight shook his head. "I do not breathe or bleed, and bread makes me ill; why should I need sleep?"

"You don't," answered Jürgen. "Not in the same way you once did. Think of it less as sleep and more as time owed to God for your continued life on Earth."

"I am alive, then?"

Jürgen chuckled dryly. "No, that's true. Your 'existence' on Earth, then." The knight was astute; that was good. If he had Embraced an idiot, he would have been very put out. "Your name, then?"

"Favst."

"Favst," Jürgen repeated, trying to pronounce the strange word. "What does it mean?"

The knight smiled and a tiny red tear came to his eye. "It means 'lucky,' sir."

Jürgen shook his head. "It may well be that the name fits, Favst. You survived an attack by those wolves—do you remember me telling you that they were demons?"

"I knew that they were, sir."

Jürgen fought the urge to correct him and instead asked, "How?"

"I have seen much worse than those wolves. I saw my brothers murdered by men who did not breathe, nor bleed, nor die when sword met flesh. I saw them call out to the forest, and I saw the wolves answer them. I saw wolves *eating* men." He tried to cough into his hand, but could not. Jürgen sympathized— mortals had easy ways to express emotions. Cainites only had the Beast. "I saw women who raised their hands and called up," and here he spoke a word that Jürgen did not understand, but just as quickly crossed himself and whispered, "Father, forgive me."

"What did the women call up, Favst?"

"I dare not say. I only know that I succumbed to cowardice and fled, and I have been running ever since. The wolves found me only tonight, and only savaged my arm. I stabbed one but lost my sword, and then ran." Favst clutched at a cross around his neck and quavered.

Jürgen reached down and lifted the knight's chin. "*Deus vult*, Favst. God wills it. Surely you fled because He wished you to find us, to find those who could avenge your brothers. You have come under the Black Cross now, and demons have no power over us."

"Because we *are* demons?"

Jürgen smiled, careful to retract his fangs first. "God moves in ways that you cannot be asked to comprehend—even I, who have done His will for centuries, am often mystified at the gifts He chooses to give us. We are not demons, we are simply changed, and I do not pretend to have all of the answers as to the extent of the change." He grimaced. "Lord knows that there are scholars among us who play at those games."

Favst relaxed slightly, but still wore a look of desperation. "But then no one knows—"

"How we go on for hundreds of years without aging? Why we must drink the blood of others to survive? Why we sleep at dawn, will we or no? No, no one *knows*. Some of us choose to wallow in self-pity, calling themselves damned while others pretend to exaltation. I know this—not once in my time after the Embrace have I ever felt that God abandoned me." *Any more than I did when I was alive*, he thought, but Favst didn't need to hear those stories tonight. "You can search, or you can *act*, Favst. And I have spoken with those who search, and none of them know anything more than I do, not with any certainty."

"But I must... follow you, yes? I gave my word that I would."

Jürgen smiled. *Perfect. This boy will make a Scion yet.* "Yes, that is exactly so, my childe. And you must acquit yourself well, for by coming under the Black Cross so quickly, you have shown yourself worthy above all these noble brothers. It was a sign from God that you came to us."

"What does it mean... father?" Favst tested the word, obviously noticing that Jürgen wasn't comfortable with "sir."

"'My lord' will do, Favst, but my name is Jürgen of Magdeburg." He looked over his knights, some rising for prayer, some bedding down for the night, and realized that now he would not need to send his message to von Salza. "And I have told you what the sign means: You can now help us to avenge your fallen brothers."

Favst's eyes grew wide. He stumbled back, and Jürgen saw his Beast fighting for control. "I won't go back there—"

Jürgen stood with such force that the chair flew backward and cracked against the floor. He grabbed his new childe by the shirt and pulled his face close. "Yes, you will, Favst. God—and I—demand it."

Chapter Thirty-Seven

Favst found his way back to the battle site admirably. Jürgen had no idea if the knight had been a skilled hunter and tracker in life or if he was simply precocious, but they reached the area in far less time than it would have taken even with Bertolt finding the path. He had difficulty carrying a torch—not surprisingly, considering his Beast was still young and railing against all it could—but the trees had not yet grown thick enough to occlude moonlight. When they arrived, however, Jürgen's heart sank—they were apparently too late.

The area was burnt. Not even a smell of blood remained; all Jürgen could scent was soot and burned flesh. Favst looked about in wonder for a moment, and then turned to his sire. "Where are the bodies?"

"Taken by wolves, perhaps. Maybe burned." He looked down at the ash-covered ground. "Maybe swallowed up by the earth."

Favst took a few steps away from the burnt clearing. "But how was this accomplished without setting fire to the entire forest?"

Jürgen nodded. "Good question." He knew that some Tremere could summon up fire, so it followed that they would be able to control it. Explaining that to his new childe, however, would have necessitated a hasty education on the Thirteen Clans, and Jürgen was in no mood. Perhaps he would foster the boy in Germany somewhere when he returned....

"They must have left here, of course. Find a trail leading away. Wolves, horses, men, anything." Jürgen and Favst had tethered their own mounts a short distance away. Favst had difficulty riding; his horse wasn't a blood steed and feared the vampires.

He'd managed to keep it under control, but only with constant attention, which made tracking impossible. Jürgen moved back towards the horses while his childe, gingerly holding a torch, searched for a trail.

Jürgen patted his steed on the nose; the other horse whinnied and shrank away. Jürgen shot it an annoyed look (which only panicked it more) and thought about their course. The Telyavs had obviously burned the battle site to hide what had happened; Jürgen doubted that he would be able to learn much by looking at the area's memories. But by burning the area, they had also revealed that the skirmish hadn't been as large as Favst had portrayed. Jürgen guessed that the poor boy might have incorporated older memories and probably legends he'd heard into his report of the battle—the burnt clearing wasn't large enough to accommodate many combatants, and there was no sign of battle outside of it.

"Favst," he called, "how many of your knightly brothers were with you?"

"Only three," he called back from the other side of the clearing. "We were scouting, looking in the forest for someone."

Jürgen walked towards his childe. "Who?"

Favst was stooped over, looking at the brush, but stood up with a puzzled look on his face. "I don't recall. Now that I think of it, I remember more of us fought here, but I know that only four of us left the house that night."

Jürgen nodded. Perhaps the shock of what happened had altered the boy's memories. Or perhaps something else was responsible—high-blooded clans could often reshape memory. *Best not to trouble about it now,* he thought.

"Where is the house, Favst? Near here?"

"Only a short walk, but how will we explain my absence? Or that I'm now—"

"We won't go there, not yet. I just wanted to know if it was close by." Jürgen kicked his feet against a tree, trying to knock the soot off. "If we engage these creatures, we'll need help, but as you say, explanations to your order might prove difficult."

"What of your order, s... my lord? The Teutons, they are called?"

Jürgen smiled. "Yes. The Grand Master of the Teutonic Order is not a man to be trifled with, however, and he knows nothing of the Black Cross. While some of his commanders are members of my order, though not my childer, making use of that order would require more time than I believe we have, especially considering that most of them are currently in Prussia."

"And the knights back at the monastery?"

"Already gone on an important errand, all those that I could spare."

Favst went back to searching. Jürgen stared off into space. The "errand," of course, was delivering Nikita to Vykos. He had sent Rosamund along with a small detachment of knights to Brasov, and had made sure that their route took them close enough to von Salza's men to deliver a message and reconnoiter with the Teutonic Knights.

Why in God's name did I send Rosamund? he asked himself, not for the first time. He answered himself as he had before— *because she is a skilled diplomat and because I had no one else to send.* He didn't believe Vykos would be foolish enough to attack her, and he had instructed her and the knights to be gone before he opened the casket, if possible. It was the journey more than the destination that worried Jürgen—if he could meet up with the knights before they got too far on their way to Brasov, perhaps they could find these Telyavs together?

The soldier in him considered the idea; the man found it abhorrent. It would put Rosamund in far too much danger. Even if diplomacy was called for, it was diplomacy between warriors, not courtiers. The Gangrel and Telyavs wouldn't understand or appreciate Rosamund's courtly manners; such behavior might even anger the low-blooded wretches. But if he did find his knights again, with Rosamund in tow, he couldn't very well send her back to the monastery alone. In all likelihood, he wouldn't be seeing her again for some time, and while the man lamented that so deeply that Jürgen winced when he thought of it, the soldier was unapologetically glad.

Something moved in the forest and Jürgen drew his sword. Favst reached for his, but Jürgen held up his hand. He knew he was being watched, and knew also that he needed to find a safe place for himself and his childe before dawn. The Sword-Brothers' house, perhaps? That would require using a liberal amount of persuasion, but it certainly wasn't beyond Jürgen's ability. Returning to the monastery was possible, but they would have to leave immediately.

"I've found a trail, I think, my lord." Favst had moved away from the clearing. "It's faint, but I think men came this way."

Jürgen nodded. "Very well. We shall follow it, but keep your wits about you and remember where you are. We need to stay within an hour of your house, no more. When the time comes, we shall ride there and take shelter for the day." He paused, looking thoughtful. "Is there a cellarer there?"

Favst nodded, looking confused. "Yes, an old man called Sigismund."

"Good. We shall need his assistance. I don't wish anyone but him to see us, at least at first." He waved a hand at his childe's questions. "Later. For now, follow the trail, but keep a sharp lookout. I shall ride and lead your horse." They walked back towards their mounts; Favst's horse shied away from them.

"Do they sense evil?" asked Favst.

Jürgen rolled his eyes. "They sense power. Now, follow the trail."

Chapter Thirty-Eight

Following the trail was difficult, but Jürgen knew they were on the right path. Favst's tracking skills were superb, and with Jürgen occasionally reading the memories of the trees to make sure they hadn't lost their way, they continued on at a decent pace.

Jürgen decided, however, that he should have brought Bertolt along. The knight was not so impressive a tracker as Favst, but that was due chiefly to his still-mortal status. Besides, he could ride a horse without frightening it half to death. Jürgen's Beast had already demanded more than once that Jürgen put the poor, frightened creature out of its misery; only Jürgen's detestation of wasting resources allowed him to ignore that demand. For what he guessed was the sixth time, Jürgen took a moment while Favst searched for another clue to look at the memories of the area.

Snow. Hard, frozen ground. People running, but not being chased. Running to find someone, help someone, save someone. It had been the same each time. The memories were old enough that the people running were gray and faded in the vision, but still potent enough that he could make out their direction. Still, he didn't like to rely on memories—he knew how easily they could be changed in a mortal or even a Cainite's mind. The visions, coupled with a trail, however, were a good enough lead for him.

"How far are we from your house, Favst?"

"Not too far, my lord. Perhaps an hour's walk on this ground." The ground, quite in contrast to the frigid earth in the visions, was soft and pulpy.

"If we continue on this trail, will we move away from the house?"

Favst pursed his lips. "Hard to say, my lord. The trail hasn't been in a completely straight line."

Jürgen frowned. That was odd, considering the impressions he'd received from the trees. Why take a roundabout route if the end goal was urgent? But then, perhaps taking a straight line would have led the runners into a bog, or a pack of Lupines, or some equally primitive danger. "We'll chance it for a bit longer. Keep your bearings; if we're caught here during the day we probably won't survive." His own Beast hardly moved; it had long since grown used to Jürgen's attempts to inure it to the threat of the sun. Favst, on the other hand, grew wide-eyed and his mouth dropped open in a feral leer as his Beast wailed in terror. Jürgen caught his attention. "Trail, boy."

From behind them, Favst's horse gave a shrill whinny and snapped its tether. It charged straight for Jürgen and Favst. The younger vampire leapt for safety; Jürgen simply drew back a fist and punched the horse in the head. It fell dead at his feet, splashing to the muddy ground, blood running out of its nostrils.

Favst stood, his mantle soiled, and opened his mouth to speak. "Quiet," hissed Jürgen. "We are not alone." If the horse had snapped its tether in fear, Jürgen reasoned, it would have run *away* from the Cainites, not towards them. He clucked his tongue to call his own steed closer. The horse did not move. Jürgen walked towards it; it stared at him with more malice than he had seen from any creature in his unlife. Jürgen looked around the forest for signs of whatever was making the horses behave this way, but saw no one. He heard his horse move slightly, but the sound was so familiar that he paid it no mind.

"Look out!" Favst's warning came just in time. Jürgen jumped backwards just as his steed reared up and lashed out with both hooves. Jürgen drew his sword, but held back. He had no wish to kill his steed if it was possible to avoid it. Favst drew his own blade and rushed to his sire's defense; the steed's hoof lanced downwards and caught him in the temple, knocking him backwards. Jürgen drew back his sword to impale the rampaging stallion, but it backed up as if anticipating the blow.

Jürgen kept a wary eye on the horse, but glanced over to his childe. Favst lay flat on his back, a chunk of white bone visible through the gash on his forehead. He had apparently had the foresight to jam his torch into the wet ground before charging into the fray, however. Jürgen saw no other movement in the forest, and advanced on his steed slowly.

The horse continued backing up, and Jürgen tensed himself to spring. He couldn't allowed the horse to flee—any creature that could command a blood-steed to turn on its master could certainly coax information from it as well. Just as he was about to leap forward and sever the horse's head, a body landed at his feet.

The body was clearly a Cainite of the Gangrel clan. It was pale and thin, like most vampires, but tufts of fur protruded from its ears and its hands were black and padded like a dog's. It wasn't moving, but Jürgen could see no stake in its heart. He glanced to his left, from where the body had come, and saw that the forest there was brighter, as though the shadows fled from that small area.

Jürgen smiled. "Gotzon," he said, turning his attention back to the horse.

The horse looked down at the body, and then shuddered and collapsed to its knees. Almost immediately, the Gangrel's body began to stir. Gotzon stepped from the trees, grabbed the vampire by his scraggly hair and threw him against a tree. "Immobilize him, quickly," he murmured.

Not having a stake to hand, Jürgen jammed his sword through the Gangrel's chest into the tree behind him. He screamed in pain, now fully awake, and clutched at the blade, but only managed to slice his hands open. Jürgen noticed that his screams sounded very much like a horse's whinny, and glanced back at his steed. The horse stood there as placidly as ever, unaware, apparently, that anything had happened. Jürgen offered his hand. The horse nuzzled against it.

Jürgen rounded on the Gangrel in fury. "You cowardly bastard, you'd strike at me through my *horse*?"

The Gangrel spit out a curse in his native tongue. Jürgen cuffed him across the head and went to revive Favst. His childe was sitting up groggily, gingerly feeling at the wound on his head. Jürgen knelt down beside him. "The wound would kill a normal man, my childe, but you are under the Black Cross now. Simply will the wound to be gone, and it will heal in seconds." Favst looked up at his sire, confused, but the wound did indeed begin to close. Jürgen heard a series of crunching sounds as the bone beneath reset itself, and then the gash sealed without even a scar. "Perfect. Now get up. I need you to translate what this creature is saying."

Favst stood, but stumbled. "My lord, I... this feeling..." He parted his lips and Jürgen saw his fangs had extended. He glanced around the clearing hungrily. Jürgen ground his teeth in frustration. He hadn't had time to discern what sort of blood appealed to his childe. The boy was not even a week from his Embrace; likely as not those preferences weren't even set yet, and ingesting any mortal blood at all would simply leave him ill and smelling of congealed humors. Jürgen bit open his own wrist and held it to Favst's mouth, watching momentary disgust change to rabid hunger. He allowed Favst to drink enough to keep him sane and functional, and then pulled his wrist away. Time enough to explain the problems of refined tastes later.

They walked back to the prisoner. Gotzon stood behind them, unnoticed. Favst winced a bit when he saw the Gangrel trying to extract Jürgen's sword from his chest, and a bit more when the feral vampire lurched out with his arms. "Ask if it is the same creature that chased you on the night of your Embrace."

Favst spoke to the Gangrel. The Gangrel merely laughed and spit blood at Jürgen. Favst asked the question again, and it answered with a rapid-fire string of strange syllables.

Favst turned back to Jürgen. "He says that it was his brother that pursued me, but that they are all one with the land. I don't think he means "brother" as a literal relative though; the word he used is one that..." he frowned, thinking. "It's much the same as we might call a fellow soldier 'brother.'"

"Brothers in arms, then." Jürgen suppressed the urge to curse. If the Gangrel here considered themselves a military force, then they were better organized than Jürgen had thought. "Ask him where the Telyavs are."

Favst asked the question, but the Gangrel did not answer. His eyes rolled back in his head and his hands began to flex.

Jürgen listened carefully and heard rustling in the forest, a good distance off, but growing closer. He leapt forward and sank his fangs into the Gangrel's neck, drinking his coarse, bitter blood, holding his head against the tree to prevent any counterattack. The blood began to run dry all too soon, and Jürgen felt something there beyond the blood, something potent, a taste that he had never—

He stopped and withdrew. The Gangrel, now bled dry, roared in rage and pulled even harder at the sword. Jürgen planted a foot against his stomach and jerked the sword free, then swung it around and lopped off the Cainite's head.

Favst gaped at his sire, staring at the blood still smeared across his lips. "Those taken in battle, alive or dead, I own, and will claim my tribute," Jürgen muttered. "You'll find your way of claiming tribute some night soon." He turned to Gotzon and waited expectantly.

"I see you've taken someone else under the Black Cross," the Lasombra remarked.

Favst glanced at Gotzon and peered closely at his eyes. "My... God..." he gasped. He backed up against a tree and crossed himself. "It's true... we really are demons. I see Hell... in his eyes." He fell to his knees, trying to clasp his hands, but didn't seem to be able to move them.

Jürgen turned to his confessor. "What on God's Earth did you do to him?"

Gotzon shook his head. "Nothing. He looked."

Jürgen pulled his childe up to standing and locked eyes with him. "Lie still and at peace, and do not think, until I awaken you," he hissed. He barely felt resistance from his childe's mind, and Favst dropped over into a catatonic slumber. He turned back to Gotzon. "What are you doing here?"

"You seem somewhat ungrateful. Had I not arrived, you might have had to kill—or worse, chase—your prized steed."

"I am grateful, forgive me." Jürgen checked himself. Gotzon was a peer, not a servant, and he had no right to treat him as one. "But I still would like to know how you found me."

"Serendipity," said Gotzon, "or God's will. I was hunting for the same demons as you, the Telyavs and their pagan herd, or whatever remains of it. I found them, but then I heard your horses screaming, so I decided to find you."

"You found them?"

Gotzon nodded. "Not far from here. Most of them are dead, but not all. The survivors look to the Gangrel chieftain as a leader."

"The chieftain," mused Jürgen. *The one that killed Alexander.*

Chapter Thirty-Nine

"What did you do to him?" gasped Favst as the cellarer, Sigismund, wandered out of the kitchen, dazed.

"Nothing permanent, childe," hissed Jürgen. "He'll sleep soundly tonight, and he'll behave as if he never saw us, but he won't open this door until an hour after sunset."

"We shall burn in Hell for bringing a demon here," moaned Favst quietly.

"Gotzon is not a demon, boy." Jürgen was losing patience. "He is a man and a Cainite, much like us, he simply hails from different lands and follows a different road."

"His eyes..."

Jürgen's Beast snarled that leaving the boy here as a decaying corpse would be preferable to listening to his moaning. Jürgen shushed the voice, but agreed that the general attitude towards Gotzon wasn't acceptable. He tapped his childe on the shoulder and locked eyes with him, then looked back into his recent memories for what he had seen in Gotzon's eyes.

He didn't have to look long; the image hadn't left Favst's head for an instant. He'd looked too deeply into the Lasombra's eyes and seen, as he'd said, Hell therein. Jürgen understood— looking at Gotzon for any length of time was disconcerting and, with the heightened perceptions that his childe probably possessed, it was apt to be downright horrifying. Still, Jürgen could fix that horror.

He reached into Favst's mind and closed his will around the memory as a gardener might close his hand around a weed, and then concentrated, pulling the image from his childe's mind. The memory floated free for a moment, threatening to become part of Jürgen's own consciousness, but he released it, and the memory winked out like a candle flame.

He was about to release his childe from his mental grip, but then looked a bit deeper. Perhaps some memory of the battle with the Telyavs lingered; perhaps he could see why the details were so blurry. He peered into his childe's mind, looking past the memories of the last night, the pain of the horse's strike, the trek through the woods, and came upon a memory of blackness.

A memory of hunger, cold, emptiness, pain. A memory of light, beckoning, and then washed away by a torrent of blood.

The memory of the Embrace.

Jürgen ignored it. He had been fortunate in his Embrace; he knew as much. Though he had chosen his sire, Hardestadt had not Embraced him right away. He had been under his sire's blood for some time before Hardestadt granted him undeath, and during that time he had prepared meticulously for what would happen to him. Favst had never had that chance, and his Embrace was a black hole in his mind, the single most important event in his existence.

That will change, my childe, thought Jürgen as he plumbed deeper. *You'll see such things as to make your own death and resurrection seem nothing more important than a piss in the woods.*

He found the battle then, but seeing the memory was like trying catch a minnow in his fist. He could see some of the things he expected—men, horses, swords, chaos—but none of it came clearly. Jürgen was reminded of Albin the Ghost's memory, how it had been cut away so brutally, and wondered what had happened to Favst to cause this. He looked further back, and saw Favst and three other knights, still mortal, still breathing, walking through the woods. One of the knights beckoned, speaking in the local tongue, following something...

Following a light...

A trap, Jürgen realized. *They weren't out hunting or on orders, they were led into a trap.* The light bobbed and weaved through the trees, and then vanished, and the three knights stood there blinking for a moment. Then the chaos began.

Jürgen watched Favst's fragmented memories of the battle, but he wasn't sure exactly what had happened. Battle *was* chaos, and so of course a memory of it wouldn't be terribly revealing. But Jürgen couldn't accurately guess how many combatants there had been and whether everyone involved had fought the knights or if the combatants had fought each other as well. He saw bodies in the chaos too large to be human, but standing on two legs. He heard snarls of wolves and snarls that *sounded* like wolves, but were just slightly… *wrong* somehow. The pitch was too high for an animal, or one particular sound in a growl was drawn out too long. *Lupines, then?* But why wouldn't those cursed creatures ally with the Gangrel and the Telyavs?

Because, decided Jürgen, *the* Telyavs *are pagan, while the Lupines are debased servants of Lucifer. The pagans can be taught, after all.*

He tried to watch the rest of the battle, but it did not clear until something very large and very strong hit Favst, knocking him from the clearing into the woods. He stood up and began to run, but was immediately knocked to the ground by a wolf. He stabbed it and it rolled over, yelping in pain; it must have been one of the wolves that had accompanied the Gangrel chasing Favst, Jürgen realized.

Favst didn't have much memory of the run towards Jürgen's monastery. It had been an act of God that he'd reached it at all, bleeding, afraid, tired. Jürgen gently released his hold on his childe's mind. He was impressed; the knight was inexperienced, but tenacious and brave, and those were both qualities that Jürgen prized. Perhaps after he had made firm his holdings here, he would devote some time to teaching the neonate himself, rather than fobbing him off on another Cainite lord. *Rosamund could help with that instruction, if she's willing. It might be good for both of them.*

Jürgen's Beast howled in rage, and Jürgen did not know why. He ignored its protests and helped Favst out of the reverie.

Favst blinked, calmed, and then his attention snapped to the door. Gotzon, who had been checking around the chapter house for any sign that the Telyavs or the Gangrel had been there, entered the room.

"We should sleep," he said, and with that, he lay down in the corner and shut his eyes.

"Who is that?" whispered Favst.

Chapter Forty

The next evening, Gotzon was gone from the cellar when the two Ventrue awoke. Jürgen wasn't surprised; Gotzon was never comfortable being in close proximity to anyone for long. He shook Favst awake and then led him out of the chapter house, deftly avoiding notice. They caught up with Gotzon a few minutes away; he was standing near Jürgen's horse.

"Amazing," said Favst. "He stayed."

Jürgen smiled and bit his fingers, then offered them to his steed. The horse chewed on the bloody offering and nuzzled at his master. "He has his reasons." Jürgen turned to Gotzon. "You say you know where the Telyavs are. How many are they? Could we three—"

"Yes." Gotzon kept his eyes downcast. Jürgen hadn't explained that he had altered his childe's memory, but Gotzon had probably realized it, and in any case didn't wish to let the curious neonate see his eyes again. "I think we could, if your childe slays the mortals, what few remain, and you and I destroy the heathen Cainites."

"What of the chieftain?"

"Not in the area. They will summon him the instant we attack, of course—I have no doubt that their sorcery allows this—but it will take time for him to reach us." Gotzon didn't speak further, but Jürgen knew what he was thinking. *And then we can add his ashes to the forest.*

Jürgen shook his head. "We must leave the chieftain intact, and slay the Telyavs first before attacking the other Gangrel."

Gotzon glanced up, but did not speak.

"I have my reasons, Gotzon." Jürgen gave a glance to Favst,

but the young knight was staring back at his former home. "How far is it from here?"

Gotzon did not answer, but simply began walking. Jürgen clucked his tongue at his horse and followed, and Favst fell into step beside him.

"Should we not bring knights from my order, my lord?"

"I had considered it," answered Jürgen, "but that would require more time, more exertion and more explanation than I think we can afford. Besides, if Gotzon feels that we can win this battle without outside help, I'll trust his judgment."

Favst looked unconvinced. He still wasn't sure who Gotzon was or why they were following him, but the blood oath was now too strong for him to risk disrespecting his sire by asking. Jürgen decided to change the subject.

"Doubtless you've guessed at our diet, Favst." The young knight winced. "Well, there's nothing for it. Some Cainites feel it is a sort of purity—'the blood is the life,' after all. Some of us feel that we are damned and the fact that we feed on blood and blood only is merely one more way this damnation shows itself."

"You don't know?"

"I do not. No Cainite I have ever met knows." He shrugged. "I merely accept it as what God demands—I drink the blood of the warriors that I and my knights best in war."

"And none other?"

"Those taken in battle, alive or dead, I own, and will claim my tribute," recited Jürgen. "I said before that you would find your own ways to claim tribute, remember?" Favst nodded. "Not all blood will sustain you. You'll feel your hunger purify itself soon, and then you'll know what tribute best serves you, Favst, Knight of the Black Cross."

"But your blood—"

"Yes, my blood will always sustain you." Jürgen smiled. "But I have other uses for it, my childe."

Favst fell into thought, probably trying to chase down his hunger, to decide upon his prey. Jürgen had faced this search himself, but it had taken only moments—his chosen prey had been clear to him from long before his Embrace. But then, he had been given much more time to consider such things before entering the night.

Ahead of them, Gotzon raised a hand and then silently drew his sword. Jürgen concentrated, and heard people moving. It sounded like very few, but he wasn't foolish enough to think that assessment correct. Rather than speak, he glanced at his childe and forced a thought into his mind. *Remember, childe, you kill the mortals. Leave any like ourselves to Gotzon and I.* Favst, to his credit, started but did not cry out.

Jürgen was expecting Gotzon to creep quietly to a place where he could best strike, to act with the stealth befitting a member of his benighted clan. Instead, Gotzon burst forth into the clearing. Jürgen heard the activity in the clearing change, and heard sounds like small trees being torn up from their roots.

An ambush? Jürgen rushed forward, Favst directly behind him. *How could they have known?* Of course, a spy could have followed them to the chapter house, but—

Jürgen broke off these thoughts as he entered the clearing. Gotzon was battling six people, at least three of them Cainites. They were naked and dripping in blood; a corpse lying on the ground nearby, eyes blank, throat slit, revealed that they had been in the midst of some unholy ceremony. Small wonder that Gotzon had attacked.

Jürgen pointed at the three mortals in the group and barked an order to Favst in Latin. Favst charged in and ran the first one through; the two other mortals (who had been attempting to wrestle Gotzon to the ground from behind) turned on the young knight.

Jürgen turned his attention away from that battle. He knew his childe could defeat two unarmed mortals, and the three Cainites should pose no real threat to Gotzon. But something was wrong—he couldn't account for the noises he had heard, and while he knew the Telyavs' numbers were diminished, he had expected more than three of them.

He heard a wet crunch and a body hit the ground. The gasp of breath told him it was one of the mortal pagans. He heard footsteps running for the trees and a voice screaming in a local tongue. Favst chased after the man, both of them running towards the trees.

The trees? Jürgen leapt forward, meaning to stop his childe before he broke the tree line, but was too late. The bark on the tree nearest to Favst split like a woman giving birth, and a blurred pale form tackled him. It knocked him deeper into the woods, and Jürgen heard a cry of pain and then silence. He ran harder, trusting that Gotzon could handle himself.

Upon leaving the clearing, he saw what he expected—his childe lying on the ground, heart pierced by a long, jagged branch. *Strange that they didn't try to drag him away,* thought Jürgen, *for interrogation or simply destruction.* He took a step forward, trying to listen for movement, but heard nothing except the battle behind him. He reached down carefully, meaning to pull the stake from his childe's heart.

The yawning, tearing sound from above told him he'd made a mistake. The woman burst forth from the tree as before, planting both feet on Jürgen's chest and knocking him backwards. Her hands remained melded with the grain of the wood, however, allowing her the firm handhold she needed to twist her body and stamp down on the stake in Favst's chest. He gasped slightly as it loosened, and then his body froze again, the look of pain etched on his face, as she drove the stick deeper into his heart.

Jürgen righted himself. The Telyav—if indeed she was one— pulled her hands from the tree. Jürgen took a moment to size her up. She was naked, and her body was caked in earth and a glistening coat of sap. She crouched low, her hands only inches away from Favst's throat, although what threat she was making Jürgen did not understand. She couldn't strangle him, after all. She smiled at Jürgen, but he saw desperation behind that smile. She knew her time had come.

And yet, something about her disturbed him. He took a step forward and raised his sword; she took a step back towards her tree and grabbed Favst by the neck. Her eyes never quite made contact with his. That wasn't so surprising. She probably knew what the result of that would be. But still, there was a delib- eration about what she did that made Jürgen uneasy. He had fought naked savages before, but had never seen this kind of method in them.

Behind him in the clearing, he heard a shriek of pain. Gotzon was winning, apparently. He glared at the naked woman. "If you surrender, I'll spare you."

His Beast lashed out in fury, and he actually raised his sword arm a little before taking control. *Spare her?* She straightened up a bit. Apparently she'd understood. Her eyes held none of the mindless fury that Masha, the Tzimisce woman's, had. She was well aware of what was happening. "And then what?" she asked.

"Do what you like. I intend to take power in these lands, but I cannot begrudge Cainites who wish to dwell in the forest." He did not tell her, of course, that von Salza and his knights were not likely to be as understanding to her people. His Beast approved.

"Why have you come here?" Her eyes were hard, angry, but somehow sad at the same time. Her face was heart-shaped, Jürgen noticed, and she looked... newborn, somehow, with the moonlight sparking off her body. She was caked in dirt and blood and sap, yes, but somehow familiar, somehow beautiful.

"I... have come for power," he said. "I have come for revenge."

She nodded.

"Hunger," she said. "I know hunger."

Chapter Forty-One

By the time Jürgen had finished speaking with the Telyav woman and removing the stake from his childe's heart, Gotzon had slain the others. The Telyav refused to give them her name, but when Favst found out that she had made a bargain with Jürgen, he called her "Varka," and the name stuck. They seemed to feel the name was ironic; Jürgen didn't understand, but didn't press the issue. He had more important things in mind.

He didn't trust Varka, but did admire her sense of self-preservation and her courage. She had fought well and with intelligence, and her decision to surrender had been wise, but surely she must have felt some loyalty to the Cainites and mortals that they had slain? Gotzon, of course, advocated killing her outright, and said as much to Jürgen later, while the four of them were walking back to Jürgen's monastery.

"She can merge with any of these trees," Gotzon muttered quietly, "and God only knows what else she can do. Beyond that, she is a pagan and a demon. Remember the *koldun*—her magic seems only a small step removed."

"She could convert to our faith," said Jürgen.

"Cainites do not find faith easily."

Jürgen gave his confessor a stern look. Gotzon had, of course, himself found faith. "Be that as it may, I need her for the moment. I need to arrange a meeting with the Gangrel chieftain. We were lucky today—the enclave we found was small."

"We should burn it. Who knows how many of those trees might have hidden those demons?"

Jürgen shook his head. "No, I think that might well be the last of the Telyavs. I think they have other enemies in these forests, and the same is true of the Gangrel." He thought of Favst's memories of the huge, powerful creatures in the battle, tearing everything they could reach limb from limb. "I have no desire to fight with Qarakh, and if he's truly a wise leader as well as a powerful warrior, he'll listen to what I have to say."

"That requires that you find him."

"That is why the woman still has her head."

If Varka heard, she did not acknowledge them. She stood behind them, talking with Favst in their native language. Jürgen wondered what Favst thought of her; clearly, he saw "pagan" and "woman" before "Cainite" and "Telyav." *How long has it been,* thought Jürgen, *since I saw another Cainite as more than their clan, more than their beliefs?*

Since Rosamund left. And perhaps the sense of familiarity he felt when he looked at Varka...

He shook off the thought. "What are we?" he said aloud.

"Damned," replied Gotzon immediately.

Jürgen glanced at him. "That isn't what I mean. I mean... you, for instance."

Gotzon stiffened noticeably. He wasn't at all comfortable talking about himself, and Jürgen knew it. What he had revealed in Kybartai had been quite out of character.

"You aren't typical of your clan." Gotzon crossed himself. "You aren't even what most Cainites expect out of even the most pious of us."

"Your point, Jürgen?"

"I'm not sure." He thought of Rosamund. His first impression of her, more than a decade ago in Magdeburg, had been that she was a pretty Toreador. But now he knew more of her—knew *her*—and she was more than the blood in her veins. "Is blood so important?"

"Blood is life, and ultimately death, to us," muttered Gotzon. "Everything we do is stained with it."

"But does it define us?" Jürgen felt he was unsuited to this discussion, but then, Gotzon wasn't exactly a church scholar, either.

"It does," he said. "It spells our damnation, which is of great importance, at least to us."

"What of salvation?"

"You and I, Jürgen, have all the salvation that we are ever likely to see." He threw a glance back at the two young Cainites behind them, and then dropped his voice low enough that Jürgen had to strain to hear it. "And I am unsure, sometimes, about you." With that, he quickened his pace, and was soon lost in the darkness ahead.

Jürgen pondered this for a moment, looking for some sign within himself that he had slipped from any chance of salvation. It was true that he was a soldier, and therefore killed of necessity. Gotzon killed only out of holy duty, or so he believed. But the wars upon which Jürgen embarked were just; he would never attack a truly Christian foe.

His Beast laughed.

Shaking his head, he slowed his pace until Favst and Varka caught up with him. "Why did you agree?"

Favst opened his mouth, and then realized his sire was talking to Varka. Varka furrowed her brow. "I don't understand."

"Are you unfaithful to your gods or your clan? Why did you agree to my offer?"

"When the alternative was to die?" She laughed dryly. "I value what life I have."

Favst's eyes widened a bit, but Jürgen frowned at him and he stayed quiet. "But dying for faith—"

"Is something fools do," she responded. "Ask me as a mother to die for my children or as a woman to die for my lover. Don't ask me to die for my gods. Martyrdom is something that people do when all that's left are symbols."

Favst crossed himself. Varka seemed not to notice. Despite the implied blasphemy, Jürgen was intrigued. "We killed your clanmates—"

She laughed, and the sound was so bitter that Jürgen's Beast cringed. "You killed what? My clan? My family died many years ago. What you killed back there were monsters, blood-drinkers, who one night decided that I should join them in their insane quest."

"What quest was that?" asked Favst timidly.

Varka dropped her gaze to the forest floor. "To be what we

once were," she answered. "They made me a monster to make me help them become human."

A memory tickled at the back of Jürgen's mind, something he had heard from a guest in his court, a rumor of the Heresy... "Golconda?"

Varka stopped, and stared at Jürgen in horror. "You... you, too? Are all of us so possessed?"

Jürgen raised his hands and shook his head vigorously. "No, no. Golconda is a fantasy. We are what we are because of God's will, and no fervent wishes otherwise will change that."

Varka began to walk again. "No blood-magic or sacrifice, either. Nothing changes." She dragged a fingernail down her forearm and watched the furrow close immediately after. "Nothing."

Favst shot a worried glance at his sire. Jürgen decided to change the subject. "There is a chieftain of sorts here, a Cainite. A Gangrel."

Varka nodded. "Qarakh. He comes from the East. I know little about him."

"I wish to meet with him."

"To kill him?"

"No, simply to... redirect him. As I told you, I intend on taking these lands for my own, and I don't wish to have to contend with him or his people."

Varka smirked. "He has slain conquerors before."

"Yes, because the conqueror did not give him the choice—he had either to fight or die. I intend to give him a way out, a way for him to retain honor and still leave these lands without having to oppose me." He gestured towards the south. "The world is wide, and surely there are others more deserving of his wrath than me."

"You bring what he fears and hates most, though. You bring people, churches, civilization."

Jürgen rolled his eyes. *These rustic idiots*, he thought. *Where people are, there too is food, and yet that never occurs to them.* "Yes, well, I suppose I'll have to address those concerns when I speak with him. Surely even his culture has some form of protocol for parley."

Varka kicked at the mud. Her feet were so filthy that Jürgen had forgotten she wasn't wearing shoes. "He has agreed to such meetings before. Our high priestess met with him, I have heard, and brought together a meeting between him and other enemies."

Jürgen didn't answer. He knew what had happened to their high priestess, though he suspected Jervais had kept a few details to himself about his trip to Livonia. "Can you contact him, or someone who can?"

Varka stopped, and cleared away some leaves from the forest floor at her feet. She said something to Favst in her own language and Favst handed her a small knife. She knelt, and stabbed the knife through her hand.

Jürgen watched as her vitae dripped to the ground, and the ground itself seemed to sigh in pleasure as the blood soaked into the earth. Varka stood and pulled the knife from her palm with a grunt, and handed it back to Favst. The young knight quickly began wiping the blood from the blade, his face shocked.

"Qarakh will know soon enough that you wish a meeting," said Varka.

"My thanks," said Jürgen carefully. He was stifling a laugh. *One of my clan could have accomplished the same thing with no pain, no blood, and no blade*, he thought. *The low-blooded are so... primitive.*

Chapter Forty-Two

It was another fortnight before the Gangrel came. Jürgen had expected them to come as wolves, and listened every night for their howls. When they arrived, though, they did so as bats.

Jürgen was in the room that had once held Nikita of Sredetz when the bats arrived. He was staring at the patch of floor that had served as the archbishop's resting place and trying to remember what he looked like. Jürgen had no idea why he was doing this, and when the shrieks from outside began, he forgot that he had ever been there.

He ran outside and found his knights running for cover. Some of them were waving torches at the bats, but with little success. Favst stood his ground, hiding behind a shield, sword ready, but obviously with very little idea what to do.

Varka stood out in the open. She wasn't naked anymore— Jürgen had insisted she wear clothes and she had torn a monk's robe to fit her—but her hair fell long around her shoulders and Jürgen could see her bare feet. She stood on open ground and bats dove towards her and then swirled around her like a cloak.

For a moment, Jürgen knew fear. *They can't all be Cainites,* he thought desperately. *It's not possible. The whole of Livonia couldn't hold so many Gangrel.* He had seen the way Gangrel fought. They called up swarms of animals to confuse their foes.

Jürgen's Beast urged him to run. His horse was faster than any bat. He could reach Jovirdas's keep before morning. He fought the urge, but it was difficult. He thought his Beast might have a strong point.

Varka turned to face Jürgen and the bats surged away from her like a chittering black cloud. Jürgen fought with all his might to keep his hands at his sides rather than flinging them up to protect his face, but the bats veered off before striking him. One of them landed on two legs, growing horribly into human form in the space of a few seconds. The Gangrel was a woman, but was so completely feral in appearance that Jürgen had to look twice to make sure. Wolf-like fur covered her face and her body, which, Jürgen noted with amused resignation, was unencumbered by clothes. Jürgen wondered what the Gangrel had against clothes—some ill-conceived rebellion against God and His Church, perhaps, that incited them to travel as naked as the first people of Eden? He noted that something about her was familiar before turning his attention to the forest behind her.

A man came riding from the trees, flanked by the cloud of bats. He rode slowly, and carried no weapon; Jürgen imagined this was to show that he was not attacking, but kept his hand near the hilt of his sword anyway. The rider passed Varka and snarled; the Telyav fled towards the monastery.

Once the man reached Jürgen, he dismounted and the bats settled in the trees. Jürgen did not recognize the man's garb or his features, but knew immediately that the dark-skinned vampire standing in front of him was Qarakh. The chieftain regarded Jürgen in the same way one hound might regard another—rivals for prey, rivals for attention, of the same kind but ready to kill one another just the same.

Jürgen could find no fault with that.

Favst took a few steps towards his sire. The woman took a step forward. As one, Jürgen and Qarakh raised their hands to warn their servants off. Jürgen nearly smiled, but had no idea how Qarakh might take such a gesture. As he did not know what language the Gangrel chieftain might speak, he waited for Qarakh to begin the discussion.

But Qarakh didn't speak right away. He stared into Jürgen's eyes, as if daring the Sword-Bearer to command him, to take his mind, to look at his memories and reshape them. Jürgen stared back, but did not make any attempt to control the Gangrel. He wasn't sure it was possible, and in any event, the chieftain would fight. Jürgen had no desire to turn this into a battle; he wasn't certain that the bats waiting in the trees didn't hide Cainites among them, nor was he certain that, even if Qarakh and his fellows were the only enemy Cainites here that he and his knights could defeat them. *Remember that this savage destroyed Alexander,* thought Jürgen, and the Beast gave an icy whimper to punctuate that thought.

Qarakh stared for another moment, and then snarled something in a bestial tongue that Jürgen had never heard. The woman approached, spoke to Qarakh quietly in their shared language, and then addressed Jürgen in German. "The *khan* does not understand your tongue, nor the tongue of scholars, and he refuses to speak through the traitor-witch."

"Varka?" Jürgen cast a glance around for the Telyav, but did not see her. All three Gangrel broke out laughing, and Jürgen reminded himself that "Varka" wasn't her real name. "Very well, then. If you're to be our interpreter, I should like to know your name."

The woman cocked her head slightly, and the feeling of recognition grew stronger. He had seen this woman before, somewhere, not long ago, but not in a forest. It had been in court, in Magdeburg....

"Morrow," he said. She nodded curtly. He refrained from asking what she was doing here, but guessed that since Jervais hadn't mentioned her (and had met her the same night that Jürgen had) she had recently joined Qarakh's tribe. He waited for her to speak on Qarakh's behalf.

The chieftain spoke in his strange tongue, and Morrow translated. "The traitor-bitch says that you come here out of hunger. The *khan* respects that, but wishes you to know that you will meet the same fate as the last hungry Ventrue."

So this is the brute that killed Alexander. Jürgen hadn't wanted to believe it, but decided not to pursue the issue. If he did, he might be honor-bound to avenge his predecessor, and he didn't know if he could stomach that. "It seems, though, that Tremere appetites aren't met with such hostility."

Morrow bared her teeth, but translated this. Qarakh took a moment to respond. Jürgen imagined that he was choosing his words carefully; admitting that Jervais had been quite successful in his mission without losing face would be difficult for the chieftain. Finally, he spoke and Morrow repeated, "The Tremere you sent ate his fill and left. Have you a similar hunger, or will you not stop until all the world rests in your gullet?"

Jürgen wished Rosamund was here; while this sort of parley was perhaps more brutal than what she was accustomed to, no doubt she would have appreciated the word play. "I have heard a saying among Cainites—'Vengeance is best when the blood is still hot.' I have struggled for years to keep the blood hot enough to be savory between myself and my enemy, and when that meal is finished, I think I shall be satisfied."

Morrow repeated this to Qarakh, who took a moment before answering. Jürgen thought he looked confused. "Who," asked Morrow, "is this enemy?"

"Someone who I think both the," Jürgen struggled to remember the term she had used, "*khan* and I could agree is an enemy to us both." He paused for a few seconds. In a few words, he was about to make a daring move. A lesser soldier would have paused to consider backing out. Jürgen of Magdeburg paused to savor the moment. "Vladimir Rustovitch."

Jürgen had considered this move every night since Varka had sent his message. He had originally thought to lay an ambush for the Gangrel, but dismissed the idea because they knew the land and its secrets so much better than he did. He had considered setting them against all manner of enemies here, including the Tremere, since he knew that many of them hated the sorcerers anyway. What had finally decided him, though, was something Varka had said—that Qarakh hated and feared civilization above all else.

Jürgen, after all, was an unknown. He was bringing change, after a fashion. Rustovitch was already entrenched, and representative of civilization in a way that, Jürgen hoped, the Gangrel already knew and hated. It was a gamble, true, but one that he felt would work well.

And so Jürgen was not at all prepared for the way that Morrow reacted.

She took a half step back, as though about to pounce, and bared her teeth like a great cat. Then she seemed to remember herself and turned to Qarakh, translating what Jürgen had said.

He heard Rustovitch's name in her speech, but more than that, heard the bitterness and hatred with which she spoke. While Jürgen hoped that this vitriol was directed at Rustovitch, he somehow felt that he had made an error.

Qarakh answered, but much more calmly than his interpreter. The two of them conversed for a moment, and Jürgen glanced off to his right and saw Favst listening. From the look on his face, Jürgen guessed that he understood the language they were using, and that the topic was alarming. *Of course,* thought Jürgen, *everything alarms Favst.*

Finally, Morrow spoke. "Rustovitch has enemies in common with us already—you included, Sword-Bearer. I told you once that Rustovitch holds lands here only at our sufferance."

"True," replied Jürgen. "And yet, battle was still joined and more than one Gangrel's ashes lie mixed with the mud in Hungary to this night."

"Alongside Ventrue and Tzimisce," she shot back. He briefly reflected how well-traveled this savage woman was.

"And others besides, and what of it?" Jürgen raised his voice slightly; if these animals required a bit of brutal emotion in their diplomacy, so be it. "The point is, Rustovitch couldn't keep my forces out of his lands, and your people weren't any kind of deciding factor. Rustovitch has lost support here already—I've seen to that—and he will continue to lose it. The elder who once inhabited this place is gone—"

Morrow began translating and Jürgen stopped to let her finish. Qarakh's expression changed when she stopped speaking; he looked, if not fearful, then more concerned than before. He rasped a question to Morrow, who repeated it: "You destroyed the Cainite who slept here?"

Jürgen smiled smugly. "I defeated him. He is no longer here."

Another exchange followed between the Gangrel, and then Morrow asked, "That was the contents of the wagon that left here some weeks ago, then? Along with some of your knights and a pretty woman—Rosamund of Islington, if memory serves?"

Jürgen's Beast suggested that he tear the woman's tongue out with his teeth for daring to speak Rosamund's name. *Is my Beast now my lady's champion?* he thought. "Yes. I trust you left the wagon unmolested." He called up power into his gaze and let it wash over the Gangrel. They felt it, even if they would never acknowledge it, and Morrow translated Jürgen's words for Qarakh.

The chieftain responded, and Morrow said, "We have not stopped that wagon, nor do we intend to." Jürgen had the feeling that the words 'now that we know what it contains' might have fit neatly onto the end of her sentence. "What has this to do with Rustovitch, and why should we view him as an enemy?"

If you have to ask, you are stupider than I thought. Jürgen glanced at Favst and reached out into his mind, pulling what he could understand from the Gangrel's conversation.

They fear the Cainite that once dwelt here, came Favst's thoughts.

Jürgen needed to know more. "Why not view me as an ally? I have already slain the monks who lived here—probably not for the same reasons you would wish, but they are dead nonetheless."

Morrow translated, and Jürgen reached to Favst's mind again. *The Cainite who dwelt here used to hunt the Gangrel, and they left the monks alone, hoping to avoid his wrath.*

Perfect, thought Jürgen.

"What have the monks to do with this?" Morrow asked. Jürgen could hear her control slipping. She was confused, her Beast close to the surface.

"Why, didn't you know? The monks work for Rustovitch," he answered. "They carry messages for him, they perform research for him. The Cainite that dwelt here was of Rustovitch's clan, if not his very line. And it's Vykos, Rustovitch's vassal, who controls the Obertus order." He paused to gauge her reaction. She looked furious, as though she had been betrayed. "All of this," gesturing towards the monastery, "goes back to the *voivode* of *voivodes*."

The two Gangrel began speaking in their odd tongue, quickly, furiously, and Jürgen simply watched. He knew that Nikita had been feeding on Cainites, and so it followed that the archbishop had destroyed some Gangrel—perhaps some Telyavs—in his time. Jürgen actually doubted any direct connection between

Rustovitch and Nikita, but the connection between Rustovitch and the Obertus was real enough. *The choice is simple,* he thought. *Either battle me, who defeated Nikita, or battle Rustovitch, who supported him and his monks.*

In his heart, Jürgen prayed that Qarakh would make the right choice. If he chose to fight Jürgen, whether here and now or in the future, Jürgen didn't know what the outcome would be.

After long moments of conversation, Morrow turned once again to face the Sword-Bearer. "You have taken Kybartai?"

Jürgen nodded. "I have. The *kunigaikstis,* Geidas, is dead, now replaced by his childe Jovirdas, who is loyal to me." *Unless it was he who broke an oath to me,* Jürgen reminded himself. *But the Gangrel don't know that—unless of course he broke it while speaking with them.*

"The messenger Geidas sent traveled to Bistritz. We let him pass because Rustovitch is there."

As is Geidas's sire, thought Jürgen, *but they don't need to know that.*

Qarakh and Morrow spoke again, but this time the speech was slow, almost weary. Finally, Morrow asked, "The woods will remain wild? Those Gangrel who choose to stay can stay?"

Jürgen nodded. "Those who obey the Traditions of Caine are welcome. The land is vast. Of course, those who choose to follow pagan gods should do so carefully, for many reasons." Morrow nodded, and glanced at Qarakh.

"We will go, then," she said. "We will not battle Rustovitch in your name, but if he has betrayed us, he will feel our wrath." Qarakh took a step towards Jürgen, looked him up and down, and then growled something in his guttural tongue and mounted his horse. Jürgen could hear the shrieking of the bats as they took wing again, and watched as Morrow tensed her body, presumably to join them. Jürgen called out to her.

"Morrow," he said. "Out of curiosity, what does 'Varka' mean?"

Morrow smiled, not without malice. "It means 'martyr,'" she said. And then she was gone, flying off to join her people in the forest.

Chapter Forty-Three

During the winter, the Livonian nights had been silent. Jürgen remembered the eerie quiet that had blanketed the monastery when first he'd seen it.

During the spring, the forest had been alive, even at night, but the howls of wolves had often silenced the sounds of birds and animals in their nightly doings. Jürgen moved quill across parchment and remembered the noises and scents of the forest in spring, muddy, waking after the long icy months.

Now it was summer. The nights were short and humid, and the forests were often deafening to Jürgen's acute senses, but not because of the animals. The Sword-Bearer had made good on his name and his vow.

Jürgen surveyed the maps of the area. The Gangrel, true to their word, had moved south. Some had stayed, of course—even if Qarakh was a leader, Jürgen hadn't expected all of the savages to follow him. The loss was theirs. They and the pagans upon which they fed were falling before the Sword-Brothers by day, and before the Order of the Black Cross by night. Jürgen still didn't have enough Cainite soldiers here to mount any kind of large-scale assaults, and so contented himself with nudging von Salza's men towards the largest pockets of resistance and then sending his own men in to clean up afterwards. The monastery's larders had been converted into prisons. Wiftet, newly arrived from Kybartai, wasted no time in pointing out that the rooms' functions really hadn't changed much. Jürgen had his tribute, once again.

Between the monastery in Ezerelis and the town of Auce, more than a hundred miles north, four towns now held troops loyal to Jürgen. Auce was the largest of them; he meant to travel there himself, but was waiting for Rosamund to return. The outpost was secure enough. Bertolt had been installed as a commander there, and he was so competent that Jürgen had been able to move troops from the village to other, less secure venues.

Jürgen opened a letter from Heinrich in Magdeburg. More troops were en route, Cainites among them. Other letters from various courts across the Empire promised other Scions hoping to swear fealty to the Sword-Bearer. *Perfect,* he thought. He would need more vassals when this war was over; he had no intention of staying out here himself, but wished to place trustworthy Cainites in command of his new holdings. Anyone willing to fight by his side would have ample opportunity to prove himself.

In the letter, Heinrich mentioned that Christof was eager to journey east herself. *Perhaps I could let her rule here,* Jürgen thought, *make her overlord of these territories?* He had been agonizing over whom to leave in his stead when at last he returned home; it had to be someone strong and capable, for whomever it was would undoubtedly face immediate attack by Tzimisce forces. He had considered Jovirdas, but decided against it—the Tzimisce's wrath for the Ventrue was nothing compared to the venom they reserved for one of their own turned traitor.

He shook off the thought. It wasn't an issue yet; the area wasn't nearly stable enough for him to consider leaving. He leaned out the door to the abbot's office and called for Favst.

The knight had come along well in the months since his Embrace, adapting as well as could be expected. Jürgen had hoped that he might take a position of rulership here, but had decided against it—although Favst was intelligent and brave, he lacked the initiative and necessary brutality to make a leader. It pained Jürgen to admit it, but his newest childe was likely to be forever a soldier, never a commander. The worst part was that it didn't seem to chafe him, but then, he'd only had a few months. A century might change his mind.

Favst entered, and Jürgen noted that his tunic was splattered with fresh blood. The Sword-Bearer shook his head and pointed to the spots; Favst glanced down and his eyes grew sheepish, but he could do nothing but tug at his shirt. Favst had finally found the blood that would sustain him, but apparently had yet to learn to feed neatly. Jürgen recalled the night Favst had made that discovery. Scant hours before dawn, they had discovered a knight of Favst's former order rutting with a pagan girl. Jürgen was merely amused—he had no illusions as to what a vow of chastity meant to many knights. Favst, however, was incensed, and fell upon them. When he rose at last, leaving behind only bloodied corpses, Jürgen had asked him what it was he tasted on their blood.

"Sin," he'd said, and Jürgen had asked him nothing further.

Jürgen looked his childe over, and wondered at the fury against sin that lurked beneath his otherwise quiet demeanor. *Maybe you should have been Gotzon's childe*, he thought.

"Favst," he said aloud, "anything to report?"

Favst nodded. "Our outposts at Auce and Taurag send word that they've faced increased resistance."

"Just after I pulled troops from both," muttered Jürgen.

"Yes. Also, I received word from Sigismund." Favst looked uncomfortable. Jürgen decided not to let that feeling fester.

"Favst, I know you don't approve of using the old man this way."

"My lord, I—"

Jürgen cut him off with a wave of his hand. "Please, let me finish. Sigismund has no idea that he is even writing the letters. He is not using parchment or ink from your order—your former order—and for all he knows, he might as well be sleeping while he writes. Using him, a cellarer, is much more palatable to me than using one of the knights thusly. I should think you would feel that way as well."

"Yes, my lord."

"The alternative would be to put him under the blood, induct him into the order, and I'm not sure he is worthy."

Favst shook his head. "I do not think he is, my lord."

Jürgen gave his childe a piercing look; Favst seemed contrite. "Go on, then."

"Sigismund sends word that my... former order has taken losses lately. They have lost men and horses, and all within the same area that we found Varka."

"I see. What has Varka to say?" The Telyav had been most

helpful over the months. Jürgen had insisted that she remain on the monastery grounds, ostensibly because she wasn't safe in the forests.

"She says that the grove is sacred to her people and that it will always have defenders."

"I see."

"Do you trust her?"

Jürgen laughed. "Never. The question isn't whether she's trustworthy; she isn't and never has been. The question is whether she has anything to gain by lying to us, and for that we need to understand her."

"Do you?"

Jürgen glanced over at the Letters of Acindynus. He'd been reading through them the night before, looking at the footnotes of Julia Antasia. The Antasian Ventrue were convinced that they could shackle their Beasts into subservience by mimicking mortal behavior. It was an endeavor doomed to failure, in Jürgen's opinion, because Cainites were *not* mortal and never could be. It also meant that since Antasia's "Prodigals" did not abide by Cainite codes of conduct, they were not trustworthy in vampiric circles.

Varka, by her behavior, was such a Prodigal, even if she didn't know the term. Jürgen had never asked her—indeed, the primitive Telyav might not even know that she walked a moral road at all, let alone which one.

"My lord, do you understand her?" Favst repeated.

Jürgen looked down at his maps. "No, I do not."

Chapter Forty-Four

When Rosamund arrived the next night, Jürgen's first emotion was surprise that he hadn't received a letter in advance telling him that she was returning. He was sitting once again in the abbot's room, looking over the Letters of Acindynus. The night was quiet, the only sound from outside was a gentle rain, and Jürgen had deliberately kept his senses muted to mortal levels.

The footnotes in the Letters included a rather lengthy diatribe from a Latin Cainite on the nature of soldiers, spies, and assassins. Jürgen had his own feelings on the subject.

Spies, he wrote, *might be necessary, but Scions do not make effective spies. For a spy to excel in his work, he must be able to lie, to break oaths with impunity, to bear false witness even against Cainites that, only a night previously, he has sworn fealty to. Thus, a spy on the Via Regalis risks not only his unlife, but his soul as well, for the Beast does not understand such things as 'necessity' or 'intrigue.' It knows only that an oath is broken, and broken oaths are its meat and drink. Better, then, to assign such tasks to other Cainites, perhaps those who call themselves 'Prodigals' and ape mortal behavior? After all, mortals lie, do they not?*

Jürgen fully expected some mewling Prodigal to respond with a petulant note, something to the effect of "we risk their souls by lying as well," but that was actually the point. He didn't know much about the so-called Road of Humanity and the philosophies that it boasted, but clearly the Prodigals were dangerous in their own way. They also seemed to be among the most numerous of Cainites among the low-blooded.

And although he would admit it to no one, Jürgen was curious about them.

What drove a Cainite to emulate its prey? He imagined that, for many Prodigals, they simply aped humanity because it was all they knew. But he had met just as many vampires willing to teach neonates among the peasant clans as among the Cainite nobility. That led him to believe that many Prodigals remained so voluntarily. Why? Fear, perhaps, of the unknown, or fear of losing what soul they believed remained.

But then Cainites like Julia Antasia not only chose *Humanitatis*, but made it the focus of their unlives. *Julia Antasia is on a par with my sire in age and influence, even if Hardestadt would never admit it,* thought Jürgen, poring over her words in the Letters. *How has she staved off the Beast for so long?*

This was the thought in Jürgen's head when he heard a knock at the office door. Immediately he sharpened his senses and listened, but heard no breath outside. A Cainite, then. He sniffed the air deeply, but smelled only rain and mud.

He crossed the room and opened the door, reasoning that anyone who posed a threat to him would have caused alarms to be raised.

Rosamund stood before him, soaked from the rain, feet muddied, and looking absolutely beautiful.

"My lord," she said quietly, and the soldier within politely left Jürgen alone. He took her hands and kissed them, tasting the rainwater on her fingers, smelling the perfume that hadn't quite been washed away. He led her into the office, not bothering to close the door, and kissed her.

The kiss was strange, tense at first, but Jürgen imagined this was because they were not entirely in private. Besides, they hadn't seen each other in months—perhaps the shared blood between them was fading? He kissed her more deeply, hands tracing down her back, fingers entwined in her damp hair, and her lips softened as she returned the kiss. He felt her hands on his sides, the moisture soaking through his shirt—a Cainite's cold fingers did not dry as fast as a mortal's would. He kissed her cheeks and her eyes, and gazed down at her for the first time in almost two seasons.

I love her.

The Beast railed, the Beast screamed, the Beast beat at its cage and demanded that he take her blood, take her soul, violate her body and burn it to ash. Jürgen barely batted an eye. The Beast had no power over what he felt. The Beast could go hang. It had no part of this, the soldier had no part of this. Jürgen kissed her again, and opened his mouth to tell her.

"Doing the Lord's work, Jürgen?"

Jürgen's head snapped up. Gotzon was standing in the hallway behind them. The look on anyone else's face might have been amusement or polite embarrassment. Given Gotzon's position, Jürgen wouldn't have been surprised to see anger. Instead he saw resignation, and that frightened him most of all.

Rosamund coughed slightly and moved out from between them, seating herself in one of the chairs in front of Jürgen's desk. Jürgen took a step towards his confessor. "I trust you have something important to tell me, Gotzon?"

Gotzon pursed his lips. "Yes, but would you listen, I wonder?"

Jürgen narrowed his eyes. "When I wish for your counsel in personal matters, I will ask for it. What do you want?"

"I have returned to tell you that I was right."

"Regarding what?"

Gotzon turned and began to walk. Jürgen gave Rosamund a pained glance, but followed. The soldier had returned, as quietly as he'd gone, sensing he was needed. Gotzon didn't look at Jürgen when he spoke. "Regarding the Telyav witch. I was right; you should have burned her when you had the chance."

"Meaning I don't have the chance now?" Now Jürgen was concerned—if Varka had fled, she could potentially do his cause great damage.

"No, she is still here. She did not see me enter. She has already caused you enough harm to merit destroying her." They left the monastery and Favst ran up to Jürgen.

"My lord, Auce has fallen."

Jürgen stopped dead. "What?"

"It's true, my lord. Last night. Everyone there is dead. One of our knights became separated from his fellows and discovered it by accident, and rode all day to inform us."

The Beast, probably still smarting from Jürgen's earlier disregard of its tantrum, only growled menacingly.

"Where is Varka?" he hissed in Latin.

Favst looked momentarily confused, but then nodded. "This way," he said.

Varka was on the outskirts of the monastery grounds. The instant she saw the three Cainites walking towards her, she bolted for the trees.

Jürgen, however, had expected that. He called forth the vitae in his veins and his limbs surged with speed and power. She was almost a hundred yards away when she began to run; he crossed the distance in seconds and leaped for her, sword drawn. The Beast suggested he aim for her head. He admitted that the idea was attractive, but Jürgen had other ideas. He stabbed the sword downwards and pierced her hip; the sword blade stretched the flesh of her thigh, protruded just above her knee, and then slammed into the earth.

Varka shrieked in pain. Jürgen removed the sword with a grunt and then stabbed it through the small of her back, pinning her to the ground. Favst sprinted up behind him, already carrying a jagged stick, and forced it through her back. The Telyav froze in mid-struggle. Jürgen pulled the sword from her back. "Take her back to the monastery and put her in one of the cells, but make sure she remains immobile. Chain her securely. I'll be there shortly."

Favst shouldered the torpid Cainite and staggered back towards the monastery. Jürgen could hear others coming to help him, but did not turn to face them. He was afraid of seeing Gotzon.

"Thank you," he said after a long moment.

"You'll come to give confession?" The voice was black ice on Jürgen's neck. He actually shuddered, considering what he had already lost because of his mistake and what he might have lost if she had remained undetected.

"I will."

"You never looked at her thoughts?"

"I…" He stopped. Why hadn't he? He hated doing it, yes, but

that had never stopped him when the need was there.

Because she reminded me of Rosamund. In my lady's absence, I couldn't bring myself to violate the private mind of one who so resembled her.

Jürgen turned and walked back towards the monastery. If Gotzon followed, he made no sound, and Jürgen didn't turn to look.

Chapter Forty-Five

Varka was chained to the wall, her faced pressed into the stone. The stake protruded from her back; apparently the knights hadn't wanted to chance removing it. Jürgen didn't blame them. He had seen firsthand what the Telyav was capable of doing. He needed information, however, and so he stared at her, forcing his way into her mind, brushing aside her thoughts....

And found he could not.

Jürgen frowned. He should have been able to see her mind with no difficulty; he knew that her blood was thinner than his, and that didn't make any difference anyway. *Perhaps her mind is simply blank while the stake paralyzes her?* Jürgen was sure that he'd read the minds of Cainites thus immobilized before, but then, every Cainite was different. Perhaps her magic protected her.

He stepped forward and gripped the stake, and then decided to weaken her a bit first. He sank his fangs into her shoulder and drank.

He shut his eyes, and the soldier disappeared quite suddenly. Jürgen moved forward and pressed his body against hers, savoring the taste of blood, the feel of her against his hips, even the stake nudging him as he fed. *She cannot push me away,* he thought. *She cannot refuse, she has no notion of propriety, she doesn't even know what I'm doing.*

The Beast purred its approval, and the soldier returned. Jürgen stepped back, wiping his lips, staring at the angry but bloodless wound on her shoulder. He turned around; no one had followed him here, so no one had seen what he'd done.

And what have I done, he thought, *besides take my tribute?* Still, he felt uncomfortable. He shouldn't feel this way, he knew. He had taken blood from enemy Cainites often enough to be able to resist the feelings a single drink would engender. Steeling himself, he stepped forward and jerked the stake from her back.

Varka immediately screamed in pain and rage, fighting against the chains with all her might. It did her no good. Her leg and back were still grievously wounded and she had no leverage with which to free herself. She tried craning her neck to look behind her, but cried out in pain at the attempt. Finally she quieted, resting her forehead against the wall silently. A mortal would have panted; she simply waited.

"Bound and determined to be a martyr, then?" Jürgen asked. Varka responded with what he assumed to be a curse in her language.

"What have you told, Varka, and to whom?"

"You'll kill me anyway. Why should I tell you?" She didn't sound as defiant as Jürgen would have expected—perhaps she'd been acting under someone else's control?

"You'll tell me anyway, Varka." The words sounded hollow. The threat had no meaning. "You'll tell me, because if you don't, death will begin to look a welcome change very soon."

"I'm sure it would," she said. She tried to turn her head again and whimpered from the pain. Jürgen, to his horror, actually winced when she did so. *What is wrong with me?* "But you forget, Lord Jürgen, I do not share your notions of Hell. Send me on. We'll see where I go." She continued speaking, and from the timbre of her voice she seemed to be praying, but Jürgen could make no sense of her words.

He concentrated again, forcing his perceptions past her mind, but saw nothing but trees, blood and wind. He felt a force pushing him out of her mind, and when his vision cleared he was outside the door, as though her magical defenses had repelled his body as well as his Cainite powers.

The Sword-Bearer ground his teeth. If he could not take what he wanted from her, she would give it to him. He unhitched the chains from the wall, spun her around, and fastened them again. She struggled, but didn't have enough strength to fight through the pain or enough blood in her body to heal her wounds. Jürgen reached up and gripped her jaw, thinking to crush it, and then decided against it. She needed to be able to speak, after all.

And I don't really want to hurt her, he thought. His Beast wailed in anguish. He shut his eyes tight, and then snapped them open and peered into hers. She stared at him calmly, the same sort of sad resignation on her face as he'd seen on Gotzon's earlier when he'd found Jürgen with Rosamund.

God help me, she does so look like my lady.

Jürgen shook off the thought and stared deeper, trying this time to bend her will to his. "Tell me what I want to know," he muttered through clenched teeth. He saw her lips begin to move, and then stop. She could not muster the strength to break his gaze, but shook her head. She did not speak, but the look on her face held her thoughts clearly enough: *You cannot break me.*

Many parts of Jürgen, the soldier, the Beast, the vampire, the Sword-Bearer... all of these knew better. They knew that they could snap her bones one at a time, burn off her features with heated metal, strap her down so that the sun moved over her body, apply fire to her palms, and any of a thousand other methods of torture that Jürgen had learned, invented and perfected over nearly a quarter-millennium of experience.

But the one part of Jürgen that held control still—the man— knew she was right. He could not break her, not because of her strength or her magic, but because she looked too much like Rosamund for Jürgen to proceed. He had seen it before, but now the feeling was strengthened by the blood he had taken.

Or perhaps I am simply growing weak.

Jürgen turned and stumbled out of the room. He shut the door, but he heard her triumphant laugh behind him. Varka probably didn't know what she had just won, only that she had, and in the face of what was to come, that was enough cause to laugh.

Favst ran up to attend his sire. Jürgen waved him close. "Find out what she knows, Favst. Use any method of persuasion you must, and remember that your sin may be absolved." Jürgen felt his voice weakening, as though he was about to cry... or scream. Favst sensed the tension in his sire and backed away a few steps. Jürgen continued. "When you are finished, and convinced she knows no more—" he paused. He opened his mouth to finish the sentence several times, but the words caught in his throat. His heart, which hadn't beaten except at his occasional whim in over two centuries, ached at the thought.

Finally, he worked up the courage to finish the sentence. "Burn her." He barely heard Favst answer him as he walked back into the monastery to find Gotzon.

Chapter Forty-Six

"Doing the Lord's—" Jürgen didn't let him finish.

"I wish confession, Father," he said. No longer able to stand, he fell to his knees.

"Very well, my son." Gotzon sat next to him, blessed him, and waited patiently.

For a long time, Jürgen said nothing. He merely knelt there, bloody tears streaming down his cheeks, the sound of his Beast laughing in his skull deafening him.

I have failed as a Scion, he thought. His Beast agreed. *I have failed as a soldier. I have allowed my feelings for a woman to prevent me from my duties to God and my troops. Men have died because of my failures.*

His Beast lapped at his grief like a wolf at a stream. It glutted itself on his failure and sank its fangs into his soul. He felt it grow stronger. *God help me*, he thought.

"God help me," he whispered. "I have failed."

"Tell me," murmured Gotzon. The rumble of his voice soothed Jürgen's pain, and Jürgen continued.

He told Gotzon everything, the love he felt for Rosamund, the way he'd felt when Lucretia had drunk from him so many months ago in Magdeburg, the way he'd dreaded to leave Rosamund behind but had felt it the best choice, the way he'd agonized over sending her to Brasov but how he'd rejoiced when he'd seen her. He told Gotzon of Varka and the way he'd felt when he'd seen her at first, of how godly men now lay dead because of the resemblance she bore to Rosamund.

He told Gotzon of the two drinks that he and Rosamund

had shared, and that he planned to share a third with her.

Gotzon was silent for a moment. In that moment, a century passed. Jürgen heard whispers from outside the room, too quiet to identify, too loud to ignore. Finally, the Lasombra spoke.

"You still intend on sharing blood with her again?"

Jürgen looked up at him helplessly. "I intend on marrying her." Cainites sometimes married, Jürgen knew, though they usually approached it differently than mortals.

Gotzon shook his head. "The sacrament of marriage is for mortals, who can enter a union and multiply, as God commanded. You can do nothing of the kind."

"But…" Jürgen had no way to explain what he felt, except to tell the simple truth. "I want to. I love her."

The shadows in the room darkened. Jürgen looked at his confessor's eyes and saw angry, blackened waters. The darkness, indeed, was not empty, and what lurked therein was furious.

"Did I not tell you, Jürgen? Love God, and that is all."

"I know, and I have tried, but I cannot deny—"

"You can, you have and you will again." Gotzon's voice dropped even lower than usual and Jürgen felt the sound echo through every shadow in the room, in the monastery, in the world. "I will deny you if I have to kill her. I have made such sacrifices for you, Jürgen. My time, my blood, my honor."

Jürgen stood. A horrible realization had struck him. "Your… honor?"

"One wax seal is not worth your soul." He set the letter to Rosamund down next to Jürgen, the seal broken, the ink inside smeared.

"You betrayed me. That was the oath I heard breaking." Under other circumstances, that fact would have made Jürgen furious. But his fury was the Beast, and the Beast was as placid as a well-fed dog.

"I am true to God."

"But not to *me*, who trusted you?" The scent of a broken oath lured the Beast, and Jürgen felt his fangs extend. "Not to me, who hunted demons and sinners beside you, shielded you, put my very mind and soul at risk for you?"

"Did you stop to consider who helped you in the duel with Geidas, Jürgen?"

"I don't believe it. You were paralyzed." Jürgen knew it was true, knew that Gotzon had somehow sent a part of himself away to aid him, and then to push Jovirdas towards killing Geidas. He did not wish to believe it, not now. "How could you possibly have helped?"

"I do not care what you believe. I did what I had to do for God. Now you must. If you wish to fall from your road, do so with an eye towards your soul. Come with me, onto the true path, and perhaps there is hope for you. I lost one childe, one would-be Prince of Magdeburg, to ego and false faith, and I will not lose another."

Jürgen thought, confused, and the realization dawned. "Norbert von Xanten," he said. "You took him into your Embrace? Him, the Archbishop of Magdeburg?"

"I was mistaken in my assessment of the man. His faith was powerful, but he did not have your strength." He took a step towards Jürgen, and the Sword-Bearer reached for his blade and realized he'd left it outside the room where Varka was chained. "Come with me," he repeated, "or fall, and love like a mortal."

Jürgen backed up until he felt the door behind him. Gotzon was taller than he was, and although Jürgen had never feared him before, (the darkness in his eyes, perhaps, but never Gotzon himself), his Beast now asked that he run away from the specter before him.

He will not harm me, thought Jürgen. *I will continue to do God's work, but I must do so… differently.*

As a man.

As a man who loves.

He looked at Gotzon's eyes again, but this time felt no fear. "Go," he said.

"What?"

Jürgen nodded to himself. "Leave. You are no longer welcome in any of the lands I claim as my own. If you are captured in my lands, you will be treated as an enemy. You have violated a sworn oath to me, and thus I banish you, as Lord Jürgen Sword-Bearer, Prince of Magdeburg, Lord of Saxony and Brandenburg,

Protector of the Burzenland, *Kunigaikstis* of Livonia and Prussia, and Overlord of Acre, I banish you from these lands, and charge you never to set foot in them again upon pain of Final Death."

Gotzon stared at him for a moment, and Jürgen fixed his gaze on the older Cainite's eyes. If Gotzon decided to force his will on him now, Jürgen knew, he wouldn't be able to resist. But he couldn't look away now. He called up all of the will he had, all of the power as a leader, a Cainite and even a soldier, and forced it into his gaze.

Gotzon's eyes, which could drive a man to madness with a glance, fell. The shadows in the room darkened again, then thinned in the torchlight.

Then he walked past Jürgen without so much as a word, out into the Livonian night.

Chapter Forty-Seven

Rosamund found Jürgen later in the monastery's chapel, staring at the simple cross there. "God alone knows what defilements this place has seen," he whispered as she sat beside him.

"And so only God should worry over them," she said. "You can do nothing for the past, only be sure that it does not happen anew."

Jürgen turned to face her. "You are right, of course. The past is gone." He held the letter in his hand. "I wish to read you something."

"Lord Jürgen, have you become a poet?" Rosamund smiled, but stopped when she looked more closely at his face. Bloody tears still stained his cheeks. "My lord, what—"

"Oh, please use my name," he whispered. He lowered his eyes to the paper. "I wrote this for you before leaving for Ezerelis. I sealed it with my blood, such that anyone except you who broke the seal would break an oath to me, and I would hear it. I heard an oath break, but could not identify it—" He stopped, trying to compose himself. "I just want you to hear what I wrote to you."

"Then, please, Jürgen, tell me." Jürgen began to read, shakily, softly, never looking up from the paper:

"My dearest Rosamund,

"If your eyes ever read these words, it means that I have fallen. It means that Magdeburg has lost its prince, and all of my other vassals are freed of their vows. It means that many Cainites across the world will rejoice and, dare I hope, a few will even mourn.

"But it also means I will never see you again.

"That thought is terrifying—but terror isn't quite the right sensation. I suppose 'dread' might be closer to the truth, for the feeling isn't sharp and vicious as when the Beast drives me from fire or the sun. The feeling is insidious, it sticks in my mind like a tick. Never see my Rose again? Never again to see my native lands, never again to take my tribute of enemies, never again to battle, to ride, to claim territory?

"All of those things, I think I could accept. But never to see you again… the notion makes me ask myself why I am doing this? Why leave for battles, why claim more at all? I have more lands to my name than I could ever see.

"I am leaving, my lady, because I have to. I swore that I would, and I cannot break my word, not even for you. Especially for you, my Rose, because in you is the purest honor of the Road of Kings. In you is the reason I became a Scion, the beauty of an untainted oath. You were, you once said, a maid upon your Embrace, and so locked in that innocence forever. But that is what an oath is—it is a virgin's promise, and only by breaking it can a Scion know what a Scion truly is.

"I have broken oaths in my time, both deliberately and inadvertently. I have broken oaths to myself and others and I have confessed those sins. But I am leaving again, and only God knows what I might find at the end of this road. If you are reading it, I have found my final reward, or punishment, whatever God sees fit.

"And so consider this a last confession of sorts, my Rose—"

Jürgen stopped reading. "I can't. The paper is smudged, I can't read what I wrote."

Rosamund had been sitting, staring at him, face unmoving. "Do you remember what it was you said?"

"Not in the words I used then, I'm afraid."

Rosamund took the letter and set it aside. "Then tell me in the words that matter now."

Jürgen shut his eyes. "I love you," he said. "That is what matters. Mortals speak of eternity, but we truly *have* eternity. Can we love each other so long?"

Rosamund leaned in close and kissed him. "We can try," she said. "We can but try."

Epilogue

Jürgen slipped the ring on her finger and kissed her.

He was amazed at how long a kiss could last, and what he saw in those few seconds. He saw his return to Magdeburg, saw his last battles in Livonia, saw the installment of his vassals... but mostly he saw her.

He saw her holding him close after Gotzon had left. He heard her accepting his proposal... heard himself finally tell her that he loved her.

Jürgen kissed Rosamund, and he felt the Beast melt away, and felt the man return.

He understood the Prodigals now, even if he could never join them. *Scions can feel this, too,* he thought. *Even a prince may feel this purity.*

The guests at the celebration included Cainite nobility from all over Europe. Hardestadt attended, breaking his schedule for once and taking his traveling court to Magdeburg. Queen Isouda de Blaise, Rosamund's sire, attended on behalf of the Courts of Love, but other French Cainites had come to see "the marriage of the Rose and the Scepter." Mithras of London had not, of course, made the journey himself, but sent a representative. Rudolphus had been waiting for Jürgen when he'd returned from Livonia, but had graciously allowed him to keep the Letters of Acindynus (with notes, as promised, from a Tzimisce Scion; Jovirdas's penmanship had improved considerably) until the festivities were over.

Jürgen, when asked about it later, was seldom able to recount a list of who had attended without consulting a written record. He had engaged in no politicking, no discussion of borders or wars. The soldier once would have been horrified at letting such opportunities slip away, but the soldier was tempered more and more by the man.

They kissed, and then the ceremony ended and he took her away to his chambers—their chambers. Jürgen carried her across the threshold and laid her down on the bed, shut the door, and bolted it.

The room was cold, and though neither of them mentioned it, they both thought back to the night in Livonia when they had shared a cold wagon underneath a mound of snow, and also shared their precious blood for the second time.

And this is to be my third, thought Jürgen as he undid her clothing. *After this, she truly is my lady, for I will no longer have the heart to deny her anything.*

His Beast, in other times, might have complained. It didn't bother now, for it knew that he couldn't deny her anything as it was.

Her hands came up and undid his clothes, sharpened senses compensating for the darkness. He was naked in a few seconds, and climbed into bed next to her, pressing his body to hers.

They were cold, both of them. His Beast took the opportunity to remind him that they were dead, that all desire for them was thought, because bodily desire was long gone.

Jürgen could not know Rosamund's mind at the moment, of course, but for his part, thought was enough.

He kissed her shoulder, kissed down to her fingertips. She did not sigh as a mortal girl would have, but responded by stroking the back of his neck, playing her fingers down his back, and then leaning over to kiss his cheek and the side of his face.

Who will drink first? They had not partaken of each other's blood during the ceremony, although such was the usual practice in Cainite marriages. They had agreed that the final drink, the third drink, the one that would bind them together for always, should be done in private. That was their wedding night, and no one should see that.

Jürgen rolled over onto his back and pulled her on top of him. Cold skin slid against cold skin, scars and textures unchanged in decades met in the dark, and underneath it all, they both could feel warmth.

The blood was there, but buried deeply. Love, Jürgen decided, was not too dissimilar.

Rosamund leaned down and nipped at his neck, gently, not nearly enough to draw blood. Jürgen slid a hand behind her neck and pulled her towards him, letting his fangs draw across her neck and her shoulder.

He let his fangs pierce her skin, but waited to drink until she, too, had bitten down upon his neck.

The sensation was nothing like what he could have imagined.

He saw her, *knew* her, felt her from inside her own mind and soul. He wondered for a second if she was feeling him the same way… and then knew that she was. He felt her blood flow from her into him only to be taken out again, felt the two of them merge, felt the whole of God's Creation in the two of them, there together on the bed.

The blood is the life, he thought.

Oh, yes, she thought in response.

The moment lasted centuries, but when it ended and they broke away from their Kiss, Jürgen saddened to think it would never come again. He lay there next to his lady, savoring the blood in his mouth and the sweet pain in his shoulder, waiting to rise and light a candle and behold her beauty for the first time after the third drink.

Finally, he did. He found his way to the table and struck a stone for a spark, and lit one of the candles sitting there. He turned to see her, and nearly fell.

"An artist," he whispered.

"What?" she asked, and at the sound of her voice, he shut his eyes and shuddered.

"A poet," he said.

"What do you mean?"

He opened his eyes again, and crossed the room towards her. He sat on the bed and looked over her, naked in the cold candlelight, flesh pale and luminous. "If I were either artist or poet, I would be worthy to see you and hear your voice. I am neither."

Rosamund smiled. "I name you worthy," she said. "You may look, and hear. You must. You cannot hide from me now, behind your mind. You must share with me your thoughts, and I will weep at their beauty and brilliance just as you do now over my rude form."

Jürgen hadn't even realized he was crying, but at her remark reached up and wiped the blood from his eyes. "Yes," was all he managed to say in response.

And then, "I love you, my lady Rosamund." He said it in French, and then again in English, and then in Latin, and finally in German. He told her she could pick the one she liked best.

She chose English. Jürgen wasn't surprised—it was his favorite, as well.

They stayed up and talked until the candle burned down, and Jürgen asked to make a few final notes in the Letters of Acindynus before morning. He lit another candle, opened the Letters and skimmed through the notes he'd made.

He'd outlined a chronicle of the war in Livonia—his strategies, his thoughts, his victories and defeats. He had not, of course, related enough information to give any future enemies an advantage, but had hinted at (if not stated directly) the humiliation he'd suffered at Varka's hands. He had also spent several nights adding Armin Brenner's thoughts to the book. Several pages of the Letters were now devoted to "The Last Wisdom of a Condemned Scion," with Jürgen and Rosamund's mark both inscribed prominently at the top. Now he merely added a few notes to other parts of the Letters, reread some favorite sections, and reminisced. These Letters had been with him for a year now; he was going to miss them after handing them over to Rudolphus tomorrow night.

He stopped over a few paragraphs by a Genoese Lasombra called Fioré. He had skipped many of the Lasombra's passages. He told himself that it was because the Italian's writing was difficult to read, but the real reason was that Fioré followed the Road of Heaven, and the memory of Gotzon's betrayal was too fresh. *And yet, I pity more than despise him,* thought Jürgen, *because he hates what I feel. What must he have seen in his life and since to make him hate love so?*

Knowing that he would not have another chance, Jürgen read Fioré's words carefully. The section in question was a quote from another source, a Cainite holy scripture called *The Book of Nod*:

And then, through dread Uriel, God Almighty cursed me, saying:

Then, for as long as you walk this earth, you and your children will cling to Darkness.

You will drink only blood

You will eat only ashes

You will always be as you were at death,

Never dying, living on.

You will walk forever in Darkness,

All you touch will crumble into nothing,

Until the last days.

Fioré's notes continued. *This section of Caine's Gospel,* he wrote, *is a reminder to all Cainites, but especially to all Scions. Know this: No matter what you build, no matter what you take or destroy, no matter what lands you claim to control or what titles you add to your name, your place is foreordained. All you touch will crumble, and this means you cannot improve the world. You can only leave it poorer than you found, and this is true for all Cainites. We can only wait for the last days, and try though we might, we shall all have much to answer for then.*

Jürgen picked up a quill, but set it down. He had nothing to add to that. He shut the Letters and stood up from his table, and turned to his rooms. An ornate map showing his territories, vividly colored and painstakingly lettered, hung on the wall across from him, a gift from someone in the Courts of Love. He walked across the room, slowly, haltingly, and ran a finger down the map, stopping in Magdeburg.

All you touch will crumble into nothing.

"Jürgen?"

He turned to face his new bride, stood helplessly staring at her, loving her, worshipping her, yet not able to say a word. He couldn't identify the feeling he had, but pulled on his shirt, held up a hand (he hoped) to comfort her, and left the chamber.

He didn't see a soul as he left the building and walked into the darkened streets of Magdeburg, the Prince, the Sword-Bearer, naked but for a bloodied shirt and a dazed expression. He looked helplessly at the city around him, wanting to cry out to it, to ask the city if it was even now crumbling into nothing at his touch.

He felt a hand on his shoulder. He turned, and found Rosamund standing there. He collapsed into her arms, there in the shadow of his city, blood streaming from his eyes. She whispered to him, asking what was wrong, but he could not answer.

He could not find words to tell her he was afraid. He could not find the courage to admit that he feared his love for her would doom them both. He could not quell the nagging feeling that somewhere in his travels, he had made a horrible mistake.

But when?

About the Author

Matthew "BlackHatMatt" McFarland resides in Ohio with his wife, Michelle Lyons-McFarland, and is the proud father of two children. In addition to his day job as an SLP Matt is a former developer and current freelance author for White Wolf. He is a noted and respected author and game developer within the gaming community at large, and regular convention visitor.

Curious about other Crossroad Press books?
Stop by our site:
http://store.crossroadpress.com
We offer quality writing
in digital, audio, and print formats.

www.ingramcontent.com/pod-product-compliance
Lightning Source LLC
Chambersburg PA
CBHW070659180626
46817CB00006B/2437